Louise Penny is the Number One *New York Times* bestselling author of the Inspector Gamache series, including *Still Life*, which won the CWA John Creasey Dagger in 2006. Recipient of virtually every existing award for crime fiction, Louise was also granted The Order of Canada in 2014 and received an honorary doctorate of literature from Carleton University and the Ordre Nationale du Québec in 2017. She lives in a small village south of Montreal.

Praise for Louise Penny

'A delight for all who love crime fiction' Reginald Hill

'Penny keeps you guessing until the very last' *Guardian*

'She is in the first rank of crime writers in the world'
Toronto Globe & Mail

'Full of twists and turns' Kate Mosse

'Haunting, puzzling, brilliant' Linda Fairstein

'Terrific atmosphere . . . impressive' *The Times*

The Gamache series

Still Life
A Fatal Grace
(*prev. Dead Cold*)
The Cruellest Month
A Rule Against Murder
(*prev. The Murder Stone*)
The Brutal Telling
Bury Your Dead
Trick of the Light
The Beautiful Mystery
How the Light Gets In
The Long Way Home
The Nature of the Beast
A Great Reckoning
Glass Houses

LOUISE PENNY

STILL LIFE

A CHIEF INSPECTOR GAMACHE MYSTERY

sphere

SPHERE

First published in Great Britain in 2005 by Headline Book Publishing
Paperback published in 2006 by Headline Publishing Group
Published in 2011 by Sphere
This reissue published by Sphere in 2018

5 7 9 10 8 6

Map by Rhys Davies

'Herman Melville' © 1940 and renewed 1968 by W.H. Auden,
'For the Time Being' © 1944 and renewed 1972 by W.H. Auden,
from *Collected Poems* by W.H. Auden. Used with permission of Random House, Inc.
'I Need to Say' © 1995 by Liz Davidson, from *In the Cave of My Heart I Found . . .*
by Liz Davidson. Used with permission of the author.
'Lady Mink', 'Apology', © 2000 by Marylyn Plessner, from *Vapour Trails* by
Marylyn Plessner. Used with permission of Stephen Jarislowsky.

A CIP catalogue record for this book
is available from the British Library.

ISBN 978-0-7515-7302-2

Typeset in Janson by Palimpsest Book Production Limited,
Falkirk, Stirlingshire

Printed and Bound by LSC Communications

Sphere
An imprint of
Little, Brown Book Group
Carmelite House
50 Victoria Embankment
London EC4Y 0DZ

An Hachette UK Company
www.hachette.co.uk

www.littlebrown.co.uk

A Letter from Louise

When I was thirty-five, I thought the best was behind me.

I was lonely, and tired, and empty. Plodding through life. At thirty-five.

By the time I was forty-five, I was married to the love of my life, and my first book was about to be published.

And now I'm sixty. Living in a beautiful Quebec village, surrounded by friends, with thirteen books to my name. And counting.

This milestone birthday gives me a chance to look back in wonderment. And gratitude. And amazement. That I should be here, happy, joyous, and free.

No one quite appreciates, and recognises, the light like those who've lived in darkness. That awareness is what I try to bring to the books. The duality of our lives. The power of perception. The staggering weight of despair, and the amazement when it is lifted.

The gap between how we appear and how we really feel.

Those are foundations of the Gamache books.

Initially they were called the Three Pines books, which, of course, they are. Three Pines is the tiny hidden village in Québec. Not on any map, it is only ever found by those who are lost.

But, once found, never forgotten.

At their core, though, these books are about the profound decency of Armand Gamache, and the struggles he has to remain a good person. When 'good' is subjective, and 'decent' is a matter of judgement.

These books might appear, superficially, as traditional crime novels. But they are, I believe, more about life than death. About choices. About the price of freedom. About the struggle for peace.

Armand Gamache, of the Sûreté du Quebec, is inspired by my husband, Michael Whitehead. A doctor who treated children with cancer. Who spent his life searching for cures. Who saved countless young lives, boys and girls who now have children of their own.

Despite the dreadful deaths and broken hearts all around him, Michael was the happiest man alive. Because he understood the great gift that life is.

Michael gave that perception to Armand.

Michael died of dementia. And it broke my heart. But I still have Armand. And Clara, and Jean-Guy. Myrna and Gabri and Olivier. And crazy old Ruth.

At thirty-five, I thought the best was behind me.

As I celebrate my sixtieth birthday, I can hardly wait to see what happens next.

Ring the bells that still can ring
Forget your perfect offering
There's a crack in everything.
That's how the light gets in.

Welcome to the very cracked world of Armand Gamache and Three Pines. I am overjoyed to be able to share it with you.

Meet you in the bistro . . .

Louise Penny
March 2018

This book is given, along with all my heart, to Michael

The World of Three Pines

Rivière Bella Bella

Du Moulin

Old Stage Road

Du Moulin

ONE

～

Miss Jane Neal met her maker in the early morning mist of Thanksgiving Sunday. It was pretty much a surprise all round. Miss Neal's was not a natural death, unless you're of the belief everything happens as it's supposed to. If so, for her seventy-six years Jane Neal had been walking toward this final moment when death met her in the brilliant maple woods on the verge of the village of Three Pines. She'd fallen spread-eagled, as though making angels in the bright and brittle leaves.

Chief Inspector Armand Gamache of the Sûreté du Quebec knelt down; his knees cracking like the report of a hunter's rifle, his large, expressive hands hovering over the tiny circle of blood marring her fluffy cardigan, as though like a magician he could remove the wound and restore the woman. But he could not. That wasn't his gift. Fortunately for Gamache he had others. The scent of mothballs, his grandmother's perfume, met him

1

halfway. Jane's gentle and kindly eyes stared as though surprised to see him.

He was surprised to see her. That was his little secret. Not that he'd ever seen her before. No. His little secret was that in his mid-fifties, at the height of a long and now apparently stalled career, violent death still surprised him. Which was odd, for the head of homicide, and perhaps one of the reasons he hadn't progressed further in the cynical world of the Sûreté. Gamache always hoped maybe someone had gotten it wrong, and there was no dead body. But there was no mistaking the increasingly rigid Miss Neal. Straightening up with the help of Inspector Beauvoir, he buttoned his lined Burberry against the October chill and wondered.

Jane Neal had also been late, but in a whole other sense, a few days earlier. She'd arranged to meet her dear friend and next-door neighbor Clara Morrow for coffee in the village bistro. Clara sat at the table by the window and waited. Patience was not her long suit. The mixture of *café au lait* and impatience was producing an exquisite vibration. Throbbing slightly, Clara stared out the mullioned window at the village green and the old homes and maple trees that circled the Commons. The trees, turning breathtaking shades of red and amber, were just about the only things that did change in this venerable village.

Framed by the mullions, she saw a pick-up truck drift down rue du Moulin into the village, a beautiful dappled doe draped languidly over its hood. Slowly the truck

2

circled the Commons, halting villagers in mid-step. This was hunting season and hunting territory. But hunters like these were mostly from Montreal or other cities. They'd rent pick-ups and stalk the dirt roads at dawn and dusk like behemoths at feeding time, looking for deer. And when they spotted one they'd slither to a stop, step out of the truck and fire. Not all hunters were like that, Clara knew, but enough of them were. Those same hunters would strap the deer on to the hood of their truck and drive around the countryside believing the dead animal on the vehicle somehow announced that great men had done this.

Every year the hunters shot cows and horses and family pets and each other. And, unbelievably, they sometimes shot themselves, perhaps in a psychotic episode where they mistook themselves for dinner. It was a wise person who knew that some hunters – not all, but some – found it challenging to distinguish a pine from a partridge from a person.

Clara wondered what had become of Jane. She was rarely late, so she could easily be forgiven. Clara found it easy to forgive most things in most people. Too easy, her husband Peter often warned. But Clara had her own little secret. She didn't really let go of everything. Most things, yes. But some she secretly held and hugged and would visit in moments when she needed to be comforted by the unkindness of others.

Croissant crumbs had tumbled on top of the *Montreal Gazette* left at her table. Between flakes Clara scanned the headlines: 'Parti Quebecois Vows to Hold Sovereignty

Referendum', 'Drug Bust in Townships', 'Hikers Lost in Tremblant Park'.

Clara lifted her eyes from the morose headlines. She and Peter had long since stopped subscribing to the Montreal papers. Ignorance really was bliss. They preferred the local *Williamsburg County News* where they could read about Wayne's cow, or Guylaine's visiting grandchildren, or a quilt being auctioned for the seniors' home. Every now and then Clara wondered if they were copping out, running away from reality and responsibility. Then she realised she didn't care. Besides, she learned everything she really needed to survive right here at Olivier's Bistro, in the heart of Three Pines.

'You're a million miles away,' came the familiar and well-loved voice. There was Jane, out of breath and smiling, her laugh-lined face pink from the autumn chill and the brisk trot from her cottage across the village green.

'Sorry I'm late,' she whispered into Clara's ear as the two hugged, one tiny, plump and breathless, the other thirty years younger, slim, and still vibrating from the caffeine high. 'You're trembling,' said Jane, sitting down and ordering her own *café au lait*. 'I didn't know you cared so much.'

'Filthy old hag,' laughed Clara.

'I was this morning, that's for sure. Did you hear what happened?'

'No, what happened?' Clara leaned forward eager for the news. She and Peter had been in Montreal buying canvases and acrylics for their work. Both were artists.

Peter, a success. Clara as yet was undiscovered and, most of her friends secretly felt, was likely to remain that way if she persisted in her unfathomable works. Clara had to admit her series of warrior uteruses were mostly lost on the buying public, though her household items with bouffant hair and huge feet had enjoyed a certain success. She'd sold one. The rest, roughly fifty of them, were in their basement, which looked a lot like Walt Disney's workshop.

'No,' whispered Clara a few minutes later, genuinely shocked. In the twenty-five years she'd lived in Three Pines she'd never, ever heard of a crime. The only reason doors were locked was to prevent neighbors from dropping off baskets of zucchini at harvest time. True, as the *Gazette* headline made clear, there was another crop that equaled zucchini in scope: marijuana. But those not involved tried to turn a blind eye.

Beyond that, there was no crime. No break-ins, no vandalism, no assaults. There weren't even any police in Three Pines. Every now and then Robert Lemieux with the local Sûreté would drive around the Commons, just to show the colors, but there was no need.

Until that morning.

'Could it have been a joke?' Clara struggled with the ugly image Jane had painted.

'No. It was no joke,' said Jane, remembering. 'One of the boys laughed. It was kind of familiar, now that I think of it. Not a funny laugh.' Jane turned her clear blue eyes on Clara. Eyes full of wonderment. 'It was a sound I'd heard as a teacher. Not often, thank God. It's the sound boys make when they're hurting something and enjoying it.' Jane shivered at the recollection, and pulled her cardigan around her. 'An ugly sound. I'm glad you weren't there.'

She said this just as Clara reached across the round dark wood table and held Jane's cold, tiny hand and wished with all her heart she had been there instead of Jane.

'They were just kids, you say?'

'They wore ski masks, so it was hard to tell, but I think I recognised them.'

'Who were they?'

'Philippe Croft, Gus Hennessey and Claude LaPierre,' Jane whispered the names, looking around to make sure no one could overhear.

'Are you sure?' Clara knew all three boys. They weren't exactly the Boy Scout types, but neither were they the sort to do this.

'No,' admitted Jane.

'Better not tell anyone else.'

'Too late.'

'What do you mean, "too late"?'

'I said their names this morning, while it was happening.'

'Said their names in a whisper?' Clara could feel the blood tumbling from her fingers and toes, rushing to her core, to her heart. Please, please, please, she silently begged.

'I yelled.'

Seeing Clara's expression, Jane hurried to justify herself. 'I wanted to stop them. It worked. They stopped.'

Jane could still see the boys running away, tripping up du Moulin, out of the village. The one in the brilliant-green mask had turned to look back at her. His hands were still dripping duck manure. The manure put there as autumn mulch for the flower beds on the village green, and not yet spread. She wished she could have seen the boy's expression. Was he angry? Scared? Amused?

'So you were right. About their names, I mean.'

'Probably. I never thought I'd live to see the day this would happen here.'

'So that was why you were late? You had to clean up?'

'Yes. Well, no.'

'Could you be more vague?'

'Maybe. You're on the jury for the next Arts Williamsburg show, right?'

'Yes. We're meeting this afternoon. Peter's on it too. Why?' Clara was almost afraid to breathe. Could this be it? After all her cajoling and gentle ribbing, and sometimes not-so-gentle shoving, was Jane about to do it?

'I'm ready.' Jane gave the biggest exhale Clara had ever seen. The force of it sent a squall of croissant flakes from the front page of the *Gazette* on to Clara's lap.

'I was late,' said Jane slowly, her own hands beginning to tremble, 'because I had to decide. I have a painting I'd like to enter into the show.'

With that she started to cry.

Jane's art had been an open secret in Three Pines for ever. Every now and then someone walking in the woods or through a field would stumble upon her, concentrating on a canvas. But she'd made them swear that they wouldn't

7

approach, wouldn't look, would avert their eyes as though witnessing an act almost obscene, and certainly would never speak of it. The only time Clara had seen Jane angry was when Gabri had come up behind her while she'd been painting. He thought she'd been joking when she'd warned them never to look.

He was wrong. She'd been deadly serious. It had actually taken a few months for Jane and Gabri to get back to a normal friendship; both had felt betrayed by the other. But their natural good nature and affection for each other had healed the rift. Still, it had served as a lesson.

No one was to see Jane's art.

Until now, apparently. But now the artist was overcome with an emotion so strong she sat in the Bistro and wept. Clara was both horrified and terrified. She looked furtively around, partly in hopes no one was watching, and partly desperately hoping someone was, and would know what to do. Then she asked herself the simple question that she carried with her and consulted like a rosary. What would Jane do? And she had her answer. Jane would let her cry, would let her wail. Would let her throw crockery, if she needed to. And Jane would not run away. When the maelstrom passed, Jane would be there. And then she would put her arms around Clara, and comfort her, and let her know she was not alone. Never alone. And so Clara sat and watched and waited. And knew the agony of doing nothing. Slowly the crying subsided.

Clara rose with exaggerated calm. She took Jane in her

arms and felt the old body creak back into place. Then she said a little prayer of thanks to the gods that give grace. The grace to cry and the grace to watch.

'Jane, if I'd known it was this painful I'd never have kept at you to show your art. I'm so sorry.'

'Oh, no, dear,' Jane reached across the table where they were sitting once again, and took Clara's hands, 'you don't understand. Those weren't tears of pain. No. I was surprised by joy.' Jane gazed far off and nodded, as though carrying on a private conversation. 'Finally.'

'What's it called, your painting?'

'*Fair Day*. It's of the closing parade of the county fair.'

And so it was that on the Friday before Thanksgiving the painting was lifted on to an easel in the gallery of Arts Williamsburg. It was wrapped in butcher's paper and tied with string, like a child's bundle, against the cold, cruel elements. Slowly, meticulously, Peter Morrow picked at the knot, tugging the string until it came loose. Then he wound the old string around his palm as though winding yarn. Clara could have killed him. She was ready to shriek, to jump from her chair and shove him aside. To fling the pathetic bundle of string to the ground, and perhaps Peter with it, and tear the waxed paper from the canvas. Her face became even more placid, though her eyes had begun to bulge.

Peter neatly unfolded first one corner of the paper then the other, smoothing the creases with his hand. Clara had no idea a rectangle had so many corners. She could feel the edge of her chair cutting into her bottom. The rest

9

of the jury, assembled to judge the submissions, looked bored. Clara had enough anxiety for them all.

Every last corner was finally smooth and the paper was ready to be removed. Peter turned around to face the other four jurors and make a little speech before revealing the work beneath. Something short and tasteful, he felt. A bit of context, a bit of – he caught his wife's bulging eyes in her purple face and knew that when Clara became abstract it was no time for speechifying.

He quickly turned back to the painting and whipped the brown paper off, revealing *Fair Day*.

Clara's jaw dropped. Her head jerked down as though suddenly insupportable. Her eyes widened and her breathing stopped. It was as though she'd died, for an instant. So this was *Fair Day*. It took her breath away. And clearly the other jurors felt the same way. There were varying degrees of disbelief on the semi-circle of faces. Even the chairperson, Elise Jacob, was silent. She actually looked like she was having a stroke.

Clara hated judging other people's work, and this was the worst so far. She'd kicked herself all the way there for convincing Jane to enter her first work ever for public viewing in an exhibition she herself was judging. Was it ego? Was it mere stupidity?

'This work is called *Fair Day*,' read Elise from her notes. 'It's being submitted by Jane Neal of Three Pines, a long-time supporter of Arts Williamsburg, but her first submission.' Elise looked around. 'Comments?'

'It's wonderful,' Clara lied. The others looked at her in astonishment. Facing them on the easel was an unframed canvas and the subject was obvious. The horses looked like horses, the cows were cows, and the people were all recognisable, not only as people but as specific people from the village. But they were all stick figures. Or at least perhaps one evolutionary notch up from stick figures. In a war between a stick figure army and these people in *Fair Day*, the *Fair Day* people would win, only because they had a little more muscle. And fingers. But it was clear that these people lived in only two dimensions. Clara, in trying to grasp what she was looking at, and trying not to make the obvious comparisons, felt that it was a little like a cave drawing put on canvas. If Neanderthals had county fairs, this was what they'd have looked like.

'*Mon Dieu*. My four-year-old can do better than that,' said Henri Lariviere, making the obvious comparison. Henri had been a laborer in a quarry before discovering that the stone spoke to him. And he listened. There was no going back after that, of course, though his family longed for the day when he made at least the minimum wage instead of huge stone sculptures. His face now, as ever, was broad and rough and inscrutable, but his hands spoke for him. They were turned up in a simple and eloquent gesture of appeal, of surrender. He was struggling to find the appropriate words, knowing that Jane was a friend of many of the jurors. 'It's awful.' He'd clearly given up the struggle and reverted to the truth. Either that or his description was actually kind compared to what he really thought.

In bold, bright colors Jane's work showed the parade

just before the closing of the fair. Pigs were distinguishable from goats only because they were bright red. The children looked like little adults. In fact, thought Clara leaning tentatively forward as though the canvas might deal her another blow, those aren't children. They're small adults. She recognised Olivier and Gabri leading the blue rabbits. In the stands beyond the parade sat the crowd, many of them in profile, looking at each other, or looking away from each other. Some, not many, looked straight at Clara. All the cheeks had perfect round red circles, denoting, Clara supposed, a healthy glow. It was awful.

'Well, that's easy enough at least,' said Irenée Calfat. 'That's a reject.'

Clara could feel her extremities grow cold and numb.

Irenée Calfat was a potter. She took hunks of clay and turned them into exquisite works. She'd pioneered a new way to glaze her works and was now sought out by potters worldwide. Of course, after they'd made the pilgrimage to Irenée Calfat's studio in St Rémy and spent five minutes with the Goddess of Mud, they knew they'd made a mistake. She was one of the most self absorbed and petty people on the face of this earth.

Clara wondered how a person so devoid of normal human emotions could create works of such beauty. While you yourself struggle, said the nasty little voice that kept her company.

Over the rim of her mug she peeked at Peter. He had a piece of chocolate cupcake stuck to his face. Instinctively, Clara wiped her own face, inadvertently smearing a walnut into her hair. Even with that hunk of chocolate on his face Peter was riveting. Classically handsome. Tall, broad-shouldered like a lumberjack, not the delicate artist he was. His wavy hair was gray now, and he wore glasses all the time, and lines scored the corners of his eyes and his clean-shaven face. In his early fifties, he looked like a businessman on an outward bound adventure. Most mornings Clara would wake up and watch while he slept, and want to crawl inside his skin and wrap herself around his heart and keep him safe.

Clara's head acted as a food magnet. She was the Carmen Miranda of baked goods. Peter, on the other hand, was always immaculate. It could be raining mud and he would return home cleaner than when he went out. But sometimes, some glorious times, his natural aura failed him and a piece of something stuck to his face. Clara knew she should tell him. But didn't.

'Do you know,' said Peter and even Irenée looked at him, 'I think it's great.'

Irenée snorted and shot a meaningful look at Henri who just ignored her. Peter sought out Clara and held her gaze for a moment, a kind of touchstone. When Peter walked into a room he always swept it until he found Clara. And then he relaxed. The outside world saw a tall, distinguished man with his disheveled wife, and wondered why. Some, principally Peter's mother, even seemed to consider it a violation of nature. Clara was his centre and all that was good and healthy and happy about him. When he looked at her he didn't see the wild, untamable hair, the billowing frocks, the Dollar-rama store horn-rimmed spectacles. No. He saw his safe harbor. Although, granted, at this moment he also saw a walnut in her hair, which was pretty much an identifying characteristic. Instinctively, he put his hand up to brush his own hair, knocking the piece of cupcake from his cheek.

'What do you see?' Elise asked Peter.

'Honestly, I don't know. But I know we need to accept it.'

This brief answer somehow gave his opinion even more credibility.

'It's a risk,' said Elise.

'I agree,' said Clara. 'But what's the worst that can happen? That people who see the show might think we've made a mistake? They always think that.'

Elise nodded in appreciation.

'I'll tell you what the risk is,' said Irenée, the 'you idiots' implied as she plowed on. 'This is a community group and we barely make ends meet. Our only value is our credibility. Once it's believed we accept works based not on their value as art but because we like the artist, as a clique of friends, we're ruined. That's the risk. No one will take us seriously. Artists won't want to show here for fear of being tainted. The public won't come because they know all they'll see is crap like—' Here words failed her and she merely pointed at the canvas.

Then Clara saw it. Just a flash, something niggling on the outer reaches of her consciousness. For the briefest moment *Fair Day* shimmered. The pieces came together, then the moment passed. Clara realised she'd stopped breathing again, but she also realised that she was looking at a work of great art. Like Peter, she didn't know why or how, but in that instant that world which had seemed upside down righted. She knew *Fair Day* was an extraordinary work.

'I think it's more than wonderful, I think it's brilliant,' she said.

'Oh, please. Can't you see she's just saying that to support her husband?'

'Irenée, we've heard your opinion. Go on, Clara,' said Elise. Henri leaned forward, his chair groaning.

Clara got up and walked slowly to the work on the easel. It touched her deep down in a place of such sadness and loss it was all she could do not to weep. How could this be? she asked herself. The images were so childish, so simple. Silly almost, with dancing geese and smiling people. But there was something else. Something just beyond her grasp.

'I'm sorry. This is embarrassing,' she smiled, feeling her cheeks burning, 'but I actually can't explain it.'

'Why don't we set *Fair Day* aside and look at the rest of the works. We'll come back to it at the end.'

The rest of the afternoon went fairly smoothly. The sun was getting low, making the room even colder by the time they looked at *Fair Day* again. Everyone was wiped out and just wanted this to be over. Peter flipped on the overhead spotlights and lifted Jane's work on to the easel.

'*D'accord.* Has anyone changed their mind about *Fair Day*?' Elise asked.

Silence.

'I make it two in favor of accepting and two against.'

Elise stared quietly at *Fair Day*. She knew Jane Neal in passing and liked what she saw. She'd always struck Elise as a sensible, kind and intelligent woman. A person you'd want to spend time with. How was it this woman had created this slapdash, childish work? But. And a new thought entered her head. Not, actually, an original thought or even new to Elise, but a new one for this day.

'*Fair Day* is accepted. It'll be shown with the other works of art.'

Clara leapt up with delight, toppling her chair.

'Oh, come on,' said Irenée.

'Exactly! Well done. You've both proven my point.' Elise smiled.

'What point?'

'For whatever reason, *Fair Day* challenges us. It moves us. To anger,' here Elise acknowledged Irenée, 'to confusion,' a brief but meaningful look at Henri who nodded his grizzled head slightly, 'to . . .' a glance at Peter and Clara.

'Joy,' said Peter at the very moment Clara said, 'Sorrow.' They looked at each other and laughed.

'Now, I look at it and feel, like Henri, simply confused. The truth is I don't know whether *Fair Day* is a brilliant example of naive art, or the pathetic scrawling of a superbly untalented, and delusional, old woman. That's the tension. And that's why it must be part of the show. I can guarantee you it's the one work people will be talking about in the cafés after the *vernissage*.'

*

16

'Hideous,' said Ruth Zardo later that evening, leaning on her cane and swigging Scotch. Peter and Clara's friends were gathered in their living room, around the murmuring fireplace for a pre-Thanksgiving dinner.

It was the lull before the onslaught. Family and friends, invited or not, would arrive the next day and manage to stay through the Thanksgiving long weekend. The woods would be full of hikers and hunters, an unfortunate combination. The annual touch football game would be held on the village green on Saturday morning, followed by the harvest market in the afternoon, a last ditch effort to download tomatoes and zucchini. That evening the bonfire would be lit filling Three Pines with the delicious scent of burning leaves and wood, and the suspicious undercurrent of gazpacho.

Three Pines wasn't on any tourist map, being too far off any main or even secondary road. Like Narnia, it was generally found unexpectedly and with a degree of surprise that such an elderly village should have been hiding in this valley all along. Anyone fortunate enough to find it once usually found their way back. And Thanksgiving, in early October, was the perfect time. The weather was usually crisp and clear, the summer scents of old garden roses and phlox were replaced by musky autumn leaves, woodsmoke and roast turkey.

Olivier and Gabri were recounting that morning's events. Their description was so vivid everyone in the snug living room could see the three masked boys picking up handfuls of duck manure from the edge of the village green: the boys lifted their hands, the manure sliding between their fingers, and then hurled the stuff at the old brick building. Soon the blue and white Campari awnings were dripping. Manure was sliding off the walls. The 'Bistro' sign was splattered. In moments, the pristine face of the café in the heart of Three Pines was filthy, and not just with duck poop. The village had become soiled by the words that filled the startled air: 'Fags! Queers! *Dégueulasse!*' the boys screamed.

As Jane listened to Olivier and Gabri, she recalled how she had emerged from her tiny stone cottage across the green and, hurrying over, had seen Olivier and Gabri come out of the Bistro. The boys had roared their delight and aimed at the two men, striking them with the manure.

Jane had picked up her pace, wishing her stout legs longer. Then she'd seen Olivier do the most extraordinary thing. As the boys screamed and hauled off handfuls of mulch, Olivier had slowly, deliberately, gently taken Gabri's hand and held it before gracefully lifting it to his lips. The boys had watched, momentarily stunned, as Olivier had kissed Gabri's manure-stained hand with his manure-stained lips. The boys had seemed petrified by this act of love and defiance. But just for a moment. Their hatred triumphed and soon their attack had re-doubled.

'Stop that!' Jane had called firmly.

Their arms had halted in mid-swing, instinctively reacting to a voice of authority. Turning as one they'd seen little Jane Neal, in her floral dress and yellow cardigan, bearing down on them. One of the boys, wearing an orange mask, had lifted his arm to toss at her.

'Don't you dare, young man.'

He hesitated just long enough for Jane to look them all in the eyes.

'Philippe Croft, Gus Hennessey, Claude LaPierre,' she'd said, slowly and distinctly. That had done it. The boys dropped their handfuls and ran, shooting past Jane and tripping up the hill, the one in the orange mask laughing. It was a sound so foul it even eclipsed the manure. One boy turned and looked back as the others careered into him and shoved him back up du Moulin.

It had happened only that morning. It already seemed like a dream.

'It was hideous,' said Gabri, agreeing with Ruth as he dropped into one of the old chairs, its faded fabric warmed by the fire. 'Of course they were right; I *am* gay.'

'And,' said Olivier, lounging on the arm of Gabri's chair, 'quite queer.'

'I have become one of the stately homos of Quebec,' Gabri paraphrased Quentin Crisp. 'My views are breathtaking.'

Olivier laughed and Ruth threw another log on the fire.

'You did look very stately this morning,' said Ben Hadley, Peter's best friend.

'Don't you mean estately?'

'More like the back forty, it's true.'

In the kitchen, Clara was greeting Myrna Landers.

'The table looks wonderful,' said Myrna, peeling off her

19

coat and revealing a bright purple kaftan. Clara wondered how she squeezed through doorways. Myrna then dragged in her contribution to the evening, a flower arrangement. 'Where would you like it, child?'

Clara gawked. Like Myrna herself, her bouquets were huge, effusive and unexpected. This one contained oak and maple branches, bulrushes from the Rivière Bella Bella which ran behind Myrna's bookshop, apple branches with a couple of McIntoshes still on them, and great armfuls of herbs.

'What's this?'

'Where?'

'Here, in the middle of the arrangement.'

'A kielbassa.'

'A sausage?'

'Hummuh, and look in there.' Myrna pointed into the tangle.

'*The Collected Works of W. H. Auden*,' Clara read. 'You're kidding.'

'It's for the boys.'

'What else is in there?' Clara scanned the immense arrangement.

'Denzel Washington. But don't tell Gabri.'

In the living room, Jane continued the story: '. . . then Gabri said to me, "I have your mulch. This is just the way Vita Sackville West always wore it."'

Olivier whispered in Gabri's ear, 'You are queer.'

'Aren't you glad one of us is?' A well-worn and comfortable jest.

'How are you?' Myrna came in from the kitchen, followed by Clara, and hugged Gabri and Olivier while Peter poured her Scotch.

'I think we're all right.' Olivier kissed Myrna on both cheeks. 'It's probably surprising this didn't happen sooner. We've been here for what? Twelve years?' Gabri nodded, his mouth full of Camembert. 'And this is the first time we've been bashed. I was gay bashed in Montreal when I was a kid, by a group of grown men. That was terrifying.' They'd grown silent, and there was just the crackling and muttering of the fire in the background as Olivier spoke.

'They hit me with sticks. It's funny, but when I think back that's the most painful part. Not the scrapes and bruises, but before they hit me they kind of poked, you know?' He jabbed with one arm to mimic their movements. 'It was as though I wasn't human.'

'That's the necessary first step,' said Myrna. 'They dehumanise their victim. You've put it well.'

She spoke from experience. Before coming to Three Pines she'd been a psychologist in Montreal. And, being black, she knew that singular expression when people saw her as furniture.

Ruth turned to Olivier, changing the subject. 'I was in the basement and came across a few things I thought you could sell for me.' Ruth's basement was her bank.

'Great. What?'

'There's some cranberry glass—'

'Oh, wonderful.' Olivier adored colored glass. 'Hand blown?'

'Do you take me for an idiot? Of course they're hand blown.'

'Are you sure you don't want them?' He always asked this of his friends.

'Stop asking me that. Do you think I'd mention them if there was a doubt?'

'Bitch.'

'Slut.'

'OK, tell me more,' said Olivier. The stuff Ruth hauled up from her basement was incredible. It was as though she had a porthole to the past. Some of it was junk, like the old broken-down coffee makers and burned-out toasters. But most made him tremble with pleasure. The greedy antique dealer in him, which composed a larger part of his make-up than he'd ever admit, was thrilled to have exclusive access to Ruth's treasures. He'd sometimes daydream about that basement.

If he was excited by Ruth's possessions, he was positively beside himself with lust after Jane's home. He'd kill to see beyond her kitchen door. Her kitchen alone was worth tens of thousands of dollars in antiques. When he'd first come to Three Pines, at the Drama Queen's insistence, he was reduced almost to incoherence when he saw the linoleum on Jane's mudroom floor. If the mudroom was a museum and the kitchen a shrine, what in the world lay beyond? Olivier shook off the thought, knowing he would probably be disappointed. IKEA. And shag carpet. He'd long since stopped thinking it strange that Jane had never invited anyone through the swinging door into her living room and beyond.

'About the mulch, Jane,' Gabri was saying, his bulk bending over one of Peter's jigsaw puzzles, 'I can get it to you tomorrow. Do you need help cutting back your garden?'

'No, almost done. But this might be the last year. It's getting beyond me.' Gabri was relieved he didn't have to help. Doing his own garden was work enough.

'I have a whole lot of hollyhock babies,' said Jane, fitting in a piece of the sky. 'How did those single yellows do for you? I didn't notice them.'

'I put them in last fall, but they never called me mother. Can I have some more? I'll trade you for some monarda.'

'God, don't do that.' Monarda was the zucchini of the flower world. It, too, figured prominently in the harvest market and, subsequently, the Thanksgiving bonfire, which would give off a hint of sweet bergamot so that it smelled as though every cottage in Three Pines was brewing Earl Grey tea.

'Did we tell you what happened this afternoon after you'd all left?' Gabri said in his stage voice, so that the words fell neatly into every ear in the room. 'We were just getting the peas ready for tonight' – Clara rolled her eyes and mumbled to Jane, 'Probably lost the can opener.' – 'when the doorbell rang and there were Matthew Croft and Philippe.'

'No! What happened?'

'Philippe mumbled, "I'm sorry about this morning."'

'What did you say?' Myrna asked.

'Prove it,' said Olivier.

'You didn't,' hooted Clara, amused and impressed.

23

'I most certainly did. There was a lack of sincerity about the apology. He was sorry he got caught and sorry there were consequences. But I didn't believe he was sorry about what he did.'

'Conscience and cowardice,' said Clara.

'What do you mean?' asked Ben.

'Oscar Wilde said that conscience and cowardice are the same thing. What stops us from doing horrible things isn't our conscience but the fear of getting caught.'

'I wonder if that's true,' said Jane.

'Would you?' Myrna asked Clara.

'Do terrible things if I could get away with it?'

'Cheat on Peter,' suggested Olivier. 'Steal from the bank. Or better still, steal another artist's work?'

'Ah, kids stuff,' snapped Ruth. 'Now, take murder, for instance. Would you mow someone down with your car? Or poison them, maybe, or throw them into the Bella Bella during spring run off? Or,' she looked around, warm firelight reflecting off slightly concerned faces, 'or we could set a fire and then not save them.'

'What do you mean, "we", white woman?' said Myrna. Myrna brought the conversation back from the edge.

'The truth? Sure. But not murder.' Clara looked over at Ruth who simply gave her a conspiratorial wink.

'Imagine a world where you could do anything. Anything. And get away with it,' said Myrna, warming to the topic again. 'What power. Who here wouldn't be corrupted?'

'Jane wouldn't,' said Ruth with certainty. 'But the rest of you?' she shrugged.

'And you?' Olivier asked Ruth, more than a little annoyed to be lumped in where he secretly knew he belonged.

'Me? But you know me well enough by now, Olivier. I'd be the worst. I'd cheat, and steal, and make all your lives hell.'

'Worse than now?' asked Olivier, still peeved.

'Now you're on the list,' said Ruth. And Olivier remembered that the closest thing they had to a police force was the volunteer fire brigade, of which he was a member but of which Ruth was the chief. When Ruth Zardo ordered you into a conflagration, you went. She was scarier than a burning building.

'Gabri, what about you?' Clara asked.

'There've been times I've been mad enough to kill, and may have, had I known I would get away with it.'

'What made you that angry?' Clara was astonished.

'Betrayal, always and only betrayal.'

'What did you do about it?' asked Myrna.

'Therapy. That was where I met this guy.' Gabri reached out and patted Olivier's hand. 'I think we both went to that therapist for about a year longer than we had to just to see each other in the waiting room.'

'Is that sick?' said Olivier, smoothing a lock of his immaculate, thinning blond hair off his face. It was like silk, and kept falling into his eyes, no matter what products he used.

'Mock me if you will, but everything happens for a reason,' Gabri said. 'No betrayal, no rage. No rage, no therapy. No therapy, no Olivier. No Olivier no—'

'Enough.' Olivier held up his hands in surrender.

'I've always liked Matthew Croft,' said Jane.

'Did you teach him?' asked Clara.

'Long time ago. He was in the second to last class at the old schoolhouse here, before it closed.'

'I still think that was a shame they closed it,' said Ben.

'For God's sake, Ben, the school closed twenty years ago. Move on.' Only Ruth would say this.

When she first came to Three Pines, Myrna had wondered whether Ruth had had a stroke. Sometimes, Myrna knew from her practice, stroke victims had very little impulse control. When she asked about it, Clara said if Ruth had had a stroke it was in the womb. As far as she knew, Ruth had always been like this.

'Then why does everyone like her?' Myrna had asked.

Clara had laughed and shrugged, 'You know there are days I ask myself the same thing. What a piece of work that woman can be. But she's worth the effort, I think.'

'Anyway,' Gabri huffed now, having temporarily lost the spotlight. 'Philippe agreed to work for fifteen hours, volunteer, around the Bistro.'

'Bet he wasn't happy about that,' said Peter, getting to his feet.

'You got that right,' said Olivier with a grin.

'I want to propose a toast,' said Gabri. 'To our friends, who stood by us today. To our friends who spent all morning cleaning the Bistro.' It was a phenomenon Myrna had noticed before, some people's ability to turn a terrible event into a triumph. She'd thought about it that morning, manure under her fingernails, pausing for a moment to look at the people, young and old, pitching in. And she was one of them. And she blessed, again, the day she'd decided to quit the city and come here and sell books to these people. She was finally home. Then another image came back to her, one that had gotten lost in the activity of the morning. Of Ruth leaning on her cane, turning away from the others, so that only Myrna could see the wince of pain as the elderly woman lowered herself to her knees, and silently scrubbed. All morning.

'Dinner's ready,' Peter called.

'Formidable. Just like dear Mama. *Le Sieur*?' Jane asked a few minutes later, bringing a forkful of mushy peas and gravy to her mouth.

'*Bien sûr*. From Monsieur Beliveau.' Olivier nodded.

'Oh, for God's sake,' Clara called down the groaning pine table. 'They're canned peas! From the general store. You call yourself a chef!'

'*Le Sieur* is the gold standard for canned peas. Keep this up, missy, and you'll get the no-name brand next year. No gratitude,' Olivier stage-whispered to Jane, 'and on Thanksgiving, too. Shameful.'

They ate by candlelight, the candles of all shapes and sizes flickering around the kitchen. Their plates were piled high with turkey and chestnut stuffing, candied yams and potatoes, peas and gravy. They'd all brought something to eat, except Ben, who didn't cook. But he'd brought bottles of wine, which was even better. It was a regular get-together, and pot-luck was the only way Peter and Clara could afford to hold a dinner party.

Olivier leaned over to Myrna, 'Another great flower arrangement.'

'Thank you. Actually, there's something hidden in there for you two.'

'Really!' Gabri was on his feet in an instant. His long legs propelled his bulk across the kitchen to the arrangement. Unlike Olivier, who was self-contained and even fastidious, like a cat, Gabri was more like a St Bernard, though mostly without the slobber. He carefully examined the complex forest and then shrieked. 'Just what I've always wanted.' He pulled out the kielbassa.

'Not that. That's for Clara.' Everyone looked at Clara with alarm, especially Peter. Olivier looked relieved. Gabri reached in again and gingerly extracted the thick book.

'*The Collected Works of W. H. Auden.*' Gabri tried to keep the disappointment out of his voice. But not too hard. 'I don't know him.'

'Oh, Gabri, you're in for a treat,' said Jane.

'All right, I can't stand it any more,' Ruth said suddenly, leaning across the table to Jane. 'Did Arts Williamsburg accept your work?'

'Yes.'

It was as though the word triggered springs in their chairs. Everyone was catapulted to their feet, shooting toward Jane who stood and accepted their hugs with enthusiasm. She seemed to glow brighter than any of the candles in the room. Standing back for an instant and watching the scene, Clara felt her heart contract and her spirit lighten and felt fortunate indeed to be part of this moment.

'Great artists put a lot of themselves into their work,' said Clara when the chairs had been regained.

'What's *Fair Day*'s special meaning?' Ben asked.

'Now, that would be cheating. You have to figure it out. It's there.' Jane turned to Ben, smiling. 'You'll figure it out, I'm sure.'

'Why's it called *Fair Day*?' he asked.

'It was painted at the county fair, the closing parade.' Jane gave Ben a meaningful look. His mother, her friend, Timmer, had died that afternoon. Was it only a month ago? The whole village had been at the parade, except Timmer, dying of cancer alone in bed, while her son Ben was away in Ottawa at an antiques auction. Clara and Peter had been the ones to break the news to him. Clara would never forget the look on his face when Peter told him his mother was dead. Not sadness, not even pain, yet. But utter disbelief. He wasn't the only one.

'Evil is unspectacular and always human, and shares our bed and eats at our own table,' Jane said almost under her breath. 'Auden,' she explained, nodding to the book in Gabri's hand and flashing a smile that broke the unexpected, and unexplained, tension.

'I might just sneak down and take a look at *Fair Day* before the show,' said Ben.

Jane took a deep breath. 'I'd like to invite you all over for drinks after the opening of the exhibition. In the living room.' Had she said 'In the nude' they wouldn't have been more amazed. 'I have a bit of a surprise for you.'

'No kidding,' said Ruth.

Stomachs full of turkey and pumpkin pie, port and espresso, the tired guests walked home, their flashlights bobbing like huge fireflies. Jane kissed Peter and Clara goodnight. It had been a comfortable, unremarkable early Thanksgiving with friends. Clara watched Jane make her way along the winding path through the woods that joined their two homes. Long after Jane had disappeared from view her flashlight could be seen, a bright white light, like Diogenes. Only when Clara heard the eager barking of Jane's dog Lucy did she gently close her door. Jane was home. Safe.

TWO

———

Armand Gamache got the call Thanksgiving Sunday just as he was leaving his Montreal apartment. His wife Reine-Marie was already in the car and the only reason he wasn't on the way to his grand-niece's christening was because he suddenly needed to use the facilities.

'*Oui, allô?*'

'*Monsieur L'Inspecteur?*' said the polite young voice at the other end. 'This is Agent Nichol. The Superintendent asked me to call. There's been a murder.'

After decades with the Sûreté du Quebec, most of them in homicide, those words still sent a frisson through him. 'Where?' he was already reaching for the pad and pen, which stood next to every phone in their flat.

'A village in the Eastern Townships. Three Pines. I can be by to pick you up within a quarter hour.'

'Did you murder this person?' Reine-Marie asked her

husband when Armand told her he wouldn't be at the two-hour service on hard benches in a strange church.

'If I did, I'll find out. Want to come?'

'What would you do if I ever said yes?'

'I'd be delighted,' he said truthfully. After thirty-two years of marriage he still couldn't get enough of Reine-Marie. He knew if she ever accompanied him on a murder investigation she would do the appropriate thing. She always seemed to know the right thing to do. Never any drama, never confusion. He trusted her.

And once again she did the right thing, by declining his invitation.

'I'll just tell them you're drunk, again,' she said when he asked whether her family would be disappointed he wasn't there.

'Didn't you tell them I was in a treatment center last time I missed a family gathering?'

'Well, I guess it didn't work.'

'Very sad for you.'

'I'm a martyr to my husband,' said Reine-Marie, getting into the driver's seat. 'Be safe, dear heart,' she said.

'I will, *mon coeur*.' He went back to his study in their second-floor flat and consulted the huge map of Quebec he had tacked to one wall. His finger moved south from Montreal to the Eastern Townships and hovered around the border with the United States.

'Three Pines . . . Three Pines,' he repeated, as he tried to find it. 'Could it be called something else?' he asked himself, unable for the first time with this detailed map to find a village. '*Trois Pins*, perhaps?' No, there was nothing. He wasn't worried since it was Nichol's job to find the place. He walked through the large apartment they'd bought in the Outremont quartier of Montreal when the children had been born and even though they'd long since moved out and were having children of their own now, the place never felt empty. It was enough to share it with Reine-Marie. Photos sat on the piano and shelves bulged with books, testament to a life well lived. Reine-Marie had wanted to put up his commendations, but he'd gently refused. Each time he came across the framed commendations in his study closet he remembered not the formal Sûreté ceremony, but the faces of the dead and the living they left behind. No. They had no place on the walls of his home. And now the commendations had stopped completely, since the Arnot case. Still, his family was commendation enough.

Agent Yvette Nichol raced around her home, looking for her wallet.

'Oh, come on, Dad, you must have seen it,' she pleaded, watching the wall clock and its pitiless movement.

Her father felt frozen in place. He had seen her wallet. He'd taken it earlier in the day and slipped twenty dollars in. It was a little game they played. He gave her extra money and she pretended not to notice, though every now and then he'd come home from the night shift at the brewery and there'd be an éclair in the fridge with his name on it, in her clear, almost childlike, hand.

He'd taken her wallet a few minutes ago to slip the money in, but when the call had come through for his daughter to report for a homicide case he'd done something he never dreamed he'd do. He hid it, along with her Sûreté warrant card. A small document she'd worked years to earn. He watched her now, throwing cushions from the sofa on to the floor. She'll tear the place apart looking for it, he realised.

'Help me, Dad, I've got to find it.' She turned to him, her eyes huge and desperate. Why's he just standing in the room not doing anything? she wondered. This was her big chance, the moment they'd talked about for years. How many times had they shared this dream of her one day making it on to the Sûreté? It had finally happened, and now, thanks to a lot of hard work and, frankly, her own natural talents as an investigator, she was actually being handed the chance to work on homicide with Gamache. Her Dad knew all about him. Had followed his career in the papers.

'Your Uncle Saul, now he had a chance to be on the police force, but he washed out,' her father had told her, shaking his head. 'Shame on him. And you know what happens to losers?'

'They lose their lives.' Yvette knew the right answer to that. She'd been told the family story since she'd had ears to hear.

'Uncle Saul, your grandparents. All. Now you're the bright one in the family, Yvette. We're counting on you.'

And she'd exceeded every expectation, by qualifying for the Sûreté. In one generation her family had gone from victims of the authorities in Czechoslovakia, to the ones who made the rules. They'd moved from one end of the gun to the other.

She liked it there.

But now the only thing standing between the fulfillment of all their dreams and failure, like stupid Uncle Saul, was her missing wallet and her warrant card. The clock was ticking. She'd told the Chief Inspector she'd be at his place in fifteen minutes. That was five minutes ago. She had ten minutes to get across town, and to pick up coffee on the way.

'Help me,' she pleaded, dumping the contents of her purse on to the living-room floor.

'Here it is.' Her sister Angelina came out of the kitchen holding the wallet and the warrant card. Nichol practically fell on Angelina and, kissing her, she rushed to put her coat on.

Ari Nikulas was watching his beloved youngest child, trying to memorise every inch of her precious face and trying not to give in to the wretched fear nesting in his stomach. What had he done, planting this ridiculous idea into her head? He'd lost no family in Czechoslovakia. Had made it up to fit in, to sound heroic. To be a big man in their new country. But his daughter had believed it, had believed there had once been a stupid Uncle Saul and a slaughtered family. And now it had gone too far. He couldn't tell her the truth.

She flew into his arms and kissed him on his stubbled cheek. He held her for a moment too long and she paused, looking into his tired, strained eyes.

'Don't worry, Dad. I won't let you down.' And she was off.

He'd just had time to notice how a tiny curl of her dark hair hooked on to the side of her ear, and hung there.

Yvette Nichol rang the doorbell within fifteen minutes of hanging up the phone. Standing awkwardly on the stoop she looked around. This was an attractive quartier, within an easy walk of the shops and restaurants along Rue Bernard. Outremont was a leafy neighborhood populated by the intellectual and political elite of French Quebec. She'd seen the Chief Inspector at headquarters, bustling through the halls, always with a group of people in his slipstream. He was very senior and had a reputation for acting as a mentor to the people lucky enough to work with him. She counted herself fortunate.

He opened the door promptly, just fixing his tweed cap to his head and gave her a warm smile. He held out his hand and after a slight hesitation she shook it.

'I'm Chief Inspector Gamache.'

'It's an honour.'

As the passenger door of the unmarked car was opened for him, Gamache caught the unmistakable fragrance of Tim Horton's coffee in cardboard cups and another aroma. Brioche. The young agent had done her homework. Only while on a murder case did he drink fast-food coffee. It was so associated in his mind with the teamwork, the long hours, the standing in cold, damp fields, that his heart raced every time he smelt industrial coffee and wet cardboard.

'I downloaded the preliminary report from the scene.

A hard copy is in the file back there.' Nichol waved toward the back seat while negotiating Blvd St Denis to the autoroute which would take them over the Champlain Bridge and into the countryside.

The rest of the trip was made in silence, as he read the scant information, sipped coffee, ate pastry and watched the flat farmlands around Montreal close in and become slowly rolling hills, then larger mountains, covered with brilliant autumn leaves.

About twenty minutes after turning off the Eastern Townships autoroute they passed a small pockmarked sign telling them Three Pines was two kilometers off this secondary road. After a tooth-jarring minute or two along the washboard dirt road they saw the inevitable paradox. An old stone mill sat beside a pond, the mid morning sun warming its fieldstones. Around it the maples and birches and wild cherry trees held their fragile leaves, like thousands of happy hands waving to them upon arrival. And police cars. The snakes in Eden. Though, Gamache knew, the police were not the evil ones. The snake was already here.

Gamache walked straight toward the anxious crowd that had gathered. As he approached he could see the road dip down, gently sloping into a picturesque village. The growing crowd stood on the brow of the hill, some looking into the woods, where they could just make out the movement of officers in bright yellow jackets, but most were looking at him. Gamache had seen their expression countless times, people desperate for news they desperately didn't want to hear.

'Who is it? Can you tell us what happened?' A tall, distinguished man spoke for the others.

'I'm sorry, I haven't even seen for myself yet. I'll tell you as soon as I can.'

The man looked unhappy with the answer but nodded. Gamache checked his watch: 11 a.m., Thanksgiving Sunday. He turned from the crowd and walked to where they were staring, to the activity in the woods and the one spot of stillness he knew he'd find.

A yellow plastic tape circled the body and within that circle the investigators worked, bowing down like some pagan ritual. Most had been with Gamache for years, but he always kept one position open for a trainee.

'Inspector Jean Guy Beauvoir, this is Agent Yvette Nichol.'

Beauvoir gave a relaxed nod. 'Welcome.'

At thirty-five years old, Jean Guy Beauvoir had been Gamache's second in command for more than a decade. He wore cords and a wool sweater under his leather jacket. A scarf was rakishly and apparently randomly whisked around his neck. It was a look of studied nonchalance which suited his toned body but was easily contradicted by the cord-tight tension of his stance. Jean Guy Beauvoir was loosely wrapped but tightly wound.

'Thank you, sir.' Nichol wondered whether she would ever be as comfortable at a murder scene as these people.

'Chief Inspector Gamache, this is Robert Lemieux,' Beauvoir introduced a young officer standing respect-fully just outside the police cordon. 'Agent Lemieux was the duty officer with the Cowansville Sûreté. He got the call and came here immediately. Secured the scene then called us.'

'Well done.' Gamache shook his hand. 'Anything strike you when you arrived?'

Lemieux looked dumbfounded by the question. At best he'd hoped to be allowed to hang around and watch, and not be shooed away from the scene. He'd never expected to meet Gamache, never mind actually answer a question.

'*Bien sûr*, I saw that man there. An *Anglais*, I suspected by his clothes and his pallor. The English, I have noticed, have weak stomachs.' Lemieux was pleased to pass this insight on to the Chief Inspector, even though he'd just made it up. He had no idea whether *Les Anglais* were more prone to pallor than the Quebecois, but it sounded good. It had also been Lemieux's experience that the English had no clothes sense, and this man in his plaid flannel shirt could not possibly be francophone. 'His name is Benjamin Hadley.'

On the far side of the circle, half sitting against a maple tree, Gamache could see a middle-aged man. Tall, slim, looking very, very ill. Beauvoir followed Gamache's gaze.

'He found the body,' said Beauvoir.

'Hadley? As in Hadley's Mills?'

Beauvoir smiled. He couldn't imagine how he knew this, but he did. 'That's the one. You know him?'

'No. Not yet.' Beauvoir cocked his eyebrow at his chief and waited. Gamache explained, 'The mill has faded writing at the top.'

'Hadley's Mills.'

'Well deduced, Beauvoir.'

'A wild guess, sir.'

Nichol could have kicked herself. She'd been everywhere Gamache had been and he had noticed that and she hadn't. What else did he see? What else didn't she? Damn. She looked suspiciously at Lemieux. He seemed to be ingratiating himself to the Chief Inspector.

'*Merci*, Agent Lemieux,' she said, putting out her hand while the Chief Inspector's back was turned, watching the wretched '*Anglais*'. Lemieux took it, as she hoped he would. '*Au revoir.*' Lemieux stood uncertainly for a moment, looking from her to Gamache's broad back. Then he shrugged and left.

Armand Gamache turned his attention from the living to the dead. He walked a few paces and knelt down beside the body that had brought them there.

A clump of hair had fallen into Jane Neal's open eyes. Gamache wanted to brush it away. It was fanciful, he knew. But he was fanciful. He had come to allow himself a certain latitude in that area. Beauvoir, on the other hand, was reason itself, and that made them a formidable team.

Gamache stared quietly at Jane Neal. Nichol cleared her throat, thinking perhaps he'd forgotten where he was. But he didn't react. Didn't move. He and Jane were frozen in time, both staring, one down, one up. Then his eyes moved along her body, to the worn camel-hair cardigan, the light-blue turtleneck. No jewelry. Was she robbed? He'd have to ask Beauvoir. Her tweed skirt was where you'd expect it to be, in someone who'd fallen. Her leotards, patched in at least one place, were otherwise unmarred. She might have been robbed, but she hadn't been violated. Except for being killed, of course.

His deep brown eyes lingered on her liver-spotted brown hands. Rough, tanned hands that had known seasons in a garden. No rings on her fingers, or sign there had ever been. He always felt a pang when looking at the hands of the newly dead, imagining all the objects and people those hands had held. The food, the faces, the doorknobs. All the gestures they'd made to signal delight or sorrow. And the final gesture, surely, to ward off the blow that would kill. The most poignant were the hands of young people who would never absently brush a lock of gray hair from their own eyes.

He stood up with Beauvoir's help and asked, 'Was she robbed?'

'We don't think so. Mr Hadley says she never wore jewelry, and rarely carried a handbag. He thinks we'll find it in her home.'

'Her house key?'

'No. No key. But again, Mr Hadley says people don't lock up around here.'

'They will now.' Gamache stooped over the body and stared at the tiny wound, hardly large enough, you'd have thought, to drain the life from a whole human being. It was about the size of the tip of his little finger.

'Any idea what did this?'

'It's hunting season, so perhaps a bullet, though it doesn't look like any bullet wound I've ever seen.'

'It's actually bow-hunting season. Guns don't start for two weeks,' said Nichol.

The two men looked at her. Gamache nodded and the three of them stared at the wound as though perhaps with enough concentration it would talk.

'So where's the arrow?' Beauvoir asked.

'Is there an exit wound?'

'I don't know,' said Beauvoir. 'We haven't let the medical examiner move her.'

'Let's get her over here,' said Gamache as Beauvoir waved to a young woman in jeans, field coat and carrying a medical bag.

'*Monsieur L'Inspecteur*,' said Dr Sharon Harris, nodding and kneeling. 'She's been dead about five hours, perhaps slightly less. That's just a guess.' Dr Harris rolled Jane over. Dried leaves clung to the back of her sweater. A retching noise was heard and Nichol looked over to see Ben Hadley, his heaving back turned to them, throwing up.

'Yes, there's an exit wound.'

'Thank you, doctor. We'll leave you to it. Now, walk with me, Beauvoir, you too, Agent Nichol. Tell me what you know.'

In all the years Jean Guy Beauvoir had worked with Gamache, through all the murders and mayhem, it never ceased to thrill him, hearing that simple sentence. 'Tell me what you know.' It signaled the beginning of the hunt. He was the alpha dog. And Chief Inspector Gamache was Master of the Hunt.

'Her name's Jane Neal. Aged seventy-six. Never been

married. We got this information from Mr Hadley who says she was the same age as his mother who died a month ago.'

'That's interesting. Two elderly women die within a month of each other in this tiny village. I wonder.'

'I wondered too, so I asked. His mother died after a long battle with cancer. They could see it coming for a year.'

'Go on.'

'Mr Hadley was walking in the woods at about eight this morning, a regular occurrence. Miss Neal's body was lying across the path. Impossible to miss.'

'What did he do?'

'He says he recognised her immediately. He knelt down and shook her. He thought she'd had a stroke or heart attack. Says he was about to begin CPR when he noticed the wound.'

'Didn't he notice she was staring blank-eyed and was cold as marble?' Nichol was feeling more confident.

'Would you?'

'Of course. You couldn't miss it.'

'Unless . . .' Here Gamache was inviting her to argue against herself. She didn't want to. She wanted to be right. Clearly he thought she wasn't.

'Unless. Unless I was in shock, I suppose.' She had to admit that was a remote possibility.

'Look at the man. It's been three hours since he found her and he's still sick. He just threw up. This woman was important to him,' said Gamache, looking over at Ben Hadley. 'Unless he's faking it.'

43

'Sorry, sir?'

'Well, it's easy enough to stick a finger down your throat and throw up. Makes quite an impression.' Gamache turned to Beauvoir. 'Do any others know about the death of Miss Neal?'

'There was a group of villagers on the road, sir,' said Nichol. Gamache and Beauvoir looked at her. She'd done it again, she realised. In an effort to impress and redeem herself she'd in fact done the opposite. She'd answered a question not directed at her, interrupting a senior officer with information obvious to a three-year-old. Inspector Gamache had seen those people as well as she had. Damn! Nichol knew with a creeping chill that in trying to impress them with her brilliance she was having the opposite effect. She was proving herself a fool.

'Sorry, sir.'

'Inspector Beauvoir?'

'I've tried to keep this a sterile site.' He turned to Nichol. 'No outsiders, and none of our people talking about the crime outside our perimeter.' Nichol blushed a deep red. She hated that he felt he had to explain it to her, and she hated even more that she needed the explanation.

'But—' Beauvoir shrugged.

'Time to speak with Mr Hadley,' said Gamache, walking with a measured pace in his direction.

Ben Hadley had been watching them, understanding clearly that the boss had arrived.

'Mr Hadley, I'm Chief Inspector Armand Gamache of the Sûreté du Quebec.'

Ben had been expecting a francophone, perhaps even a unilingual French detective, so he'd spent a few minutes practicing his French, and how to describe his movements. Now this immaculate man with the trimmed moustache, the deep-brown eyes looking at him over the rim of his half-moon glasses, the three-piece suit (could that possibly be a Burberry coat?), the tweed cap with graying, groomed hair underneath, was extending his large hand – as though this was a slightly formal business occasion – and speaking English with a British accent. Yet he'd heard snippets of his conversation with his colleagues and that was definitely in fast and fluid French. In Quebec it was far from unusual that people spoke both languages, even fluently. But it was unusual to find a francophone speaking like a hereditary member of the House of Lords.

'This is Inspector Jean Guy Beauvoir and Agent Yvette Nichol.' They all shook hands, though Nichol was slightly leery, not sure what he'd wiped his face with after throwing up.

'How can I help?'

'Let's walk,' Gamache pointed down the path through the woods, 'just a little away from here.'

'Thank you,' said Ben, genuinely grateful.

'I'm sorry about the death of Miss Neal. Was she a close friend?'

'Very. She actually taught me at the school house here.'

Gamache was watching him attentively, his dark brown eyes on Ben's face, taking in what was being said, without judgment or accusation. Ben could feel himself relax for the first time in hours. Gamache said nothing, just waited for Ben to continue.

'She was a wonderful woman. I wish I was good with words, I could begin to describe her for you.' Ben turned his face away, ashamed of the tears that came up again. He balled his hands into fists and could feel the welcome pain of his fingernails biting into his palms. That was a pain he could understand. The other was beyond his comprehension. Strangely it was so much greater than when his mother had died. He gathered himself again, 'I don't understand what's happened. Jane's death wasn't natural, was it?'

'No, Mr Hadley, it wasn't.'

'Someone killed her?'

'Tell us about this morning, please.'

By now their walking had slowed and petered to a stop.

'I found Jane just lying—'

Gamache interrupted, 'From the time you woke up, please.' Ben raised an eyebrow but did as he was asked.

'I woke up at about seven. I always get up with the sun. The light comes into my bedroom and I never bothered to get curtains. I got up, had a shower and the rest, and fed Daisy.' He watched their faces closely, looking for some sign that he was giving too much or too little detail. The woman agent looked as puzzled as he felt. The tall good-looking Inspector (Ben had already forgotten their names) was writing everything down. And the boss looked interested and encouraging. 'Then we went outside for a walk, but she has arthritis and this morning she was very sore. Daisy's a dog, by the way. Anyway, I let her back in the house and took myself off for a walk. This was a quarter to eight.' Ben figured, correctly, they'd be interested in the timing. 'It takes just a few minutes to walk here, up the road and past the school house then into the woods.'

'Did you see anyone?' Beauvoir asked.

'No, I didn't. It's possible someone saw me, but I missed them. I tend to walk with my head down, lost in thought. I've passed right by people without noticing them. My friends know that about me and don't take offense. I was walking along the path and something made me look up.'

'Please try to remember, Mr Hadley. If you normally walk with your head down, why would you raise it?'

'Odd, isn't it? I can't remember. But unfortunately, as I said, I'm normally lost in thought. Never deep or important thoughts. My mother used to laugh and say some people try to be in two places at once. I, on the other hand, am generally nowhere.' Ben laughed, but Nichol privately thought that was an awful thing for a mother to say.

'She was right, of course. Look at today. Beautiful sunshine. I'm walking through the gorgeous woods. It's like a postcard, but I don't notice anything, don't appreciate it, except perhaps sometime later when I'm somewhere else and thinking about this walk. It seems my mind is constantly one step behind my body.'

'Looking up, sir,' Beauvoir prompted.

'I really can't think what made me look up, but it's a good thing I did. I might have fallen right over her. Funny but it never occurred to me that she was dead. I was

47

reluctant to disturb her. I kind of tiptoed up and called her name. Then I noticed a stillness and my mind just kind of exploded. I thought she'd had a stroke, or heart attack.' He shook his head, still in disbelief.

'Did you actually touch the wound?' Beauvoir asked.

'I think I might have. I just remember leaping up and wiping my hands on my pants. I panicked and like a – I don't know what – an hysterical child I ran in circles. Idiot! Anyway, I finally got a hold of myself and dialed 911 on my cell phone.'

'I'm curious,' said Gamache. 'Why did you bring a cell phone to walk in the woods?'

'These woods belong to my family and every fall hunters trespass. I'm not a brave man, I'm afraid, but I can't tolerate killing. Killing anything. I have spiders in my home with names. In the mornings when I go for a walk I bring a cell phone. Partly out of fear that I'll get shot by some drunken hunter and need to call for help and partly to call Natural Resources and get a warden up here if I do spot someone.'

'And what would that number be?' asked Chief Inspector Gamache pleasantly.

'I don't know. I have it on my speed dial. I know that my hands shake when I'm nervous, so I just programmed the number in.' Ben looked concerned for the first time and Inspector Gamache took him by the arm and led him further up the path.

'I'm sorry about these questions. You're an important witness and, frankly, the person who finds the body is near the top of our list of suspects.'

Ben stopped in his tracks and looked at the Inspector, incredulous.

'Suspected of what? What are you saying?' Ben turned around and looked back in the direction they'd come, toward Jane's body. 'That's Jane Neal over there. A retired schoolteacher who tended roses and ran the ACW, the Anglican Church Women. It can't be anything other than an accident. You don't understand. Nobody would kill her on purpose.'

Nichol was watching this exchange and now waited with some satisfaction for Chief Inspector Gamache to set this stupid man straight.

'You're absolutely right, Mr Hadley. That's by far the likeliest possibility.' Yvette Nichol couldn't believe her ears. Why didn't he just tell Hadley to get off his soapbox and let them do their jobs? After all, he was the idiot who disturbed the body then ran around messing up and contaminating the whole site. He was hardly in a position to lecture a man as senior and respected as Gamache.

'In the few hours you've been standing here, has anything about the scene or about Miss Neal seemed out of place?'

Gamache was impressed that Ben chose not to say the obvious. Instead he thought for a minute.

'Yes. Lucy, her dog. I can't remember Jane ever going for a walk without Lucy, especially a morning walk.'

'Did you call anyone else on your cell?'

Ben looked as though he'd been presented with a totally new, and brilliant, idea.

'Oh. Such an idiot! I can't believe it. It never occurred

to me to call Peter, or Clara or anyone. Here I was all alone, not wanting to leave Jane, but having to wave down the police. And it never occurred to me to call for help, except 911. Oh my God, the shock, I suppose.'

Or maybe, thought Nichol, you really are an idiot. So far it would be difficult to find a human being less effective than Ben Hadley.

'Who are Peter and Clara?' Beauvoir asked.

'Peter and Clara Morrow. My best friends. They live next door to Jane. Jane and Clara were like mother and daughter. Oh, poor Clara. Do you think they know?'

'Well, let's find out,' said Gamache suddenly, walking with surprising speed back down the path toward the body. Once at the scene he turned to Beauvoir.

'Inspector, take over here. You know what you're looking for. Agent, stay with the Inspector and help him. What time is it?'

'Eleven-thirty, sir,' said Nichol.

'Right. Mr Hadley, is there a restaurant or café in the village?'

'Yes, there's Olivier's Bistro.'

Gamache turned to Beauvoir. 'Assemble the team at Olivier's at one-thirty. We'll miss the lunch rush and should have the place almost to ourselves. Is that correct, Mr Hadley?'

'Hard to say, really. It's possible as word gets out the village will congregate there. Olivier's is the Central Station of Three Pines. But he has a back room he opens only for dinner. It overlooks the river. He'd probably open it for you and your team.'

Gamache looked at Ben with interest. 'That's a good idea. Inspector Beauvoir, I'll stop by and speak with Monsieur Olivier—'

'It's Olivier Brulé,' Ben interrupted. 'He and his partner Gabriel Dubeau run it and the only B&B in the village.'

'I'll speak with them and arrange a private room for lunch. May I walk with you, Mr Hadley, to the village? I haven't been there yet.'

'Yes, of course.' Ben almost said, 'It would be a pleasure', but stopped himself. Somehow this police officer emitted and invited courtesy and a certain formality. Though they must have been about the same age, Ben felt it was very like being with his grandfather.

'There's Peter Morrow.' Ben pointed into the crowd which had turned as though choreographed in their direction as the two men made their way out of the woods. Ben was pointing to the tall worried-looking man who'd spoken to Gamache earlier.

'I'm going to tell you all I can right now,' Gamache spoke to the crowd of about thirty villagers. He noticed Ben walk over to stand next to Peter Morrow.

'The dead woman's name is Jane Neal.' Gamache knew it was a false kindness to cushion a blow like this. A few of the people started to cry, some brought their hands up to their mouths as though covering a wound. Most dropped their heads as though the information was too heavy. Peter Morrow stared at Gamache. Then at Ben.

Gamache took all this in. Mr Morrow showed no surprise. And no sorrow. Anxiety, yes. Concern, without doubt. But sadness?

'How?' someone asked.

'We don't know yet. But it wasn't natural.'

A moan escaped the crowd, involuntary and heartfelt. Except Peter Morrow.

'Where's Clara?' Ben looked around. It was unusual to see one without the other.

Peter tilted his head toward the village. 'St Thomas's.'

The three men found Clara alone in the chapel, eyes closed, head bowed. Peter stood at the open door looking at her hunched back, braced against the blow that was to fall. He quietly walked up the short path between the pews, feeling as though he was floating above his body, watching his movements.

It was the minister who had brought the news earlier that morning that the police were active in the woods behind the old school house. Then, as the service of Thanksgiving progressed, their unease grew. Soon the tiny church was sick with rumors of a hunting accident. A woman. Injured? No, killed. Don't know who. Terrible. Terrible. And deep down in her stomach Clara knew just how terrible it was. With each opening of the door, each shaft of sunlight, she begged Jane to appear, late and flustered and apologetic. 'I've just slept in. Silly of me. Lucy, poor dear, woke me with a little cry to go out. So sorry.' The minister, either oblivious to the drama or out of his depth, just kept droning on.

Sun poured in through the stained-glass boys in uniforms from the Great War, scattering blues and deep reds and yellows across the pine floor and oak pews. The chapel smelled like every small church Clara had ever known. Pledge and pine and dusty old books. As the choir stood to sing the next hymn Clara turned to Peter.

'Can you go see?'

Peter took Clara's hand and was surprised to feel it freezing cold. He rubbed it between his own hands for a moment.

'I'll go. It'll be all right. Look at me,' he said, trying to get her frantic mind to stop its twirling.

'Praise, my soul, the King of heaven,' sang the choir.

Clara blinked, 'It will be all right?'

'Yes.'

'Alleluia, Alleluia. Praise the everlasting King.'

That had been an hour ago and now everyone had left, including the minister, late for Thanksgiving service in Cleghorn Halt. Clara heard the door open, saw the square of sunlight grow down the aisle, and saw the shadow appear, the outline familiar even in its distortion.

Peter hesitated then slowly made his way to her pew. She knew then.

THREE

Clara sat in her kitchen drained and stunned with the overwhelming need to call Jane and tell her what had happened. What had happened was inconceivable. A world suddenly, violently, without Jane. Without that touch, that comfort, that kindness. Clara felt that someone had scooped not just her heart but her brain right out of her body. How is it possible, Clara wondered, looking down at her hands folded neatly in her lap, that my heart can still beat? I must call Jane.

After leaving the church they had, with Gamache's permission, gone to get Jane's golden retriever Lucy, who was now curled at Clara's feet as though hugging her own inconceivable loss.

Peter was willing the water to boil so he could make tea and then all this would go away. Maybe, said his brain and his upbringing, if you make enough tea and small talk, time reverses and all bad things are undone. But he'd lived too long with Clara to be able to hide in denial.

Jane was dead. Killed. And he needed to comfort Clara and somehow make it all right. And he didn't know how. Rummaging through the cupboard like a wartime surgeon frantically searching for the right bandage, Peter swept aside Yogi Tea and Harmony Herbal Blend, though he hesitated for a second over chamomile. But no. Stay focused, he admonished himself. He knew it was there, that opiate of the Anglos. And his hand clutched the box just as the kettle whistled. Violent death demanded Earl Grey. Glancing out the window as he splashed boiling water into the pot and felt the painful pricks of scalding water bouncing on to his hand, he saw Chief Inspector Gamache sitting alone on the bench on the village green. The inspector appeared to be feeding the birds, but that couldn't be right. His attention returned to the important task of making tea.

Armand Gamache sat on the bench, watching the birds but mostly watching the village. Before his eyes the village of Three Pines seemed to slow right down. The insistence of life, the bustle and energy became muffled. The voices dropped, gaits slowed. Gamache sat back and did what he did best. He watched. He took in the people, their faces, their actions, and where possible he took in what they said, though people stayed far enough away from his wooden bench on the grass that he couldn't hear much. He noticed who touched and who didn't. Who hugged and who shook hands. He noticed who had red eyes and who gave the appearance of business as usual.

Three huge pine trees faced him at the far end of the

green. Between him and them was a pond, a bunch of sweater-clad children circling it, hunting for frogs, he supposed. The village green sat, not surprisingly, in the center of the village, a road called The Commons circling it with homes, except behind him, which seemed to be the commercial district. It was a very short commercial. It consisted, as far as Gamache could see, of a *dépanneur* whose Pepsi sign read 'Beliveau'. Beside that was a *boulangerie*, the Bistro and a bookstore. Four roads led off The Commons, like the spokes of a wheel, or the directions of a compass.

As he sat quietly and let the village happen around him he was impressed by how beautiful it was, these old homes facing the green, with their mature perennial gardens and trees. By how natural everything looked, undesigned. And the pall of grief that settled on this little community was worn with dignity and sadness and a certain familiarity. This village was old, and you don't get to be old without knowing grief. And loss.

'They say it's supposed to rain tomorrow.' Gamache looked up and saw Ben holding an ancient and, by the aroma, perhaps decomposing dog on a leash.

'Is that right?' Gamache indicated the seat next to him and Ben sat down, Daisy collapsing gratefully at his feet.

'Starting in the morning. And getting colder.'

The two men sat silently for a moment or two.

'That's Jane's home.' Ben pointed to a small stone cottage off to the left. 'And that place beside it belongs to Peter and Clara.' Gamache shifted his gaze. Their home was slightly larger than Jane's and while hers was made of fieldstone, theirs was red brick, in the style known as Loyalist. A simple wooden veranda ran along the front of the home and held two wicker rocking chairs. A front door was flanked by windows and upstairs he could see two more windows, with shutters painted a warm and deep blue. The pretty front garden was planted with roses and perennials and fruit trees. Probably crab apple, thought Gamache. A stand of trees, mostly maple, separated Jane Neal and the Morrows. Though more than the trees separated them now.

'My place is over there.' Ben nodded at a charming old white clapboard home, with a veranda below and three dormers above. 'But I guess that place up there is also mine.' Ben waved vaguely into the sky. Gamache thought it possible Ben was speaking metaphorically, or even meteorologically. Then his eyes dropped from the puffy clouds and landed on the roof of a home on the side of the hill leading out of Three Pines.

'Been in my family for generations. My mother lived there.'

Gamache didn't quite know what to say. He'd seen homes like that before. Many times. They were what he'd heard referred to during his time at Christ's College, Cambridge as Victorian piles. Quite descriptive, he'd always thought. And Quebec, notably Montreal, boasted its share of piles, built by the Scottish robber barons, of railway, booze and banking money. They were held together with hubris, a short-term binder at best since many of them had long ago been torn down or donated to McGill University, which needed another Victorian monstrosity like it needed the Ebola virus. Ben was looking at the home with great affection.

'Will you move to the big house?'

'Oh yes. But it needs some work. Parts of it are straight out of a horror movie. Gruesome.'

Ben remembered telling Clara about the time he and Peter had played war in the basement as kids and had come across the snake's nest. He'd never seen a person turn green, but Clara had.

'Is the village named after those trees?' Gamache looked at the cluster on the green.

'You don't know the story? Those pines aren't the originals, of course. They're only sixty years old. My mother helped plant them when she was a kid. But there have been pines here since the village was founded, more than two hundred years ago. And always in a group of three. Three Pines.'

'But why?' Gamache leaned forward, curious.

'It's a code. For the United Empire Loyalists. They settled all the land around here, except for the Abenaki, of course.' In a sentence, Gamache noticed, Ben had dismissed a thousand years of native habitation. 'But we're only a couple of kilometers from the border with the States. When the people loyal to the crown during and after the War of Independence were fleeing, they had no way of knowing when they were safe. So a code was designed. Three pines in a cluster meant the loyalists would be welcome.'

'*Mon Dieu, c'est incroyable*. So elegant. So simple,' said Gamache, genuinely impressed. 'But why haven't I heard of this? I'm a student of Quebec history myself, and yet this is completely unknown to me.'

'Perhaps the English want to keep it a secret, in case we need it again.' Ben at least had the grace to blush as he said this. Gamache turned in his seat and looked at the tall man, slumping as was his nature, his long sensitive fingers loosely holding the leash of a dog who couldn't possibly leave him.

'Are you serious?'

'The last sovereignty referendum was perilously close, as you know. And the campaign was ugly at times. It's not always comfortable being a minority in your own country,' said Ben.

'I appreciate that, but even if Quebec separates from Canada, surely you wouldn't feel threatened? You know your rights would be protected.'

'Do I? Do I have the right to put up a sign in my own language? Or work only in English? No. The language police would get me. The Office de la Langue Française. I'm discriminated against. Even the Supreme Court agrees. I want to speak English, Chief Inspector.'

'You are speaking English. And so am I. And so are all my officers. Like it or not, Mr Hadley, the English are respected in Quebec.'

'Not always, and not by everyone.'

'True. Not everyone respects police officers either. That's just life.'

'You're not respected because of your actions, what Quebec police have done in the past. We're not respected just by virtue of being English. It's not the same thing.

Do you have any idea how much our lives have changed in the last twenty years? All the rights we've lost? How many of our neighbors and friends and family members have left because of the draconian laws here? My mother barely spoke French, but I'm bilingual. We're trying, Inspector, but still the English are the laughing stock. Blamed for everything. The *tête carrée*. No,' Ben Hadley nodded toward the three sturdy pine trees swaying slightly in the wind, 'I'll put my faith in individuals, not the collective.'

It was, reflected Gamache, one of the fundamental differences between anglophone and francophone Quebecers; the English believed in individual rights and the French felt they had to protect collective rights. Protect their language and culture.

It was a familiar and sometimes bitter debate, but one that rarely infected personal relationships. Gamache remembered reading in the *Montreal Gazette* a few years ago an article by a columnist who observed that Quebec worked in reality, just not on paper.

'Things change, you know, Monsieur Hadley,' Gamache said gently, hoping to lift the tension that had settled on their little park bench. The French-English debate in Quebec was a polarising force. Best, in Gamache's opinion, leave it to politicians and journalists, who had nothing better to do.

'Do they, Chief Inspector? Are we really growing more civilised? More tolerant? Less violent? If things had changed, you wouldn't be here.'

'You're referring to Miss Neal's death. You believe it

was murder?' Gamache himself had been wondering just that.

'No, I don't. But I know whoever did that to her intended murder of some sort this morning. At the very least the murder of an innocent deer. That is not a civilised act. No, inspector, people don't change.' Ben dipped his head and fiddled with the leash in his hands. 'I'm probably wrong.' He looked at Gamache and smiled disarmingly.

Gamache shared Ben's feelings about hunting but couldn't have disagreed more about people. Still, it had been a revealing exchange, and that was his job. To get people to reveal themselves.

He'd been busy in the two hours since leaving Beauvoir. He'd walked with Peter Morrow and Ben Hadley to the church, where Peter had broken the news to his wife. Gamache had watched, standing back by the door, needing to see how she reacted, and not wanting to interfere. He'd left them then and he and Mr Hadley had continued down the road into the village.

He'd left Ben Hadley at the entrance to the charming village and made straight for the Bistro. It was easy to spot with its blue and white awnings and round wooden tables and chairs on the sidewalk. A few people were sipping coffee, all eyes on him as he made his way along the Commons.

Once his eyes adjusted to the inside of the Bistro he saw not the one largish room he'd expected but two rooms, each with its own open fireplace, now crackling with cheery fires. The chairs and tables were a comfortable mishmash of antiques. A few tables had armchairs in faded heirloom materials. Each piece looked as though it had been born there. He'd done enough antique hunting in his life to know good from bad, and that diamond point in the corner with the display of glass and tableware was a rare find. At the back of this room the cash register stood on a long wooden bar. Jars of licorice pipes and twists, cinnamon sticks and bright gummy bears shared the counter with small individual boxes of cereal.

Beyond these two rooms French doors opened on to a dining room, no doubt, thought Gamache; the room Ben Hadley had recommended.

'May I help you?' a large young woman with a bad complexion was asking him in perfect French.

'Yes. I'd like to speak with the owner please. Olivier Brulé, I believe.'

'If you'd like a seat, I'll get him. Coffee while you wait?'

The woods had been chilly and the thought of a *café au lait* in front of this open fire was too good. And maybe a licorice pipe, or two. Waiting for Mr Brulé and the coffee, he tried to figure out what was unusual or unexpected about this lovely bistro. Some small thing was a little off.

'I'm sorry to disturb you,' came a throaty voice slightly above him. He looked up and saw an elderly woman with cropped white hair leaning on a gnarled cane. As he shot to his feet he noticed she was taller than he'd expected. Even leaning she was almost as tall as he, and he had the impression she was not as frail as she appeared.

Armand Gamache gave a subtle bow and indicated the

other chair at his small table. The woman hesitated, but finally the ramrod bent and sat down.

'My name is Ruth Zardo,' she spoke loudly and slowly, as though to a dull child. 'Is it true? Is Jane dead?'

'Yes, Madame Zardo. I'm very sorry.'

A great bang, so sudden and violent it made even Gamache jump, filled the Bistro. None of the other patrons, he noticed, even flinched. It took him just an instant to realise that the noise came from Ruth Zardo whacking her cane against the floor, like a caveman might wield a club. He'd never seen anyone do that before. He'd seen people with canes lift them up and rap on the floor in an annoying bid for attention, which generally worked. But Ruth Zardo had picked up her cane in a swift and apparently practiced move, taken hold of the straight end, and swung the cane over her head until the curved handle whacked the floor.

'What are you doing here while Jane is lying dead in the woods? What kind of police are you? Who killed Jane?'

The Bistro grew momentarily silent, then slowly the murmur of conversation started up again. Armand Gamache held her imperious stare with his own thoughtful eyes and leaned slowly across the table until he was sure only she could hear. Ruth, believing he might be about to actually whisper the name of the person who had killed her friend, leaned in as well.

'Ruth Zardo, my job is to find out who killed your friend. And I will do that. I will do it in the manner I see fit. I will not be bullied and I will not be treated with disrespect.

This is my investigation. If you have anything you'd like to say, or to ask, please do. But never, ever, swing that cane in my company again. And never speak to me like that again.'

'How dare I! This officer is obviously hard at work.' Both Ruth and her voice rose. 'Mustn't disturb the best the Sûreté has to offer.'

Gamache wondered whether Ruth Zardo really believed this sarcasm would be fruitful. He also wondered why she would take this attitude at all.

'Mrs Zardo, what can I get you?' the young waitress asked as though none of the dramatics had happened. Or perhaps it was simply intermission.

'A Scotch, please, Marie,' said Ruth, suddenly deflating and sinking back into the chair. 'I'm sorry. Forgive me.'

She sounded to Gamache like someone used to apologising.

'I suppose I could blame Jane's death for my poor behavior, but as you'll discover, I'm just like this. I have no talent for choosing my battles. Life seems, strangely, like a battle to me. The whole thing.'

'So I can expect more where that came from?'

'Oh, I think so. But you'll have plenty of company in your foxhole. And I promise not to whack my cane, at least around you.'

Armand Gamache leaned back in his chair, just as the Scotch and his *café au lait* and candy arrived. He took them and with all the dignity he could muster, turned to Ruth. 'Pipe, Madame?'

Ruth took the largest one and immediately bit the red candy end off.

'How did it happen?' Ruth asked.

'It looks like a hunting accident. But can you think of anyone who would want to deliberately kill your friend?'

Ruth told Gamache about the boys throwing manure. When she'd finished, Gamache asked, 'Why do you think these boys might have killed her? I agree it was a reprehensible thing to do, but she'd already announced their names, so it's not as though killing her would stop that. What's gained?'

'Revenge?' suggested Ruth. 'At that age, humiliation could be considered a capital offense. True, they were the ones who were trying to humiliate Olivier and Gabri, but the tables turned. And bullies don't much like getting some of their own back.'

Gamache nodded. It was possible. But surely, unless you're psychotic, the revenge would take a different form, something short of cold-blooded murder.

'How long did you know Mrs Neal?'

'Miss. She never married,' said Ruth. 'Though she almost did, once. What was his name?' She consulted the yellowing Rolodex in her head. 'Andy. Andy Selchuk. No. Sel . . . Sel . . . Selinsky. Andreas Selinsky. That was years ago. Fifty or more. Doesn't matter.'

'Please, tell me,' said Gamache.

Ruth nodded and absently stirred her Scotch with the butt end of her licorice pipe.

'Andy Selinsky was a logger. These hills were full of logging operations for a hundred years. Most of them are closed now. Andy worked on Mont Echo at the Thompson operation. The lumberjacks could be violent men. They'd work all week on the mountain, sleeping rough through storms and bear season, and the blackflies must have driven them crazy. They'd smear themselves with bear grease to keep away bugs. They were more afraid of blackflies than black bears. On weekends they'd come out of the woods, like living filth.'

Gamache was listening closely, genuinely interested, though not sure whether it was all pertinent to the investigation.

'Kaye Thompson's operation was different, though. I don't know how she did it, but somehow she kept those huge men in line. Nobody messed with Kaye,' said Ruth, in admiration.

'Andy Selinksy worked his way up to foreman. A natural leader. Jane fell in love with him, though I must admit most of us had a crush on him. Those huge arms and that rugged face . . .' Gamache could feel himself receding as she spoke and drifted back in time. 'He was immense but gentle. No, gentle isn't right. Decent. He could be tough, even brutal. But not vicious. And he was clean. Smelled like Ivory soap. He'd come to town with the other lumberjacks from the Thompson mill and they'd stand out because they didn't stink of rancid bear fat. Kaye must have scrubbed them with lye.'

Gamache wondered how low the bar was set when all a man had to do to attract a woman was not smell of decomposing bears.

'At the opening dance of the County Fair Andy chose Jane.' Ruth fell quiet, remembering. 'Still don't understand it,' said Ruth. 'I mean, Jane was nice and

66

all. We all liked her. But, frankly, she was ugly as sin. Looked like a goat.'

Ruth laughed out loud at the image she'd conjured up. It was true. Young Jane's face seemed to stretch out ahead of her, as though reaching for something, her nose elongating and her chin receding. She was also short-sighted, though her parents hated to admit they'd produced anything other than a perfect child, so they ignored her weak eyesight. This only accentuated the peering look, sticking her head out to the limits of her neck, trying to bring the world into focus. She always had a look on her face as though asking, 'Is that edible?' Young Jane was also chubby. She would remain chubby her whole life.

'For some unfathomable reason, Andreas Selinsky chose her. They danced all night. It was quite a sight.' Ruth's voice had hardened.

Gamache tried to imagine the young Jane, short, prim and plump, dancing with this huge muscled mountain man.

'They fell in love but her parents found out and put a stop to it. Caused quite a little stir. Jane was the daughter of the chief accountant for Hadley's Mills. It was inconceivable she'd marry a lumberjack.'

'What happened?' he couldn't help but ask. She looked at him as though surprised he was still there.

'Oh, Andy died.'

Gamache raised an eyebrow.

'No need to get excited, Inspector Clouseau,' said Ruth. 'An accident in the woods. A tree fell on him. Lots of witnesses. Happened all the time. Though there was some romantic notion at the time that he was so heartbroken he became deliberately careless. Bullshit. I knew him too. He liked her, perhaps even loved her, but he wasn't nuts. We all get dumped at sometime or another and don't kill ourselves. No, it was just an accident.'

'What did Jane do?'

'She went away to school. Came back a couple of years later with her teaching degree and took over at the school here. School House Number six.'

Gamache noticed a slight shadow at his arm and looked up. A man in his mid-thirties was standing there. Blond, trim, well-dressed in a casual way as though he'd walked out of a Lands End catalogue. He looked tired, but eager to help.

'I'm sorry I was so long. I'm Olivier Brulé.'

'Armand Gamache, I'm the Chief Inspector of Homicide with the Sûreté du Quebec.'

Unseen by Gamache, Ruth's eyebrows rose. She'd underestimated the man. He was the big boss. She'd called him Inspector Clouseau, and that was the only insult she could remember. After Gamache arranged for lunch, Olivier turned to Ruth, 'How are you?' he touched Ruth lightly on the shoulder. She winced as though burned.

'Not bad. How's Gabri?'

'Not good. You know Gabri, he wears his heart on his sleeve.' In fact, there were times Olivier wondered whether Gabri hadn't been born inside out.

Before Ruth left, Gamache got the bare outline of Jane's life. He also got the name of her next of kin. A niece named Yolande Fontaine, a real estate agent working

68

out of St Rémy. He looked at his watch: 12.30. St Rémy was about fifteen minutes away. He could probably make it. As he fished in his pocket for his wallet he saw Olivier just leaving and wondered if he couldn't do two things at once.

Grabbing his hat and coat from the rack he noticed a tiny white tag hanging from one of the hooks. It twigged. The thing that was out of place, unusual. He turned around, putting on his coat, and peered at the tables and chairs and mirrors and all the other antiques in the Bistro. Every one of them had a tag. This was a shop. Everything was for sale. You could eat your croissant and buy your plate. He felt a wave of pleasure at solving the little riddle. A few minutes later he was in Olivier's car heading for St Rémy. It wasn't hard to convince Olivier to give him a lift. Olivier was anxious to help.

'Rain on the way,' said Olivier, bumping along the gravel road.

'And turning colder tomorrow,' Gamache added. Both men nodded silently. After a couple of kilometers, Gamache spoke. 'What was Miss Neal like?'

'It's just so unbelievable that anyone would kill her. She was a wonderful person. Kind and gentle.'

Unconsciously, Olivier had equated the way people lived with the way they died. Gamache was always impressed with that. Almost invariably people expected that if you were a good person you shouldn't meet a bad end, that only the deserving are killed. And certainly only the deserving are murdered. However well hidden and subtle, there was a sense that a murdered person had somehow asked for it. That's why the shock when someone they knew to be kind and good was a victim. There was a feeling that surely there had been a mistake.

'I've never met anyone uniformly kind and good. Didn't she have any flaws? Anyone she rubbed the wrong way?'

There was a long pause and Gamache wondered whether Olivier had forgotten the question. But he waited. Armand Gamache was a patient man.

'Gabri and I have only been here twelve years. I didn't know her before that. But I have to say, honestly, I've never heard anything bad about Jane.'

They arrived in St Rémy, a town Gamache knew slightly, having skied at the mountain that grew behind the village when his children were young.

'Before you go in, do you want me to tell you about her niece Yolande?'

Gamache noticed the eagerness in Olivier's voice. Clearly there were things to tell. But that treat would have to wait.

'Not now, but on the way back.'

'Great.' Olivier parked the car and pointed to the real estate office in the little mall. Where nearby Williamsburg was self-consciously quaint, St Rémy was just an old Townships town. Not really planned, not designed, it was working-class, and somehow more real than the far prettier Williamsburg, the main town in the area. They arranged to meet back at the car at 1.15. Gamache noticed that even though Olivier had a few things in the back seat he didn't lock the car. Just strolled away.

A blonde woman with a great big smile greeted Chief Inspector Gamache at the door.

'M. Gamache, I'm Yolande Fontaine.' Her hand was out and pumping before he'd even slipped his into it. He felt a practiced eye sweep over him, assessing. He'd called to make sure she was in the office before leaving Three Pines and clearly he, or his Burberry, measured up.

'Now, please have a seat. What kind of property are you interested in?' She maneuvered him into an orange-upholstered cupped chair. Bringing out his warrant card he handed it across the desk and watched the smile fade.

'What's that goddamned kid done now? *Tabarnac.*' Her impeccable French had disappeared as well, replaced by street French, twangy and harsh, the words covered in grit.

'No, Madame. Is your aunt Jane Neal? Of Three Pines?'

'Yes. Why?'

'I'm sorry, but I have bad news. Your aunt was found dead today.'

'Oh, no,' she responded, with all the emotion one greets a stain on an old T-shirt. 'Heart?'

'No. It wasn't a natural death.'

Yolande Fontaine stared as though trying to absorb the words. She clearly knew what each individual word meant, but put together they didn't make any sense.

'Not natural? What does that mean?'

Gamache looked at the woman sitting in front of him. Lacquered nails, blonde hair puffed up and soldered into place, her face made up as though for a ball, at noon. She'd be in her early thirties, he figured, but perversely the heavy make-up made her look about fifty. She didn't appear to be living a natural life.

'She was found in the woods. Killed.'

'Murdered?' she whispered.

'We don't know. I understand you're her closest relative. Is that right?'

'Yes. My mother was her younger sister. She died of breast cancer four years ago. They were very close. Like this.' Here Yolande attempted to cross her fingers but the nails kept knocking into each other making it look like a finger puppet version of All Star Wrestling. She gave up and looked at Gamache knowingly.

'When can I get into the house?' she asked.

'I'm sorry?'

'In Three Pines. Aunt Jane always said it would be mine.'

Gamache had seen enough grief in his time to know that people handle it in different ways. His own aunt, upon waking up next to her husband of fifty years dead in the bed, called her hairdresser first to cancel her appointment. Gamache knew better than to judge people based upon what they do when presented with bad news. Still, it was an odd question.

'I don't know. We haven't even been in yet.'

Yolande became agitated.

'Well, I have a key. Can I go in before you, just to kind of tidy up?'

He wondered briefly whether this was a real estate agent's learned response.

'No.'

Yolande's face became hard and red, matching her nails. This was a woman not used to hearing 'no', and a woman without mastery of her anger.

'I'm calling my lawyer. The house is mine and I do not give you permission to enter. Got it?'

'Speaking of lawyers, do you happen to know who your aunt used?'

'Stickley. Norman Stickley.' Her voice brittle. 'We use him too from time to time for house transactions around Williamsburg.'

'May I have his co-ordinates, please?'

While she wrote them down in a florid hand Gamache glanced around and noticed some of the listings on the 'For Sale' board were estates, beautiful, sprawling ancestral homes. Most were more modest. Yolande had a lot of condos and trailer homes. Still, someone had to sell them, and it probably took a far better salesperson to sell a trailer home than a century home. But you'd have to sell a lot of trailers to make ends meet.

'There.' She shoved it across her desk. 'You'll hear from my lawyer.'

Gamache found Olivier waiting for him in the car. 'Am I late?' he asked, checking his watch. It said 1.10.

'No, a little early, in fact. I just had to pick up some shallots for tonight's dinner.' Gamache noticed a distinct and very pleasant odor in the car. 'And, to be honest, I didn't figure the interview with Yolande would take long.'

Olivier smiled as he pulled the car on to rue Principale. 'How'd it go?'

'Not quite as I expected,' admitted Gamache. Olivier gave a bark of a laugh.

'She's quite a piece of work is our Yolande. Did she cry hysterically?'

'Actually, no.'

'Well, that is a surprise. I would've thought given an audience, and the police at that, she'd make the most of her role as sole survivor. She's a triumph of image over reality. I'm not even sure if she knows what reality is anymore, she's so busy creating this image of herself.'

'Image as what?'

'A success. She needs to be seen as a happy and successful wife and mother.'

'Don't we all?'

Here Olivier gave him an arch and openly gay look. Gamache caught it and realised what he'd said. He raised his eyebrow to Olivier as though returning the look and Olivier laughed again.

'I meant' – Gamache smiled – 'we all have our public images.'

Olivier nodded. It was true. Especially true in the gay community, he thought, where you had to be entertaining, clever, cynical and, above all, attractive. It was exhausting looking so bored all the time. It was one of the things that made him flee to the country. He felt in Three Pines he had a shot at being himself. What he hadn't counted on was it taking so long to figure out who 'he' was.

'That's true. But it goes deeper with Yolande, I think. She's like a Hollywood set. This big fake front and all sort of empty and ugly behind. Shallow.'

'What was her relationship with Miss Neal?'

'Well, apparently they were quite close when Yolande was small, but there was a rupture of sorts. No idea what it was. Yolande eventually pisses everyone off, but it must have been pretty big. Jane even refused to see Yolande.'

'Really? Why?'

'Not a clue. Clara might know. Timmer Hadley could certainly have told you, but she's dead.'

There it was again. Timmer's death, so close to Jane's.

'And yet Yolande Fontaine seems to think Miss Neal left everything to her.'

'Well, she might have. For some blood is thicker, etc.'

'She seemed particularly anxious to get into Miss Neal's home before we do. Does that make any sense to you?'

Olivier considered. 'Can't say. I don't think anyone can answer that question since no one has ever been into Jane's home.'

'Pardon?' Gamache thought he must have misheard.

'Funny, I'm so used to it I never even thought to mention it. Yes. That's the only thing that was weird about Jane. She'd have us into the mudroom and kitchen. But never, ever, beyond the kitchen.'

'Surely Clara—'

'Not even Clara. Not Timmer. Nobody.'

Gamache made a note to make that the first activity after lunch. They arrived back with a few minutes to spare. Gamache settled into the bench on the green and watched Three Pines go about its life and its singular death. Ben joined him for a few minutes chat then dragged Daisy back home. Before heading to the Bistro for lunch

75

Gamache reflected on what he'd heard so far, and who would want to kill kindness.

Beauvoir had set up a large stand with paper and magic markers. Gamache took a seat next to him in Olivier's private back room and looked out through the wall of French doors. He could see tables, their umbrellas down, and beyond them the river. Bella Bella. He agreed.

The room filled with hungry and cold Sûreté officers. Gamache noticed Agent Nichol was sitting by herself and wondered why she chose her isolated position. Beauvoir reported first between bites of a ham sandwich, made with thick-sliced ham carved from what must have been a maple-cured roast, with honey-mustard sauce and slabs of aged cheddar on a fresh croissant.

'We scoured the site and found' – Beauvoir checked his notebook, smearing a bit of mustard on the page – 'three old beer bottles.'

Gamache raised his eyebrows. 'That's it?'

'And fifteen million leaves.'

'This is the wound.' Beauvoir drew a circle using a red magic marker. The officers watched without interest. Then Beauvoir raised his hand again and completed the drawing, marking in four lines radiating from the circle, as though marking compass points. Several officers lowered their sandwiches. Now they were interested. It looked like a crude map of Three Pines. Contemplating the macabre image Gamache wondered if the killer could possibly have done that intentionally.

'Would an arrow make this wound?' Beauvoir asked. No one seemed to know.

If an arrow had made that wound, thought Gamache, then where was it? It should be in the body. Gamache had an image from Notre Dame de Bon Secours, the church he and Reine-Marie attended sporadically. The walls were thick with murals of saints in various stages of pain and ecstasy. One of those images floated back to him now. St Sebastien, writhing, falling, his body stuffed full of arrows. Each one pointing out of his martyred body like accusing fingers. Jane Neal's body should have had an arrow sticking out of it, and that arrow should have pointed to the person who did this. There should not have been an exit wound. But there was. Another puzzle.

'Let's leave this and move on. Next report.'

The lunch progressed, the officers sitting around listening and thinking out loud, in an atmosphere that encouraged collaboration. He strongly believed in collaboration, not competition, within his team. He realised he was in a minority within the leadership of the Sûreté. He believed a good leader was also a good follower. And he invited his team to treat each other with respect, listen to ideas, support each other. Not everyone got it. This was a deeply competitive field, where the person who got results got promoted. And being second to solve a murder was useless. Gamache knew the wrong people were being rewarded within the Sûreté, so he rewarded the team players. He had a near-perfect solution rate and had never risen beyond the rank he now held and had held for twelve years. But he was a happy man.

Gamache bit into a grilled chicken and roasted vegetable baguette and decided he was going to enjoy mealtimes in this place. Some of the officers took a beer, but not Gamache, who preferred ginger beer. The pile of sandwiches quickly disappeared.

'The coroner found something odd,' reported Isabelle Lacoste. 'Two bits of feather imbedded in the wound.'

'Don't arrows have feathers?' asked Gamache. He again saw St Sebastien and his arrows, all with feathers.

'They used to,' said Nichol quickly, glad of the opportunity to show expertise. 'Now they're plastic.'

Gamache nodded. 'I didn't know that. Anything else?'

'There was very little blood, as you saw, consistent with instant death. She was killed where she was found. The body wasn't moved. Time of death, between six-thirty and seven this morning.'

Gamache told them what he'd learned from Olivier and Yolande and handed out assignments. First up was searching Jane Neal's home. Just then Gamache's cell phone rang. It was Yolande Fontaine's lawyer. Gamache never raised his voice, but his frustration was obvious.

'We won't be getting into Jane Neal's home just yet,' he reported after clicking his cell closed. 'Ms Fontaine's lawyer has unbelievably found a justice willing to sign an injunction stopping us from searching the home.'

'Until?' Beauvoir asked.

'Until it's proven to be murder or Ms Fontaine is proven not to have inherited the home. The new priorities are as follows. Find Jane Neal's will, get information on local archers, and I want to know why a hunter, if he accidentally shot Miss Neal, would bother removing the arrow. And we need to find out more about Timmer Hadley's death. I'll get us an Incident Room somewhere in Three Pines. I'm also going to speak with the Morrows. Beauvoir, I'd like you with me. You too, Agent Nichol.'

'It's Thanksgiving,' said Beauvoir. Gamache stopped in his tracks. He'd forgotten.

'Who here has plans for Thanksgiving dinner?'

All hands went up. He did too, come to that. Reine-Marie had asked their best friends over for dinner. Intimate, so he'd certainly be missed. And he doubted the treatment center excuse would fly with them.

'Change of plans. We'll be on the road back to Montreal by four – that's in an hour and a half. Cover as much ground as you can between now and then. We don't want this going cold because the turkey wouldn't wait.'

Beauvoir opened the wooden gate leading up the winding path to the cottage door. Hydrangea, turning pink now in the cold weather, bloomed around the house. The walk itself was lined with old garden roses, under-planted with some purple flower Gamache thought might be lavender. He made a mental note to ask Mrs Morrow, at a better time. The foxgloves and hollyhocks he knew immediately. His only regret about their apartment in Outremont was having only window boxes to plant. He'd love a garden exactly like this. It perfectly suited the modest brick home he was approaching. The deep blue door was opened by Peter even before they'd knocked and they stepped into a small mudroom with its collection of outdoor coats on pegs and boots stuffed under a long wooden bench.

'The Burlington news says rain's on the way,' said Peter as he took their coats and led them through to the big country kitchen. ''Course, they're almost always wrong. We seem to have a microclimate here. Must be the mountains.'

The room was warm and comfortable, with shiny dark wood counters and open shelving revealing crockery and tins and glasses. Rag throw rugs looked as though they had literally been thrown here and there on the vinyl floor, lending the room a relaxed charm. A huge bouquet, almost an island, sat at one end of the pine dining table. Clara sat at the other, wrapped in a multi-coloured afghan. She looked wan and disconnected.

'Coffee?' Peter wasn't at all sure of the etiquette, but all three declined.

Clara smiled slightly and rose, holding out her hand, the afghan slipping off her shoulder. So ingrained, Gamache knew, was our training to be polite that even in the midst of a terrible personal loss people still smiled.

'I'm so sorry,' he said to Clara.

'Thank you.'

'I'd like you to sit over there,' Gamache whispered to Nichol, pointing to a simple pine chair by the mudroom door, 'and take notes.'

Notes, Nichol said to herself. He's treating me like a secretary. Two years in the Sûreté du Quebec and I'm asked to sit and take notes. The rest of them sat at the kitchen table. Neither Gamache nor Beauvoir took out their notebooks, she observed.

'We think Jane Neal's death was an accident,' Gamache began, 'but we have a problem. We can't find a weapon, and no one's come forward, so I'm afraid we're going to have to investigate this as a suspicious death. Can you think of anyone who would want to harm your friend?'

'No. Not a soul. Jane ran bake sales and rummage sales for the ACW here at St Thomas's. She was a retired schoolteacher. She led a quiet, uneventful life.'

'Mrs Morrow?'

Clara thought a moment, or appeared to. But her brain was numb, incapable of giving a clear answer.

'Does anyone gain by her death?' Gamache thought maybe a clearer question would help.

'I don't think so,' Clara rallied, feeling a fool for feeling so much. 'She was comfortable, I think, though we never talked about it. Out here a little money goes a long way, thankfully. She grew her own vegetables but she gave most of them away. I always thought she did it more for fun than necessity.'

'How about her home?' Beauvoir asked.

'Yes, that would be worth quite a lot,' said Peter. 'But quite a lot by Three Pines standards, not by Montreal standards. She could get, maybe, a hundred and fifty thousand for it. Perhaps a little more.'

'Could there be another way someone could gain by her death?'

'Not an obvious one.'

Gamache made to get up. 'We need what we call an

Incident Room. A private place we can make our tempo-
rary headquarters here in Three Pines. Can you think of
a suitable spot?'

'The railway station. It's not used for that anymore.
The volunteer fire department has its headquarters there.
I'm sure they wouldn't mind sharing it.'

'We need something more private, I'm afraid.'

'There's the old schoolhouse,' Clara suggested.

'The one where Miss Neal worked?'

'That's it,' said Peter. 'We passed it walking down this
morning. It's owned by the Hadleys, but the archery club
uses it these days.'

'Archery club?' Beauvoir asked, hardly able to believe
his ears.

'We've had one here for years. Ben and I started it
years ago.'

'Is it locked? Do you have a key?'

'I have a key somewhere, I guess. Ben has one too, I
think. But it's never locked. Maybe it should have been.'
He looked at Clara, seeking her thoughts or comfort. He
only found a blank face. Gamache nodded to Beauvoir
who picked up his cell phone and placed a call while the
others spoke.

'I'd like to call a community meeting in the morning,'
said Gamache, 'at St Thomas's at eleven-thirty. But we
need to get the word out.'

'That's easy. Tell Olivier. They'll have the whole province
there, and the cast of Cats. And his partner Gabri's the
choir director.'

'I don't think we'll need music,' said Gamache.

'Neither do I, but you do need to get in. He has a set of keys.'

'The archery club is open but the church is locked?'

'The minister's from Montreal,' explained Peter.

Gamache said his goodbyes and the three of them walked across the now familiar village green. Instinctively, they kicked their feet slightly as they walked through the fallen leaves, sending up a slight flutter and a musky autumn scent.

The bed and breakfast was kitty-corner to the row of commercial buildings, at the corner of the Old Stage Road, another route out of Three Pines. It had once served as a stagecoach stop on the well-traveled route between Williamsburg and St Rémy. Long since unnecessary, it had, with the arrival of Olivier and Gabri, rediscovered its vocation of housing weary travelers. Gamache told Beauvoir he intended to get both information and reservations.

'For how long?' Beauvoir asked.

'Until this is solved, or we're taken off the case.'

'That must have been one hell of a good baguette.'

'I'll tell you, Jean Guy, had he put mushrooms on it I would have bought the damned bistro and moved right in. This'll be a whole lot more comfortable than some places we've found ourselves.'

It was true. Their investigations had taken them far from home, to Kuujjuaq and Gaspé and Shefferville and James Bay. They had had to leave home for weeks on end. Beauvoir had hoped this would be different, being so close to Montreal. Apparently not.

'Book me in.'

'Nichol?' he called over his shoulder. 'Want to stay too?'

Yvette Nichol felt she'd just won the lottery.

'Great. I don't have any clothes but that's not a problem, I could borrow some and wash these in the tub tonight—'

Gamache held up his hand.

'You weren't listening. We're going home tonight and starting here tomorrow.'

Damn. Every time she showed enthusiasm it kicked her in the ass. Would she never learn?

Carved pumpkins squatted on each step up to the sweeping veranda of the B&B. Inside, worn oriental rugs and overstuffed chairs, lights with tassels and a collection of oil lamps gave Gamache the impression of walking into his grandparents' home. To add to the impression, the place smelled of baking. Just then a large man in a frilly apron that said, 'Never Trust a Skinny Cook' made his entrance through a swinging door. Gamache was startled to see more than a passing resemblance to his grandmother.

Gabri sighed hugely and put a wan hand up to his forehead in a gesture not often seen this side of Gloria Swanson.

'Muffins?'

The question was so unexpected even Gamache was thrown off guard.

'Pardon, Monsieur?'

'I have carrot, date, banana and a special tribute to Jane called "Charles de Mills".' And with that Gabri disappeared and reappeared a moment later with a platter holding rings of muffins marvelously decorated with fruit and roses.

'They aren't Charles de Mills roses, of course. They're long dead,' Gabri's face dissolved into tears and the platter lurched perilously. Only Beauvoir's quick action, fueled by desire, saved the food. '*Désolé. Excusez-moi.* I'm just so sad.' Gabri collapsed on to one of the sofas, arms and legs flopping. Gamache had the feeling that for all the dramatics, the man was sincere. He gave Gabri a moment to compose himself, fully realising it was possible Gabri had never been composed. He then asked Gabri to spread the word about the public meeting the next day, and to open the church. He also booked rooms in the bed and breakfast.

'Bed and brunch,' Gabri corrected. 'But you may have your brunch at breakfast, if you like, since you're helping bring the brute to justice.'

'Any idea who might have killed her?'

'It was a hunter, wasn't it?'

'We don't actually know. But if it wasn't, who comes to mind?'

Gabri reached for a muffin. Beauvoir took that as permission to take one himself. They were still warm from the oven.

Gabri was silent for two muffins, then said softly, 'I can't think of anyone, but,' he turned intense brown eyes on Gamache, 'am I likely to? I mean, isn't that what's so horrible about murder? We don't see it coming. I'm not saying this very well.' He reached for another muffin and ate it, rose and all. 'The people I've been angriest at probably never even realised. Does that make sense?'

He seemed to be pleading with Gamache to understand.

'It does. It makes perfect sense,' said Gamache, and he meant it. Few people understood so quickly that most premeditated murders were about rancid emotions, greed, jealousy, fear, all repressed. As Gabri said, people don't see it coming, because the murderer is a master at image, at the false front, at presenting a reasonable, even placid exterior. But it masked a horror underneath. And that's why the expression he saw most on the faces of victims wasn't fear, wasn't anger. It was surprise.

'Who knows what evil lurks in the hearts of men?' Gabri asked and Gamache wondered if he knew he was quoting an old radio drama. Then Gabri winked.

Gabri disappeared again, and returned, handing Gamache a small bag of muffins.

'One more question,' said Gamache at the door, the bag of muffins in one hand and the door handle in the other. 'You mentioned the Charles de Mills rose.'

'Jane's favorite. He's not just any rose, Chief Inspector. He's considered by rosarians to be one of the finest in the world. An old garden rose. Only blooms once a season but with a show that's spectacular. And then it's gone. That's why I made the muffins from rose water, as a homage to Jane. Then I ate them, as you saw. I always eat my pain.' Gabri smiled slightly. Looking at the size of the man, Gamache marveled at the amount of pain he must have. And fear perhaps. And anger? Who knows, indeed.

Ben Hadley was waiting for them outside the schoolhouse, as Beauvoir had requested in his call.

'Is everything as it should be from the outside, Mr Hadley?' Gamache asked.

Ben, a little surprised at the question, looked around. Gamache wondered whether Ben Hadley wasn't a little surprised all the time.

'Yes. Do you want to see inside?' Ben reached for the knob, but Beauvoir quickly brought his own hand down on Ben's arm and stopped him. Instead, Beauvoir pulled a roll of yellow police tape from his jacket and handed it to Nichol. While Nichol put the yellow 'Do not cross, crime scene' tape around the door and windows Beauvoir explained.

'It looks as though Miss Neal was killed by an arrow. We need to go over your clubhouse carefully in case the weapon came from here.'

'But that's ridiculous.'

'Why?'

Ben simply looked around as though the peaceful setting was reason enough. Into Beauvoir's outstretched hand he deposited the keys.

As Agent Nichol maneuvered the car on to the Champlain Bridge and back into Montreal she looked past Chief Inspector Gamache, silent and thinking in the seat beside her, and toward the Montreal skyline, the huge cross just beginning to glow on the top of Mont Royal. Her family would have held back Thanksgiving dinner for her. They'd do anything for her, she knew, both comforted and bound by the certainty. And all she had to do was succeed.

Walking into his own home that evening Gamache smelt roasting partridge. It was one of Reine-Marie's holiday specialties, the small game birds wrapped in bacon and slowly cooked in a sauce of mulled wine and juniper berries. Normally he'd have made the wild rice stuffing, but she'd probably have done that herself. They exchanged news while he stripped and took a shower. She told him about the baptism and the finger food afterward. She was almost certain she was at the right baptism, though she didn't recognise all that many people. He told her about his day and the case. He told her everything. In this he was unusual, but he couldn't quite see how he could have a deep partnership with Reine-Marie and keep this part of his life secret. So he told her everything, and she told him everything. So far, after thirty-five years, it seemed to be working.

Their friends came, and it was a comfortable, easy night. A couple of good bottles of wine, an outstanding Thanksgiving meal, and warm and thoughtful company. Gamache was reminded of the beginning of Virginia Woolf's *Orlando*. Orlando, through the ages, wasn't looking for wealth or fame, or honors. No, all Orlando wanted was company.

Clara rocked back and forth, back and forth, cradling her loss. Earlier in the day she'd felt someone had scooped her heart and her brain right out of her body. Now they were back, but they were broken. Her brain jumped madly about the place, but always back to that one scorched spot.

Peter crept to the bedroom door and looked in. God help him, part of him was jealous. Jealous of the hold Jane had over Clara. He wondered whether Clara would have been like this had he died. And he realised that, had he died in the woods, Clara would have had Jane to comfort her. And Jane would have known what to do. In that instant a door opened for Peter. For the first time in his life he asked what someone else would do. What would Jane do if she was here and he was dead? And he had his answer. Silently he lay down beside Clara and wrapped himself around her. And for the first time since getting the news, her heart and mind calmed. They settled, just for one blessed instant, on a place that held love, not loss.

FOUR

~

'Toast?' Peter ventured next morning to Clara's blubbering back.

'High doan whan doast,' she sobbed and slobbered, a fine thread of spittle descending to the floor to pool, glistening, at her feet. They were standing barefoot in the kitchen where they'd begun to make breakfast. Normally they'd have already showered and if not dressed at least put on slippers and a dressing gown over their flannel pajamas. But this morning wasn't normal. Peter simply hadn't appreciated how far from normal it was until this moment.

Lying all night, holding Clara, he'd dared to hope that the worst was over. That maybe the grief, while still there, would today allow some of his wife to be present. But the woman he knew and loved had been swallowed up. Like Jonah. Her white whale of sorrow and loss in an ocean of body fluid.

'Clara? We need to talk. Can we talk?' Peter yearned to

crawl back into their warm bed with a pot of coffee, some toast and jam, and the latest Lee Valley catalogue. Instead, he stood barefoot in the middle of their cold kitchen floor wielding a baguette like a wand at Clara's back. He didn't like the wand image. Maybe a sword. But was that appropriate? To wield a sword at your wife? He gave it a couple of swishes through the air and the crisp bread broke. Just as well, he thought. The imagery was getting too confusing.

'We need to talk about Jane.' He remembered where he really was, placed the tragically broken sword on the counter and put his hand on her shoulder. He felt the soft flannel for an instant before her shoulder jerked away from his hand. 'Remember when you and Jane would talk and I'd make some rude comment and leave?' Clara stared ahead, snorting every now and then as a fresh drip left her nose. 'I'd go into my studio to paint. But I left the door open. You didn't know that, did you?'

For the first time in twenty-four hours he saw a flicker of interest. She turned to face him, wiping her nose with the back of her hand. Peter resisted the urge to get a Kleenex.

'Every week while you and Jane talked I'd listen and paint. For years, and years. Did my best work in there, listening to you two. It was a little like when I was a kid lying in bed, listening to Mom and Dad downstairs, talking. It was comforting. But it was more than that. You and Jane talked about everything. Gardening, books, relationships, cooking. And you talked about your beliefs. Remember?'

Clara looked down at her hands.

'You both believed in God. Clara, you have to figure out what you believe.'

'What do you mean? I know what I believe.'

'What? Tell me.'

'Screw off. Leave me alone!' Now she rounded on him. 'Where're your tears? Eh? You're more dead than she is. You can't even cry. And now what? You want me to stop? It hasn't even been a day yet, and you're what? Bored with it? Not the center of the universe anymore? You want everything to go back to the way it was, like that.' Clara snapped her fingers in his face. 'You disgust me.'

Peter leaned away from the assault, wounded, and wanting to say all the things he knew would hurt her the way she'd just hurt him.

'Go away!' she screamed through hiccups and gasps. And he wanted to. He'd wanted to go away since this time yesterday. But he'd stayed. And now, more than ever, he wanted to flee. Just for a little while. A walk around the Commons, a coffee with Ben. A shower. It sounded so reasonable, so justified. Instead, he leaned toward her again, and took her snot-smeared hands in his and kissed them. She tried to pull away, but he held on firmly.

'Clara, I love you. And I know you. You have to figure out what you believe, what you really, truly believe. All these years you've talked about God. You've written about your faith. You've done dancing angels, and yearning goddesses. Is God here, now, Clara? Is he in this room?'

Peter's kind voice calmed Clara. She began to listen.

'Is he here?' Peter slowly brought his forefinger to her chest, not quite touching. 'Is Jane with him?'

Peter pressed on. He knew where he had to go. And this time it wasn't somewhere else. 'All those questions you and Jane debated and laughed about and argued over, she has the answer to. She's met God.'

Clara's mouth dropped open and she stared straight ahead. There. There it was. Her mainland. That's where she could put her grief. Jane was dead. And she was now with God. Peter was right. She either believed in God, or she didn't. Either was OK. But she could no longer say she believed in God and act otherwise. She did believe in God. And she believed that Jane was with him. And suddenly her pain and grief became human and natural. And survivable. She had a place to put it, a place where Jane was with God.

It was such a relief. She looked at Peter, his face bent to her. Dark rings under his eyes. His gray wavy hair sticking out. She felt in her hair and found a duck clip buried in the chaos of her head. Taking it out, and with it some of her own hair, she placed her hand on the back of Peter's head. Silently she drew it toward her and with her other hand she smoothed a section of his unruly hair, and put her clip on it. And as she did so she whispered in his ear, 'Thank you. I'm sorry.'

And Peter started to cry. To his horror he felt his eyes sting and well up and there was a burning in the back of his throat. He couldn't control it any longer and it came bursting out. He cried like he'd cried as a child when, lying in bed listening to the comfort of his parents talking downstairs, he realised they were talking about divorce. He took Clara in his arms and held her to his chest and prayed he would never lose her.

The meeting at the Sûreté headquarters in Montreal didn't last long. The coroner hoped to have a preliminary report that afternoon and would bring it by Three Pines on her way home. Jean Guy Beauvoir reported his conversation with Robert Lemieux, of the Cowansville Sûreté, still eager to help.

'He says Yolande Fontaine herself is clean. Some vague suspicions of slippery practices as a real estate agent, but nothing against the law, yet. But her husband and son are quite popular with the police, both the local and the Sûreté. Her husband is André Malenfant, aged thirty-seven. Five counts of drunk and disorderly. Two of assault. Two of breaking and entering.'

'Has he done any jail time?' Gamache asked.

'Couple of stretches at Bordeaux and lots of single nights in the local lock-up.'

'And the son?'

'Bernard Malenfant. Age fourteen. Seems to be apprenticing to his father. Out of control. Lots of complaints from the school. Lots of complaints from parents.'

'Has the boy ever actually been charged with anything?'

'No. Just a couple of stern talkings to.' A few officers in the room snorted their cynicism. Gamache knew Jean Guy Beauvoir well enough to know he always kept the best for last. And his body language told Gamache there was more to come.

'But,' said Beauvoir, his eyes lit in triumph, 'André Malenfant is a hunter. Now with his convictions he isn't allowed a gun-hunting permit. But –'

Gamache enjoyed watching Beauvoir indulge his flamboyant side, and this was about as flamboyant as Beauvoir got. A dramatic pause.

' – this year, for the first time, he applied for and got a bow-hunting permit.'

Ta da.

The meeting broke up. Beauvoir handed out the assignments and the teams went off. As the room cleared Nichol made to get up but Gamache stopped her. They were alone now and he wanted a quiet talk. He'd watched her during the meeting, again choosing a seat one removed from the next person, not grabbing a coffee and Danish with the others. In fact, not doing anything anyone else did. It was almost willful, this desire to separate herself from the team. The clothes she was wearing were plain, not the kind you might expect from a Montreal woman in her mid-twenties. There was none of the characteristic Quebecoise flamboyance. He realised he'd grown used to a certain individuality among his team members. But Nichol seemed to strive to be invisible. Her suit was dull blue and made of cheap material. The shoulders were slightly padded, the lumps of foam screamed bargain bin. Creeping out from her armpits was a thin white line where the tide of perspiration had reached the last time she'd worn this suit. And not cleaned it. He wondered if she made her own clothes. He wondered if she still lived at home with her parents. He wondered how proud they must be of her, and how much pressure she felt to succeed. He wondered if all that explained the one thing that did distinguish her from everyone else. Her smugness.

'You're a trainee, here to learn,' he said quietly, directly into the slightly pursed face. 'Therefore a certain teaching is necessary. Do you enjoy learning?'

'Yes, sir.'

'And how do you learn?'

'Sir?'

'The question is clear. Think about it, please, and answer.'

His deep brown eyes, as always, were lively and warm. He spoke calmly, but firmly. Without hostility but with an expectation. His tone was clearly one of boss and trainee. She was taken aback. He had been so friendly yesterday, so courteous, she thought she could take advantage of that. Now she began to realise her mistake.

'I learn by watching and listening, sir.'

'And?'

And what? They sat there, Gamache looking as though he had all day, though she knew he had to conduct the public meeting in Three Pines in just two hours and they still had to drive there. Nichol's mind froze. And . . . and . . .

'Think about it. Tonight you can tell me what you've come up with. For now, though, let me tell you how I work. And what my expectations of you are.'

'Yes sir.'

'I watch. I'm very good at observing. Noticing things.

And listening. Actively listening to what people are saying, their choice of words, their tone. What they aren't saying. And this, Agent Nichol, is the key. It's choice.'

'Choice?'

'We choose our thoughts. We choose our perceptions. We choose our attitudes. We may not think so. We may not believe it, but we do. I absolutely know we do. I've seen enough evidence, time after time, tragedy after tragedy. Triumph after triumph. It's about choice.'

'Like choice of schools? Or dinner?'

'Clothes, hairstyle, friends. Yes. It starts there. Life is choice. All day, everyday. Who we talk to, where we sit, what we say, how we say it. And our lives become defined by our choices. It's as simple and as complex as that. And as powerful. So when I'm observing, that's what I'm watching for. The choices people make.'

'What can I do, sir?'

'You can learn. You can watch and listen, and do as you're told. You're a trainee. Nobody expects you to know anything. If you pretend to know you aren't going to actually learn.'

Nichol could feel herself blush and cursed her body, which had betrayed her for as long as she could remember. She was a blusher. Maybe, came some voice from deep down below blushing level, maybe if you stop pretending you'll also stop blushing. But it was a very weak voice.

'I watched you yesterday. You did some good work. You got us on to the arrow possibility early. Excellent. But you also have to listen. Listen to the villagers, listen to the suspects, listen to gossip, listen to your instincts and listen to your colleagues.'

Nichol liked the sound of that. Colleagues. She'd never had them before. In the Highway Division of the Sûreté she'd worked more or less on her own, and before that in the local Repentigny force she'd always felt people were waiting to undermine her. It would be nice to have colleagues. Gamache leaned toward her.

'You need to learn that you have choices. There are four things that lead to wisdom. You ready for them?'

She nodded, wondering when the police work would begin.

'They are four sentences we learn to say, and mean.' Gamache held up his hand as a fist and raised a finger with each point. 'I don't know. I need help. I'm sorry. And one other.' Gamache thought for a moment but couldn't bring it to mind. 'I forget. But we'll talk more about it tonight, right?'

'Right, sir. And thank you.' Oddly enough, she realised she meant it.

After Gamache had left, Nichol brought out her note-book. She hadn't wanted to take notes while he was talking. She figured it would make her look foolish. Now she quickly wrote: I'm sorry, I don't know, I need help, I forget.

When Peter got out of the shower and came into the kitchen he noticed two things. The coffee was brewing and Clara was wrapped around Lucy who herself was a tight ball of Golden Retriever, her nose between her back legs.

'It worked for me last night,' said Clara, arching her head back to look at Peter's slippers, and instinctively up his bathrobe.

Peter knelt down and kissed Clara. Then he kissed Lucy's head. But the dog didn't stir. 'Poor one.'

'I offered her some banana but she didn't even look up.'

Everyday for Lucy's entire dog life Jane had sliced a banana for breakfast and had miraculously dropped one of the perfect disks on to the floor where it sat for an instant before being gobbled up. Every morning Lucy's prayers were answered, confirming her belief that God was old and clumsy and smelt like roses and lived in the kitchen.

But no more.

Lucy knew her God was dead. And she now knew the miracle wasn't the banana, it was the hand that offered the banana.

After breakfast Peter and Clara both got into their fall clothing and headed across the village green to Ben's place. The gray clouds were threatening rain and the wind had a dampness and a bite. The aroma of sautéed garlic and onions met them as they stepped on to Ben's front veranda. Clara knew if she was struck blind she'd always be able to tell when she was in Ben's home. It smelled of stinky dog and old books. All of Ben's dogs had smelled, not just Daisy, and it seemed to have nothing to do with age. Clara wasn't sure if he created or attracted them. But now, suddenly, his place smelled of home cooking. Instead of welcoming it, Clara felt a little queasy, as though one more certainty had been removed. She wanted the old smell back. She wanted Jane back. She wanted everything to stay the same.

'Oh, I wanted to surprise you,' said Ben, coming over to hug Clara. 'Chili con carne.'

'My favorite comfort food.'

'I've never made it before but I have some of my mother's recipe books and found it in *The Joy of Cooking*. It won't bring Jane back, but it might ease the pain.'

Clara looked at the huge cookbook open on the counter, and felt revolted. It had come from that house. Timmer's place. The home that repulsed love and laughter and welcomed snakes and mice. She wanted nothing to do with it, and she realised her revulsion stretched even to objects that had come from there.

'But Ben, you loved Jane too. And you found her. It must have been a nightmare.'

'It was.' He told them briefly about it, his back to them, not daring to face Peter and Clara as though he was responsible. He stirred the ground meat as it cooked while Clara opened the tins of ingredients and listened to Ben. After a moment she handed the can opener to Peter and had to sit down. Ben's story was playing in her head like a movie. But she kept expecting Jane to get up. As Ben finished Clara excused herself and went through the kitchen into the living room.

She put another small log on the fire and listened to the quiet murmur of Peter and Ben. She couldn't make out the words, just the familiarity. Another wave of sadness enveloped her. She'd lost her murmuring partner. The one with whom she made comforting noises. And she felt something else, a wisp of jealousy that Peter still had Ben. He could visit any time, but her best friend was gone. She knew it was unspeakably petty and selfish but there it was. She took a deep breath and inhaled garlic and onions and frying mince and other calming smells. Nellie must have cleaned recently because there was the fresh aroma of detergents. Cleanliness. Clara felt better and knew that Ben was her friend too, not just Peter's. And that she wasn't alone, unless she chose to be. She also knew Daisy could best sautéed garlic any day and her smell would re-emerge triumphant.

St Thomas's was filling up when Peter, Clara and Ben arrived. The rain was just beginning so there wasn't much milling about. The tiny parking lot at the side of the chapel was packed, and trucks and cars lined the circular Commons. Inside, the small church was overflowing and warm. It smelled of damp wool and the earth trod in on boots. The three squeezed in and joined the line of people leaning against the back wall. Clara felt some small knobs pushing into her and turning around she saw she'd been leaning against the cork bulletin board. Notices of the semi-annual tea and craft sale, the Brownie meeting, Hanna's exercise classes Monday and Thursday mornings, the bridge club Wednesdays at 7.30, and old yellowed announcements of 'new' church hours, from 1967.

'My name is Armand Gamache.' The big man had taken center stage. This morning he was dressed in a tweed jacket and gray flannel slacks with a simple and elegant burgundy tie around the neck of his Oxford shirt. His hat was off and Clara saw he was balding, without attempt to hide it. His hair was graying, as was his trimmed moustache. He gave the impression of a county squire addressing the village. He was a man used to being in charge, and he wore it well. The room hushed immediately, save for a persistent cough at the back. 'I'm the chief inspector of homicide for the Sûreté du Quebec.' This produced quite a buzz, which he waited out.

'This is my second in command, Inspector Jean Guy Beauvoir.' Beauvoir stepped forward and nodded. 'There are other Sûreté officers around the room. I expect they're obvious to you.' He didn't mention that most of his team were off turning the archery clubhouse upside down.

It struck Clara that the person who had killed Jane was probably among the crowd gathered in St Thomas's. She looked around and spotted Nellie and her husband Wayne, Myrna and Ruth, Olivier and Gabri. Matthew and Suzanne Croft sat in the row behind them. But no Philippe.

'We think the death of Jane Neal was an accident, but so far no one has come forward.' Gamache paused and Clara noticed how still and focused he could become. His intelligent eyes quietly swept the room before he continued. 'If this was an accident, and the person who killed her is here, I want you to know a few things.' Clara didn't think the room could get any quieter, but it did. Even the coughing stopped, miraculously cured by curiosity.

'It must have been horrible when you realised what

you'd done. But you need to come forward and admit it. The longer you wait the harder it will be. For us, for the community and for yourself.' Chief Inspector Gamache paused and slowly looked around the room, each and every person feeling that he was looking inside them. The room waited. There was a frisson, an idea each person held that maybe the one responsible would get up.

Clara caught the eye of Yolande Fontaine, who smiled weakly. Clara disliked her intensely, but smiled back. André, Yolande's scrawny husband, was there picking his cuticles and occasionally nibbling them. Their remarkably unattractive son Bernard sat slack-jawed and sullen, slumped in his pew. He looked bored and was making faces at his friends across the way between mouthfuls of candy.

Nobody moved.

'We will find you. That's what we do.' Gamache took a deep breath, as though changing the subject. 'We're investigating this as though it was a murder, though we doubt that. I have the coroner's preliminary report here.' He flipped open his palm pilot. 'It confirms that Jane Neal died between six-thirty and seven yesterday morning. The weapon appears to have been an arrow.'

This produced more than a few murmurs.

'I say "appears" because no weapon was found. And that's a problem. It argues against this being just an accident. That, combined with the fact that nobody has taken responsibility, is why we need to treat this as suspicious.'

Gamache paused and looked at the gathering. A sea

of well-meaning faces looked back, with a few rocks of petulance thrown in here and there. They have no idea what's about to happen to them, thought Gamache.

'This is how it starts. You'll see us everywhere. We'll be asking questions, checking backgrounds, talking – not just to you, but your neighbors and your employers and your family and your friends.'

Another murmur, this one with an edge of hostility. Gamache was pretty sure he heard 'fascist' from his lower left side. He stole a look and saw Ruth Zardo sitting there.

'You didn't ask for any of this to happen but it's here now. Jane Neal is dead and all of us need to deal with it. We need to do our job and you need to help us, and that means accepting things you wouldn't normally accept. That's just life. I'm sorry for it. But it doesn't change the facts.'

The murmuring diminished and there were even nods of agreement.

'We all have secrets, and before this is over I'll know most of yours. If they're not pertinent then they'll die with me. But I will find them out. Most days in the late afternoon I'll be at Mr Brulé's bistro, reviewing notes. You're welcome to join me for a drink and a talk.'

Crime was deeply human, Gamache knew. The cause and the effect. And the only way he knew to catch a criminal was to connect with the human beings involved. Chatting in a café was the most pleasant, and disarming, way to do it.

'Any questions?'

'Are we in danger?' Hanna Parra, the local elected representative, asked.

Gamache had been expecting this. It was a tough one since they really didn't know whether it was an accident or murder.

'I don't think so. Should you be locking your doors at night? Always. Should you be careful walking in the woods or even around the Common? Yes. Should you not do these things?'

He paused and saw a whole congregation of concern.

'Did you lock the door last night?' Clara whispered to Peter. He nodded and Clara gave his hand a relieved squeeze. 'Did you?' she asked Ben, who shook his head, 'No, but I will tonight.'

'That's up to you,' Gamache was saying. 'The reaction I see most is caution for about a week after an event of this sort. Then people go back to the way of life that's most comfortable. Some continue the precautions all their lives, others revert to their old way of doing things. Most find a middle ground of prudence. There's no right or better way. Frankly, I would take care right now, but there is absolutely no need for panic.'

Gamache smiled and added, 'You don't look like the panicking kind.' And they didn't, though most did have slightly wider eyes then when they had walked in. 'Besides, I'll be staying at the B&B here, if you have any concerns.'

'My name's Old Mundin.' A man aged about twenty-five got up. He was impossibly handsome with curly dark hair, chiseled, rugged face, and a body that spoke of lots of lifting. Beauvoir shot Gamache a look both amused and confused. Was this man's name really 'Old' Mundin? He wrote it down but without conviction.

'Yes, Mr Mundin?'

'I heard as that Lucy weren't with Jane when she died. Is that right?'

'Yes. I understand that's very unusual.'

'You're right there, boy. She went everywhere with that dog. She wouldn't have gone into the woods without Lucy.'

'For protection?' Gamache asked.

'No, just because. Why would you have a dog and not take it on your walk? And first thing in the morning, when a dog yearns to run and do its business. No, sir. Makes no sense.'

Gamache turned to the gathering. 'Can any of you think why Jane would leave Lucy behind?'

Clara was impressed by the question. Here was the head of the investigation, a senior Sûreté officer, asking for their opinion. There was suddenly a shift, from mourning and a kind of passivity, to involvement. It became 'their' investigation.

'If Lucy was sick or in heat Jane might leave her,' Sue Williams called out.

'True,' called Peter, 'but Lucy's fixed and healthy.'

'Could Jane have seen some hunters and put Lucy back in the house so they didn't shoot her by mistake?' Wayne Robertson asked, then a coughing jag caught him and he sat down. His wife Nellie put her generous arm around him, as though flesh could ward off sickness.

'But', asked Gamache, 'would she go back alone into the woods to confront a hunter?'

'She might,' Ben said. 'She's done it before. Remember a couple of years ago when she caught –' he stopped and grew flustered. Some uncomfortable laughter and a hum followed his aborted remarks. Gamache raised his brows and waited.

'That was me, as you all know.' A man rose from his seat. 'My name's Matthew Croft.' He was in his mid-thirties, Gamache guessed, medium build, pretty nondescript. Beside him sat a slim, tense woman. The name was familiar.

'Three years ago I was hunting illegally on the Hadley property. Miss Neal spoke to me, asked me to leave.'

'Did you?'

'Yes.'

'Why were you there at all?'

'My family has been here for hundreds of years and we were raised to believe that private property doesn't exist in hunting season.'

'That's not right,' a voice resonated from the back of the room. Beauvoir busily made notes.

Croft turned to face the interruption. 'That you, Henri?'

Henri Lariviere, the stone artist, rose majestically to his feet.

'It's the way I was raised,' Croft continued. 'I was taught it was only right to be able to hunt where you chose, since your very survival depended upon getting enough meat for the season.'

'Grocery stores, Matthew. Loblaws not good enough?' Henri said, quietly.

'IGA, Provigo,' others yelled.

'Me,' said Jacques Beliveau, the owner of the local general store. Everyone laughed. Gamache was letting this go on, watching, listening, seeing where it would go.

'Yes, times change,' an exasperated Croft agreed. 'It's no longer necessary, but it's a fine tradition. And a fine philosophy of neighbor helping neighbor. I believe in that.'

'No one says you don't, Matt,' said Peter, stepping forward. 'And I can't think you have to justify yourself or your actions, especially from years ago.'

'He does, Mr Morrow,' Gamache broke in just as Beauvoir handed him a note. 'Jane Neal was probably killed by a hunter trespassing on Mr Hadley's property. Anyone with a history of this needs to explain.' Gamache glanced at the note. In block letters Beauvoir had printed, 'Philippe Croft threw manure. Son?' Gamache folded the note and put it in his pocket.

'Do you still hunt where you choose, Mr Croft?'

'No, sir, I don't.'

'Why not?'

'Because I respected Miss Neal, and because I finally heard what people have been telling me for years and years. And I agreed. In fact I don't hunt at all anymore, anywhere.'

'Do you own a bow-hunting set?'

'Yes sir, I do.'

Gamache looked around the room. 'I'd like everyone here who owns a bow hunting set, even if you haven't used it in years, to give your name and address to Inspector Beauvoir here.'

'Just hunting?' Peter asked.

'Why? What do you have in mind?'

'The bows and arrows for recreational archery are called recurve and are different to the hunters' equipment. Those are compound.'

'But they would bring the same results, if used against a person?'

'I think so.' Peter turned to Ben who thought for an instant.

'Yes,' said Ben. 'Though the arrows are different. You'd have to be amazingly lucky, or unlucky, I guess, to kill with a target-shooting arrow.'

'Why?'

'Well, a target-shooting arrow has a very small head, not unlike the tip of a bullet. But a hunter's arrow, well, that's different. I've never shot one, but Matt, you have.'

'A hunter's arrow has four, sometimes five razors at the end, tapering into a tip.'

Beauvoir had set up the easel with paper near the altar. Gamache went to it and quickly drew a big black circle, with four lines radiating from it, a duplicate of the one Beauvoir had drawn at lunch the day before.

'Would it produce a wound like that?'

Matthew Croft walked forward a bit, appearing to drag the gathering with him as everyone swayed forward in their seats.

'Exactly like that.'

Gamache and Beauvoir locked eyes. They had at least part of their answer.

'So,' said Gamache almost to himself, 'this would have to have been done by a hunting arrow.'

Matthew Croft wasn't sure if Gamache was speaking to him, but he answered anyway, 'Yes, sir. No question.'

'What's a hunting arrow like?'

'It's made of metal, very light and hollow, with wings at the back.'

'And the bow?'

'A hunter's bow is called a compound and it's made from alloys.'

'Alloy?' Gamache asked. 'That's metal of some sort. I thought they were wood.'

'They used to be,' agreed Matthew.

'Some still are,' someone called from the crowd to general laughter.

'They're mocking me, Inspector,' admitted Ben. 'When I set up the archery club it was with old bows and arrows. The traditional recurve sort—'

'Robin Hood,' someone called, again to some chuckles.

'And his merry men,' Gabri chimed in, pleased with his contribution. More quiet chuckles, but Gabri didn't hear them, he was concentrating on getting Olivier's vice-like grip off his leg.

'It's true,' continued Ben. 'When Peter and I started the club we had a fascination with Robin Hood, and cowboys and Indians. We used to dress up.' Beside him, Peter groaned and Clara snorted at the long-forgotten memory of these two friends stalking the forests, in green tights and ski toques doubling as medieval caps. They were in their mid-twenties at the time. Clara also knew that sometimes, when they thought no one was watching, Peter and Ben still did it.

'So we only used wooden recurve bows and wooden arrows,' said Ben.

'What do you use now, Mr Hadley?'

'The same bows and arrows. Saw no reason to change. We only use it for target shooting out behind the school-house.'

'So let me get this straight. Modern bows and arrows are made of some metal or other. The old ones are wood, right?'

'Right.'

'Would an arrow go through a body?'

'Yes, right through,' said Matthew.

'But, well, Mr Hadley, you talked about cowboys and Indians. In all those old movies the arrows stay in the body.'

'Those movies weren't actually real,' said Matthew. Behind him Gamache heard Beauvoir give a brief laugh. 'Believe me, an arrow would go straight through a person.'

'Alloy and wood?'

'Yup. Both.'

Gamache shook his head. Another myth exploded. He wondered if the church knew. But at least they had an answer to the exit wound puzzle, and it was now more certain than ever that Jane Neal had been killed by an arrow. But where was it?

'How far would the arrow go?'

'Humm, that's a good question. Ten, fifteen feet.'

Gamache looked at Beauvoir and nodded. The arrow would have gone right through her chest, out her back and flown into the woods behind. Still, they'd searched there and found nothing.

'Would it be hard to find?'

'Not really. If you're an experienced hunter you know exactly where to look. It'll be sticking up from the ground a bit, and the feathering makes it slightly easier. Arrows are expensive, Inspector, so we always look for them. Becomes second nature.'

'The coroner found a few slivers of real feathers in the wound. What could that mean?' Gamache was surprised to see the hubbub created by his simple statement. Peter was looking at Ben who was looking confused. Everyone, in fact, seemed to suddenly pop into activity.

'If it was an arrow then it could only be an old arrow, a wooden one,' said Peter.

'Wouldn't you find real feathers on an alloy arrow?' Gamache was asking, finally feeling like he was getting a grasp on the subject.

'No.'

'So. Forgive me for going over the ground several times, I just need to be sure. Since there were real feathers in the wound we're talking about a wooden arrow. Not alloy, but wood.'

'Right,' half the congregation spoke up, sounding like a revival meeting.

'And,' said Gamache, edging another small step forward in the case, 'not a target-shooting arrow, like the archery club uses, but a hunting arrow? We know that because of the shape of the wound.' He pointed to the drawing. Everyone nodded. 'It would have to have been a wooden arrow with a hunting tip. Can you use wooden hunting arrows with the new alloy bows?'

'No,' said the congregation.

'So it would have to be a wooden bow, right?'

'Right.'

'A Robin Hood bow.'

'Right.'

'I've got it, thank you. Now, I have another question. You keep using the words "recurve" and "compound". What's the difference?' He looked over at Beauvoir, hoping he was taking good notes.

'A recurved,' said Ben, 'is the Robin Hood bow. The cowboys and Indians bow. It's a long slim piece of wood that's thicker in the middle where there's a sort of carved grip for your hand. And on either end of the stick there are notches. You put your string on one end then the other and the wood curves to make a bow. Simple and effective. The design is thousands of years old. When you've finished you take the string off and store the bow, which is now back to being a slightly curved stick. The name "recurved" is because you recurve it every time you use it.'

Simple enough, thought Gamache.

'Compound,' said Matthew 'is a fairly new design. Basically, it looks like a really complex bow, with pulleys at both ends and lots of strings. And a very sophisticated sighting mechanism. It also has a trigger.'

'Is a recurved as powerful and accurate as, what was the name of the other bow?'

'Compound,' about twenty people said at once, including at least three of the officers in the room.

'As accurate . . . yes. As powerful, no.'

'You hesitated over accuracy.'

'With a recurved you have to release the string with your fingers. A rough release would affect the accuracy. A compound bow has a trigger so it's smoother. It also has a very accurate device for sighting.'

'There are hunters today who choose to use the wooden recurve bows and wooden arrows. Is that right?'

'Not many,' said Helene Charron. 'It's very rare.'

Gamache turned back to Matthew. 'If you were going to kill someone, which would you use? Recurve or compound?'

Matthew Croft hesitated. He clearly didn't like the question. André Malenfant laughed. It was a humorless, snarky sound.

'No question. A compound. I can't imagine why anyone would be hunting in this day and age with an old wooden recurved bow, and with arrows with real feathers. It's like someone stepped out of the past. Target practice, sure. But hunting? Give me modern equipment. And frankly, if you were going to kill someone deliberately? Murder? Why take chances with a recurve? No, a compound is far more likely to do the job. Actually, I'd use a gun.'

And that's the puzzle, thought Gamache. Why? Why an arrow and not a bullet? Why an old-fashioned wooden bow and not the state-of-the-art hunting bow? At the end of the investigation there was always an answer. And one that made sense, at least on some level. To someone. But for now it seemed nonsense. An old-fashioned

114

wooden arrow with real feathers used to kill an elderly retired country schoolteacher. Why?

'Mr Croft, do you still have your hunting equipment?'

'Yes, sir, I do.'

'Perhaps you could give me a demonstration this afternoon.'

'With pleasure.' Croft didn't hesitate, but Gamache thought he saw Mrs Croft tense. He looked at his watch: 12.30.

'Does anyone have any other questions?'

'I have one.' Ruth Zardo struggled to her feet. 'Actually, it's more a statement than a question.' Gamache looked at her with interest. Inside he steeled himself.

'You can use the old train station if you think it would be suitable as a headquarters. I heard you were looking. The volunteer fire department can help you set things up.'

Gamache considered for a moment. It wasn't perfect, but it seemed like the best option now that the schoolhouse was cordoned off.

'Thank you, we will use your fire hall. I'm most grateful.'

'I want to say something.' Yolande rose. 'The police will no doubt tell me when I can have the funeral for Aunt Jane. I'll let you all know when and where it will be.'

Gamache suddenly felt deeply sorry for her. She was dressed head to toe in black and seemed to be waging an internal battle between being weak with grief, and the need to claim ownership of this tragedy. He'd seen it many times, people jockeying for position as chief mourner. It was always human and never pleasant and often misleading.

Aid workers, when handing out food to starving people, quickly learn that the people fighting for it at the front are the people who need it least. It's the people sitting quietly at the back, too weak to fight, who need it the most. And so too with tragedy. The people who don't insist on their sorrow can often be the ones who feel it most strongly. But he also knew there was no hard and fast rule.

Gamache wrapped the meeting up. Just about everyone sprinted through the gusty rain to the Bistro for lunch, some to cook, some to serve, most to eat. Gamache was anxious to hear the results of the search of the archery clubhouse.

FIVE

～

With trembling hands, Agent Isabelle Lacoste reached into the plastic bag and carefully withdrew a lethal weapon. In her fingers, wet and numb with cold, she held an arrowhead. The other Sûreté officers around the room sat in silence, many squinting, trying to get a clear look at the tiny tip, designed to kill.

'We found it and others in the clubhouse,' she said, passing it around. She'd arrived early that morning, leaving her husband to look after the kids and driving through the rain and dark from Montreal. She liked her quiet time at the office, and today the office was a cold and silent former schoolhouse. Inspector Beauvoir had given her the key and as she let herself past the yellow police tape she pulled out her thermos of coffee, dropped her police bag with 'scene of crime' paraphernalia on the floor, switched on the light and looked around. The tongue-in-groove walls were covered with quivers hanging from what must once have been hooks for little coats. At the front of the room the blackboard still dominated, no doubt permanently attached to the wall. On it someone had drawn a target, an 'X' and an arc between the two with numbers written below. Agent Lacoste had done her homework on the Internet the night before and recognised this as a pretty basic archery lesson on wind, distance and trajectory. Still, she took out her camera and photographed it. Pouring herself a coffee, she sat down and drew the diagram in her notebook. She was a careful woman.

Then, before any of the other officers assigned to the search arrived, she did something only she knew about: she went back outside and in the strained light of the rainy morning she walked to the spot where Jane Neal had died. And she told Miss Neal that Chief Inspector Gamache would find out who had done this to her.

Agent Isabelle Lacoste believed in 'do unto others' and knew she'd want someone to do this for her.

She then returned to the unheated archery clubhouse. The other officers had arrived and together they searched the single room, fingerprinting, measuring, photographing, bagging. And then Lacoste, reaching into the back of a drawer in the only desk remaining in the room, had found them.

Gamache held it in the palm of his hand, as though holding a grenade. The arrowhead clearly meant for hunting. Four razors tapered to a fine tip. Now, finally, he could appreciate what had been said in the public meeting. This arrowhead seemed to yearn to cut through his palm. Hurtled from a bow with all the force thousands

118

of years of need could produce, it would without a doubt pass straight through a person. It's a wonder guns were ever invented when you already had such a lethal and silent weapon.

Agent Lacoste wiped a soft towel through her dripping dark hair. She stood with her back to the lively fire perking in the stone fireplace, feeling warm for the first time in hours, and she smelt the homemade soup and bread and watched the deadly weapon progress around the room.

Clara and Myrna stood in line at the buffet table, balancing mugs of steaming French Canadian pea soup and plates with warm rolls from the boulangerie. Just ahead Nellie was piling food on to her plate.

'I'm getting enough for Wayne too,' Nellie explained unnecessarily. 'He's over there, poor guy.'

'I heard his cough,' said Myrna. 'A cold?'

'Don't know. It's gone to his chest. This is the first time I've been out of the house in days, I've been that worried. But Wayne cut Miss Neal's lawn and looked after odd jobs and he wanted to go to the meeting.' The two women watched as Nellie took her huge plate over to Wayne, who sat slouched and exhausted in a chair. She wiped his brow and then got him to his feet. The two of them left the Bistro, Nellie concerned and in charge, and Wayne docile and happy to be led. Clara hoped he'd be all right.

'What did you think of the meeting?' Clara asked Myrna as they edged along.

'I like him, Inspector Gamache.'

'Me too. But it's strange, Jane being killed by a hunting arrow.'

'Though if you think about it, it makes sense. It's hunting season, but I agree the old wooden arrow gave me the shivers. Very weird. Turkey?'

'Please. Brie?' asked Clara.

'Just a sliver. Perhaps a bigger sliver than that.'

'When does a sliver become a hunk?'

'If you're a hunk, size doesn't matter,' Myrna explained.

'I'll remember that next time I go to bed with a hunk of Stilton.'

'You'd cheat on Peter?'

'With food? I cheat on him everyday. I have a very special relationship with a gummy bear who shall remain nameless. Well, actually his name is Ramon. He completes me. Look at that.' Clara pointed to the floral arrangement on the buffet.

'I did that this morning,' said Myrna, happy that Clara had noticed. Clara noticed most things, Myrna realised, and had the wit to mostly mention just the good.

'I thought perhaps you had. Anything in it?'

'You'll see,' said Myrna, with a smile. Clara leaned into the arrangement of annual monarda, helenium and artist's acrylic paint brushes. Nestled inside was a package wrapped in brown waxed paper.

'It's sage and sweetgrass,' said Clara back at the table, unwrapping the package. 'Does this mean what I think?'

'A ritual,' said Myrna.

'Oh, what a fine idea.' Clara reached over and touched Myrna's arm.

'From Jane's garden?' Ruth asked, inhaling the musky, unmistakable aroma of sage, and the honey-like fragrance of the sweetgrass.

'The sage, yes. Jane and I cut it in August. The sweetgrass I got from Henri a couple of weeks ago, when he cut back his hay. It was growing around Indian Rock.'

Ruth passed them to Ben who held them at arm's length.

'Oh, for God's sake, man, they won't hurt you.' Ruth snatched them up and whipped them back and forth under Ben's nose. 'As I recall, you were even invited to the Summer Solstice ritual.'

'Only as a human sacrifice,' said Ben.

'Come on, Ben, that's not fair,' said Myrna. 'We said that probably wouldn't be necessary.'

'It was fun,' said Gabri, swallowing a deviled egg. 'I wore the minister's frocks.' He lowered his voice and darted his eyes around, in case the minister should have actually decided to come and minister.

'Best use they've been put to,' said Ruth.

'Thank you,' said Gabri.

'It wasn't meant as a compliment. Weren't you straight before the ritual?'

'As a matter of fact, yes.' Gabri turned to Ben. 'It worked. Magic. You should definitely go to the next one.'

'That's true,' said Olivier, standing behind Gabri and massaging his neck. 'Ruth, weren't you a woman before the ritual?'

'Weren't you?'

*

121

'And you say this,' Gamache held the arrowhead up so the tip was pointing to the ceiling, 'was found in an unlocked drawer along with twelve others?' He examined the hunting tip with its four razor edges coming to an elegant and lethal point. It was a perfect, silent, killing device.

'Yes, sir,' said Lacoste. She'd firmly claimed the spot directly in front of the fire. From where she stood in the back room of the Bistro she could see out the French doors as rain, almost sleet, whipped against the glass. Her hands, now free of lethal weapons, cradled a mug of hot soup and a warm roll stuffed with ham, melting brie and a few leaves of arugula.

Gamache carefully placed the arrowhead on to Beauvoir's open palm. 'Can this be put on to the end of any arrow?'

'What do you have in mind?' Beauvoir asked the boss.

'Well, that clubhouse is full of target-shooting arrows, right?'

Lacoste nodded, her mouth full.

'With little stubby heads, like bullet tips?'

'Phreith,' Lacoste managed, nodding.

'Can those tips be removed and this put on?'

'Yes,' said Lacoste, swallowing hard.

'Forgive me.' Gamache smiled. 'But how do you know?'

'I read up on it on the Internet last night. The tips are made to be interchangeable. 'Course you have to know what you're doing or you'll cut your fingers to ribbons. But, yes, take one out, put the other in. That's the design.'

'Even the old wooden ones?'

'Yes. I suspect these hunting heads came originally from

the old wooden arrows in the clubhouse. Someone took them off and replaced them with the target heads.'

Gamache nodded. Ben had told them that he'd picked up the old wooden arrows from families who were upgrading their hunting equipment. The arrows would have come originally with hunting heads and he'd have to replace them with the target ones.

'Good. Get them all to the lab.'

'Already on their way,' said Lacoste, taking a seat next to Nichol, who moved her chair slightly away.

'What time is our appointment with Notary Stickley about the will?' Gamache asked Nichol. Yvette Nichol knew very well it was at one-thirty, but saw an opportunity to prove she'd heard his little lecture that morning.

'I forget.'

'I'm sorry?'

Ha, she thought, he gets it. He'd given her one of the key statements in response. She quickly went through the other statements, the ones that lead to promotion. I forget, I'm sorry, I need help and what was the other one?

'I don't know.'

Now Chief Inspector Gamache was looking at her with open concern.

'I see. Did you happen to write it down?'

She considered trying out the last phrase but couldn't bring herself to say, 'I need help.' Instead she lowered her head and blushed, feeling she'd somehow been set up.

Gamache looked in his own notes. 'It's at one-thirty. With any luck we'll get into Miss Neal's home after we sort out the will.'

He had called his old friend and classmate Superintendent Brébeuf earlier. Michel Brébeuf had been promoted beyond Gamache, into a job they'd both applied for, but it hadn't affected their relationship. Gamache respected Brébeuf and liked him. The Superintendent had sympathised with Gamache, but couldn't promise anything.

'For God's sake, Armand, you know how it works. It was just stinking bad luck she actually found someone dense enough to sign the injunction. I doubt we'll find a judge willing to overturn a colleague.'

Gamache needed evidence, either that it was murder or that the home didn't go to Yolande Fontaine. His phone rang as he contemplated the interview with the notary.

'*Oui, allô?*' He got up to take the call in a quiet part of the room.

'I think a ritual would be perfect,' said Clara, picking at a piece of bread but not really hungry. 'But I have this feeling it should just be women. And not necessarily just Jane's close friends, but any women who'd like to take part.'

'Damn,' said Peter, who'd been to the Summer Solstice ritual and had found it embarrassing and very strange.

'When would you like it?' Myrna asked Clara.

'How about next Sunday?'

'One week to the day Jane died,' said Ruth.

Clara had spotted Yolande and her family arriving at the Bistro and knew she'd have to say something. Gathering her wits she walked over. The Bistro grew so silent Chief Inspector Gamache heard the sudden drop off in noise next door after he'd hung up from the call. Tiptoeing around the back he stood just inside the servers' entrance. From there he could see and hear everything, but not be observed. You don't get to be that good at this job, he thought, without being a sneak. He then noticed a server standing patiently behind him with a tray of cold cuts.

'This should be good,' she whispered. 'Black forest ham?'

'Thank you.' He took a slice.

'Yolande,' Clara said, extending her hand. 'I'm sorry for your loss. Your aunt was a wonderful woman.'

Yolande looked at the extended hand, took it briefly and then released it, hoping to give the impression of monumental grief. It would have worked had she not been playing to an audience well acquainted with her emotional range. Not to mention her real relationship with Jane Neal.

'Please accept my condolences,' Clara continued, feeling stiff and artificial.

Yolande bowed her head and brought a dry paper napkin to her dry eye.

'At least we can re-use the napkin,' said Olivier, who was also looking over Gamache's shoulder. 'What a pathetic piece of work. This is really awful to watch. Pastry?'

Olivier was holding a tray of mille feuilles, meringues, slices of pies and little custard tarts with glazed fruit on top. He chose one covered in tiny wild blueberries.

'Thank you.'

'I'm the official caterer for the disaster that's about to happen. I can't imagine why Clara is doing this, she knows what Yolande has been saying behind her back for years. Hideous woman.'

Gamache, Olivier and the server stared at the scene unfolding in the silent bistro.

'My aunt and I were extremely close, as you know,' Yolande said straight into Clara's face, appearing to believe every word she said. 'I know you won't be upset if I mention that we all think you took her away from her real family. All the people I talk to agree with me. Still, you probably didn't realise what you were doing.' Yolande smiled indulgently.

'Oh my God,' Ruth whispered to Gabri, 'here it comes.'

Peter was gripping the arms of his chair, wanting with all his being to leap up and scream at Yolande. But he knew Clara had to do that herself, had to finally stand up for herself. He waited for Clara's response. The whole room waited.

Clara took a deep breath and said nothing.

'I'll be organising my aunt's funeral,' Yolande plowed on. 'Probably have it in the Catholic church in St Rémy. That's André's church.' Yolande reached out a hand to take her husband's, but both his hands were taken up clutching a huge sandwich, gushing mayo and meat. Her son Bernard yawned, revealing a mouth full of half-chewed sandwich and strings of mayo glopping down from the roof of his mouth.

'I'll probably put a notice in the paper which I'm sure

you'll see. But maybe you can think of something for her headstone. But nothing weird, my aunt wouldn't have liked that. Anyway, think about it and let me know.'

'Again, I'm so sorry about Jane.'

When she'd gone over to speak with Yolande, Clara had known this would happen. Known that Yolande, for some unfathomable reason, could always get to her. Could hurt her where most others couldn't reach. It was one of life's little mysteries that this woman she had absolutely no respect for, could lay her flat. She thought she'd been ready for it. She'd even dared to harbour a hope that maybe this time would be different. But of course it wasn't.

For many years Clara would remember how it felt standing there. Feeling again like the ugly little girl in the schoolyard. The unloved and unlovable child. Flatfooted and maladroit, slow and mocked. The one who laughed in the wrong places and believed tall stories, and was desperate for someone, anyone, to like her. Stupid, stupid, stupid. The polite attention and the balled up fist under the school desk. She wanted to run to Jane, who'd make it better. Take her in those full, kindly arms and say the magic words, 'There, there.'

Ruth Zardo would also remember this moment and turn it into poetry. It would be published in her next volume called, 'I'm FINE':

You were a moth
brushing against my cheek
in the dark.
I killed you,

not knowing
you were only a moth,
with no sting.

But more than anything, Clara would remember André's toxic laugh ringing in her ears as she silently made her way back to her table, so far away. A laugh such as a maladjusted child might make on seeing a creature hurt and suffering. It was a familiar sound.

'Who was on the phone?' Beauvoir asked when Gamache slipped back into his seat. Beauvoir was unaware the boss had gone anywhere other than the washroom.

'Dr Harris. I didn't know she lives close to here, in a village called Cleghorn Halt. She said she'd bring her report by on her way home, at about five.'

'I've assigned a team to set up the Incident Room and I've sent a team back to the woods to do another search. I figure the arrow is in one of three places, stuck into the ground in the woods, picked up by the killer and probably destroyed by now, or, with any luck, it's among the arrows Lacoste found in the clubhouse.'

'Agreed.'

Beauvoir handed out the assignments, and sent a couple of agents to interview Gus Hennessey and Claude LaPierre about the manure incident. He would interview Philippe Croft himself. Then he joined Gamache outside and the two strolled around the village green, head to head under their umbrellas.

'Miserable weather,' said Beauvoir, lifting the collar of

his jacket and shrugging his shoulders against the driving rain.

'More rain on the way and turning colder,' Gamache said automatically, and suddenly realised the villagers were getting into his head, or at least their incessant forecasts were.

'What do you think of Agent Nichol, Jean Guy?'

'I can't figure out how she got into the Sûreté, with an attitude like that, not to mention recommended for a promotion to homicide. No skill as a team member, almost no people skills, no ability to listen. It's amazing. I have to think it backs up what you've been saying for years, that the wrong people are promoted.'

'Do you think she can learn? She's young, right? About twenty-five?'

'That's not so young. Lacoste isn't much older. I'm far from convinced it's an issue of age and not personality. I think she's going to be like this, and worse, at fifty if she isn't careful. Can she learn? Undoubtedly. But the real question is can she unlearn? Can she get rid of her bad attitudes?' He noticed the rain dripping from the chief inspector's face. He wanted to wipe it away, but resisted the impulse.

Even as he spoke, Beauvoir knew he'd made a mistake. It was like honey to a bear. He could see the chief's face change, from the somber problem-solving mode into mentor mode. He'd try to fix her. God, here it comes, thought Beauvoir. He respected Gamache more than any other human being, but saw his flaw, perhaps a fatal flaw, as a desire to help people, instead of just firing them. He was far too compassionate. A gift Beauvoir sometimes envied, but mostly watched with suspicion.

'Well, maybe her need to be right will be tempered by her curiosity.'

And maybe the scorpion will lose its sting, thought Beauvoir.

'Chief Inspector?' The two men looked up and saw Clara Morrow running through the rain, her husband Peter fighting with their umbrella and struggling to keep up. 'I've thought of something odd.'

'Ahh, sustenance.' Gamache smiled.

'Well this is a pretty small nugget, but who knows. It just struck me as a strange coincidence and I thought you should know. It's about Jane's art.'

'I don't think it's that big a deal,' said Peter, soaked and sullen. Clara shot him a surprised look which wasn't lost on Gamache.

'It's just that Jane painted all her life but never let anyone see her work.'

'That's not so strange, is it?' said Beauvoir. 'Lots of artists and writers keep their work secret. You read about it all the time. Then after their deaths their stuff is discovered and makes a fortune.'

'True, but that's not what happened. Last week Jane decided to show her work at Arts Williamsburg. She just decided Friday morning, and the judging was Friday afternoon. Her painting was accepted.'

'Got accepted and got murdered,' murmured Beauvoir. 'That is odd.'

'Speaking of odd,' said Gamache, 'is it true Miss Neal never invited anyone into her living room?'

'It's true,' said Peter. 'We've gotten so used to it it doesn't seem strange. It's like a limp or a chronic cough, I guess. A small abnormality that becomes normal.'

'But why not?'

'Don't know,' admitted Clara, herself baffled. 'Like Peter said I've gotten so used to it it doesn't seem strange.'

'Didn't you ever ask?'

'Jane? I suppose we did, when we first arrived. Or maybe we asked Timmer and Ruth, but I know for sure we never got an answer. No one seems to know. Gabri thinks she has orange shag carpet and pornography.'

Gamache laughed. 'And what do you think?'

'I just don't know.'

Silence greeted this. Gamache wondered about this woman who had chosen to live with so many secrets for so long, then chosen to let them all out. And died because of it? That was the question.

Maître Norman Stickley stood at his desk and nodded his hello, then sat down without offering a seat to the three officers in front of him. Putting on large round glasses and looking down at his file he launched into speech.

'This will was drawn up ten years ago and is very simple. After a few small bequests the bulk of her estate goes to her niece, Yolande Marie Fontaine, or her issue. That would be the home in Three Pines, all its contents, plus whatever monies are left after paying the bequests

131

and burial fees and whatever bills the executors incur. Plus taxes, of course.'

'Who are the executors of her estate?' Gamache asked, taking the blow to their investigation in his stride, but inwardly cursing. Something wasn't right, he felt. Maybe it's just your pride, he thought. Too stubborn to admit you were wrong and this elderly woman quite understandably left her home to her only living relative.

'Ruth Zardo, née Kemp, and Constance Hadley, née Post, known, I believe, as Timmer.'

The list of names troubled Gamache, though he couldn't put his finger on it. Was it the people themselves? he wondered. The choice? What?

'Had she made other wills with you?' Beauvoir asked.

'Yes. She'd made a will five years before this one.'

'Do you still have a copy of it?'

'No. Do you think I have space to keep old documents?'

'Do you remember what was in it?' Beauvoir asked, expecting to get another defensive, snippy, answer.

'No. Do you—' but Gamache headed him off.

'If you can't remember the exact terms of the first will can you perhaps remember, in broad strokes, her reasons for changing it five years later?' Gamache asked in as reasonable and friendly a tone as possible.

'It's not unusual for people to make wills every few years,' said Stickley, and Gamache was beginning to wonder if this slightly whiny tone was just his way of speaking. 'Indeed, we recommend that clients do this every two to five years. Of course,' said Stickley, as though answering an accusation, 'it's not for the notarial fee, but because situations tend to change every few years. Children are born, grandchildren come, spouses die, there's divorce.'

'The great parade of life.' Gamache jumped in to stop the parade.

'Exactly.'

'And yet, Maître Stickley, her last will is ten years old. Why would that be? I think we can assume she made this one because the old one was no longer valid. But,' Gamache leaned forward and tapped the long thin document in front of the notary, 'this will is also out of date. Are you certain this is the most recent?'

'Of course it is. People get busy and a will is often not a priority. It can be an unpleasant chore. There are any number of reasons people put them off.'

'Could she have gone to another notary?'

'Impossible. And I resent the implication.'

'How do you know it's impossible?' Gamache persevered. 'Would she necessarily tell you?'

'I just know. This is a small town and I would have heard.' *Point final.*

As they were leaving, a copy of the will in hand, Gamache turned to Nichol, 'I'm still not convinced about this will. I want you to do something.'

'Yes, sir,' Nichol was suddenly alert.

'Find out if this is the latest copy. Can you do that?'

'*Absolument.*' Nichol practically levitated.

'Hello,' Gamache called, poking his head through the door of Arts Williamsburg. After they'd been to the notary they'd walked over to the gallery, a wonderfully preserved

133

and restored former post office. Its huge windows let in what little light the sky offered and that gray light sat on the narrow and worn wood floors and rubbed against the pristine white walls of the small open room, giving it an almost ghostly glow.

'*Bonjour,*' he called again. He could see an old pot-bellied wood stove in the center of the room. It was beautiful. Simple, direct, nothing elegant about it, just a big, black stove that had kept the Canadian cold at bay for more than a hundred years. Nichol had found the light switches and turned them on. Huge canvases of abstract art lunged off the walls. It surprised Gamache. He'd been expecting pretty country watercolors, romantic and salable. Instead he was surrounded by brilliant stripes and spheres ten feet tall. It felt youthful and vibrant and strong.

'Hello.'

Nichol started, but Gamache just turned around and saw Clara coming toward them, a duck barrette clinging to a few strands of hair, getting ready for the final flight.

'We meet again,' she said, smiling. 'After all that talk about Jane's art I wanted to come and see it again, and sit with it quietly. It's a bit like sitting with her soul.'

Nichol rolled her eyes and groaned. Beauvoir noticed this with a start and wondered if he had been that obnoxious and closed-minded when the Chief talked about his feelings and intuition.

'And the smell,' Clara inhaled deeply and passionately, ignoring Nichol, 'every artist responds to this smell. Gets the heart going. Like walking into Grandma's and smelling fresh chocolate-chip cookies. For us it's that combination of varnish, oils and fixative. Even acrylics have a scent, if you've got a good shnozz. You must have smells like that, that cops respond to.'

'Well,' Gamache said, laughing, and remembering yesterday morning, 'when Agent Nichol here picked me up at my home, she brought along Tim Horton's coffee. Double double. That gets my heart racing' – here he brought his hand to his chest and held it there – 'totally and exclusively associated with investigations. I can walk into a concert hall, but if I smell Tim Horton's double double I'll start looking at the floor for a body.'

Clara laughed. 'If you like chalk outlines you're going to love Jane's work. I'm glad you've come to see it.'

'Is this it?' Gamache looked around the vibrant room.

'Not even close. This is another artist. Their show is ending in a week, then we hang the members' exhibition. That opens in about ten days. Not this Friday, but next.'

'That's the *vernissage*?'

'Exactly. Two weeks after the judging.'

'May I see you for a moment?' Beauvoir steered Gamache a few steps away.

'I spoke with Lacoste. She just got off the phone with Timmer Hadley's doctor. Her death was completely natural, as far as he's concerned. Kidney cancer. It spread to the pancreas and liver and then it was just a matter of time. She actually survived longer than he expected.'

'Did she die at home?'

'Yes, on September second of this year.'

'Labour day,' said Nichol, who'd wandered over and been listening in.

'Ms Morrow,' Gamache called to Clara who had been keeping a respectful distance, one that allowed her to appear to be out of earshot, while actually hearing their entire conversation, 'what do you think?'

Oh, oh. Copped. Literally, this time. No use, she realised, being coy.

'Timmer's death was expected, but still a bit surprising,' said Clara, joining their little circle. 'Well, no, that's overstating it. It's just that we took turns sitting with her. That day it was Ruth's turn. They'd arranged beforehand that if Timmer was feeling good Ruth would steal away to the closing parade of the County Fair. Ruth said Timmer told her she was feeling fine. Ruth gave her her meds, brought a fresh glass of Ensure and then left.'

'Just left a dying woman alone,' Nichol stated. Clara answered quietly.

'Yes. I know it sounds uncaring, even selfish, but we'd all been looking after her for so long and we'd gotten to know her ups and downs. We all slipped away for a half hour at a time, to do her laundry, or shopping, or to cook a light meal. So it wasn't as unusual as it sounds. Ruth would never have left' – now Clara turned to Gamache – 'had she had the slightest hint Timmer was in trouble. It was terrible for her when she came back and found Timmer dead.'

'So it was unexpected,' said Beauvoir.

'In that sense, yes. But we since found out from the

doctors that it often happens that way. The heart just gives out.'

'Was there an autopsy?' Gamache wanted to know.

'No. No one saw any need. Why are you interested in Timmer's death?'

'Just being thorough,' said Beauvoir. 'Two elderly women dying within a few weeks of each other in a very small village, well, it begs some questions. That's all.'

'But as you said, they were elderly. It's what you'd expect.'

'If one hadn't died with a hole in her heart,' said Nichol. Clara winced.

'May I see you for a moment?' Gamache led Nichol outside. 'Agent, if you ever treat anyone the way you've been treating Mrs Morrow, I'll have your badge and send you home on the bus, is that clear?'

'What's wrong with what I said? It's the truth.'

'And do you think she doesn't know that Jane Neal was killed with an arrow? Do you really not know what you've done wrong?'

'I only spoke the truth.'

'No, you only treated another human being like a fool, and from what I can see deliberately hurt her. You are to take notes and remain silent. We'll talk about this further tonight.'

'But—'

'I've been treating you with courtesy and respect because that's the way I choose to treat everyone. But never, ever mistake kindness for weakness. Never debate with me again. Got it?'

'Yes, sir.' And Nichol pledged to keep her opinions to herself if that was the thanks she got for having the courage to say what everyone was thinking. When asked directly she'd answer in monosyllables. So there.

'So there's Jane's picture,' said Clara, hauling a medium-size canvas out from the storage room and putting it on an easel. 'Not everyone liked it.'

Nichol was on the verge of saying, 'No kidding', but remembered her pledge.

'Did you like it?' Beauvoir asked.

'Not at first, but the longer I looked the more I liked it. Something sort of shimmered into place. It went from looking like a cave drawing to something deeply moving. Just like that.' And Clara snapped her fingers.

Gamache thought he'd have to stare at it for the rest of his life before it looked anything other than ridiculous. And yet, there was something there, a charm. 'There are Nellie and Wayne,' he said pointing, surprised, to two purple people in the stands.

'Here's Peter.' Clara pointed to a pie with eyes and a mouth, but no nose.

'How'd she do it? How could she get these people so accurately with two dots for eyes and a squiggly line for a mouth?'

'I don't know. I'm an artist, have been all my life, and I couldn't do that. But there's more to it than that. There's a depth. Though I've been staring at it for more than an hour now and that shimmering thing hasn't happened again. Maybe I'm too needy. Maybe the magic only works when you're not looking for it.'

'Is it good?' Beauvoir asked.

'That's the question. I don't know. Peter thinks it's brilliant, and the rest of the jury, with one exception, was willing to risk it.'

'What risk?'

'This might surprise you, but artists are temperamental so-and-sos. For Jane's work to be accepted and shown, someone else's had to be rejected. That someone will be angry. As will his relatives and friends.'

'Angry enough to kill?' Beauvoir asked.

Clara laughed. 'I can absolutely guarantee you the thought has crossed and even lodged in all our artistic brains at one time or another. But to kill because your work was rejected at Arts Williamsburg? No. Besides, if you did, it would be the jury you'd murder, not Jane. And, come to think of it, no one except the jury knew this work had been accepted. We'd only done the judging last Friday.'

It seems so long ago now, thought Clara.

'Even Miss Neal?'

'Well, I told Jane on Friday.'

'Did anyone else know?'

Now Clara was getting a little embarrassed. 'We talked about it over dinner that night. It was a sort of pre-Thanksgiving dinner with our friends at our place.'

'Who was at the dinner?' Beauvoir asked, his notepad out. He no longer trusted Nichol to take proper notes. Nichol saw this and resented it almost as much as she'd resented it when they'd asked her to take notes. Clara ran down the list of names.

Gamache, meanwhile, was staring at the picture.

'What's it of?'

'The closing parade at the county fair this year. There,' and Clara pointed to a green-faced goat with a shepherd's crook, 'that's Ruth.'

'By God, it is,' said Gamache, to Beauvoir's roar of laughter. It was perfect. He must have been blind to miss it. 'But wait,' Gamache's delight suddenly disappeared, 'this was painted the very day, at the very time, Timmer Hadley was dying.'

'Yes.'

'What does she call it?'

'*Fair Day.*'

SIX

~

Even in the rain and wind Gamache could see how beautiful the countryside was. The maples had turned deep reds and oranges, and leaves blown down in the storm were spread along the road and gully like a tapestry. Their drive had taken them out of Williamsburg toward Three Pines, through the mountain range that separated the two. The road, like most sensible ones, followed the valleys and the river and was probably the old stagecoach route, until Beauvoir turned off on to an even smaller dirt road. Huge potholes jarred their car and Gamache could barely read his notes. He'd long since trained his stomach not to lurch with whatever vehicle he was in, but his eyes were proving more recalcitrant.

Beauvoir slowed down at a large metal mailbox painted sunny yellow. Hand printed in white was the number and the name, 'Croft'. He turned in. The huge maples continued up the drive, creating a Tiffany tunnel.

Through the furious windscreen wiper Gamache saw

a white clapboard farmhouse. The home had a comfortable, lived-in look. Tall, end-of-season sunflowers and hollyhocks leaned against it. Woodsmoke whispered out of the chimney to be grabbed away by the wind and taken home to the woods beyond.

Homes, Gamache knew, were a self-portrait. A person's choice of color, furnishing, pictures. Every touch revealed the individual. God, or the Devil, was in the details. And so was the human. Was it dirty, messy, obsessively clean? Were the decorations chosen to impress, or were they a hodgepodge of personal history? Was the space cluttered or clear? He felt a thrill every time he entered a home during an investigation. He was desperate to get into Jane Neal's home, but that would have to wait. For now the Crofts were about to reveal themselves.

Gamache turned to look at Nichol. 'Keep your eyes open and take detailed notes of what's being said. And just listen, got it?'

Nichol glared back.

'I asked you a question, Agent.'

'Got it.' Then after a significant pause, she added, 'Sir.'

'Good. Inspector Beauvoir, will you take the lead?'

'Right,' replied Beauvoir, getting out of the car.

Matthew Croft was waiting at the screen door. After taking their sodden coats he led them straight into the kitchen. Bright reds and yellows. Cheery tableware and dishes in the hutch. Clean white curtains with flowers embroidered on the border. Gamache looked across the table at Croft who was straightening the rooster salt and pepper shakers. His clever eyes couldn't seem to rest and he held himself as though waiting. Listening. It was all very subtle, hidden below the friendly exterior. But it was there, Gamache was sure of it.

'I've got the archery set in the screen porch. It's wet out, but if you'd still like a demonstration I could show you how they're fired.' Croft had said this to Gamache but Beauvoir answered, dragging Croft's eyes away from his chief.

'That would be very useful, but I have a few questions first, just some background I'd like to get straight.'

'Sure, anything.'

'Tell me about Jane Neal, your relationship with her.'

'We weren't that close. I'd sometimes go over to her place to visit. It was quiet. Peaceful. She was my teacher, long ago now, up at the old schoolhouse.'

'What was she like as a teacher?'

'Remarkable. She had this really amazing ability to look at you and make you feel you were the only person on earth. You know?'

Beauvoir knew. Armand Gamache had the same ability. Most people when talking are also watching the rest of the room, and nodding to others, waving. Never Gamache. When he looked at you, you were the universe. Though Beauvoir knew the boss was also taking in every detail of what was happening. He just didn't show it.

'What do you do for a living?'

'I work for the township of St Rémy in the road department.'

'Doing what?'

'I'm the head of road maintenance. I assign crews, assess

problem areas. Sometimes I just drive, looking for problems. Don't want to find a problem at the same time as I find an overturned car.'

It happened far too often. Normally death came at night, taking a person in their sleep, stopping their heart or tickling them awake, leading them to the bathroom with a splitting headache before pouncing and flooding their brain with blood. It waits in alleys and metro stops. After the sun goes down plugs are pulled by white-clad guardians and death is invited into an antiseptic room.

But in the country death comes, uninvited, during the day. It takes fishermen in their longboats. It grabs children by the ankles as they swim. In winter it calls them down a slope too steep for their budding skills, and crosses their skies at the tips. It waits along the shore where snow met ice not long ago but now, unseen by sparkling eyes, a little water touches the shore, and the skater makes a circle slightly larger than intended. Death stands in the woods with a bow and arrow at dawn and dusk. And it tugs cars off the road in broad daylight, the tires spinning furiously on ice or snow, or bright autumn leaves.

Matthew Croft was always called to road accidents. Sometimes he was the first there. As he worked to free the body Matthew Croft's bruised heart and brain would go home to poetry. He would recite poems learned by heart from books borrowed from Miss Neal. And Ruth Zardo's poetry was his favorite.

On quiet days off he would often visit Miss Neal and

sit in her garden in an Adirondack chair looking across the phlox to the stream beyond, and memorise poems, to be used to ward off the nightmares. As he memorised, Miss Neal would make pink lemonade and deadhead her perennial borders. She was aware of the irony of dead-heading while he banished death from his head. For some reason Matthew was loath to tell the police about this, to let them that far in.

Before he could say more he tensed, slightly. A moment later Gamache heard it too. Suzanne opened the door from the basement which led into the kitchen and came in.

Suzanne Croft didn't look well at all. She'd looked strained at the public meeting, but nothing compared to this. Her skin was almost translucent, except for the blotches. And a thin layer of sweat lent it a sheen, not unlike a reptile. Her hand, when shaken by Gamache, was ice-cold. She was terrified, he realised. Scared sick. Gamache looked over at Croft, who now wasn't even trying to hide his own fear. He was looking at his wife the way one might look at a specter, a ghost with a particularly awful and personal message.

Then the moment passed. Matthew Croft's face fell back to 'normal', with only a pall to the skin evidence of what lay beneath. Gamache offered Mrs Croft his seat but Matthew had grabbed a stool and sat while his wife took his chair. No one spoke. Gamache was willing Beauvoir not to speak. To let the silence stretch to breaking. This woman was holding on to something horrible and her grip was slipping.

'Would you like a glass of water?' Nichol asked Suzanne Croft.

'No, thank you, but let me make some tea.' And with that Mrs Croft leapt from her chair and the moment was broken. Gamache looked at Nichol, perplexed. If she had wanted to sabotage the case and her career she couldn't have done a better job.

'Here, let me help,' said Nichol, bouncing off her seat and grabbing the kettle.

Beauvoir had allowed his face to show a flash of fury when Nichol spoke, then it too was replaced by his familiar, reasonable, mask.

Stupid, stupid woman, he cursed to himself, even as his face took on a benevolent half-smile. He stole a glance at Gamache, and saw with satisfaction the boss was also staring at Nichol, but not angrily. To Beauvoir's disgust, he saw a look he took to be tolerance on the chief's face. Will he never learn? What in God's name drives him to want to help such fools?

'What do you do for a living, Mrs Croft? Do you work?' Now that the silence was fractured, Beauvoir figured he might as well grab back control. Even as he asked the question he could hear the insult. The easy assumption motherhood wasn't work. But he didn't care.

'I help out three times a week at the photocopy store in St Rémy. Helps make ends meet.'

Beauvoir felt badly for the question now it was asked. He wondered whether he'd balled up his anger at Nichol and pitched it into Mrs Croft's face. He looked around the room and realised all the homey touches were made by hand, even the plastic covers of the chairs were inexpertly stapled on, a few coming loose. These people made a little go a long way.

'You have two children, I believe.' Beauvoir shook off his momentary shame.

'That's right,' Matthew jumped in.

'And what are their names?'

'Philippe and Diane.'

'Nice names,' he said into the gathering stillness. 'And how old are they?'

'He's fourteen, she's eight.'

'And where are they?'

The question hovered in the air, as the earth stopped turning. He had been marching inexorably toward this question, as the Crofts must have known. He hadn't wanted to surprise them with it, not out of delicacy for their parental feelings, but because he wanted them to see it coming toward them from a great distance, and to have to wait, and wait. Until their nerves were taut to breaking. Until they both longed for and dreaded this instant.

'They're not here,' said Suzanne, strangling a teacup.

Beauvoir waited, looking steadily at her. 'When are you having your Thanksgiving dinner?'

The swift shift left Suzanne Croft gaping, as though he'd suddenly switched to Pig Latin. Xnay on the erdinnaye.

'I'm sorry?'

'One of the great things I've noticed in my home is that the smell of the turkey hangs around for a couple of days. Then of course, my wife and I make soup the next day, and that's hard to miss too.' He took a deep breath, and then slowly, slowly scanned the clean counters of the kitchen.

'We were going to have Thanksgiving yesterday, Sunday,' said Matthew, 'but with the news of Miss Neal and all we've decided to put it off.'

'For ever?' Beauvoir asked, incredulous. Gamache wondered if it wasn't a little overdone, but the Crofts were beyond critiquing his performance.

'Where's Diane, Mrs Croft?'

'She's at a friend's home. Nina Levesque's.'

'And Philippe?'

'He's not here, I told you. He's out. I don't know when he'll be back.'

OK, thought Beauvoir, joke's over.

'Mrs Croft, we're going to go out with your husband in a minute and look at the bows and arrows. While we're out there I'd like you to think about something. We need to speak with Philippe. We know he was involved in the manure incident in Three Pines, and that Miss Neal identified him.'

'And others,' she said defiantly.

'Two days later she's dead. We need to speak to him.'

'He had nothing to do with it.'

'I'm willing to accept that you believe that. And you might be right. But did you think he was capable of attacking two men in Three Pines? Do you really know your son, Mrs Croft?'

He'd hit a nerve, but then he'd expected to. Not because Beauvoir had any particular insight into the Croft family, but because he knew every parent of a teenage boy fears they're housing a stranger.

'If we can't speak with your son by the time we're ready to leave then we'll get a warrant and have him brought to the police station in St Rémy to be questioned. Before today is over, we will speak with him. Here or there.'

Chief Inspector Gamache watched all this and knew they had to somehow get into that basement. These people were hiding something, or someone. And whatever it was was in the basement. Yet it was odd, thought Gamache. He could have sworn Matthew Croft had been relaxed and natural in the public meeting. It was Suzanne Croft who had been so upset. Now they both were. What had happened?

'Mr Croft, may we see those bows and arrows now?' Beauvoir asked.

'How dare you—' Croft was vibrating with rage.

'It's not a question of "dare".' Beauvoir looked him hard in the face. 'At the meeting this morning Chief Inspector Gamache made it clear that unpleasant things would be asked of each and every one of you. That's the price you'll pay for finding out who killed Miss Neal. I understand your anger. You don't want your children traumatised by this. But, frankly, I think they already are. I'm giving you a choice. We can speak with your son here, or we can speak with him at the St Rémy station.'

Beauvoir paused. And paused. And in his mind dared Nichol to offer cookies. Finally he continued. 'The rules of normal life are suspended when there's a violent death.

149

You two and your family are among the first casualties. I have no illusions about what we do, and we do it as painlessly as possible' – Matthew Croft sputtered in disgust – 'which is why I've offered you the choice. Now, the bows and arrows please.'

Matthew Croft took a deep breath, 'This way.'

He led them out of the kitchen on to the screen porch.

'Mrs Croft,' Gamache said, and poked his head back into the kitchen just as Suzanne Croft was stepping toward the basement door, 'would you join us, please?'

Suzanne Croft's shoulders sagged.

'There.' It was all Matthew Croft could do to be civil. 'That's a recurve and that's a compound, and there're the arrows.'

'Are these two the only bows you have?' Beauvoir asked, picking up the arrows and noting they were the target-shooting kind.

'Yes, they are,' said Croft without hesitation.

They looked exactly as they had been described, only larger. Beauvoir and Gamache lifted each bow in turn. They were heavy, even the simple recurve.

'Could you put the string on the recurve, please?' Beauvoir asked.

Matthew grabbed the recurve, took a long string with loops on either end, put the 'stick' between his legs and bent the bow down until the string could reach the little notch at the top. Gamache could see it took some strength. Suddenly, there stood a 'Robin Hood' bow.

'May I?'

Croft handed Gamache the bow and as he took it he

noticed dust. But no dirt. Gamache then turned his attention to the compound. It looked more like a traditional bow than he'd expected. He picked it up, noticing the wisps of cobwebs between some of the strings. This bow too hadn't been used in some time. And it was far heavier than he'd expected. He turned to Mrs Croft.

'Do you bow hunt or target shoot?'

'I sometimes target shoot.'

'Which bow do you use?'

After a breath of hesitation Suzanne Croft pointed to the recurve.

'Would you mind taking off the string?'

'Why?' Matthew Croft stepped forward.

'I'd like to see your wife do it.' Gamache turned to Suzanne. 'Please.'

Suzanne Croft picked up the recurve, and swiftly putting it around her leg she leaned on the bow and popped the string off. She'd clearly done this many times before. Then Gamache had an idea.

'Could you restring the bow, please?'

Suzanne shrugged and replaced the now straight bow around her leg and leaned on the upper part. Not much happened. Then she gave a huge thrust down and slipped the string over the top, recreating the recurve. She handed it to Gamache without a word.

'Thank you,' he said, puzzled. He'd had a hunch, but it didn't seem to be right.

'Would you mind if we shot a few arrows?' Beauvoir asked.

'Not at all.'

After putting their outside rain gear on again all five trooped into the light drizzle. Fortunately the heavy rain had let up. Matthew had put up a round archery target made of hay encased in canvas with target circles painted in red. He picked up the recurve, put a new wooden target arrow in the slot and pulled the string back. Croft spent a moment aiming then he released the arrow. It hit the second ring. Croft then handed the bow to Gamache who handed it with a slight smile to Beauvoir. Beauvoir took it with relish. He'd been raring to try it, and even daring to imagine himself getting bull's-eye after bull's-eye until the Canadian Archery team invited him to compete in the Olympics. This so-called sport looked like a no-brainer, especially since he was a crack shot with a gun.

The first sign of trouble came almost immediately. He almost didn't get the string all the way back. It was far harder than he imagined. Then the arrow, held tentatively in place between two of his fingers, started jumping all over the bow, refusing to stay snug on the little peg at the front. Finally he was ready to shoot. He released the string and the arrow shot out of the bow and missed the target by a country mile. What didn't miss was the string itself. A millisecond after being released, it hit Beauvoir's elbow with such force he thought his arm had been severed. He yelped and dropped the bow, hardly daring to look at his arm. The pain was searing.

'What happened, Mr Croft?' Gamache snapped, going to Beauvoir. Croft wasn't exactly laughing, but Gamache could see the pleasure this was giving him.

'Not to worry, Chief Inspector. He's just got a bruised arm. Happens to all amateurs. The string caught his elbow. As you said, we must all be prepared for unpleasantness.' Croft gave him a hard look, and Gamache remembered he'd offered the bow to him first. This injury had been meant for him.

'Are you all right?' Beauvoir was cradling his arm and straining to see the arrow. Unless he'd split Croft's arrow, his own had missed the target. That hurt almost as much as the bruise.

'I'm fine, sir. It was more the surprise than the pain.'

'Sure?'

'Yes.'

Gamache turned to Croft. 'Can you show me how to shoot the arrow without hitting my arm?'

'Probably. You willing to risk it?'

Gamache just looked expectantly at Croft, refusing to play.

'Right. Take the bow like this.' Croft stood beside Gamache and held his arm up as Gamache gripped the bow. 'Now twist your elbow so it's perpendicular to the ground. There, that's right,' said Croft. 'Now the string will shoot right by your elbow instead of hitting it. It makes a much smaller target. Probably.'

Gamache grinned. If the string hit, it hit. At least, unlike Beauvoir, he'd be prepared.

'What else should I be doing?'

'Now, with your right hand, put the arrow in so its tip is resting on that little wooden notch on the bow, and fit the back of the arrow on to the string. Good. Now you're ready to pull back. What you don't want to do is to have to hold the string back for too long before firing. You'll see why in a moment. Get yourself lined up, your body like this.' He turned Gamache so his body was sideways to the target. His left arm was getting tired holding the heavy bow in place.

'Here's the sight.'

Croft, incredibly, was pointing to a tiny pin like Gamache took out of his shirts after they'd been dry cleaned. 'You line the knob of the pin up with the bull's-eye. Then you draw the string back in one fluid motion, realign the sight, and let go.'

Croft stood back. Gamache lowered the bow to give his arm a break, took a breath, reviewed the steps in his mind then did it. Smoothly he brought his left arm up, and before placing the arrow he twisted his elbow out of the way of the string. He then placed the arrow on the knob, put the arrow butt in the string, lined the head of the pin up with the bull's-eye, and pulled back on the string in one fluid motion. Except it wasn't exactly fluid. It felt as though the Montreal Canadiens were playing tug of war with him, yanking the string in the other direction. With his right arm trembling slightly he managed to get the string all the way back until it was almost to his nose, then he released. By then he didn't much care whether it took his whole elbow off, he just wanted to let the damn thing go. The arrow flew wildly off, missing the target by at least as much as Beauvoir's. But the string also missed. It twanged back into place without even grazing Gamache's arm.

'You're a good teacher, Mr Croft.'

'You must have low standards. Look where your arrow went.'

'I can't see it. Hope it isn't lost.'

'It isn't. They never are. Haven't lost one yet.'

'Mrs Croft,' said Gamache, 'your turn.'

'I'd rather not.'

'Please, Mrs Croft.' Chief Inspector Gamache handed her the bow. He was thankful he'd shot the bow and arrow. It had given him a thought.

'I haven't used it in a while.'

'I understand,' said Gamache. 'Just do your best.'

Suzanne Croft lined up her shot, put the arrow in, grabbed the string and pulled. And pulled. And pulled until she started crying and collapsed on to the muddy ground, overwhelmed by an emotion that had nothing to do with failing to shoot the arrow. Instantly Matthew Croft was kneeling beside her, holding her. Swiftly Gamache took Beauvoir's arm and led him a step or two away. He spoke in an urgent whisper.

'We need to get into that basement. I'd like you to offer them a deal. We won't take Philippe to the police station, if they take us to the basement right now.'

'But we have to speak with Philippe.'

'I agree, but we can't do both and the only way we'll get to the basement is if we give them something they really want. They want to protect their son. We can't have both and I think this is the best we can do.'

Beauvoir thought about it while watching Croft console

155

his wife. The Chief Inspector was right. Philippe would probably wait. What was in the basement probably wouldn't. After that demonstration it was clear Mrs Croft knew her way around a bow and arrow, but she'd never shot that particular bow. There must be another one somewhere, one that she was used to using. And one that Philippe might have used. Probably in the basement. His nose caught the woodsmoke wafting out of the chimney. He hoped it wasn't too late.

Peter and Clara were walking Lucy along the footpath through the woods across the Bella Bella from their home. Once over the small bridge they released her. She trudged along, showing no interest in the wealth of new scents. The rain had stopped but the thick grass and ground were sodden.

'Weather network says it's supposed to clear,' said Peter, kicking a stone along with his feet.

'But getting colder,' agreed Clara. 'Hard frost's on the way. Have to get into the garden.' She wrapped her arms around herself, feeling the chill. 'I have a question for you. It's advice, really. You know when I went over to Yolande?'

'At lunch? Yes. Why did you do that?'

'Well, because she was Jane's niece.'

'No, really. Why?'

Damn Peter, thought Clara. He actually knows me.

'I wanted to be kind –'

'But you knew what would happen. Why would you choose to walk right into a situation where you know the person is going to be hurtful? It kills me to see you do that, and you do it all the time. It's like a form of insanity.'

'You call it insanity, I call it optimism.'

'Is it optimism to expect people to do something they've never done before? Every time you approach Yolande she's horrible to you. Every time. And yet you keep doing it. Why?'

'What's all this about?'

'Have you ever thought how it makes me feel to watch you do this time after time, and to not be able to do anything except pick up the pieces? Stop expecting people to be something they're not. Yolande is a horrible, hateful, petty little person. Accept that and stay away from her. And if you choose to walk into her space, be prepared for the consequences.'

'That's unfair. You seem to think I'm this moron who had no idea what was about to happen. I knew perfectly well she'd do that. And I did it anyway. Because I had to know something.'

'Know what?'

'I had to hear André's laugh.'

'His laugh? Why?'

'That's what I wanted to talk about. Remember Jane described that horrible laugh when the boys threw manure at Olivier and Gabri?' Peter nodded. 'I heard a laugh like that this morning, at the public meeting. It was André. That's why I had to go up to their table, to get him to laugh again. And he did. One thing I'll say for Yolande and André, is that they're predictable.'

'But Clara, André's a grown man, he wasn't one of those masked boys.'

Clara waited. Peter wasn't normally this obtuse, so it was fun to watch. His furrowed brow eventually cleared.

'It was André's son Bernard.'

'Atta boy.'

'Jane got it wrong, it wasn't Philippe, Gus and Claude. One of them wasn't there, but Bernard was.'

'Should I tell Chief Inspector Gamache? Could he see it as me just bad-mouthing Yolande?' asked Clara.

'Who cares? Gamache needs to know.'

'Good. I'll go over to the Bistro this afternoon, during his, "at home".' Clara picked up a stick and threw it, hoping Lucy would follow. She didn't.

The Crofts accepted the deal. They really had little choice and now Gamache, Beauvoir, Nichol and the Crofts were making their way down the narrow steps. The entire basement was well organised, not the kind of labyrinth of confusion he'd seen, and sifted through, so often. When he commented on it Croft answered, 'It's one of Philippe's chores, cleaning the basement. We did it together for a few years, but on his fourteenth birthday I told him it was now all his.' Then Croft had added, perhaps realising how it sounded, 'It wasn't his only birthday present.'

For twenty minutes the two men methodically searched. Then, amid the skis, tennis rackets and hockey gear, hanging on the wall half hidden by goalie pads, they found a quiver. Carefully lifting it off its hook using one of the tennis rackets, Beauvoir looked inside. Five old wooden hunting arrows. What wasn't in the quiver was a single cobweb. This quiver had been out recently.

'Whose is this, Mr Croft?'

'That belonged to my father.'

'There are only five arrows. Is that usual?'

'That's how it came to me. Dad must have lost one.'

'And yet you said it was rare. I believe you said that hunters almost never lose an arrow.'

'That's true, but "almost never" and "never" are two different things.'

'May I?' Beauvoir handed him the tennis racket with the quiver hanging from it. Gamache held the racket as high as he could and strained to look at the round leather bottom of the old quiver.

'Have you got a flashlight?'

Matthew took a bright yellow Eveready from a hook and handed it over. Gamache switched it on and saw six shadowy points on the belly of the quiver. He showed them to Beauvoir.

'There were six arrows until recently,' said Beauvoir.

'Recently? How do you figure that, Inspector?' Listening to Matthew Croft's attempt at calm Gamache felt for the man. He was clamping down for control, tighter and tighter. So tight his hands were trembling slightly now and his voice was rising.

'I know leather, Mr Croft,' Beauvoir lied. 'This is thin calves' leather, used because it's supple, yet durable. These arrows, which I assume are hunting arrows' – Croft shrugged – 'these arrows can sit in this leather-bottomed

159

quiver, tip down and neither dull the tip nor break through the bottom. And, now this is important, Mr Croft, the leather will not keep the form of whatever it holds. It's so supple it will slowly go back to its original shape. These six blemishes have been made by six arrow tips. Yet only five arrows remain. How is that possible?'

Now Croft was silent, his jaw clamped shut.

Beauvoir handed the tennis racket and quiver to Nichol with instructions to hold it while he and Gamache continued the search. Now Croft had joined his wife, and side by side they awaited whatever was coming their way. The two men spent the next half-hour searching the basement inch by inch. They'd just about given up when Beauvoir wandered over to the furnace. Once there he actually stepped on it. Sitting practically in plain sight was a recurve bow, and beside it an axe.

A search warrant was sought and issued and the Croft farm was scoured from the attic to the barn to the chicken coop. Philippe was found in his bedroom plugged in to his Sony 'Discman'. Beauvoir checked the ash bin under the wood-burning furnace and found a metal arrowhead, charred by the fire, but still intact. At this discovery Matthew Croft's legs gave way and he sank to the cold concrete floor, to a place no rhyming verse existed. He had finally been hurt beyond poetry.

Beauvoir arranged for all the things they'd collected to go to the Sûreté labs in Montreal. Now the team sat around the fire hall once again.

'What do we do about the Crofts?' Lacoste wanted to know, sipping a Tim Horton's double double.

'Nothing for now,' replied Gamache, biting into a chocolate donut. 'We wait for the report to come back from the labs.'

'They'll have results for us tomorrow,' said Beauvoir.

'About Matthew Croft. Shouldn't we take him into custody?' Lacoste spoke up, smoothing back her shiny auburn hair with her wrist, trying not to get chocolate glaze into it.

'Inspector Beauvoir, what do you think?'

'You know me, I always want to be on the safe side.'

Gamache was reminded of a cartoon he'd cut from the *Montreal Gazette* years ago. It showed a judge and the accused. The punch line read, 'The jury has found you "not guilty" but I'm giving you five years just to be on the safe side.' Everyday he looked at it, chuckled, and knew deep down the truth of it. Part of him yearned for 'the safe side', even at the cost of other people's freedom.

'What risk are we running by leaving Matthew Croft free?' Gamache looked around the table.

'Well,' ventured Lacoste, 'there might be more evidence in that house, evidence he could destroy between now and tomorrow.'

'True, but couldn't Mrs Croft destroy it just as easily? After all, she was the one who threw the arrow in the furnace and was about to chop up the bow. She's admitted as much. In fact, if there's anyone we should bring in it's her, for destroying evidence. I'll tell you my thinking.' He took a paper napkin and wiped his hands, then, leaning

161

forward, he put his elbows on the table. Everyone else, except Nichol, did the same, giving it the appearance of a highly secretive gathering.

'Let's say the bow and arrow tip are the ones that killed Jane Neal. Right?'

Everyone nodded. As far as they were concerned they were home free.

'But which of them did it? Was it Matthew Croft? Inspector Beauvoir, what do you think?' Beauvoir with all his might wanted Matthew Croft to be the guilty one. Yet, damn it, it didn't fit.

'No. He was far too relaxed in the public meeting. His panic didn't kick in until later. No. If it'd been him he'd have been more evasive earlier. He has very little skill at hiding how he's feeling.'

Gamache agreed. 'Scratch Mr Croft. How about Suzanne Croft?'

'Well, she could have done it. She clearly knew about the bow and arrow during the public meeting, and she destroyed the arrow and would have chucked the bow in the furnace if she'd had time. But, again, it doesn't fit.'

'If she killed Jane Neal she'd have destroyed the arrow and the bow long before now,' said Nichol, leaning into the group. 'She'd have gone right home and burned the whole lot. Why wait until they know the police are about to arrive?'

'You're right,' said Gamache, surprised and pleased. 'Go on.'

'OK. Suppose it's Philippe. He's fourteen, right? This is an old bow, not as powerful as the newer ones. Doesn't take as much strength. So he takes the old wooden bow and the old wooden arrows and he heads off to hunt. But he shoots Miss Neal by mistake. He picks up his arrow and runs back home. But Maman figures it out –'

'How?' Gamache asked.

'How?' This stopped Nichol. She had to think. 'He might have had blood on his clothing, or his hands. She'd have gotten it out of him eventually, maybe just before the public meeting. She had to go to hear what the police had, but she'd have kept Philippe back at home. That explains her increasing agitation in the meeting.'

'Any holes in this theory?' Beauvoir asked the gathering, trying not to sound hopeful. While he hoped Nichol would prove not a total liability, this was a disastrously good showing. He tried not to look at her, but couldn't help it. Sure enough she was staring straight at him with a tiny smile. She leaned back in her chair, slowly, luxuriously.

'Well done, Nichol.' Gamache rose and nodded to her.

Wait, just wait, she thought, till Dad hears about this.

'So the Croft family stays put for today, until we get the results of the lab tests,' said Gamache.

The meeting broke up, each one looking forward to wrapping up the investigation the next day. Still, Armand Gamache knew better than to count on one theory. He wanted to keep the investigation active. Just to be on the safe side.

It was almost five and time to head to the Bistro. But there was something he wanted to do first.

SEVEN

~

Gamache walked through the bistro, nodding to Gabri who was setting tables. Each business connected to the next in the row of shops and at the back of the bistro he found the door into the next store. Myrna's Livres, Neufs et Usagés.

And there he found himself, holding a worn copy of *Being*. He'd read *Being* when it first came out a few years before. The title always reminded him of the day his daughter Annie had come home from first grade with her English homework which was to name three types of beans. She'd written, 'green beans, yellow beans and human beans'.

He turned the book over and looked at the back, with its 'blurb' and brief bio of the author, the famous McGill University doctor and geneticist, Dr Vincent Gilbert. Dr Gilbert glared back, strangely stern for a man who wrote about compassion. This particular book was about his work with Brother Albert Mailloux at 'La Porte', mostly with men and women with Down's syndrome. It was really a meditation on what he'd learned watching these people. What he'd learned about them and the nature of humanity and what he'd learned about himself. It was a remarkable study of arrogance and humility and, above all, forgiveness.

The walls of the shop were lined with bookcases, all ordered and labeled and filled with books, some new, some already read, some French, most English. Myrna had managed to make it feel more like the library in a cultured and comfortable country home than a store. She'd set up a couple of rocking chairs beside an open fire, with a couch facing it. Gamache sank into one of the rockers and reminded himself of the beauty of *Being*.

'Now there's a good book,' said Myrna, dropping into the chair opposite. She'd brought a pile of used books and some price stickers. 'We haven't actually met. I'm Myrna Landers. I saw you at the public meeting.'

Gamache got up and shook her hand, smiling. 'I saw you too.'

Myrna laughed. 'I'm hard to miss. The only black in Three Pines and not exactly a slip of a woman.'

'You and I are well matched.' Gamache smiled, rubbing his stomach.

She picked a book out of her pile. 'Have you read this?' She held a worn copy of Brother Albert's book, *Loss*. Gamache shook his head and figured it probably wasn't the cheeriest of reads. She turned it over in her huge hands and seemed to caress it.

'His theory is that life is loss,' said Myrna after a moment.

'Loss of parents, loss of loves, loss of jobs. So we have to find a higher meaning in our lives than these things and people. Otherwise we'll lose ourselves.'

'What do you think of that?'

'I think he's right. I was a psychologist in Montreal before coming here a few years ago. Most of the people came through my door because of a crisis in their lives, and most of those crises boiled down to loss. Loss of a marriage or an important relationship. Loss of security. A job, a home, a parent. Something drove them to ask for help and to look deep inside themselves. And the catalyst was often change and loss.'

'Are they the same thing?'

'For someone not well skilled at adapting they can be.'

'Loss of control?'

'That's a huge one, of course. Most of us are great with change, as long as it was our idea. But change imposed from the outside can send some people into a tailspin. I think Brother Albert hit it on the head. Life is loss. But out of that, as the book stresses, comes freedom. If we can accept that nothing is permanent, and change is inevitable, if we can adapt, then we're going to be happier people.'

'What brought you here? Loss?'

'That's hardly fair, Chief Inspector, now you've got me. Yes. But not in a conventional way, since of course I always have to be special and different.' Myrna put back her head and laughed at herself. 'I lost sympathy with many of my patients. After twenty-five years of listening to their complaints I finally snapped. I woke up one morning bent out of shape about this client who was forty-three but acting sixteen. Every week he'd come with the same complaints, "Someone hurt me. Life is unfair. It's not my fault." For three years I'd been making suggestions, and for three years he'd done nothing. Then, listening to him this one day, I suddenly understood. He wasn't changing because he didn't want to. He had no intention of changing. For the next twenty years we would go through this charade. And I realised in that same instant that most of my clients were exactly like him.'

'Surely, though, some were trying.'

'Oh, yes. But they were the ones who got better quite quickly. Because they worked hard at it and genuinely wanted it. The others said they wanted to get better, but I think, and this isn't popular in psychology circles' – here she leaned forward and whispered, conspiratorially – 'I think many people love their problems. Gives them all sorts of excuses for not growing up and getting on with life.'

Myrna leaned back again in her chair and took a long breath.

'Life is change. If you aren't growing and evolving you're standing still, and the rest of the world is surging ahead. Most of these people are very immature. They lead "still" lives, waiting.'

'Waiting for what?'

'Waiting for someone to save them. Expecting someone to save them or at least protect them from the big, bad world. The thing is no one else can save them because the problem is theirs and so is the solution. Only they can get out of it.'

'"The fault, dear Brutus, lies not in our stars, but in ourselves that we are underlings."'

Myrna leaned forward, animated, 'That's it. The fault lies with us, and only us. It's not fate, not genetics, not bad luck, and it's definitely not Mom and Dad. Ultimately it's us and our choices. But, but' – now her eyes shone and she almost vibrated with excitement – 'the most powerful, spectacular thing is that the solution rests with us as well. We're the only ones who can change our lives, turn them around. So all those years waiting for someone else to do it are wasted. I used to love talking about this with Timmer. Now there was a bright woman. I miss her.' Myrna threw herself back in her chair. 'The vast majority of troubled people don't get it. The fault is here, but so is the solution. That's the grace.'

'But that would mean admitting there was something wrong with them. Don't most unhappy people blame others? That's what was so stark, so scary about that line from *Julius Caesar*. Who among us can admit that the problem is us?'

'You got it.'

'You mentioned Timmer Hadley. What was she like?'

'I only met her near the end of her life. Never knew her when she was healthy. Timmer was a smart woman, in every way. Always well turned out, trim, elegant, even. I liked her.'

'Did you sit with her?'

'Yes. Sat with her the day before she died. Took a book to read but she wanted to look at old pictures so I got her album down and we flipped through it. There was a picture of Jane in it, from centuries ago. She must have been sixteen, maybe seventeen. She was with her parents. Timmer didn't like the Neals. Cold, she said, social climbers.'

Myrna suddenly stopped, on the verge of saying something else.

'Go on,' prompted Gamache.

'That's it,' said Myrna.

'Now, I know that wasn't all she said. Tell me.'

'I can't. She was doped up with morphine and I know she would never have said anything had she been in her right mind. Besides, it has nothing to do with Jane's death. It happened over sixty years ago.'

'The funny thing about murder is that the act is often committed decades before the actual action. Something happens, and it leads, inexorably, to death many years later. A bad seed is planted. It's like those old horror films from the Hammer studios, of the monster, not running, never running, but walking without pause, without thought or mercy, toward its victim. Murder is often like that. It starts way far off.'

'I still won't tell you what Timmer said.'

Gamache knew he could persuade her. But why? If the lab tests exonerated the Crofts, then he'd come back, but otherwise she was right. He didn't need to know, but, God knew, he really wanted to know.

'I'll tell you what,' he said. 'I won't press. But one day I might ask again and you'll need to tell me.'

'Fair enough. You ask again, and I'll tell you.'

'I have another question. What do you think of the boys who threw the manure?'

'We all do stupid, cruel things as children. I remember I once took a neighbor's dog and shut it in my house, then told the little girl her dog had been picked up by the dog catcher and destroyed. I still wake up at three in the morning seeing her face. I tracked her down about ten years ago to say I was sorry but she'd been killed in a car accident.'

'You have to forgive yourself,' said Gamache, holding up *Being*.

'You're right, of course. But maybe I don't want to. Maybe that's something I don't want to lose. My own private hell. Horrible, but mine. I'm quite thick at times. And places.' She laughed, brushing invisible crumbs from her caftan.

'Oscar Wilde said there's no sin except stupidity.'

'And what do you think of that?' Myrna's eyes lit up, happy to so obviously turn the spotlight on him. He thought a moment.

'I've made mistakes that have allowed killers to take more lives. And each of those mistakes, upon looking back, was stupid. A conclusion jumped to, a false assumption held too firmly. Each wrong choice I make puts a community at risk.'

'Have you learned from your mistakes?'

'Yes, teacher, I believe I have.'

'Then that's all you can ask of yourself, Grasshopper. I'll make you a deal. I'll forgive myself if you forgive yourself.'

'Deal,' said Gamache, and wished it was that easy.

Ten minutes later Armand Gamache was sitting at the

table by the Bistro window looking out on to Three Pines. He'd bought just one book from Myrna, and it wasn't *Being* or *Loss*. She'd seemed slightly surprised when he put the book next to her till. He now sat and read, a Cinzano and some pretzels in front of him, and every now and then he'd lower the book to stare through the window and through the village and into the woods beyond. The clouds were breaking up, leaving patches of early evening sunshine on the small mountains that surrounded Three Pines. Once or twice he flipped through the book, looking for illustrations. Finding what he was looking for he ear-marked them and continued reading. It was a very pleasant way to pass the time.

A manila file hitting the table brought him back to the Bistro.

'The autopsy report.' The coroner, Sharon Harris, sat down and ordered a drink.

He lowered his book and picked up the dossier. After a few minutes he had a question. 'If the arrow hadn't hit her heart, would it still have killed her?'

'If it had come close to the heart, yes. But', Dr Harris leaned forward and bent the autopsy report down so she could see it, upside down, 'she was hit straight through the heart. You see? Whoever did it must have been a great shot. That wasn't a fluke.'

'And yet I suspect that's exactly the conclusion we're going to reach, that it was a fluke. A hunting accident. Not the first in Quebec history.'

'You're right, lots of hunting accidents every season with rifles. But arrows? You'd have to be a good hunter to get her through the heart and good hunters don't often make mistakes like that. Not archers. They aren't the usual yahoos.'

'What are you saying, doctor?'

'I'm saying if the death of Miss Neal was an accident the killer had very bad Karma. Of all the accidental hunting deaths I've investigated as medical examiner none has involved a good bow hunter.'

'You mean if a good hunter did this it was on purpose?'

'I'm saying a good bow hunter did this and good bow hunters don't make mistakes. You connected the dots.' She smiled warmly then nodded to the people at the next table. Gamache remembered she lived in the area.

'You have a home at Cleghorn Halt, don't you? Is it close by?'

'About twenty minutes from here toward the Abbey. I know Three Pines quite well from the Tours Des Arts. Peter and Clara Morrow live here, right? Just over there?' She pointed through the window across the green to their red-brick home.

'That's right. Do you know them?'

'Just their art. He's a member of the Royal Academy of Canada, quite a distinguished artist. Does the most amazing works, very stark. They look like abstracts, but they're actually just the opposite, they're hyper-realism. He takes a subject, say that glass of Cinzano,' she picked it up, 'and he gets really close.' She leaned in until her eyelashes were licking the moisture on the outside of his glass. 'Then he takes a microscope device and gets even closer. And he paints that.' She put his glass back on the table. 'They're absolutely dazzling. Takes him for ever, apparently, to do a single piece. Don't know where he finds the patience.'

'How about Clara Morrow?'

'I have one of her works. I think she's fabulous, but very different from him. Her art is quite feminist, a lot of female nudes and allusions to goddesses. She did the most wonderful series on Sophia's Daughters.'

'The Three Graces, Faith, Hope and Charity?'

'Very impressive, Chief Inspector. I have one of that series. Hope.'

'Do you know Ben Hadley?'

'Of Hadley Mills? Not really. We've been at a few functions together. Arts Williamsburg has an annual garden party, often on his mother's property, and he's always there. I guess it's his property now.'

'He never married?'

'No. Late forties and still single. I wonder if he'll marry now.'

'What makes you say that?'

'It just seems often the case. No woman could come between mother and son, though I don't think Ben Hadley had the hots for Mommy. Anytime he spoke of her it was of how she'd somehow put him down. Some of his stories were horrible, though he never seemed to notice. I always admired that.'

'What does he do?'

'Ben Hadley? I don't know. I always had the impression he did nothing, sort of emasculated by Mom. Very sad.'

'Tragic.' Gamache was remembering the tall, ambling,

likeable professor type, slightly befuddled all the time. Sharon Harris picked up the book he'd been reading and read the back cover.

'Good idea.' She placed it back on the table, impressed. Seems she'd been lecturing Gamache on things he already knew. It probably wasn't the first time. After she left Gamache went back to his book, flipping to the dog-eared page and staring at the illustration. It was possible. Just possible. He paid for his drink, shrugged into his field coat and left the warmth of the room to head into the cold and damp and approaching dark.

Clara stared at the box in front of her and willed it to speak. Something had told her to start work on a big wooden box. So she had. And now she sat in her studio and stared, trying to remember why building a big box had seemed such a good idea. More than that. Why had it seemed an artistic idea? In fact, what the hell was the idea anyway?

She waited for the box to speak to her. To say something. Anything. Even nonsense. Though why Clara thought the box, should it choose to speak, would say anything other than nonsense was another mystery. Who listens to boxes anyway?

Clara's art was intuitive, which wasn't to say it wasn't skilled and trained. She'd been to the best art college in Canada, even taught there for a while, until its narrow definition of 'art' had driven her away. From downtown Toronto to downtown Three Pines. That had been decades ago and so far she'd failed to set the art world on fire.

Though waiting for messages from boxes could be a reason. Clara cleared her mind and opened it to inspiration. A croissant floated through it, then her garden, which needed cutting down, then she had a tiny argument with Myrna about the prices Myrna would no doubt offer for some of Clara's used books. The box, on the other hand, remained mute.

The studio was growing cold and Clara wondered whether Peter, sitting across the hall in his own studio was also cold. He would almost certainly, she thought with a twang of envy, be working too hard to notice. He never seemed to suffer from the uncertainty that could freeze her, leave her stuck and frozen in place. He just kept putting one foot in front of the other, producing his excruciatingly detailed works that sold for thousands in Montreal. It took him months to do each piece, he was so painfully precise and methodical. She'd given him a roller for his birthday one year and told him to paint faster. He didn't seem to appreciate the joke. Perhaps because it wasn't entirely a joke. They were constantly broke. Even now, with the autumn chill seeping in through the cracks around the windows, Clara was loath to turn on the furnace. Instead she'd put on another sweater, and even that was probably worn and pilled. She longed for crisp new bed linens and one can in their kitchen with a name brand and enough firewood to see them through the winter without worry. Worry. It wears you down, she thought as she put on another sweater and sat down again in front of the big silent box.

Again Clara cleared her mind, opened it wide. And lo

and behold, an idea appeared. Fully formed. Whole and perfect and disturbing. Within moments she was out the front door and chugging up rue du Moulin. As she approached Timmer's home she instinctively crossed to the other side and averted her eyes. Once beyond it she re-crossed the road and made her way past the old schoolhouse, still bedecked in yellow police tape. Then she plunged into the woods, wondering for a moment at the folly of her actions. It was getting on dusk. The time when death waits in the woods. Not in the form of a ghost, Clara hoped, but in an even more sinister guise. A man with a weapon designed to make ghosts. Hunters crept into the woods at dusk. One had killed Jane. Clara slowed down. This was perhaps not the brightest idea she'd had. Actually, it was the box's idea, so she could blame it if she was killed. Clara heard a movement ahead. She froze.

The woods were darker than Gamache had expected. He'd entered by a route he was unfamiliar with and spent a moment looking around, getting his bearings. He had his cell phone with him in case he got lost, but he knew the cellular grid was unreliable at best in the mountains. Still, it was some comfort. He turned full circle, slowly, and spotted a small flash of yellow. The police tape circling the spot where Jane had died. He made for it, the woods still soaked from the day's downpour, and drenching his legs and feet as he went. Just outside the cordon he stopped again and listened. He knew it was the hunting hour, he'd just have to trust that it wasn't his time. Trust, and be very, very careful. Gamache spent ten minutes searching before he found it. He smiled as he made his way to the tree. How often had his mother chastised him as a child for staring down at his feet, instead of looking up? Well, she'd been right again. When they'd first searched the site he'd been looking on the ground when what he wanted wasn't down there. It was up in the trees.

A box.

Now Gamache stood at the foot of the tree contemplating the wooden structure twenty feet up. Nailed to the trunk was a series of wooden planks, rungs, their nails long since rusted and bleeding a deep orange into the wood. Gamache thought of his warm seat by the window in the Bistro. His amber Cinzano and pretzels. And the fireplace. And he started climbing. Hauling himself up one rung at a time he remembered something else, as one trembling hand reached up and strangled the next rung. He hated heights. How could he have forgotten? Or had he perhaps hoped this time would be different? As he clung to the slimy, creaky, narrow slats and looked up to the wooden platform a zillion feet above, he froze.

Had the noise come from ahead or behind? Clara wondered. It was like sirens in the city, the noise seems omnipresent. And now she heard it again. She turned and looked behind her. Back there the trees were mostly pines and held their dark needles, making the woods prickly and black. Ahead, into the red sunset, the woods were more mixed, with maples and cherry. Clara made instinctively for the light, not sure whether she should make a lot of noise, like in the spring to warn the bears, or be as quiet as possible. She supposed it depended on what she thought was with her in the woods. A bear, a deer, a hunter, or a ghost. She wished she had a box to consult. Or Peter. Yes, Peter was almost always better than a box.

Gamache willed his hands to move to the next rung. He remembered to breathe and even hummed a little song of his own devising. To ward away terror. He climbed toward the dark patch above him. Breathe, reach, step. Breathe, reach, step. Finally he made it and his head poked through the small square cut in the floor. It was as the book described. A blind. You'd have to be blind drunk to want to sit up there, thought Gamache. He hauled himself through the hole and to his feet, feeling a wave of relief, which was replaced a moment later by blinding terror. He dropped to his knees and scrambled to the tree trunk, hugging it to himself. The fragile box was perched twenty feet up the tree and hung out five feet into the air, hovering there with only a rickety old rail between Gamache and oblivion. Gamache dug his hands into the bark, feeling the wood pinch his palm, glad for the pain to concentrate on. His horrible fear, and the terrible betrayal, wasn't that he'd trip and fall, or even that the wooden blind would tumble to the ground. It was that he'd throw himself over the edge. That was the horror of vertigo. He felt pulled to the edge and over as if an anchor was attached to his leg. Unaided, unthreatened, he would essentially kill himself. He could see it all happen and the horror of it took his breath away and for a moment he gripped the tree, closed his eyes, and fought to breathe deeply, regularly, from his solar plexus.

It worked. Slowly the terror ebbed, the certainty of flinging himself to his own death diminished. He opened his eyes. And there he saw it. What he'd come for. What he'd read about in the Bistro from the book he'd bought second-hand from Myrna. *The Boys' Big Book of Hunting.* He'd read about blinds, the structures hunters built so they could see the deer coming, and shoot them. But that wasn't what had called Gamache from the safety and warmth of the village. He'd come looking for something else mentioned in the book. And from where he sat he could see it in the middle distance.

But now he heard a sound. An almost certainly human sound. Dare he look down? Dare he let go of the trunk and crawl to the edge of the blind and look over? There it was again. A kind of hum. A familiar tune. What was it? Cautiously he released the tree and, sprawling on his stomach on the platform, he inched to the edge.

He saw the top of a familiar head. Actually he saw a mushroom of hair.

Clara had decided that she should go with the worst-case scenario, but then couldn't decide which one was the worst. A bear, a hunter or a ghost? Thoughts of bear reminded her of Winnie the Pooh and the Heffalump. She started to hum. A tune Jane always hummed.

'What do you do with a drunken sailor?' Gamache called from above.

Below, Clara froze. Was that God? But surely God would

179

know exactly what to do with a drunken sailor? Besides, Clara couldn't believe God's first words to her would be any question other than, 'What on earth were you thinking?'

She looked up and saw a box. A talking box. Her knees went weak. So they did speak after all.

'Clara? It's Armand Gamache. I'm up in the blind.' Even from this great height in the dusk he could see her confusion. Now he saw a huge smile on her face.

'A blind? I'd forgotten that was there. May I come up?' But she was already climbing the rungs like an immortal six-year-old. Gamache was both impressed and appalled. Another body, no matter how slim, could be just enough to bring down the entire structure.

'Wow, this is fabulous!' Clara hopped on to the platform. 'What a view. Good thing the weather cleared. I hear tomorrow's supposed to be sunny. Why're you here?'

'Why are you?'

'I couldn't concentrate on my work and I suddenly knew I had to come here. Well, not here but down there, to where Jane died. I feel I owe Jane.'

'Hard to get on with life and not feel guilty.'

'That must be it.' She turned and looked at him, impressed. 'So what brought you here?'

'I came looking for that.' He pointed over the side of the platform, trying to sound nonchalant. White lights were dancing in front of his eyes, a familiar prelude to vertigo. He forced himself to look over the edge. The sooner this was over the better.

'What?' Clara stared into the woods beyond where Jane had been killed. Gamache could feel himself getting annoyed. Surely she could see it. Was that a crack? The sun was casting long shadows and strange light, and some of it just caught at the edge of the forest, and then she saw it.

'The opening through the woods, over there. Is that it?'

'It's a deer trail,' said Gamache, inching back from the edge and reaching behind him for the tree trunk. 'Made by deer year after year. They're like the railways in Switzerland. Very predictable. They always use the same path, for generations. Which is why the blind was built here.' He was almost forgetting to panic. 'To watch the deer move along the trail, and shoot them. But the trail is almost invisible. We had trained investigators searching this whole area yesterday and none of them saw it. None realised there was a tiny path through the woods. I didn't. You'd have to know it was there.'

'I knew it was there but I'd completely forgotten,' said Clara. 'Peter brought me here a long time ago. Right up to this blind. But you're right. Only locals would know that this is where to find deer. Did Jane's killer shoot her from here?'

'No, this hasn't been used in years. I'll get Beauvoir along, but I'm sure. The killer shot her from the woods. He was either there because he was waiting for deer –'

'Or he was there waiting for Jane. Incredible view from up here.' Clara turned her back on the deer trail and looked in the opposite direction. 'You can see Timmer's home from here.'

Gamache, surprised by the change in topic, also turned, slowly, cautiously. Sure enough there were the slate roofs of the old Victorian home. Solid and beautiful in its own way with its red stone walls and huge windows.

'Hideous.' Clara shivered and made for the ladder. 'Horrible place. And in case you're wondering,' she turned to climb down and looked at Gamache, her face in darkness now, 'I understand what you were saying. Whoever killed Jane was local. But there's more.'

'"When thou hast done, thou hast not done, for I have more",' quoted Gamache. 'John Donne,' he explained, feeling a little giddy at the thought of finally escaping.

Clara was halfway down the hole in the floor, 'I remember, from school. Frankly, Ruth Zardo's poetry comes more to mind:

> *I'll keep it all inside;*
> *festering, rotting; but I'm really a nice person, kind,*
> *loving. "Get out of my way, you motherfucker."*
> *Oops, sorry . . .'*

'Ruth Zardo, did you say?' said Gamache stunned. Clara had just quoted from one of his favorite poems. Now he knelt down and continued it:

> *'that just slipped out, escaped, I'll*
> *try harder, just watch, I will. You can't make*
> *me say anything. I'll just go further away, where*
> *you will never find me, or hurt me, or make me speak.*

You mean Ruth Zardo wrote that? Wait a minute . . .'
He thought back to the notary's office earlier in the day

and his discomfort when he'd heard the names of Jane's executors. Ruth Zardo née Kemp. Ruth Zardo is the Governor-General award-winning poet Ruth Kemp? The gifted writer who defined the great Canadian ambivalence of kindness and rage? Who put voice to the unspeakable? Ruth Zardo. 'Why does that particular Zardo poem remind you of what we're seeing?'

'Because as far as I know Three Pines is made up of good people. But that deer trail suggests one of us is festering. Whoever shot Jane knew they were aiming at a person and wanted it to look like a hunting accident, like someone was waiting for a deer to come down the trail and shot Jane by accident. But the problem is that with a bow and arrow you have to be too close. Close enough to see what you're aiming at.'

Gamache nodded. She had understood after all. Ironic, really, that from a blind they should suddenly see so clearly.

Back in the Bistro, Gamache ordered a hot cider and went to wash up, pouring the warm water over his frozen hands and picking bits of bark from the scratches. He joined Clara in the armchairs by the fireplace. She was sipping her beer and flipping through *The Boys' Big Book of Hunting*. She put the book back on the table and slid it towards him.

'Very clever of you. I'd completely forgotten about blinds and trails and things like that.'

Gamache cupped his hands around the mug holding his hot, fragrant cider and waited. He felt she needed to talk. After a comfortable minute of silence she nodded into the body of the Bistro. 'Peter's over there with Ben. I'm not sure he even knows I left.'

Gamache looked over. Peter was talking to a waitress and Ben was looking over at them. But not at them. He was looking at Clara. When he caught Gamache's eye he quickly looked away, back to Peter.

'I need to tell you something,' said Clara.

'I hope it's not a weather forecast.' Gamache grinned. Clara looked confused. 'Go on,' he encouraged. 'Something to do with the blind or the deer trail?'

'No, I'll have to think about that some more. That was pretty disturbing and I don't even have vertigo.' She smiled at him warmly and he hoped he wasn't blushing. He'd really thought he'd gotten away with that one. Well, one less person who thought he was perfect. 'What did you want to say?'

'It's about André Malenfant. You know, Yolande's husband. At lunch I went up to speak with Yolande, and I heard him laugh at me. It was an unusual sound. Sort of hollow and penetrating. Rancid. Jane described a laugh like that from one of the boys who threw manure.' Gamache absorbed this information, staring into the fire and sipping his cider, feeling the warm sweet liquid move through his chest and spread into his stomach.

'You're thinking his son Bernard was one of those boys.'

'That's it. One of those boys wasn't there. But Bernard was.'

'We interviewed Gus and Claude. Both deny being there at all, not surprisingly.'

'Philippe apologised for throwing the manure, but that might not mean anything. Every kid's afraid of Bernie. I think Philippe would have confessed to murder if it would save him a thrashing from that boy. He has them all terrified.'

'Is it possible Philippe wasn't even there?'

'Possible, not probable. But I do know absolutely that Bernard Malenfant was throwing manure at Olivier and Gabri, and enjoying it.'

'Bernard Malenfant was Jane Neal's grand-nephew,' said Gamache slowly, working through the connections.

'Yes,' agreed Clara, taking a handful of beer nuts. 'But they weren't close, as you know. Don't know the last time she saw Yolande socially. There was a rift.'

'What happened?'

'I don't know the specifics,' said Clara, hesitantly. 'I only know it had something to do with the house. Jane's home. It'd belonged to her parents, and there was some sort of dispute. Jane said she and Yolande had been close once. Yolande used to visit her as a kid. They'd play rummy and cribbage. There was another game too with the Queen of Hearts. Every night she'd put the card on the kitchen table and tell Yolande to memorise it because in the morning it would have changed.'

'And did it?'

'That's just it. It did. Every morning Yolande would come down and was sure the card was different. Still the Queen of Hearts, but the pattern would be changed.'

'But was the card actually different? I mean, did Jane change it herself?'

'No. But Jane knew that a child couldn't possibly memorise every detail. And, more than that, she knew every child longs to believe in magic. So sad.'

'What?' asked Gamache.

'Yolande. I wonder what she believes in today.'

Gamache remembered his talk with Myrna and wondered whether Jane could possibly have been sending another message to young Yolande. Change happens and it's nothing to be afraid of.

'When would Jane have seen Bernard? Would she have known him?'

'She may actually have seen him quite often in the last year or so, but from a distance,' said Clara. 'Bernard and the other kids from the area now catch the school bus from Three Pines.'

'Where?'

'Up by the old schoolhouse, so the bus doesn't have to go through the village. Some parents drop the kids off really early when it suits them and the kids have to wait. So they sometimes wander down the hill into the village.'

'What happens when it's cold or there's a storm?'

'Most parents stay with the kids in their car, keeping them warm, until the bus arrives. But then it was discovered that some parents just dropped the kids off anyway. Timmer Hadley would take them in until the bus showed up.'

'That was nice,' said Gamache. Clara looked slightly taken aback. 'Was it? I guess it was, now that I think of it. But I suspect there was some other reason for it.

She was afraid of being sued if a kid died of exposure or something. Frankly, I'd rather freeze to death than go into that house.'

'Why?'

'Timmer Hadley was a hateful woman. Look at poor Ben.' Clara tossed her head in Ben's direction and Gamache looked just in time to catch Ben staring at them again. 'Crippled by her. Needy, manipulative woman. Even Peter was terrified of her. He used to spend school holidays at Ben's. To keep Ben company and try to protect him from that woman in that monstrosity of a house. Do you wonder I love him?' For an instant he wasn't sure if Clara meant Peter or Ben. 'Peter's the most wonderful man in the world and if even he hated and feared Timmer there was something really wrong.'

'How did he and Ben meet?'

'At Abbot's, the private boys' school near Lennoxville. Ben was sent there when he was seven. Peter was also seven. The two youngest kids there.'

'What did Timmer do that was so bad?' Gamache's brow knitted, imagining the two frightened boys.

'For one, she sent a scared little boy away from home to boarding school. Poor Ben was totally unprepared for what awaited him. Have you ever been to boarding school, Inspector?'

'No. Never.'

'You're lucky. It's Darwinism at its most refined. You adapt or die. You learn that the skills that allow you to survive are cunning, cheating, bullying, lying. Either that or just plain hiding. But even that didn't last for long.'

Peter had painted for Clara a pretty clear picture of life at Abbot's. Now she saw the doorknob turning slowly, slowly. And the door to the boys' unlockable dorm room opening slowly, slowly. And the tiptoes of upper classmen sneaking in to do more damage. Peter had learned the monster wasn't under the bed after all. It broke Clara's heart every time she thought of those little boys. She looked over at their table and saw two grown men, graying, craggy heads leaning so close they almost touched. And she wanted to rush over there and keep all bad things away from them.

'Matthew ten, thirty-six.'

Clara brought herself back to Gamache, who was looking at her with such tenderness she felt both exposed and protected at the same time. The dorm door closed.

'Pardon?'

'A biblical quote. My first chief, Inspector Comeau, used to quote it. Matthew Chapter Ten, verse Thirty-six.'

'I could never forgive Timmer Hadley for doing that to Ben,' said Clara quietly.

'But Peter was there too,' Gamache said, also quietly. 'His parents sent him.'

'True. His mother's also a piece of work, but he was better equipped. And still it was a nightmare. Then there were the snakes. One holiday Ben and Peter were playing cowboys in the basement when they came across a nest of snakes. Ben said they were everywhere in the basement. And mice too. But everyone has mice around here. Not everyone has snakes.'

'Are the snakes still there?'

'I don't know.' Every time Clara had gone into Timmer's home she'd see snakes, curled in dark corners, slithering under chairs, hanging from the beams. It might have been just her imagination. Or not. Eventually Clara had refused to go into the house at all until Timmer's last weeks when volunteers were needed. Even then, she only went with Peter, and never to the bathroom. She knew the snakes were curled behind the sweating tank. And never, ever into the basement. Never close to that door off the kitchen where she could hear the sliding and slithering and smell the swamp.

Clara upgraded to a Scotch and the two of them stared out the window at the Victorian turrets just visible above the trees on the hill.

'Yet Timmer and Jane were best of friends,' said Gamache.

'True. But then, Jane got along with everyone.'

'Except her niece Yolande.'

'That's hardly revealing. Even Yolande doesn't get along with Yolande.'

'Do you have any idea why Jane didn't let anyone beyond the kitchen?'

'Not a clue,' said Clara, 'but she invited us to cocktails in her living room for the night of the Arts Williamsburg *vernissage*, to celebrate *Fair Day*.'

'When did she do that?' Gamache asked, leaning forward.

'Friday, at dinner, after she'd heard she'd been accepted for the show.'

'Wait a minute,' said Gamache, leaning his elbows on the table, as though preparing to crawl across it and into her head. 'Are you telling me on the Friday before she died she invited everyone to a party inside her home? For the first time in her life?'

'Yes. We'd been to dinner and to parties in her home thousands of times, but always in the kitchen. This time she specified the living room. Is that important?'

'I don't know. When's the show opening?'

'In two weeks.' They sat in silence, thinking about the show. Then Clara noticed the time. 'I need to go. People coming for dinner.' He stood up with her and she smiled at him. 'Thank you for finding the blind.' He gave her a small bow and watched her wind her way through the tables, nodding and waving to people, until she'd reached Peter and Ben. She kissed Peter on the top of his head and the two men stood as one, and all three left the Bistro, like a family.

Gamache picked up *The Boys' Big Book of Hunting* from the table and opened the front cover. Scrawled inside in a big, round, immature hand was 'B. Malenfant'.

When Gamache arrived back at the B&B, he found Olivier and Gabri getting ready to head over to the Morrows for a pot luck dinner.

'There's a shepherd's pie in the oven for you, if you want,' Gabri called as they left.

Upstairs, Gamache tapped on Agent Nichol's door and suggested they meet downstairs in twenty minutes to continue their talk from that morning. Nichol agreed. He also told her they'd be eating in that night, so she could dress casually. She nodded, thanked him, and shut the door, going back to what she'd been doing for the last half-hour, desperately trying to decide what to wear. Which of the outfits she'd borrowed from her sister Angelina was perfect? Which said smart, powerful, don't mess with me, future chief inspector? Which one said 'Like me'? Which one was right?

Gamache climbed the next flight to his room, opened the door and felt drawn toward the brass bed piled high with a pure white duvet and white down pillows. All he wanted to do was to sink into it, close his eyes, and fall fast and deeply asleep. The room was simply furnished, with soothing white walls and a deep cherry wood chest of drawers. An old oil portrait dominated one wall. A faded and well-loved oriental throw rug sat on the wood floor. It was a soothing and inviting room and almost more than Gamache could stand. He wavered in the middle of the room then walked determinedly to the ensuite bathroom. His shower revived him, and after getting into casual clothing he called Reine-Marie, gathered his notes, and was back in the living room in twenty minutes.

Yvette Nichol came down half an hour later. She'd decided to wear the 'power' outfit. Gamache didn't look up from his reading when she walked in.

'We have a problem.' Gamache lowered his notebook and looked at her, cross-legged and cross-armed across from him. She was a station of the cross. 'Actually, you have a problem. But it becomes my problem when it affects this investigation.'

'Really, sir? And what would that be?'

'You have a good brain, Agent.'

'And that's a problem?'

'No. That's *the* problem. You're smug and you're arrogant.' The soft-spoken words hit her like an assault. No one had dared speak to her like this before. 'I started off by saying you have a good brain. You showed fine deductive reasoning in the meeting this afternoon.'

Nichol sat up straighter, mollified, but alert.

'But a good brain isn't enough,' continued Gamache. 'You have to use it. And you don't. You look, but you don't see. You hear, but you don't listen.'

Nichol was pretty sure she'd seen that written on a coffee cup in the traffic division. Poor Gamache lived by philosophies small enough to fit a mug.

'I look and listen well enough to solve the case.'

'Perhaps. We'll see. As I said before, that was good work, and you have a good brain. But there's something missing. Surely you can feel it. Do you ever feel lost, as though people are speaking a foreign language, as though there's something going on which everyone else gets, but you don't?'

Nichol hoped her faced didn't reflect her shock. How did he know?

'The only thing I don't get, sir, is how you can dress me down for solving a case.'

'You lack discipline,' he persevered, trying to get her to see. 'For instance, before we went into the Croft home, what did I say?'

'I can't remember.' Deep down a realisation began to dawn. She might actually be in trouble here.

'I told you to listen and not to speak. And yet you spoke to Mrs Croft when she arrived in the kitchen.'

'Well somebody had to be nice to her. You'd accused me of being unkind and that isn't true.' Dear lord, don't let me cry, she thought, as the tears welled up. She put her fists into balls in her lap. 'I am nice.'

'And that's what that was about? This is a murder investigation. You do as you're told. There isn't one set of rules for you and another set for everyone else. Understand? If you're told to be quiet and take notes that is what you do.' The last few words were said slowly, distinctly, coldly. He wondered whether she even knew how manipulative she was. He doubted it. 'This morning I gave you three of the four sentences that can guide us to wisdom.'

'You gave me all four this morning.' Nichol seriously questioned his sanity now. He was looking at her sternly, without anger, but certainly without warmth.

'Repeat them for me, please.'

'I'm sorry, I don't know, I need help and I forget.'

'I forget? Where did you get that?'

'From you this morning. You said, "I forget".'

'Are you seriously telling me you thought "I forget" could be a life lesson? I clearly meant that I had forgotten the last sentence. Yes, I'm sure I said, "I forget". But think of the context. This is a perfect example of what's wrong with that good brain of yours. You don't use it. You don't think. It's not enough to hear the words.'

Here it comes, thought Nichol. Blah, blah, blah. You've got to listen.

'You've got to listen. The words don't just fall into

some sterile bin to be regurgitated later. When Mrs Croft said there was nothing in the basement, did you notice how she spoke, the inflection, what went before, the body language, the hands and eyes? Do you remember previous investigations when suspects said the same thing?'

'This is my first investigation,' said Nichol, with triumph.

'And why do you think I told you to just listen and take notes? Because you have no experience. Can you guess what the last sentence is?'

Nichol was now literally wrapped up in herself.

'I was wrong.' Gamache suspected he was talking to himself, though he had to try. All these things he was passing on to Nichol he'd heard as a 25-year-old rookie in homicide. Inspector Comeau had sat him down and told him all these things in one session, then never spoken of it again. It was a huge mountain of a gift, and one that Gamache continued to unwrap each day. He also understood, even as Comeau was speaking, that this was a gift designed to be given away. And so when he'd become an Inspector he'd started passing it on to the next generation. Gamache knew he was only responsible for trying. What they did with it was their business. There was one more thing he had to pass on.

'I asked you this morning to think about the ways you learn. What did you come up with?'

'I don't know.'

Lines from Ruth Zardo's famous poem came back to him:

'I'll just go further away, where you will never
  find me,
or hurt me, or make me speak.'

'What?' said Nichol. This was so unfair. Here she was
doing her best. Following him around, even willing to
stay in the country for the sake of the investigation. And
she'd solved the damn thing. And did she get any credit?
No. Maybe Gamache was losing it and her solving the
case had made him see how pathetic he'd become. That's
it, she thought, as her weary, wary eye spotted the island.
He's jealous. It's not my fault. She grabbed hold of the
shifting sand and scrambled out of the frigid sea just in
the nick of time. She'd felt the hands brushing against
her ankles, hoping to pull her under. But she made it on
to her island, safe and perfect.

'We learn from our mistakes, Agent Nichol.'

Whatever.

EIGHT

⁓

'Oh great,' said Ruth, looking out of Peter and Clara's mudroom door. 'The village people.'

'*Bonjour, mes amours,*' cried Gabri, waltzing into the home, 'and Ruth.'

'We have bought out the health food store.' Olivier struggled into the kitchen and deposited two shepherd's pies and a couple of paper bags on the counter.

'I was wrong,' said Ruth, 'it's just a couple of old bags.'

'Bitch,' said Gabri.

'Slut,' snarled Ruth. 'What's in them?'

'For you, my little Brillo pad . . .' Gabri grabbed the bags and, like a maniacal magician, turned them upside down with a flourish. Out spilled bags of potato chips, cans of salted cashew nuts, handmade chocolates from Maison du Chocolat Marielle, in St Rémy. There were licorice Allsorts, St André's cheese, jelly beans and Joe Louis cakes. Lune Moons tumbled to the ground, and bounced.

'Gold!' cried Clara, kneeling down and scooping up the ridiculous, fabulous yellow cream-filled cakes. 'Mine, all mine.'

'I thought you were a chocoholic,' said Myrna, grabbing up the perfect, delectable cream-filled sweets lovingly made by Madame Marielle.

'Any port in a storm.' Clara ripped open the cellophane around the Lune Moons and gobbled one down, miraculously getting at least half of it in her mouth. The rest nestled on her face and in her hair. 'Haven't had one of these in years. Decades.'

'And yet they're so becoming,' said Gabri, surveying Clara who looked as though the POM bakery had exploded in her face.

'I brought my own paper bags,' said Ruth, pointing to the counter. Peter was there, his back turned to his guests and rigid, even for him. His mother would have finally been proud, of both his physical and emotional posture.

'Who wants what?' He spoke the clipped words to the shelving. Unseen behind him his guests exchanged glances. Gabri brushed the cake from Clara's hair and cocked his head in Peter's direction. Clara shrugged and immediately knew her betrayal of Peter. In one easy movement she'd distanced herself from his bad behavior, even though she herself was responsible for it. Just before everyone had arrived she'd told Peter about her adventure with Gamache. Animated and excited she'd gabbled on about her box and the woods and the exhilarating climb up the ladder to the blind. But her wall of words hid from her a growing quietude. She failed to notice his silence, his distance, until it was too late and he'd retreated all the way to his icy island. She hated that place. From it he stood and stared, judged and lobbed shards of sarcasm.

'You and your hero solve Jane's death?'

'I thought you'd be pleased,' she half lied. She actually hadn't thought at all, and if she had, she probably could have predicted his reaction. But since he was comfortably on his Inuk island, she'd retreat to hers, equipped with righteous indignation and warmed by moral certitude. She threw great logs of 'I'm right, you're an unfeeling bastard' on to the fire and felt secure and comforted.

'Why didn't you tell me?' he asked. 'Why didn't you ask me along?'

And there it was. The simple question. Peter always did have the ability to cut through the crap. Unfortunately, today, it was her crap. He'd asked the one question she was even afraid to ask herself. Why hadn't she? Suddenly her refuge, her island, whose terrain was unremitting higher ground, was sinking.

On that note the guests had arrived. And now Ruth had made the astonishing announcement that she too had brought something to share. Jane's death must have shaken her to the marrow, thought Clara. On the counter stood her grief. Tanqueray gin, Martini & Rossi vermouth and Glenfiddich Scotch. It was a fortune in booze, and Ruth did not run to fortunes. Great poetry doesn't pay the bills. In fact, Clara couldn't remember the last time Ruth had bought her own drink. And today the elderly woman had gone all the way to the Societé des Alcools in Williamsburg and bought these bottles, then lugged them across the green to their home.

'Stop,' snapped Ruth, waving her cane at Peter who was about to unscrew the Tanqueray cap. 'That's mine. Don't touch it. Don't you have booze to offer your guests?' she demanded, elbowing Peter aside and shoving the bottles back into their paper sleeves. Cradling them she hobbled to the mudroom and laid them on the floor below her cloth coat as a mother might lay a particularly precious child.

'Pour me a Scotch,' she called from there.

Strangely, Clara felt more comfortable with this Ruth than the momentarily generous one. It was the devil she knew.

'You said there were books you wanted to sell?' said Myrna, drifting into the living room, a red wine in one hand and a bunch of Allsorts in the other.

Clara followed, grateful to be away from Peter's eloquent back. 'The murder mysteries. I want to buy some more but I need to get rid of the old ones first.' The two women inched along the floor-to-ceiling bookcases across from the fireplace, Myrna every now and then selecting one. Clara had very specific tastes. Most of them were British and all were of the village cozy variety. Myrna could spend happy hours browsing bookcases. She felt if she could just get a good look at a person's bookcase and their grocery cart, she'd pretty much know who they were.

This was not the first time she'd stood in front of these books. Every few months the frugal couple would sell some off and replace them with others, also used and also from

Myrna's shop. The titles drifted by. Spy novels, gardening, biography, literature, but mostly mysteries. The books were a jumble. Some order had been attempted at one stage, the art restoration books were alphabetical, though one had been replaced incorrectly. Without thinking, Myrna put it in its proper alphabetical home. Myrna could guess who had taken a stab at order but the rest had succumbed to everyday literary glee.

'There.' Myrna looked at her pile when they reached the end of the bookcase. From the kitchen came the promise of comfort food. Clara's mind followed her nose, and she again saw Peter, frozen in his anger. Why hadn't she told him about the blind and the trail right away?

'I'll give you a dollar each for them,' said Myrna.

'How about trading them for others?' It was a familiar and practiced dance. The two women engaged each other and emerged, both satisfied. Ruth had joined them and was reading the back of a Michael Innes.

'I'd make a good detective.' Into the stunned silence Ruth explained: 'Unlike you, Clara, I see people the way they really are. I see the darkness, the anger, the pettiness.'

'You create it, Ruth,' Clara clarified.

'It's true,' Ruth roared with laughter and unexpectedly hugged Clara in a grip that was disconcertingly strong. 'I'm obnoxious and disliked –'

'I hadn't heard,' said Myrna.

'It can't be denied. Those are my best qualities. The rest is window dressing. Actually, the real mystery is why more people don't commit murder. It must be terrible to be human. I heard in the Societé des Alcools that that great oaf Gamache had actually searched the Croft place. Ridiculous.'

They drifted back into the kitchen where dinner was on the table in steaming casseroles, ready for each to help themselves. Ben poured Clara a glass of red wine and sat down next to her. 'What have you been talking about?'

'I'm not really sure.' Clara smiled into Ben's kind face. 'Ruth said Gamache had searched the Croft place. Is that true?'

'He didn't tell you this afternoon?' Down the table, Peter snorted.

'Oh yeah, big to-do,' said Olivier, trying to ignore Peter slapping food on to his plate from the serving spoons. 'Turned the place upside down and apparently found something.'

'But they won't arrest Matthew, surely?' said Clara, her fork stopped halfway to her mouth.

'Could Matthew have killed Jane?' Ben asked, offering more chili con carne around. He meant the question for the whole group, but he naturally and instinctively turned to Peter.

'I can't believe it,' said Olivier when Peter failed to reply.

'Why not?' Ben turned again to Peter. 'Accidents happen.'

'That's true,' Peter conceded. 'Though I think he'd own up to it.'

'But, this was no ordinary mistake. I think it'd be only natural to run away.'

'Do you?' Myrna asked.

'I think so,' said Ben. 'I mean, I'm not sure how I'd react if I threw a rock, say, and it hit someone in the head and killed them, and no one saw. Can I say for sure I would admit to it? Don't get me wrong, I really hope I'd call for help and take what's coming. But can I stand here today and say for sure? No. Not till it happens.'

'I think you would,' said Peter, quietly. Ben could feel his throat constrict. Compliments always made him want to cry and left him deeply embarrassed.

'It goes back to what we were talking about Friday night. That quote of yours, Clara,' said Myrna. 'Conscience and cowardice are the same thing.'

'Oscar Wilde, actually. He was more cynical than me. I think that's true for some people, but fortunately not the majority. I think most people have a pretty good moral compass.' To her left she heard Ruth snort. 'Sometimes it just takes time to get your bearings, especially after a shock. When I try to see it from Gamache's point of view, it makes sense. Matthew's a skilled bow hunter. He knew there were deer in that area. He had the ability and the knowledge.'

'But why not admit to it?' Myrna wanted to know. 'Sure, I agree with you totally, Ben. At first it would be understandable for Matthew to run, but after a while wouldn't he admit to it? I couldn't live carrying that secret.'

'You just have to get better at keeping secrets,' said Gabri.

'I think it must have been a stranger,' said Ben. 'God

knows, the woods are full of them right now. All those hunters from Toronto and Boston and Montreal, firing away like maniacs.'

'But,' Clara turned to him, 'how would a hunter from Toronto know where to stand?'

'What do you mean? They go into the woods and stand. There's not much to it, that's why so many morons hunt.'

'But in this case the hunter knew exactly where to stand. This afternoon I was at the deer blind, you know, the one behind the schoolhouse, just by where Jane was killed. I went up and looked out. Sure enough, there was the deer trail. That's why the blind was built right there –'

'Yeah, by Matthew Croft's father,' said Ben.

'Really?' Clara was momentarily off balance. 'I didn't know that. Did you?' She appealed to the rest of the table.

'What was the question? I wasn't listening,' admitted Ruth.

'Some detective,' said Myrna.

'Matthew's father built the blind,' said Clara to herself. 'Anyway, Gamache is pretty sure it hadn't been used for a while –'

'Blinds aren't generally used by bow hunters,' said Peter in a flat voice. 'Only guns.'

'So what's your point?' Ruth was getting bored.

'A stranger, a hunter visiting from somewhere else, wouldn't know to go there.'

Clara let the implication of what she said sink in.

'Whoever killed Jane was local?' Olivier asked. Up

until that moment they'd all assumed the killer had been a visiting hunter who'd run away. Now, maybe not.

'So it might have been Matthew Croft after all,' said Ben.

'I don't think so,' Clara forged ahead. 'The very things that argue for Matthew having done it also argue against it. An experienced bow hunter wouldn't kill a person by accident. It's the sort of accident he isn't likely to have. A bow hunter standing by the deer trail would be too close. He'd know if it was a deer coming along, or – or not.'

'Or Jane, you mean.' Ruth's normally flinty voice was now as hard as the Canadian Shield. Clara nodded. 'Bastard,' said Ruth. Gabri took her hand and for once in her life Ruth didn't pull away.

Across the table, Peter laid down his knife and fork and stared at Clara. She couldn't quite make out the look on his face, but it wasn't admiration.

'One thing is true, whoever killed Jane was a very good bow hunter,' she said. 'A poor one wouldn't have got off that shot.'

'There are a lot of very good bow hunters around here, unfortunately,' said Ben. 'Thanks to the Archery Club.'

'Murder,' said Gabri.

'Murder,' confirmed Clara.

'But who would want Jane dead?' Myrna asked.

'Isn't it normally gain of some kind?' Gabri asked. 'Money, power.'

'Gain, or trying to protect something you're afraid of losing,' said Myrna. She'd been listening to this conversation, thinking it was just a desperate attempt by grieving friends to take their minds off the loss by turning it into an intellectual game. Now she began to wonder. 'If something you value is threatened, like your family, your inheritance, your job, your home—'

'We get the idea,' Ruth interrupted.

'You might convince yourself killing is justified.'

'So if Matthew Croft did it,' said Ben, 'it was on purpose.'

Suzanne Croft looked down at her dinner plate. Congealing Chef Boyardee mini-ravioli formed pasty lumps in a puddle of thick, cold sauce. On the side of her plate a single piece of pre-sliced brown Wonder Bread balanced, put there more in hope than conviction. Hope that maybe this sickness in her stomach would lift long enough for her to take a bite.

But it sat there, whole.

Across from her Matthew lined up his four squares of mini-ravioli in a precise little road, marching across his plate. The sauce made ponds on either side. The children got the most food, then Matthew, and Suzanne took what was left. Her conscious brain told her it was a noble maternal instinct. Deep down inside she knew it was a more personal instinct for martyrdom that guided the portions. An unsaid but implied contract with her family. They owed her.

Philippe sat beside Matthew in his usual place. His dinner plate was clean, all the ravioli gobbled down and the sauce soaked up by the bread. Suzanne considered exchanging her untouched plate for his, but something stopped her hand. She looked at Philippe, plugged in to his Discman, eyes closed, lips pursed in that insolent attitude he'd adopted in the last six months, and she decided the deal was off. She also felt a stirring that suggested she didn't actually like her son. Love, yes. Well, probably. But like?

Normally, in fact habitually for the past few months, Matthew and Suzanne had had to fight with Philippe to get him to remove the Discman, Matthew arguing with him in English and Suzanne speaking with him in her mother tongue, French. Philippe was bilingual and bi-cultural and equally deaf to both languages.

'We're a family,' Matthew had argued, 'and NSYNC isn't invited to dinner.'

'Who?' Philippe had huffed. 'It's Eminem.' As though that was somehow significant. And Philippe had given Matthew that look, not of anger or petulance, but of dismissal. Matthew might as well have been what? Not the refrigerator. He seemed to have a good relationship with the fridge, his bed, the TV, and his computer. No, he looked at his dad as though he was NSYNC. Passé. Discarded. Nothing.

Philippe would eventually take the Discman off, in exchange for food. But tonight was different. Tonight both his mom and dad were happy to have him plugged in and removed. He'd eaten greedily, as though this slop was the best food he'd ever been given. Suzanne had even felt resentment about that. Every night she worked hard to give them good, home-made dinners. Tonight all she could manage was to open two cans, from their emergency supply, and warm them up. And tonight Philippe wolfed it down as though it was gourmet food. She looked at her son and wondered if he did it on purpose, to insult her.

Matthew leaned closer to his plate and fine tuned the ravioli road. Each tiny ridge on the outside of the squares needed to fit into the opposing indentations. Or else? Or else the universe would explode in fire and their flesh would bubble and sear off, and he would see his whole family die in front of him, milliseconds before his own horrible death. There was a lot riding on Chef Boyardee.

He looked up and caught his wife watching him. Mesmerised by the precision of his movements. Stuck on the stutter of a decimal point. The line suddenly came to him. He'd always liked it, from the moment he'd read it at Miss Neal's. It was from Auden's Christmas Oratorio. She'd pushed it on him. She was a lifelong admirer of Auden. Even this cumbersome, somewhat strange work, she seemed to love. And understand. For himself, he'd struggled through it, out of respect for Miss Neal. But he hadn't liked it at all. Except for that one line. He didn't know what made it stand out from the gazillion other lines in the epic work. He didn't even know what it meant. Until now. He, too, was stuck on the stutter of a decimal point. His world had come down to this. To look up was to face disaster. And he wasn't ready for that.

He knew what tomorrow brought. He knew what he'd seen coming from so far off. Inexorably. Without hope of escape he waited for it to arrive. And it was almost there, on their doorstep. He looked over at his son, his little boy, who had changed so much in the last few months. They'd thought it was drugs, at first. His anger, his slipping grades, his dismissal of everything he had previously loved, like soccer, and movie night, and 'NSYNC'. And his parents. Himself in particular, Matthew felt. For some reason Philippe's rage was directed at him. Matthew wondered what was going on behind that euphoric face. Could Philippe possibly know what was coming, and be happy about it?

Matthew adjusted the ravioli, just in time, before his world exploded.

Each time the phone rang in the Incident Room activity stopped. And it rang often. Various officers checking in. Shopkeepers, neighbors, bureaucrats returning phone calls.

The old Canadian National rail station had proven perfect for their needs. A team had worked with the volunteer fire department and cleared a space in the center of what must have been the waiting room. Glowing varnished wood went a quarter of the way up the walls and the walls themselves had held posters with fire tips and past winners of the Governor-General's Literary Awards, a hint as to who the fire chief might be. The Sûreté officers had removed those, neatly rolling them up, and replaced them with flow charts and maps and lists of suspects. It now looked like any other incident room, in an old and atmospheric train station. It was a space that seemed used to waiting. All those hundreds, thousands, of people who'd sat in this room, waiting. For trains. To take them away, or to bring their loved ones home. And now men and women again sat in the space, waiting. This time for a report from the Sûreté lab in Montreal. The report that would send them home. The report that would destroy the Crofts. Gamache got up, pretended to stretch, and started to walk. The chief always paced, his hands clasped behind his back, his head down looking at his feet, when he got impatient. Now, as the others pretended to work the phones and gather information, Chief Inspector Gamache circled them, slowly, with a measured pace. Unhurried, unperturbed, unstoppable.

Gamache had risen before the sun that morning. His little travel alarm said 5.55. He was always delighted when a digital clock had all the same numbers. Half an hour later, dressed in his warmest clothes, he was tiptoeing down the stairs toward the front door of the B&B when he heard a noise in the kitchen.

'*Bonjour, M. l'Inspecteur*,' said Gabri coming out in a deep purple bathrobe and fluffy slippers, holding a thermos. 'I thought you might like a *café au lait*, to go.'

Gamache could have kissed him.

'And', Gabri whipped a small paper bag out from behind his back, 'a couple of croissants.'

Gamache could have married him. '*Merci, infiniment, patron.*'

Minutes later Armand Gamache sat on the frosted wooden bench on the green. For half an hour he sat there in the still, peaceful, dark morning, and watched the sky change. Black became royal blue and then a hint of gold. The forecasters had finally gotten it right. The day dawned brilliant, crisp, clear and cold. And the village awoke.

One by one lights appeared in the windows. It was a tranquil few minutes, and Gamache appreciated every calm moment, pouring rich, full bodied *café au lait* from the thermos into the little metal cup, and burrowing into the paper bag for a flaky croissant, still warm from the oven.

Gamache sipped and chewed. But mostly he watched.

At ten to seven a light went on over at Ben Hadley's place. A few minutes later Daisy could be seen limping around the yard, her tail wagging. Gamache knew from experience the last earthly acts of most dogs was to lick their master and wag their tail. Through the window Gamache could just make out movement in Ben's home as he prepared breakfast.

Gamache waited.

The village stirred and by seven-thirty most homes had come to life. Lucy had been let out of the Morrow home and was wandering around, sniffing. She put her nose in the air, then slowly turned and walked then trotted and finally ran to the trail through the woods that would take her home. Back to her mother. Gamache watched the golden-feathered tail disappear into the maple and cherry forest, and felt his heart break. A few minutes later Clara came out and called Lucy. A single forlorn bark was heard and Gamache watched as Clara went into the woods and returned a moment later, followed slowly by Lucy, her head down and her tail still.

Clara had slept fitfully the night before, waking up every few hours with that sinking feeling that was becoming a companion. Loss. It wasn't the shriek it had been, more a moan in her marrow. She and Peter had spoken again over the dishes while the others sat in the living room, mulling over the possibility Jane had been murdered.

'I'm sorry,' Clara said, a dish towel in her hand, taking the warm, wet plates from Peter's hand. 'I should have told you about my conversation with Gamache.'

'Why didn't you?'

'I don't know.'

'That's not good enough, Clara. Can it be that you don't trust me?'

He searched her face, his icy-blue eyes keen and cold. She knew she should hold him, should tell him how much she loved him and trusted him and needed him. But something held her back. There it was again. A silence between them. Something else unsaid. Is this how it starts? Clara wondered. Those chasms between couples, filled not with comfort and familiarity, but with too much unsaid, and too much said.

Once again her lover closed up. Became stone. Still and cold.

Ben had walked in on them at that moment, and caught them in an act more intimate than sex. Their anger and pain was fully exposed. Ben stammered and stumbled and bumbled and finally left, looking like a child who had walked in on his parents.

That night, after everyone had left, Clara said the things she knew Peter had longed to hear. How much she trusted him and loved him. How sorry she was, and how grateful she was for his patience in the face of her

211

own pain at Jane's death. And she asked for his forgiveness. And he gave it, and they'd held each other until their breathing became deep and even and in sync.

But still, something had been left unsaid.

The next morning Clara rose early, let Lucy out, and made Peter pancakes, maple syrup and bacon. The unexpected smell of cured Canadian bacon, fresh coffee and woodsmoke woke Peter. Lying in bed he resolved to try to move beyond the hard feelings of the day before. Still, it had confirmed for Peter that feelings were too dangerous to expose. He showered, put on clean clothes and his game face, and went downstairs.

'When do you think Yolande'll move in?' Clara asked Peter over breakfast.

'I guess after the will has been read. A few days, maybe a week.'

'I can't believe Jane would leave her home to Yolande, if for no other reason than she knew how much I hate her.'

'Maybe it wasn't about you, Clara.'

Zing. And maybe, thought Clara, he's still pissed off. 'I've been watching Yolande for the last couple of days. She keeps lugging stuff into Jane's place.'

Peter shrugged. He was getting tired of comforting Clara.

'Didn't Jane make a new will?' she tried again.

'I don't remember that.' Peter knew Clara enough to know this was a ruse, an attempt to take his mind off his hurt and to get him on her side. He refused to play.

'No, really,' said Clara. 'I seem to remember when

212

Timmer was diagnosed and knew it was terminal that they both talked about revising their wills. I'm sure Jane and Timmer went off to that notary in Williamsburg. What was her name? You know. The one who just had the baby. She was in my exercise class.'

'If Jane made a new will, the police'll know about it. It's what they do.'

Gamache got up from the bench. He'd seen what he needed to. What he suspected. It was far from conclusive, but it was interesting. Lies always were. Now, before the day swept him up in its imperatives, he wanted to see the blind again. Maybe not climb it, though. He walked across the green, his duck boots leaving prints in the frost-soaked grass. Up the hill he walked, past the old schoolhouse, and then into the woods. Once again he found himself at the foot of the tree. It was pretty obvious from his first, and he hoped only, visit upwards that the blind hadn't been used by the killer. But still . . .

'Bang. You're dead.'

Gamache swung around, but had recognised the voice an instant after he'd begun to turn.

'You're a sneak, Jean Guy. I'm going to have to put a cow bell on you.'

'Not again.' It wasn't often he could get the drop on the chief. But Beauvoir had begun to worry. Suppose he snuck up on Gamache sometime and he had a heart attack? It would certainly take the fun out of it. But he worried about the Chief Inspector. His rational mind, which normally had the upper hand, knew it was stupid.

The Chief Inspector was slightly overweight and he had crested fifty, but that described many people, and most did just fine without Beauvoir's help. But. But the Chief Inspector's job was stressful enough to fell an elephant. And he worked hard. But mostly Jean Guy Beauvoir's feelings couldn't be explained. He just didn't want to lose the Chief Inspector. Gamache clapped him on the shoulder and offered him the last of the *café au lait* from the thermos, but Beauvoir had had breakfast at the B&B.

'Brunch, you mean.'

'Humm. Eggs Benedict, croissants, homemade jams.' Beauvoir looked at the crumpled paper bag in Gamache's fist. 'It was awful. You're lucky to have missed it. Nichol is still there. She came down after me and sat at a different table. Odd girl.'

'Woman, Jean Guy.'

Beauvoir harrumphed. He hated Gamache's political correctness. Gamache smiled. 'It's not that.' He'd divined the reason for the harrumph. 'Don't you see? She wants us all to see her as a girl, as a child, someone who needs to be treated delicately.'

'If so she's a spoiled child. She gives me the willies.'

'Don't let her get under your skin. She's manipulative and angry. Just treat her like any other agent. That'll drive her nuts.'

'Why's she even with us? She brings nothing.'

'She came up with some very good analysis yesterday that helped convince us Philippe Croft is our killer.'

'True, but she's a dangerous character.'

'Dangerous, Jean Guy?'

'Not physically. She won't take her gun and shoot us all. Probably.'

'Not all. One of us would get her before she finished us all off, I hope.' Gamache smiled.

'I hope it's me. She's dangerous because she's divisive.'

'Yes. That makes sense. I've been thinking about it. When she picked me up at home Sunday morning I was impressed. She was respectful, thoughtful, answered thoroughly when asked a question but didn't impose or need to impress. I really thought we had a winner.'

'She brought you coffee and donuts, didn't she.'

'Brioche, actually. Almost promoted her to Sergeant on the spot.'

'That's how I made Inspector. That éclair put me over the top. But something happened to Nichol between the time she arrived and now,' agreed Beauvoir.

'All I can think is that as she met more team members she began to unravel. Some people do. They're great one on one. The individual sports types. Brilliant. But put them on a team and they're awful. I think that's Nichol, competitive when she should be collaborative.'

'I think she's desperate to prove herself and wants your approval. At the same time she sees any advice as criticism and any criticism as catastrophic.'

'Well she had a catastrophic night, then.' Gamache filled him in on his conversation with Nichol.

'Let her go, sir. You've done your best. You coming up?'

Beauvoir began climbing the ladder to the blind. 'This is great. Like a tree house.' Gamache had rarely seen Beauvoir so animated. Still, he felt no need to see the animation close up.

'Already been. Do you see the deer trail?' The night before he'd told Beauvoir about the blind and advised him to take samples. But he hadn't expected to see the Inspector so early.

'*Mais oui*. From up here it's easy. Still, something occurred to me last night.' Beauvoir was staring down at him. Oh God, I have to go up, don't I, thought Gamache. Reaching for the slimy wooden slats he started climbing. Hauling himself on to the platform, he pressed his back against the rough trunk and gripped the railing.

'Dope.'

'I beg your pardon?' For an instant Gamache thought Beauvoir had guessed his secret and was calling him . . .

'Mary Jane. Marijuana. Not just pumpkins get harvested right now. It's dope season in the townships. I think it's possible Jane Neal was killed by growers after she found their crop. She used to walk all over, right? God knows it's a multimillion dollar industry, and people are sometimes murdered.'

'True,' Gamache was intrigued by the suggestion, except for one thing, 'but most of the growing is done by the Hells Angels and the Rock Machine, the biker gangs.'

'Right. This is Hells Angels turf. Wouldn't want to mess with them. They're killers. Do you think we can transfer Nichol to narcotics?'

'Focus, Beauvoir. Jane Neal was killed by a forty-year-old arrow. When was the last time you saw a biker with a bow and arrow?'

It was a good point, and one Beauvoir hadn't thought of. He was glad he'd brought it up to the chief here, hovering above the ground, rather than in the crowded Incident Room. Gamache, clinging to the railing, was just wondering how he was going to get down when he suddenly had to use the toilet. Beauvoir swung his leg over the side, found the ladder and started climbing down. Gamache said a little prayer, inched over to the edge, and put his leg over, feeling nothing but empty air. Then a hand grabbed his ankle and guided his foot to the first rung.

'Even you need a little help now and then.' Beauvoir looked up at him then hurriedly descended.

'Right, let's have your reports.' Beauvoir brought the briefing to order a few minutes later. 'Lacoste, you first.'

'Matthew Croft. Thirty-eight,' she said, taking the pen out of her mouth. 'Head of the roads department for the county of St Rémy. I spoke with the county manager, and he's glowing in his praise. I actually haven't heard praise like that since my own evaluation.'

The place erupted. Jean Guy Beauvoir, who conducted their evaluations, was notoriously tough.

'But, a fired worker lodged a complaint. Said Croft had beaten him.'

'Who was this worker?' Gamache asked.

'André Malenfant.' There was a rumble of appreciation.

'Croft won, hands down. Thrown out. But not before Malenfant had gone to the local papers. Nasty piece of work, that man. Next, Suzanne Belanger. Also thirty-eight. Married to Croft for fifteen years. Works part time at Les Réproductions Doug, in St Rémy. Let's see, what else?' Lacoste scanned her notes for something worth saying about this woman who had led a quiet, unremarkable life.

'No arrests?' Nichol asked.

'Only the one for murdering an old woman last year.' Nichol made a sour face.

'What about Philippe?'

'He's fourteen and in grade nine. 'B plus student until last Christmas. Then something happened. His marks started slipping and his attitude changed. I spoke with the guidance counselor. She says she has no idea what's wrong. Might be drugs. Might be problems at home. She says at fourteen most boys go a little wacky. She didn't seem particularly worried.'

'Any idea whether he was on any school teams?' Gamache wanted to know.

'Basketball and hockey, though he didn't try out for basketball this term.'

'Do they have an archery team?'

'Yes, sir. He's never been on it.'

'Good,' said Beauvoir. 'Nichol, what about the will?'

Yvette Nichol consulted her notebook. Or pretended to. She'd totally forgotten. Well, not totally. She'd remembered at the end of yesterday afternoon, but by then she'd solved the case and it would be just a waste of time. Besides, she had no idea how to find out whether another will existed, and she had absolutely no intention of parading her ignorance in front of so-called colleagues who had so far proven unhelpful.

'The Stickley will is the latest,' said Nichol, looking Beauvoir in the eyes. Beauvoir hesitated before dropping his eyes.

And so the reports progressed. The tension rose in the room as the one phone they all willed to ring sat silent in Gamache's large hand.

Jane Neal, according to reports, had been a dedicated and respected teacher. She had cared about her students, enough to occasionally fail them. Her personal finances were healthy. She was a church warden at St Thomas's and active in the Anglican Church Women, organising thrift sales and socials. She played bridge and gardened with a passion.

Her neighbors saw and heard nothing on Sunday morning.

All Quiet on the Western front, thought Gamache, listening to this gentle life. His magical thinking allowed him to be surprised that when such a good soul dies it isn't remarked. The bells of the church didn't set themselves off. The mice and deer didn't cry out. The earth didn't shudder. It should have. If he were God, it would have. Instead, the line in the official report would read, 'Her neighbors noticed nothing.'

The reports finished, the team went back to their phones and their paperwork. Armand Gamache began pacing.

Clara Morrow called to tell Gamache that Matthew Croft's father had built the blind, a fact of some interest, given their suspicions.

At ten fifteen his palm rang. It was the lab.

NINE

～

Matthew Croft was to remember for the rest of his life where he was when the police cars drew up. It was three minutes past eleven on the kitchen clock. He'd expected them much earlier. Had been waiting since seven that morning.

Every fall, at canning season, Suzanne's mother Marthe would come over with her shopping bag of old family recipes. The two women would 'put up' the preserves over a couple of days and invariably Marthe would ask, 'When does a cucumber become a pickle?'

At first he'd tried to answer that question as though she genuinely wanted to know. But over the years he realised there was no answer. At what point does change happen? Sometimes it's sudden. The 'ah ha' moments in our lives, when we suddenly see. But often it's a gradual change, an evolution.

For four hours, waiting, Matthew wondered what had

happened. When did things start to go wrong? This, too, he couldn't answer.

'Good morning, Mr Croft.' Chief Inspector Gamache looked calm, solid. Jean Guy Beauvoir was standing beside Gamache, next to him was that woman officer, and slightly behind was a man Matthew hadn't met yet. Middle-aged, in a suit and tie, hair streaked with gray and conservatively cut. Gamache followed Croft's look.

'This is Claude Guimette. He's one of the provincial guardians. We've had the results of the tests from the bow and arrows. May we come in?'

Croft stepped back, and they entered his home. Instinctively he took them into the kitchen.

'It would be valuable to have you and your wife together right now.'

Croft nodded and went upstairs. Suzanne was sitting on the side of the bed. It had taken her all morning to dress, one piece of clothing at a time then flopping back on the bed, exhausted. Finally, about an hour ago, the last piece was in place. Her body looked fine but her face was a monstrosity, and there was no hiding that.

She'd tried praying, but had forgotten the words. Instead she kept repeating the only thing she could remember:

Little Boy Blue, come blow your horn,
the sheep's in the meadow, the cow's in the corn.

She'd recited it over and over to Philippe when he was little but now she couldn't remember the rest. It seemed to matter, even though it wasn't itself a prayer. It was more than that. It was proof she'd been a good mother. Proof she'd loved her children. Proof, whispered the little girl's voice inside her head, that it isn't your fault. But she couldn't remember the rest of the nursery rhyme. So maybe it was her fault.

'They're here,' said Matthew, standing at the doorway. 'They want you downstairs.'

When she appeared, Matthew at her side, Gamache got up and took her hand. She sat at the chair offered, as though she'd become a guest in her own home. In her own kitchen.

'We have the results of the lab tests.' Gamache launched right into it. It would be cruel to mince words. 'Jane Neal's blood was on the bow we found in your basement. It was also on some pieces of clothing belonging to Philippe. The arrow tip matches the wound. The feathers found in the wound were of the same type and vintage as the feathers in the old quiver. We believe your son accidentally killed Jane Neal.'

There it was.

'What will happen to him?' Matthew asked, all fight had fled.

'I'd like to talk to him,' said M. Guimette. 'My job is to represent him. I came here with the police but I don't work for them. The Quebec Guardians Office is independent of the police. In fact, I work for Philippe.'

'I see,' said Matthew. 'Would he have to go to jail?'

'We spoke in the car on our way out here. Chief Inspector Gamache has no intention of charging Philippe with manslaughter.'

'So what might happen to him?' Matthew asked again.

'He'll be taken to the police station in St Rémy and charged with "mischief".' Matthew's brows went up. Had he known you could be charged with 'mischief' his own youth might have been far different. He'd been a mischief-maker like his son. It now seemed literally true.

'But he's just a boy,' said Suzanne, who felt she should be saying something in her son's defense.

'He's fourteen. Old enough to know right from wrong,' said Gamache, gently but firmly. 'He needs to know that when he does something wrong, however unintention-ally, there's a consequence. Was Philippe one of the boys who threw manure at Messieurs Dubeau and Brulé?'

The change of subject seemed to revive Matthew.

'Yes. He came home and bragged about it.' Matthew could remember staring at his little boy in the kitchen, wondering who this stranger was.

'But are you sure? I know Miss Neal called out three names, Philippe's being one of them, but she may have gotten at least one of them wrong.'

'Really?' Suzanne said, hope reviving for a moment before she remembered it didn't matter. A few days ago she'd been mortified by the thought her son had done such a thing, and been caught. Now it was nothing compared to the next thing he'd done.

'May I see him?' M. Guimette asked. 'Just me and Chief Inspector Gamache.'

Matthew hesitated.

'Remember, Mr Croft, I don't work for the police.'

Croft really had no choice anyway and he knew it. He took them upstairs and knocked on the closed door. There was no answer. He knocked again. Still no answer. He put his hand on the knob then took it off and knocked yet again, this time calling his son's name. Gamache watched all this with interest. Finally he reached out, turned the door knob and let himself into Philippe's room.

Philippe had his back to the door and was nodding his head. Even from a distance Gamache could hear the tinny, thin line of music coming from the headphones. Philippe was wearing the uniform of the day, baggy sweatshirt and baggy pants. The walls were plastered with posters of rock and rap groups, all made up of petulant, pouting young men. Barely visible between the posters was the wallpaper. Little hockey players in red Canadiens jerseys.

Guimette touched Philippe on the shoulder. Philippe's eyes flew open and he gave them a look of such loathing both men felt momentarily assaulted. Then the look disappeared. Philippe had hit the wrong target, not for the first time.

'Yeah, what do you want?'

'Philippe, I'm Claude Guimette from the Guardians Office, and this is Chief Inspector Gamache of the Sûreté.'

Gamache had expected to meet a frightened boy, and he knew fear came in many forms. Aggression was common. People who were angry were almost always fearful. Cockiness, tears, apparent calm but nervous hands and eyes. Something almost always betrayed the fear. But

Philippe Croft didn't seem afraid. He seemed . . . what? Triumphant.

'So?'

'We're here about the death of Jane Neal.'

'Yeah. I heard about that. What's it to do with me?'

'We think you did it, Philippe.'

'Oh? Why?'

'Her blood was on the bow found in your basement, along with your prints. Her blood was also on some of your clothing.'

'That's it?'

'There was blood on your bike, too. Miss Neal's blood.'

Philippe was looking pleased with himself.

'I didn't do it.'

'How do you explain these things?' Gamache asked.

'How do you?'

Gamache sat down. 'Shall I tell you? This is what I think happened. You went out that Sunday morning, early. Something prompted you to take the old bow and arrows and ride your bike to that spot. We know it was where your grandfather used to hunt. He even built the blind in that old maple tree, didn't he?'

Philippe continued to stare at him. Or through him, really, thought Gamache.

'Then something happened. Either your hand slipped and the arrow shot out by mistake, or you deliberately shot, thinking it was a deer. Either way the result was catastrophic. What happened then, Philippe?'

Gamache watched and waited, as did M. Guimette. But Philippe was impassive, his face blank, as though listening

226

to someone else's story. Then he raised his eyebrows and smiled.

'Go on. This is getting interesting. So the old lady kacks out and I'm supposed to be beside myself with grief? But I wasn't there, remember?'

'I forgot,' said Gamache. 'So let me continue. You're a bright lad.' Here Philippe frowned. He clearly didn't like being patronised. 'You could tell she was dead. You searched for the arrow and found it, getting blood on your hands and your clothes. You then came home and hid the bow and arrow in the basement. But your mother noticed the stains on your clothes and asked about it. You probably made up some story. But she also found the bow and arrow in the basement. When she heard about Jane Neal's death she added it all up. She burned the arrow, but not the bow because it was too big to fit into the furnace.'

'Look, man. I know you're old so let me say this again, slowly. I was not there. I did not do it. *Compris?*'

'Then who did?' Guimette asked.

'Let's see, who could have done it? Well, who in this house is an expert hunter?'

'Are you saying your father killed Miss Neal?' Guimette asked.

'Are you two idiots? Of course he did it.'

'What about the blood stains on your bike? Your clothes?' Guimette asked, amazed.

'Look, I'll tell you what happened. You might want to write this down.'

But Gamache didn't budge, just watched Philippe quietly.

'My father came home all upset. He had blood all over his gloves. I went out to see if I could help. As soon as he saw me he gave me a hug, and held my hands, for support. He gave me the bloody arrow and the bow and told me to put them in the basement. I began to get a little suspicious.'

'What did you suspect?' Guimette asked.

'When my father hunted he always cleaned his equipment. So this was weird. And there was no deer in the back of the truck. I just put two and two together and figured he'd killed someone.'

Guimette and Gamache exchanged glances.

'The basement's my chore,' continued Philippe. 'So when he told me to put the bloody things down there I began to wonder whether he was, well, setting me up. But I put them down there anyway, then he started yelling at me. "Stupid kid, get your effin' bike off the driveway." Before I could wash my hands I had to move the bike. That's how the blood stains got there.'

'I'd like to see your left arm, please.' Gamache asked.

Guimette turned to Philippe. 'I advise you not to.'

Philippe shrugged and shoved back the loose sleeve, exposing a violent purple bruise. A twin for Beauvoir's.

'How'd you get that?' Gamache asked.

'How do most kids get bruises?'

'You fell down?' Guimette asked.

Philippe rolled his eyes. 'What's the other way?'

Guimette, with sadness, said, 'Your dad did that to you?'

'Duh.'

*

'He didn't. He couldn't have.' Matthew was silent, as though suddenly emptied of all that made him go. It was Suzanne who finally found her voice, and protested. They must have misheard, misunderstood, be mistaken. 'Philippe couldn't have said those things.'

'We know what we heard, Mrs Croft. Philippe says his father abuses him, and out of fear of a beating Philippe helped Matthew cover up his crime. That's how he came to have the blood on him, and his prints on the bow. He says his father killed Jane Neal.' Claude Guimette explained all this for a second time and knew he might have to do it a few more times.

Astonished, Beauvoir caught Gamache's eye and saw there something he'd rarely seen in Armand Gamache. Anger. Gamache broke eye contact with Beauvoir and looked over at Croft. Matthew realised, too late, that he had gotten it wrong. He'd thought the thing that would destroy his home and his family was marching toward them from a great way off. He never, ever, imagined it had been there all along.

'He's right,' said Croft. 'I killed Jane Neal.'

Gamache closed his eyes.

'Oh, Matthew, please. No. Don't.' Suzanne turned to the others, taking Gamache's arm in a talon grip. 'Stop him. He's lying.'

'I think she's right, Mr Croft. I still believe Philippe killed Miss Neal.'

'You're wrong. I did it. Everything Philippe says is true.'

'Including the beatings?'

Matthew looked down at his feet and said nothing.

'Will you come with us to the station in St Rémy?' asked Gamache. Beauvoir noticed, as did the others, that it was a request, not an order. And certainly not an arrest.

'Yes.' Croft seemed relieved.

'I'm coming with you,' said Suzanne, springing up.

'What about Philippe?' Claude Guimette asked.

Suzanne suppressed the urge to scream, 'What about him?' Instead she took a couple of breaths.

Gamache stepped forward and spoke with her softly, calmly. 'He's only fourteen, and as much as he might not show it, he needs his mother.'

She hesitated then nodded, afraid to speak again.

Gamache knew that while fear came in many forms, so did courage.

Gamache, Beauvoir and Croft sat in a small white interview room at the Sûreté station in St Rémy. On the metal table between them sat a plate of ham sandwiches and several tins of soft drinks. Croft hadn't eaten anything. Neither had Gamache. Beauvoir couldn't stand it any longer and slowly, as though his stomach wasn't making that whiny noise filling the room, picked up a half sandwich and took a leisurely bite.

'Tell us what happened last Sunday morning,' said Gamache.

'I got up early, as I usually do. Sunday's Suzanne's day to sleep in. I put the breakfast things on the kitchen table for the kids then went out. Bow hunting.'

'You told us you didn't hunt any more,' said Beauvoir.

'I lied.'

'Why go to the woods behind the schoolhouse?'

'Dunno. I guess because that's where my father always hunted.'

'Your father smoked unfiltered cigarettes and ran your home as a dairy farm. You don't,' said Gamache. 'You've proven you're no slave to your father's way of doing things. There must be another reason.'

'Well, there isn't. It was Thanksgiving and I was missing him. I took his old recurve bow and his old arrows and went to his old hunting grounds. To feel closer to him. *Point final.*'

'What happened?'

'I heard a sound, something coming through the trees, like a deer. Slowly and carefully. Almost on tiptoe. That's how deer walk. So I drew my bow and as soon as the shape appeared I fired. You have to be fast with deer 'cause any little thing will set them off.'

'But it wasn't a deer.'

'No. It was Miss Neal.'

'How was she lying?'

Croft stood up, put his arms and legs out, his eyes wide open.

'What did you do?'

'I ran to her, but I could see she was dead. So I panicked. I looked for the arrow, picked it up, and ran to the truck. I threw everything in the back and drove home.'

'What happened then?' In Beauvoir's experience interrogation was really just asking, 'Then what happened?' and listening closely to the reply. Listening was the trick.

'I don't know.'

'What do you mean?'

'I can't remember anything after getting in the truck and driving home. But isn't that enough? I killed Miss Neal. That's all you need to know.'

'Why didn't you come forward?'

'Well, I didn't think you'd find out. I mean, the woods are full of hunters, I couldn't believe you'd come to me. Then when you did, I didn't want to destroy my father's old bow. It means a lot to me. It's like having him in the house still. When I realised it had to be destroyed it was too late.'

'Do you beat your son?'

Croft winced, as though revolted, but said nothing.

'I sat in your kitchen this morning and told you we thought Philippe had killed Miss Neal.' Gamache leaned forward so his head hovered over the sandwiches, but he only had eyes for Croft. 'Why didn't you confess then?'

'I was too stunned.'

'Come on, Mr Croft. You were waiting for us. You knew what the lab tests would show. And yet now you're saying you were going to have your son arrested for a crime you yourself committed? I don't think you're capable of that.'

'You have no idea what I'm capable of.'

'I guess that's true. I mean, if you can beat your son you can do anything.'

Croft's nostrils flared and his lips compressed. Gamache suspected if he truly was violent he'd have taken a swing at him then.

They left Croft sitting in the interview room. 'What'd

you think, Jean Guy?' Gamache asked when they reached the privacy of the station commander's office.

'I don't know what to think, sir. Did Croft do it? Philippe's story hangs together. It's possible.'

'We found absolutely no evidence of Jane Neal's blood in Croft's truck, or Mrs Croft's car. His fingerprints weren't anywhere—'

'True, but Philippe said he wore gloves,' Beauvoir interrupted.

'You can't wear gloves and shoot a bow and arrow at the same time.'

'He could have put them on after he shot, once he saw what he'd done.'

'So he had the presence of mind to put on gloves, but not enough to call the police and admit the accident? No. On paper it makes sense. But in real life it doesn't.'

'I don't agree, sir. One thing you've always impressed on me is that we can never know what happens behind closed doors. What really goes on in the Croft home? Yes, Matthew Croft gives every impression of being a thoughtful and reasonable man, but we've found time and again that that's exactly how abusers appear to the outside world. They have to. That's their camouflage. Matthew Croft may very well be abusive.' Beauvoir felt stupid lecturing Gamache on the very things he'd learned from the man himself, but he thought they bore repeating.

'What about the public meeting, when he was so helpful?' Gamache asked.

'Arrogance. He admits himself he never thought we'd find him.'

'I'm sorry, Jean Guy. I just don't buy it. There's absolutely no physical evidence against him. Just the accusation of a very angry teenager.'

'His bruised son.'

'Yes. A bruise that's exactly like yours.'

'But he'd shot arrows before. Croft said only beginners got bruises like that.'

'True, but Croft also said he'd stopped hunting a couple of years ago, so he probably hadn't taken his son hunting since then,' Gamache reasoned. 'That's a long time in kid years. He was probably rusty. Believe me, that boy shot an arrow in the last two days.'

They had a problem and they knew it. What to do about Matthew Croft?

'I've called the prosecutor's office in Granby,' said Gamache. 'They're sending someone around. Should be here soon. We'll put it to him.'

'Her.'

Beauvoir nodded through the glass door at a middle-aged woman standing patiently, briefcase in hand. He got up and brought her in to the now cramped office.

'Maître Brigitte Cohen,' Beauvoir announced.

'Bonjour, Maître Cohen. It's almost one o'clock; have you had lunch?'

'Only a brioche on the way over. I consider that an hors d'oeuvre.'

Ten minutes later they were in a comfortable diner across from the station house, ordering lunch. Beauvoir put the situation to Maître Cohen, succinctly. She grasped the pertinent details immediately.

'So the one with all the evidence against him won't admit it, and the one with no evidence can't stop admitting it. On the surface it appears the father's protecting the son. Yet when you first arrived, Chief Inspector, he seemed willing to let his son be charged with the crime.'

'That's true.'

'What changed his mind?'

'I think he was stunned and deeply wounded by his son's accusations. I don't think he saw that coming at all. It's hard to know, of course, but I get the feeling that had once been a very happy home, but hasn't been for a while now. Having met Philippe I think the unhappiness radiates from him. I've seen it before. The angry kid runs the home because the parents are afraid of him.'

'Yes, I've seen it too. You don't mean physically afraid, do you?' asked Cohen.

'No, emotionally. I think Croft confessed because he couldn't stand what Philippe must think of him. It was a desperate, even momentarily insane action designed to win back his son. To prove to Philippe he loved him. There also seemed to be an element of, what?' Gamache thought back to Croft's face, across the kitchen table. 'It was like suicide. A resignation. I think he couldn't stand the pain of what his son had accused him of, so he just gave up.'

Gamache looked at his two companions and smiled slightly.

'This is all supposition, of course. Just an impression I got. A strong man finally broken and throwing up his hands. He'll confess to a crime he didn't commit. But

Matthew Croft is just that; a strong man. A man of convictions. He'll regret this one day, soon, I hope. From what I saw Philippe is very angry and has his family well trained not to cross him.' Gamache remembered Croft's hand on the door knob, then him taking it off. Gamache was under the impression Philippe had given his father hell for opening that door without permission in the past, and Croft had learned that lesson well.

'But why's he so angry?' Beauvoir wanted to know.

'Why is any fourteen-year-old?' Cohen countered.

'There's normal anger, then there's anger that spills out all over everyone around. Like acid.' Beauvoir told her about the manure thrown at Olivier and Gabri.

'I'm not a psychologist, but it sounds like that boy needs help.'

'I agree,' said Gamache. 'But Beauvoir's question is good. Why is Philippe so angry? Could he be abused?'

'He could. The typical reaction of an abused child, though, is to make nice to the abuser and attack the other parent. Philippe seems to scorn both, and have particular disdain for his father. It doesn't fit the profile, but I'm sure many don't. I can't tell you how many times I've prosecuted children who have killed their abusive parents. Eventually they turn. Though most don't turn to murder.'

'Could he be abused by someone else and be projecting?' Gamache was remembering Clara's comment about Bernard Malenfant. She'd said he was a bully and all the boys were terrified of him. She'd even said Philippe would probably admit to murder if it would avoid a beating by Bernard. He passed his thoughts on to Cohen.

'It's possible. We're just getting a handle on how destructive bullies and bullying can be. Philippe might be a victim of bullying and that would certainly make him angry, feel powerless, impotent. And he might become overly controlling at home. It's a familiar, sadly clichéd, reality. The abused becomes an abuser. But we don't know.'

'That's true. We don't. But I do know there's no evidence against Croft in the death of Miss Neal.'

'Though we have his confession.'

'The confession of a man who isn't in his right mind. That can't be enough. We must have evidence. Sometimes our job is to save people from themselves.'

'Inspector Beauvoir, what do you think?'

This put Beauvoir exactly where he didn't want to be.

'I think there's reason to seriously consider prosecuting Matthew Croft in the death of Jane Neal.' Beauvoir watched Gamache as he said this. Gamache was nodding. 'We have Philippe's eye-witness account,' continued Beauvoir, 'which fits all the evidence, and we have strong circumstantial evidence that the death demanded a skilled bow hunter, which Philippe isn't. Croft described the scene perfectly, even showing us how Jane Neal was lying. And he knew about the deer trail. All that combined with Croft's confession should be enough to lay charges.'

Maître Cohen ate a forkful of Caesar salad. 'I'll go over your reports and let you know this afternoon.'

On the way back to the station house Beauvoir tried to apologise to Gamache for contradicting him.

'Now, don't patronise me,' Gamache laughed, putting an arm across Beauvoir's shoulder. 'I'm glad you spoke your mind. I'm just annoyed you made such a strong case. Maître Cohen is likely to agree with you.'

Gamache was right. Cohen called from Granby at 3.30 in the afternoon, instructing Gamache to arrest Croft and charge him with manslaughter, leaving the scene of a crime, obstruction, and destroying evidence.

'Jesus, she's really going after him,' commented Beauvoir. Gamache nodded and asked Beauvoir for a few minutes of privacy in the Commander's office. Surprised, Beauvoir left. Armand Gamache dialed home and spoke with Reine-Marie, then he called his boss, Superintendent Brébeuf.

'Oh, come on, Armand, you've got to be kidding.'

'No, Superintendent. I'm serious. I won't arrest Matthew Croft.'

'Look, it's not your call. I don't need to tell you of all people how the system works. We investigate and get the evidence, lay it before the prosecutors, and they decide who to charge. It's out of your hands. You've been given your instructions, do it, for pity's sake.'

'Matthew Croft didn't kill Jane Neal. There's absolutely no evidence he did it. There's the accusation of a probably unbalanced son and his own confession.'

'What more do you need?'

'When you were investigating that serial killer in Brossard, did you arrest everyone who confessed?'

'This is different and you know it.'

'I don't know it, Superintendent. Those people who confessed were confused individuals who were fulfilling some obscure need of their own, right?'

'Right.' But Michel Brébeuf sounded guarded. He

hated arguing with Armand Gamache, and not only because they were friends. Gamache was a thoughtful man and Brébeuf knew he was a man of his convictions. But he isn't always right, Brébeuf told himself.

'Croft's confession is meaningless. I think it's his form of self-punishment. He's confused and hurt.'

'Poor baby.'

'Yes, well, I'm not saying it's noble or attractive. But it's human. And just because he's begging for punishment doesn't mean we should comply.'

'You're such a sanctimonious bastard. Lecturing me on the moral role of a police force. I know damn well what our job is. You're the one who wants to be police, judge and jury. If Croft didn't do it he'll be released. Trust the system, Armand.'

'He won't even come to trial if he continues in this ludicrous confession. And even if he's eventually released, you and I know what happens to people arrested for a crime. Especially a violent crime. They're stigmatised for the rest of their lives. Whether they did it or not. We'd be inflicting on Matthew Croft a wound that will stay with him for ever.'

'You're wrong. He's inflicting it on himself.'

'No, he's challenging us to do it. Goading us into it. But we don't have to react. That's what I'm saying. A police force, like a government, should be above that. Just because we're provoked doesn't mean we have to act.'

'So, what are you telling me, Chief Inspector? From now on you'll only arrest people if you're guaranteed a conviction? You've arrested people before who turned out not to have committed the crime. Just last year, remember the Gagné case? You arrested the uncle, but it turned out the nephew had done it?'

'True, I was wrong. But I believed the uncle had done it. That was a mistake. This is different. This would be deliberately arresting someone I believe did not commit the crime. I can't do it.'

Brébeuf sighed. He'd known from the first minute of this conversation that Gamache wouldn't change his mind. But he had to try. Really, a most annoying man.

'You know what I'm going to have to do?'

'I do. And I'm prepared for it.'

'So as punishment for insubordination you'll walk through Sûreté Headquarters wearing Sergeant LaCroix's uniform?' Mai LaCroix was the immense desk Sergeant who presided over the entry to HQ like Buddha gone bad. To add to the dimension of the horror, she wore a Sûreté-issue skirt some sizes too small.

Gamache laughed at the image. 'I'll make you a deal, Michel. If you can get that uniform off her. I'll wear it.'

'Never mind. I guess I'll just have to suspend you.' Michel Brébeuf had come close to doing this once before, after the Arnot case. His own superiors had ordered him to suspend Gamache, again for insubordination. That case had almost ended both their careers, and the stink still stuck to Gamache. He'd been wrong then, too, in Brébeuf's opinion. All he had to do was say nothing, it wasn't as though their superiors were proposing letting the criminals go. Just the opposite, really. But Gamache

240

had defied the authorities. He wondered if Gamache really believed the Arnot case was over.

Brébeuf never thought he'd be doing this. 'You're suspended from this moment for the period of one week, without pay. A disciplinary hearing will be held at that time. Don't wear a skirt.'

'Thanks for the tip.'

'*D'accord*. Give me Beauvoir.'

It took a lot to stun Jean Guy Beauvoir, but his conversation with the Superintendent did just that. Gamache knew that he cared deeply for Beauvoir, like a son, but the younger man had never shown him any feelings, except that of junior to respected superior. That had been enough. But now Gamache saw the depth of Beauvoir's pain at having to do this thing, and he received a great gift. The gift of knowing he was cared for in return.

'Is it true?'

Gamache nodded.

'Is this my fault? Did I do this by arguing against you? What a fool. Why didn't I just keep my mouth shut?' Beauvoir was pacing the small office like a leopard trapped.

'This isn't about you. You did the right thing. The only thing you could do. As did I. As did Superintendent Brébeuf, for that matter.'

'I thought he was a friend of yours.'

'He is. Look, don't feel badly about this. I knew when I called the Super he'd have to do this. I called Reine-Marie before, to run it by her.'

Beauvoir felt pricked, a tiny little point of pain that

the Chief Inspector had consulted his wife but not him. He knew it was unreasonable, but feelings so often were. It was why he tried to avoid them.

'When she said "do it" I called him with a clear conscience. I can't arrest Matthew Croft.'

'Well, if you can't, I can't. I won't do Brébeuf's dirty work for him.'

'It's Superintendent Brébeuf, and it's your job. What was that this afternoon I heard? Just some Devil's Advocate bullshit? You know how I hate that. Say what you really think, don't play pretentious little mind games. Is that all that was? Taking the other position like some empty adolescent intellectual game?'

'No, it wasn't. I believe Matthew Croft did it.'

'So arrest him.'

'There's more.' Now Beauvoir looked really miserable. 'Superintendent Brébeuf ordered me to take your badge and gun.'

This shook Gamache. Had he thought this all the way through he wouldn't have been surprised, but he hadn't seen it coming. He felt his stomach lurch. The force of his reaction stunned him. He'd have to think about why and fortunately he had a long drive home in which to consider.

Gamache pulled himself together, reached into his breast pocket and handed over both his badge and his warrant card. Then he slipped the holster off his belt.

'I'm sorry,' whispered Beauvoir. Gamache had been quick to recover, but not quick enough to hide his feelings from Beauvoir. As he took the items

Beauvoir remembered one of the many things he'd learned from Gamache. Matthew 10:36.

The funeral for Jane Neal, spinster of the village of Three Pines in the county of St Rémy, Province of Quebec, was held two days later. The bells of the Église Ste Marie rang and echoed along the valleys, heard miles away, and felt deep in the earth, where creatures lived who might not otherwise, had Jane Neal herself not lived and been the sort of person she'd been.

And now people gathered to say a formal goodbye. Armand Gamache was there, having driven in from Montreal. It made a nice break from his forced inaction. He sailed through the crowd, through the front of the small church, and found himself in the gloom inside. It always struck Gamache as paradoxical that churches were gloomy. Coming in from the sunshine it took a minute or so to adjust. And even then, to Gamache, it never came close to feeling like home. Churches were either great cavernous tributes not so much to God as the wealth and privilege of the community, or they were austere, cold tributes to the ecstasy of refusal.

Gamache enjoyed going to churches for their music and the beauty of the language and the stillness. But he felt closer to God in his Volvo. He spotted Beauvoir in the crowd, waved, then made his way over.

'I hoped you'd be here,' said Beauvoir. 'You'll be interested to hear we've arrested the entire Croft family and their farm animals.'

'You've found the safe side.'

'Damn straight, pardner.' Gamache hadn't seen Beauvoir since he'd left that Tuesday afternoon, but they'd talked on the phone several times. Beauvoir wanted to keep Gamache in the loop, and Gamache wanted to make sure Beauvoir knew there were no hard feelings.

Yolande wobbled behind the casket as it was led into the church. André, slim and greasy, was beside her and Bernard slouched behind, his furtive, active eyes darting everywhere as though in search of his next victim.

Gamache felt deeply sorry for Yolande. Not for the pain she felt, but for the pain she didn't feel. He prayed, in the silence, that one day she wouldn't have to pretend to emotions, other than resentment, but could actually feel them. Others in the church were sad but Yolande cut the saddest figure. Certainly the most pathetic.

The service was short and anonymous. The priest clearly had never met Jane Neal. No member of the family got up to speak, except André, who read one of the beautiful scriptures with less enlightenment than he might read the TV Guide listings. The service was entirely in French, though Jane herself had been English. The service was entirely Catholic, though Jane herself had been Anglican. Afterwards Yolande, André and Bernard accompanied the casket to a 'family only' burial, though Jane's friends had actually been her family.

'A real chill in the air today,' said Clara Morrow, who had appeared at his elbow, her eyes bloodshot. 'There'll be frost on the pumpkins tonight.' She managed a smile. 'We're having a memorial service for Jane at St Thomas's on Sunday. A week to the day since she died. We'd like you to be there, if you don't mind coming down again.'

Gamache didn't mind. Looking around he realised how much he liked this place and these people. Too bad one of them was a murderer.

TEN

~

The memorial service for Jane Neal was short and sweet, and had it been plump it would have been an exact replica of the woman. The service was really nothing more than Jane's friends getting up one after the other and talking about her, in French and English. The service was simple, and the message was clear. Her death was just one instant in a full and lovely life. She'd been with them for as long as she was meant to be. Not a minute longer, not a moment less. Jane Neal had known that when her time came God wouldn't ask how many committees she'd sat on, or how much money she'd made, or what prizes she'd won. No. He'd ask how many fellow creatures she'd helped. And Jane Neal would have had an answer.

At the end of the service Ruth stood at her seat and sang, in a thin, unsure, alto, 'What Do You Do With a Drunken Sailor?' She sang the unlikely sea shanty at a quarter speed, like a dirge, then slowly picked up speed. Gabri joined in, as did Ben and in the end the whole church was alive with people clapping and swinging their hips and asking the musical question, 'What do you do with a drunken sailor, err-lie in the morning?'

In the basement after the service the Anglican Church Women served up homemade casseroles and fresh apple and pumpkin pies, accompanied by the thin hum of the sea shanty heard here and there.

'Why "Drunken Sailor"?' Approaching the buffet, Armand Gamache found himself standing next to Ruth.

'It was one of Jane's favorite songs,' said Ruth. 'She was always singing it.'

'You were humming it that day in the woods,' Gamache said to Clara.

'Wards off bears. Didn't Jane learn it in school?' Clara asked Ruth.

Olivier jumped in. 'She told me she learned it for school. To teach, right, Ruth?'

'She was expected to teach every subject, but since she couldn't sing or play piano she didn't know what to do about the music course for her students. This was when she first started, back fifty years ago. So I taught her the song,' said Ruth.

'Can't say I'm surprised,' mumbled Myrna.

'It was the only song her students ever learned,' said Ben.

'Your Christmas pageants must have been something,' said Gamache, imagining the Virgin Mary, Joseph, the baby Jesus and three drunken sailors.

'They were,' laughed Ben, remembering. 'We sang all

the carols, but they were all to the tune of "Drunken Sailor". The looks on the parents' faces at the Christmas concert when Miss Neal would introduce, "Silent Night", and we'd sing!' Ben started singing, 'Silent Night, holy night, all is calm, all is bright', but to the tune of the shanty. Others in the room laughed and joined in.

'I still find it really hard to sing the carols correctly,' said Ben.

Clara spotted Nellie and Wayne and waved at them. Nellie left Wayne and made a bee-line for Ben, beginning to talk before she was halfway across the room.

'Ah, Mr Hadley, I was hoping to find you here. I'm going to be over to do your place next week. How's Tuesday?' Then she turned to Clara and said confidentially, as though passing a State secret, 'I haven't cleaned since before Miss Neal died, Wayne's had me that worried.'

'How is he now?' asked Clara, remembering Wayne's hacking and coughing during the public meeting a few days earlier.

'Now he's complaining, so there's nothing much wrong. Well, Mr Hadley? Haven't got all day, ya know.'

'Tuesday's fine.' He turned to Clara once Nellie had gone back to her pressing job, which seemed to be eating the entire buffet. 'The place is filthy. You won't believe the mess an old bachelor and his dog can create.'

As the line crawled forward, Gamache spoke to Ruth. 'When I was in the notary's office asking about Miss Neal's will, he mentioned your name. When he said, "née Kemp", something twigged, but I couldn't figure it out.'

'How did you finally get it?' Ruth asked.

'Clara Morrow told me.'

'Ah, clever lad. And from that you deduced who I was.'

'Well, it took a while after that, but eventually I got it.' Gamache smiled. 'I do love your poetry.' Gamache was just about to quote from one of his favorites, feeling himself a pimply youth in front of a matinée idol. Ruth was backing up, trying to get out of the way of her own beautiful words coming toward her.

'Sorry to interrupt,' said Clara, to two people apparently maniacally happy to see her. 'But did you say, "he"?'

'He?' repeated Gamache.

'He? The notary.'

'Yes. Maître Stickley in Williamsburg. He was Miss Neal's notary.'

'Are you sure? I thought she saw that notary who just had a baby. Solonge someone-or-other.'

'Solonge Frenette? From exercise class?' Myrna asked.

'That's her. Jane said she and Timmer were off to see her about wills.'

Gamache stood very still, staring at Clara.

'Are you sure?'

'Frankly? No. I seem to remember her saying that because I asked Jane how Solonge was feeling. Solonge would have been in her first trimester. Morning sickness. She just had her baby, so she's on maternity leave.'

'I suggest one of you get in touch with Maître Frenette as soon as possible.'

'I'll do it,' said Clara, suddenly wanting to drop

everything and hurry home to call. But there was something that had to be done first.

The ritual was simple and time-worn. Myrna led it, having grounded herself with a full lunch of casseroles and bread. Very important, she explained to Clara, to feel grounded before a ritual. Looking at her plate Clara thought there wasn't much chance she'd fly away. Clara examined the twenty or so faces gathered in a cluster on the village green, many of them apprehensive. The farm women stood in a loose semi-circle of woolen sweaters and mitts and toques, staring at this huge black woman in a bright green cape. The Jolly Green Druid.

Clara felt perfectly relaxed and at home. Standing in the group she closed her eyes, took a few deep breaths and prayed for the grace to let go of the anger and fear that hung around her, like black funeral crêpe. This ritual was designed to end that, to turn the dark into light, to banish the hate and fear and invite the trust and warmth back.

'This is a ritual of celebration and cleansing,' Myrna was explaining to the gathering. 'Its roots go back many thousands of years, but its branches reach out and touch us today, and embrace anyone who wants to be included. If you have any questions, just ask.' Myrna paused but no one spoke up. She had a few things in a bag and now she fished into it and brought out a stick. Actually, it looked more like a thick, straight branch, stripped of its bark and whittled to a sharp point at one end.

'This is a prayer stick. It might look familiar to some of you.' She waited and heard a small laugh.

'Isn't that a beaver stick?' Hanna Parra asked.

'That's exactly what it is,' laughed Myrna. She passed it around and the ice was broken. The women who'd been apprehensive, even a little frightened at what they thought might be witchcraft, thawed, and realised there was nothing to be afraid of here. 'I found it by the mill pond last year. You can see where the beaver gnawed it.'

Eager hands reached out to touch the stick and see the teeth marks and see where the beaver had eaten away the end until it was sharp.

Clara had gone home briefly to get Lucy, now standing quietly on her leash. When the prayer stick got back to Myrna she offered it to the Golden Retriever. For the first time in a week, since Jane had died, Clara saw Lucy's tail wag. Once. She gently took the stick in her teeth. And held it there. Her tail gave another tentative wag.

Gamache sat on the bench on the green. He'd come to think of it as 'his' bench, since that morning when they'd greeted the dawn together. Now he and the bench were in the sunshine, which was a few precious degrees warmer than the shade. Still, his breath was coming out in puffs. As he sat quietly he watched the women gather, form a line, and with Myrna in front and Clara behind with Lucy they walked around the green.

''Bout time for Indian Summer,' said Ben, sitting down in a way that made it look like all his bones had dissolved. 'The sun's getting lower in the sky.'

'Humm,' Gamache agreed. 'Do they do this often?' He nodded to the procession of women.

'About twice a year. I was at the last ritual. Didn't get it.' Ben shook his head.

'Perhaps if they tackled each other now and then we'd understand,' suggested Gamache, who actually understood perfectly well. The two men sat in companionable silence watching the women.

'How long have you loved her?' Gamache asked quietly, not looking at Ben. Ben turned in his seat and stared at Gamache's profile, flabbergasted.

'Who?'

'Clara. How long have you loved her?'

Ben gave a long sigh, like a man waiting all his life to exhale. 'We were all at art school together, though Peter and I were a couple of years ahead of Clara. He fell for her right away.'

'And you?'

'Took me a little longer. I think I'm more guarded than Peter. I find it harder to open up to people. But Clara's different, isn't she?' Ben was watching her, smiling.

Myrna lit the knot of Jane's sage, and it started to smoke. As they walked around the green the procession of women stopped at the four directions, North, South, East and West. And at each stop Myrna handed the smoking knot to another woman, who softly wafted her hand in front of the sage, encouraging the sweet-smelling smoke to drift toward the homes.

Myrna explained this was called 'smudging'. It was cleansing away the bad spirits and making room for the good. Gamache breathed deeply and inhaled the fragrant mix of woodsmoke and sage. Both venerable, both comforting.

'Is it obvious?' Ben asked anxiously. 'I mean, I used to dream about us getting together, but that was long ago. I could never, ever do anything like that. Not to Peter.'

'No, it isn't obvious.' Ben and Gamache watched as the line of women walked up rue du Moulin and into the woods.

It was cold and dark, dead leaves underfoot and overhead and swirling in the air in between. The women's high spirits had been replaced by restlessness. A shadow crept over the jovial gathering. Even Myrna became subdued, her smiling, friendly face growing watchful.

The forest creaked. And shivered. The poplar leaves trembled in the wind.

Clara wanted to leave. This was not a happy place.

Lucy began to growl, a long, low song of warning. Her hackles rose and she slowly sunk to the ground, her muscles bunched as though ready to spring.

'We must form a circle,' said Myrna, trying to sound casual while actually looking around the gathering trying to figure out who she could outrun if it came to that. Or would she be the straggler? Damn that grounding casserole.

The circle, the tiniest, tightest known to math, was made, the women grasping hands. Myrna picked up the prayer stick from where Lucy had dropped it and thrust it into the ground, deep. Clara half expected the earth to howl.

'I've brought these ribbons.' Myrna opened her bag. Piled there were brightly colored ribbons, all intertwined. 'We asked you all to bring something that was symbolic of Jane.'

From her pocket Myrna brought out a tiny book. She rummaged around in the bag until she found a crimson ribbon. First she tied the book to the ribbon, then she went to the prayer stick and spoke as she tied the ribbon on to it.

'This is for you, Jane, to thank you for sharing your love of the written word with me. Bless you.'

Myrna stood at the prayer stick for a moment, huge head bowed, and then she stepped away, smiling for the first time since coming to this place.

One by one the women took a ribbon, tied an item to it, tied the ribbon to the stick and spoke a few words. Some were audible, some weren't. Some were prayers, some were simple explanations. Hanna tied an old 78 record to the prayer stick, Ruth a faded photograph. Sarah tied a spoon and Nellie, a shoe. Clara reached into her head and pulled out a duck barrette. She tied that to a bright yellow ribbon and the ribbon to the now festooned prayer stick.

'This is for helping me see more clearly,' said Clara. 'I love you, Jane.' She looked up and spotted the blind, hovering above them in the near distance. Blind. How strange, thought Clara, blind, but now I see.

And Clara had an idea. An inspiration. 'Thank you, Jane,' she whispered, and felt the elderly arms around her for the first time in a week. Before moving off Clara pulled a banana out of her pocket, and tied it to the stick, for

Lucy. But she had one more item to add. From her other pocket she drew a playing card. The Queen of Hearts. Tying it to the prayer stick Clara thought of Yolande, and the wonderful gift she'd been offered as a child, and either rejected or forgot. Clara stared at the pattern on the Queen of Hearts, memorising it. She knew the magic wasn't in it staying the same, but in the changes.

By the end the prayer stick was brilliant with waving and weaving colored ribbons, dangling their gifts. The wind caught the objects and sent them dancing into the air around the prayer stick, clinking and clanging into each other, like a symphony.

The women looked around and saw their circle was no longer bound by fear, but was loose and open. And in the center, on the spot Jane Neal had last lived and died, a wealth of objects played, and sang the praises of a woman who was much loved.

Clara allowed her gaze, free now from fear, to follow the ribbons as they were caught in the wind. Her eye caught something at the end of one of the ribbons. Then she realised it wasn't attached to a ribbon at all, but to the tree behind.

High up in one of the maple trees she saw an arrow.

Gamache was just getting into his car to drive back to Montreal when Clara Morrow shot out of the woods, running toward him down du Moulin as though chased by demons. For a wild moment Gamache wondered whether the ritual had inadvertently conjured something better left alone. And, in a way, it had. The women, and their ritual, had conjured an arrow, something someone must sorely wish had been left undisturbed.

Gamache immediately called Beauvoir in Montreal then followed Clara to the site. He hadn't been there for almost a week and was impressed by how much it'd changed. The biggest changes were the trees. Where they'd been bright and bold with cheery color a week ago, now they were past their prime, with more leaves on the ground than in the branches. And that's what had revealed the arrow. When he'd stood at this spot a week ago and looked up he would never, could never, have seen the arrow. It'd been hidden by layers of leaves. But no longer.

The other change was the stick in the ground with ribbons dancing around it. He supposed it had something to do with the ritual. Either that or Beauvoir had very quickly become very weird without his supervision. Gamache walked over to the prayer stick, impressed by its gaiety. He caught at some of the items to look at them, including an old photograph of a young woman, plump and short-sighted, standing next to a rugged, handsome lumberjack. They were holding hands and smiling. Behind them a slender young woman stood, looking straight into the camera. A face taken by bitterness.

'So? It's an arrow.' Matthew Croft looked from Beauvoir to Gamache. They were in the cell at the Williamsburg jail. 'You've got five of them. What's the big deal with this one?'

'This one,' said Gamache, 'was found twenty-five feet up a maple tree two hours ago. Where Jane Neal was killed. Is this one of your father's?'

Croft examined the wood shaft, the four-bladed tip, and finally, critically, the feathering. By the time he pulled away he felt faint. He took a huge breath, and collapsed on to the side of the cot.

'Yes,' he whispered on the exhale, having difficulty focusing now. 'That was Dad's. You'll see for sure when you compare it to the others from the quiver, but I can tell you now. My father made his own feathering, it was a hobby of his. He wasn't very creative, though, and they were all the same. Once he found what he liked and what worked he saw no need to change.'

'Good thing,' said Gamache.

'Now.' Beauvoir sat on the cot opposite him. 'You have a lot to tell us.'

'I need to think.'

'There's nothing to think about,' said Gamache. 'Your son shot this arrow, didn't he?' Croft's mind was racing. He'd so steeled himself to stick to his story it was hard now to give it up, even in the face of this evidence. 'And if he shot this arrow and it ended up in that tree,' continued Gamache, 'then he couldn't have killed Jane Neal. He didn't do it. And neither did you, this arrow proves someone else did it. We need the truth from you now.'

And still Croft hesitated, afraid there was a trap, afraid to give up his story.

'Now, Mr Croft,' said Gamache in a voice that brooked

no argument. Croft nodded. He was too stunned to feel relief, yet.

'All right. This is what happened. Philippe and I had had an argument the night before. Some stupid thing, I can't even remember what. The next morning when I got up Philippe was gone. I was afraid he'd run away, but about 7.15 he comes skidding into the yard on his bike. I decided not to go out and see him, but to wait for him to come to me. That was a mistake. I found out later he went directly to the basement with the bow and arrow then took a shower and changed his clothes. He never did come to see me, but stayed in his room all day. That wasn't unusual. Then Suzanne started to act strange.'

'When did you hear about Miss Neal?' Beauvoir asked.

'That night, a week ago. Roar Parra called, said it was a hunting accident. When I went to your meeting next day I was sad, but not like it was the end of the world. Suzanne, on the other hand, couldn't sit still, couldn't relax. But honestly I didn't think much about it, women can be more sensitive than men, that's all I figured it was.'

'How'd you find out about Philippe?'

'When we got home. Suzanne had been silent in the car, then once we got back she laid into me. She was furious, violent almost, because I'd asked you back to look at the bows and arrows. She told me then. She'd found out because she found Philippe's clothes ready for the wash, blood stains on them. Then she'd gone into the basement and found the bloody arrow. She got the story from Philippe. He thought he'd killed Miss Neal, so he grabbed the bloody arrow and ran, thinking it was his. He didn't look at it, neither did Suzanne. I guess they didn't notice it wasn't the same as the others. Suzanne burned the arrow.'

'What did you do when you heard all this?'

'I burned his clothes in the furnace but then you arrived so I told Suzanne to burn the bow, to destroy everything.'

'But she didn't.'

'No. When I put the clothes in it smothered the flames, so she had to build them back up. Then she realised the bow would have to be chopped up. She didn't think she could do it without making a noise so she came upstairs, to try to warn me. But you wouldn't let her go back down. She was going to do it when we were out shooting arrows.'

'How'd you know how Miss Neal's body was lying?'

'Philippe showed me. I went to his room, to confront him, to hear the story from him. He wouldn't speak to me. Just as I was leaving his room he stood up and did that.' Croft shuddered at the memory, baffled by where this child could have come from. 'I didn't know what he meant by it at the time but later, when you asked me to show you how she was lying, it clicked. So I just did what Philippe had done. What does that mean?' Croft nodded to the arrow.

'It means,' said Beauvoir, 'someone else shot the arrow that killed Miss Neal.'

'It means,' clarified Gamache, 'that she was almost certainly murdered.'

Beauvoir tracked down Superintendent Michel Brébeuf at the Montreal Botanical Gardens, where he volunteered one Sunday a month in the information booth. The people gathered around waiting to ask where the Japanese garden was were left to wonder just how wide a mandate these volunteers had.

'I agree, it sounds like murder,' said Brébeuf over the phone, nodding and smiling to the suddenly guarded tourists waiting in front of him. 'I'm giving you the authority to treat this as a homicide.'

'Actually, sir, I was hoping it'd be Chief Inspector Gamache's investigation. He was right, Matthew Croft didn't kill Miss Neal.'

'Do you really think that's what this was about, Inspector? Armand Gamache was suspended not because we disagreed over who did it, but because he refused to carry out a direct order. And that's still true. Besides, as I recall, left to himself he would've arrested a fourteen-year-old boy.'

A tourist reached out and took the hand of his teenage son, who was so shocked he actually allowed his father to hold it, for about a nanosecond.

'Well, not arrested, exactly,' said Beauvoir.

'You're not helping your case here, Inspector.'

'Yes, sir. The Chief Inspector knows this case and these people. It's been a week already, and we've let the trail go cold by being forced to treat this as a probable accident. He's the logical person to lead this investigation. You know it, and I know it.'

'And he knows it.'

'At a guess I'd have to agree. *Voyons*, is this about punishment, or getting the best results?'

260

'All right. And tell him he's lucky to have an advocate like you. I wish I did.'

'You do.'

When Brébeuf hung up he turned his attention to the tourists at his booth and found he was alone.

'Thank you, Jean Guy.' Gamache took his warrant card, badge and gun. He'd thought about why it had stung so much to give them up. Years ago, when he'd first been issued with the card and gun, he'd felt accepted, a success in the eyes of society and, more important, in the eyes of his family. Then, when he'd had to give up the card and gun he'd suddenly felt afraid. He'd been stripped of a weapon, but more than that, he'd been stripped of approval. The feeling had passed, it was no more than an echo, a ghost of the insecure young man he'd once been.

On the way home after being suspended, Gamache had remembered an analogy someone told him years ago. Living our lives was like living in a long house. We entered as babies at one end, and we exited when our time came. And in between we moved through this one, great, long room. Everyone we ever met, and every thought and action lived in that room with us. Until we made peace with the less agreeable parts of our past they'd continue to heckle us from way down the long house. And sometimes the really loud, obnoxious ones told us what to do, directing our actions even years later.

Gamache wasn't sure he agreed with that analogy, until the moment he'd had to place his gun into Jean Guy's palm. Then that insecure young man lived again, and whispered,

You're nothing without it. What will people think? Realising how inappropriate the reaction was didn't banish the fearful young man from Gamache's long house, it just meant he wasn't in charge.

'Where to now? Jane Neal's home?' Now they could officially treat the case as a murder investigation, Beauvoir was dying to get in, as was Gamache.

'Soon. We have a stop to make first.'

'*Oui, allô?*' a cheery voice answered the phone followed by a baby's shriek.

'Solonge?' asked Clara.

'*Allô? Allô?*'

'Solange,' called Clara.

'*Bonjour?* Hello?' A wail filled Solonge's home and Clara's head.

'Solonge,' Clara shrieked.

'*C'est moi,*' cried Solonge.

'It's Clara Morrow,' yelled Clara.

'No, I can't tomorrow.'

'Clara Morrow.'

'Wednesday?'

Oh, dear, God, thought Clara, thank you for sparing me children.

'Clara!' she wailed.

'Clara? Clara who?' asked Solonge, in a perfectly normal voice, the spawn from Hell having been silenced, probably by a breast.

'Clara Morrow, Solonge. We met in exercise class. Congratulations on the child.' She tried to sound sincere.

'Yes, I remember. How are you?'

'Just fine. But I called with a question. I'm sorry to disturb you on your leave, but this has something to do with your notary practice.'

'Oh, that's all right. The office calls every day. What can I help you with?'

'Did you know that Jane Neal had died?'

'No, no, I hadn't heard. I'm sorry.'

'It was an accident. In the woods.'

'Oh, I did hear about that when I got back. I was visiting my parents in Montreal for Thanksgiving, so I missed it. You mean, that was Jane Neal?'

'Yes.'

'Weren't the police involved?'

'Yes. They seem to think Norman Stickley, in Williamsburg, was her notary. But I thought she'd come to you.'

'Could you come to my office tomorrow morning?'

'What time's good for you?'

'Say eleven? Clara, could you invite the police? I think they'll be interested.'

It took Philippe Croft a few minutes to trust it wasn't a trap before he admitted everything. His long pale fingers picked at a pill of fluff on his sweatpants as he told his story. He'd wanted to punish his father, so he'd taken the old bow and arrows and gone hunting. He'd fired just once. But that was enough. Instead of the stag he knew he'd killed, he found Jane Neal, spread-eagled. Dead. He could still see those eyes. They followed him.

'You can let them go now,' said Gamache, quietly. 'They're someone else's nightmare.'

Philippe had simply nodded and Gamache was reminded of Myrna, and the pain we choose to carry around. He wanted to take Philippe in his arms and tell him he wouldn't be fourteen for ever. Just to hold on.

But Gamache didn't. He knew that while the intention was kind, the act would be seen as an assault. An insult. Instead he stuck out his large, steady hand to the boy. After a moment Philippe slipped his own pale hand in, as though he'd never shook hands with a man before, and squeezed.

Gamache and Beauvoir arrived back in the village to find Agent Lacoste fending off Yolande. She'd been sent to Jane Neal's cottage, warrant in hand. She'd managed to get Yolande out and to lock the door, and was now practicing her impression of a Palace Guard, immutable in the face of provocation.

'I'll sue your ass. I'll get you fired, you ugly little tramp.' Spying Beauvoir, Yolande turned on him. 'How dare you kick me out of my own home?'

'Did you show Ms Fontaine the warrant, Agent?'

'I did, sir.'

'Then you know', Beauvoir turned to Yolande, 'that this is now a homicide investigation. I take it you want to find out who killed your aunt?'

It was a low blow, but almost always effective. Who could say no?

'No. I don't care. Will it bring her back? Tell me it'll bring her back and I'll let you into my home.'

'We're already in, and this isn't a negotiation. Now, I need to speak with you and your husband. Is he home?'

'How should I know?'

'Well, why don't we just go and see.'

When they'd pulled up in Gamache's car they'd seen Yolande going after Lacoste, who seemed to have been stuffed.

'Poor woman.' Gamache smiled. 'This will make a story she can bore her rookies with one day. Listen, we're both anxious to get into that house, but I'd like to get a couple of things out of the way first. Go and interview Yolande and try to get André as well. I want to speak with Myrna Landers.'

'Why?'

Gamache told him.

'I need to know what Timmer Hadley said that day you were sitting with her.'

Myrna locked the door to her bookshop and poured them each a cup of tea. Then she sat down in the comfortable chair opposite him. 'I think you'll be disappointed. I can't see that it matters to anyone now, alive or dead.'

'You'd be surprised.'

'I dare say.' She sipped her tea and looked out the window into the dusk, her mind going back to that afternoon just a few months ago. Seemed like years. Timmer Hadley a skeleton draped with flesh. Her eyes bright in the head made huge by a shriveled body. They'd sat together, Myrna perched on the side of the bed, Timmer wrapped in blankets and hot-water bottles. The big old brown album between them. The photos falling out, their glue long since turned to grit. One that had slipped out was of a young Jane Neal and her parents and sister.

Timmer told Myrna about Jane's parents, prisoners of their own insecurities and fears. Those fears passed on to the sister Irene, who had also become a social climber and searched for security in objects and the approval of others. But not Jane. And then came the story Gamache had asked about:

'This was taken on the last day of the county fair. The day after the dance. You can see how happy Jane is,' Timmer had said, and it was true. Even in the grainy photo she glowed, even more in comparison to the glum faces of her parents and sister.

'She'd become engaged to her young man that night,' said Timmer, wistfully. 'What was his name? Andreas. He was a lumberjack, of all things. Doesn't matter. She hadn't told her parents yet, but she had a plan. She'd elope. They made a wonderful couple. Rather odd to look at, until you got to know them and saw how good they were together. They loved each other. Except,' and here Timmer's brow had clouded, 'Ruth Kemp went to Jane's parents, here at the fair, and told them what Jane planned to do. She did it in secret but I overheard. I was young, and my big regret to this day was not going to Jane right away to warn her. But I didn't.'

'What happened?' Myrna asked.

'They took Jane home and broke up the relationship. Spoke to Kaye Thompson, who employed Andreas, and threatened to take away the mills' business from her operation if this lumberjack so much as looked at Jane. You could do that in those days. Kaye's a good woman, a fair woman, and she explained it all to him, but it broke his heart. He apparently tried to see Jane, but couldn't.'

'And Jane?'

'She was told she couldn't see him. No debate. She was only seventeen, and not a very headstrong person. She gave in. It was a horrible thing.'

'Did Jane ever know it was Ruth who did it?'

'I never told her. Perhaps I should have. Seemed there was enough pain, but probably I was just afraid.'

'Did you ever say anything to Ruth?'

'No.'

Myrna looked down at the photograph in Timmer's translucent hand. A moment of joy caught just before it was extinguished.

'Why did Ruth do it?'

'I don't know. For sixty years I've wondered that. Maybe she wonders the same thing. There's something about her, something bitter, that resents happiness in others, and needs to ruin it. That's probably what makes her a great poet, she knows what it is to suffer. She gathers suffering to her. Collects it, and sometimes creates it. I think that's why she likes to sit with me, she feels more comfortable in the company of a dying woman than a thriving one. But perhaps I'm being unfair.'

Listening to Myrna's narrative, Gamache thought he would've liked to meet Timmer Hadley. But too late. He was, though, about to meet Jane Neal, or at least get as close as he would ever come to doing so.

Beauvoir stepped into the perfect home. So perfect it was lifeless. So perfect a tiny part of him found it attractive. He shoved that part down and pretended it didn't exist.

Yolande Fontaine's home gleamed. Every surface glowed with polish. In his stockinged feet he was shown into the living room, a room whose only blemish sat in an overstuffed chair and read the sports section. André didn't move, didn't acknowledge his wife. Yolande made her way to him. Actually, to his pile of dumped newspaper, forming a teepee village on the tasteful area rug. She picked up the paper, folded it, and put it in a neat stack on the coffee table, all the edges lining up. Then she turned to Beauvoir.

'Now, Inspector, would you like a coffee?'

Her change in attitude almost gave him whiplash, then he remembered. They were in her home. Her territory. It was safe for the lady of the manor to make an appearance.

'No, thank you. I just need some answers.'

Yolande inclined her head slightly, a gracious gesture to a working man.

'Did you take anything out of Miss Neal's home?'

This question brought a rise, but not from Yolande. André lowered his paper and scowled. 'And what business is it of yours?'

'We now believe Miss Neal was murdered. We have a warrant to search her home and seal it off.'

'What does that mean?'

'It means no one but the police are allowed in.'

A look was exchanged between husband and wife, the first since Beauvoir had arrived. It wasn't a loving, supportive glance, more a question from him and a confirmation from her. Beauvoir was convinced. They'd done something in that home.

'Did you take anything?' he repeated.

'No,' said Yolande.

'If you're lying, I'll have you charged with interfering with the investigation and that, M. Malenfant, won't look good on your already impressive record.' Malenfant smiled. He didn't care.

'What've you been doing in there for five days, Ms. Fontaine?'

'Decorating.' She swept her arm around the living room. It screamed cheap 'taste'. The curtains struck him as a little odd, then he noticed she'd put the pattern on both sides, so it showed outside as well as in the home. He'd never seen that before, but wasn't surprised. Yolande Fontaine only really existed with an audience. She was like those novelty lamps that came on when you clapped your hands. She switched to life with applause, or the sharp clap of rebuke. Any reaction, as long as it was directed at her, was sufficient. Silence and solitude drained her of life.

'This is a lovely room,' he lied. 'Is the rest of the home as – elegant?'

She heard his clapping and sprung into action. 'Come with me,' she said, practically dragging him around the tiny home. It was like a hotel room, sterile and anonymous. It seemed Yolande had become so self-absorbed she no longer existed. She'd finally absorbed herself.

He saw a door ajar off the kitchen and made a guess. Reaching out he opened it and in a bound he was down the stairs and looking at an unholy mess.

'Don't go down there, that's André's area.' He ignored her and quickly moved around the dank room until he found what he'd been looking for. A pair of still-wet Wellingtons and a bow leaning against the wall.

'Where were you on the morning Jane Neal was killed?' Beauvoir asked André, once they'd returned to the living room.

'Sleeping, where else?'

'Well, how about hunting?'

'Mebbe. Dunno. I got a license you know.'

'That wasn't the question. Were you hunting last Sunday morning?'

André shrugged.

'I saw a dirty bow in the basement.' So like André, he thought, not to clean his equipment. But looking at the antiseptic home Beauvoir could see why André might yearn for mud. And disorder. And time away from Lemon Pledge.

'And you think it's still wet and dirty from last week?' André hooted.

'No, from today. You hunt on Sundays, don't you? Every Sunday, including one week ago, the day Jane Neal was killed. Let me make this clear. This is now a murder investigation. Who's the most likely suspect in any murder? A family member. Who's the next most likely suspect? Someone who benefits from the death. And if that person has the opportunity as well, we might as well start making your bed in the penitentiary right now. You two win. We know you're in debt.' He took a calculated guess. 'You believed you inherited everything, and you, André, know how to shoot a bow and arrow well enough to kill. Am I making myself clear?'

'Look, Inspector,' André rose from the chair, dropping the sports section a page at a time on the floor. 'I went hunting and I bagged a deer the day Jane Neal was killed. You can ask Boxleiter at the abattoir, he dressed it for me.'

'But you were out hunting today. Isn't the limit one deer?'

'What, now you're a game warden? Yes. I went out today. I'll kill as many deer as I want.'

'And your son, Bernard? Where was he last Sunday?'

'Sleeping.'

'Sleeping like you were sleeping?'

'Look, he's fourteen, that's what kids do on weekends. He sleeps, he wakes up long enough to piss me off and eat the food I put in the fridge, and then he goes back to bed. Wish I had his life.'

'What do you do for a living?'

'I'm unemployed. I was an astronaut, but I got laid off.' And André roared at his own cleverness, a putrid laugh that seemed to deaden the room even further. 'Yeah, they hired a one-armed black lesbian to replace me.'

Beauvoir left their home wanting to call his wife and

tell her how much he loved her, and then tell her what he believed in, and his fears and hopes and disappointments. To talk about something real and meaningful. He dialed his cell phone and got her. But the words got caught somewhere south of his throat. Instead he told her the weather had cleared, and she told him about the movie she'd rented. Then they both hung up. Driving back to Three Pines Beauvoir noticed an odor clinging to his clothes. Lemon Pledge.

He found the chief standing outside Miss Neal's home, the key pressed into the palm of his hand. Gamache had waited for him. Finally, exactly a week after her death, the two men walked into Jane Neal's home.

ELEVEN

~

'*Tabarnac*,' whispered Beauvoir, then after a pause during which neither man breathed. 'Christ.'

They stood on the threshold of Jane's living room, frozen in place. Riveted as to a particularly gruesome accident. But what held them fast was no mere accident, it was more aggressive, more intentional.

'If I was Jane Neal I'd keep people out, too,' said Beauvoir, regaining his secular voice. For a moment. '*Sacrament*.'

Jane's living room assaulted them with color. Huge Timothy Leary flowers daygloed, psychedelic three-dimensional silver towers and mushrooms advanced and retreated, enormous yellow Happy Faces marched around the fireplace. It was a veritable parade of bad taste.

'Shit,' whispered Beauvoir.

The room glowed in the gathering gloom. Even the ceiling between the old timbers was wallpapered. It was more than a joke, it was a travesty. Any lover of Quebecois heritage and architecture would feel wretched in this room and Gamache, who was both, could taste his lunch in his throat.

He hadn't expected this. Faced with this cacophony of color he couldn't remember what he'd expected, but certainly not this. He tore his eyes from the maniacal Happy Faces and forced himself to look down to the wide plank floors, made with timber hand-hewn by a man being chased by winter two hundred years ago. Floors like this were rare, even in Quebec, and considered by some, Gamache included, works of art. Jane Neal was fortunate enough to live in one of the tiny original field-stone homes, made from stones literally yanked from the land as it was cleared for planting. To own a home like this was to be a custodian of Quebec history.

With dread Gamache lowered his eyes from the walls to the floor.

It was painted pink. Glossy pink.

He groaned. Beside him Beauvoir almost, almost reached out to touch the Chief Inspector on the arm. He knew how upsetting this would be for any lover of heritage. It was a sacrilege.

'Why?' asked Gamache, but the Happy Faces remained mute. So did Beauvoir. He had no answer but then he was always astonished by *'les Anglais'*. This room was just one more example of their unfathomable behavior. As the silence stretched on Beauvoir felt he owed the Chief at least an attempt at an answer.

'Maybe she needed a change. Isn't that how most of our antiques ended up in other people's homes? Our grandparents sold them to rich Anglos. Got rid of pine tables and armoires and brass beds to buy junk from the Eaton's catalogue.'

'True,' agreed Gamache. That was exactly how it had happened sixty, seventy years earlier. 'But look at that.' He pointed to a corner. An astonishing diamond-point pine armoire with its original milk paint sat filled with Port Neuf pottery. 'And there.' Gamache pointed to a huge oak Welsh dresser. 'This here,' he walked over to a side table, 'is a faux Louis Quatorze table, made by hand by a woodworker who knew the style in France and was trying to duplicate it. A piece like this is almost priceless. No, Jean Guy, Jane Neal knew antiques and loved them. I can't imagine why she'd collect these pieces, then turn around and paint the floor. But that wasn't what I was asking.' Gamache turned around slowly, surveying the room. A throbbing was starting in his right temple. 'I was wondering why Miss Neal kept her friends out of here.'

'Isn't it obvious?' an amazed Beauvoir asked.

'No, it isn't. If she did this she must have liked this style. She certainly wouldn't have been ashamed of it. So why keep them out? And let's even suppose this was done by someone else, her parents, for example, back in the days this sort of thing was in –'

'Hate to tell you, but it's back.' Beauvoir had just bought a lava lamp, but didn't think he'd tell the chief about that now. Gamache brought his hands up and rubbed his face. Lowering them he still saw the acid-trip room. Shit, indeed.

'All right, let's just say her elderly and probably demented parents did this and she didn't change it for some reason, like finances or loyalty to them or something like that, well, really it's pretty awful, but it's not that bad. Embarrassing at worst, but not shameful. To keep friends out of the heart of her home for decades speaks of more than embarrassment.'

Both men looked around again. The room had beautiful proportions, Beauvoir had to admit. But that was kind of like saying a blind date had a good personality. You still wouldn't want to introduce her to your friends. Beauvoir could understand perfectly how Jane Neal felt. He thought, perhaps, he'd return the lava lamp.

Gamache walked slowly around the room. Was there anything here he shouldn't see? Why had Jane Neal, a woman who loved and trusted her friends, kept them out of this room? And why did she change her mind two days before she was killed? What secret did this room hold?

'Upstairs?' suggested Beauvoir.

'After you.' Gamache lumbered over and looked at the stairway which ascended from the rear of the living room. It was also wallpapered, this time in a burgundy velveteen effect. To say it clashed with the flowers would be to suggest there was a wallpaper in existence which wouldn't. Still, of all the colors and styles to have chosen, this was the worst. Up it went, like a strep throat, into the second floor. The steps of the stairs had also been painted. It broke Gamache's heart.

The modest second floor had a large bathroom and two good-size bedrooms. What looked to be the master bedroom had dark red painted walls. The next room had been painted a deep blue.

But something was missing in the house.

Gamache went back downstairs and searched the living room, then back out into the kitchen and mudroom.

'There're no easel, no paints. There's no studio. Where'd she do her art?'

'How about the basement?'

'Sure, go down and check, but I can guarantee you an artist isn't going to paint in a windowless basement.' Though, come to think of it, Jane Neal's work did look like it'd been done in the dark.

'There're paints down there, but no easel,' Beauvoir said, emerging from the basement. 'Her studio wasn't in the basement. There's another thing . . .' He loved being able see something the chief had missed. Gamache turned an interested face to him. 'Pictures. There are no pictures on the walls. Anywhere.'

Gamache's face opened in astonishment. He was right. Gamache spun in place, searching the walls. Nothing.

'Upstairs too?'

'Upstairs too.'

'I just don't get it. All of this is odd, the wallpaper, the painted rooms and floors, the lack of pictures. But none of it's so odd she'd have to keep her friends out. But there is something around here she didn't want anyone to see.'

Beauvoir flopped into the big sofa and looked around. Gamache subsided into the leather chair, put his hands together like steeples on his stomach, and thought. After a few minutes he rocked himself to his feet and went downstairs. The unfinished basement was replete with cardboard boxes, an old cast iron tub, a fridge with wines. He took one out. A Dunham vineyard, reputed to be quite good. Replacing the bottle he closed the fridge and turned around. Another door led to her preserves cupboard. Auburn jellies, rich red and purple jams, British racing-green dill pickles. He looked at the dates, some from the year before, most from this year. Nothing spectacular. Nothing abnormal. Nothing he hadn't found in his mother's basement after she'd died.

He closed the door and took a step backward. Just as his back brushed the rough basement wall something bit his shoe. Hard. It was at once shocking and familiar.

'*Tabarnac!*' he yelped. Above he could hear feet running to the basement door. In an instant Beauvoir was there, his hand resting on his revolver still in its holster.

'What! What is it?' He'd so rarely heard the chief swear that when he did it acted like a siren. Gamache pointed to his foot. A small wooden plank had attached itself to his shoe.

'Pretty big mouse,' said Beauvoir with a grin. Gamache bent down and removed the trap. It had been smeared with peanut butter to attract mice. He wiped a bit off his shoe and looked around. More traps became apparent, all lined up against the wall.

'She got a couple,' said Beauvoir, pointing to some upturned traps, little tails and balled up fists poking out from underneath.

'I don't think she set those. I think these are hers.' Gamache bent down and picked up a small gray box.

Opening it he found a small field mouse curled up inside. Dead. 'It's a humane trap. She caught them alive then released them. This, poor one, must have been caught after she was murdered. It starved to death.'

'So who set those other mousetraps? Wait, don't tell me. Yolande and André, of course. They were here alone for a week or so. Still, you'd think they could have at least checked the humane trap,' said Beauvoir with disgust. Gamache shook his head. Violent, intentional, death still surprised him, whether of a man or mouse.

'Come with me, little one,' he said to the curled-up mouse, as he took it upstairs. Beauvoir tossed the other traps into a plastic bag and followed the chief. The two men locked up and walked down Jane's garden path and across the Commons. A few headlights could be seen now that the sun had set. Rush hour. And a few villagers were out doing errands or walking dogs. In the silence Gamache could hear unintelligible snippets of conversations from other strollers. Off toward du Moulin he heard, 'Pee, please pee.' He hoped it was directed at a dog. The two men crossed the village green toward the brightly lit and welcoming B&B. Halfway across Gamache stopped and laid the mouse on the grass, beside him Beauvoir opened the plastic bag and released the other little bodies from the traps.

'They'll be eaten,' said Beauvoir.

'Exactly. Something will benefit at least. Abby Hoffman said we should all eat what we kill. That would put an end to war.'

Not for the first time Beauvoir was at a loss for words

with Gamache. Was he serious? Was he, perhaps, a little touched? And who was Abbé Offman? A local cleric? Sounds like exactly the sort of things some Christian mystic would say.

The next morning the team had reassembled in the incident room, been briefed on the latest developments, and given their assignments. At Gamache's desk he found a little paper bag and inside it an éclair. A note, in large childish letters, said, 'From Agent Nichol.'

Nichol watched him open the bag.

'Agent Nichol, a word please.'

'Yes, sir.' The éclair had obviously worked. He couldn't possibly continue his unreasonable behavior.

Gamache pointed to a desk at the far end of the room, well away from the others.

'Thank you for the éclair. Did you make sure Maître Stickley held the latest will for Jane Neal?'

That was it? All that effort to go across to Sarah's boulangerie early and buy the pastry? For one line? And now he's cross-examining me again? Her mind raced. This was patently unfair, but she had to think fast. She knew the truth, but that would get her into trouble. What to say? Maybe she should mention the pastry again? But no, he was expecting an answer to his question.

'Yes sir, I did. He confirmed that Maître Stickley has the latest will.'

'And who was "he"?'

'He was the guy at the other end of the phone.'

Gamache's calm face changed. He leaned forward, stern and annoyed.

'Stop using that tone with me. You'll answer my questions thoroughly, respectfully and thoughtfully. And more than that . . .' His voice grew quiet, almost to a whisper. People who had heard this tone rarely forgot it. 'You will answer my questions truthfully.' He paused and stared into her defiant eyes. He was tired of this dysfunctional person. He'd done his best. Against good advice he'd kept her on but now she'd actually lied not once, but twice.

'Stop slouching in that chair like a petulant child. Sit up straight when you talk to me. Eyes on me.'

Nichol responded immediately.

'Who did you call to ask about the will, Agent?'

'I called headquarters in Montreal and told the person who answered to check it for me. He called back with this information. Was it wrong, sir? If it was it wasn't my fault. I believed him. I trusted him to do the job properly.'

Gamache was so amazed by her response he would have felt admiration if he hadn't been so repelled.

The truth was, she hadn't called anyone because she had had no idea whom to call. The least Gamache could have done was give her guidance. He was so big on bragging how he loved to take young people under his wing and then do fuck all for them. It was his own fault.

'Who at headquarters?'

'I don't know.'

Gamache was tired of this, it was a waste of time. She was a waste of time. But there was one more thing he might try. He could show her her future, if she wasn't careful. 'Come with me.'

Ruth Zardo's home was tiny and cramped, full of papers and magazines and work books, piled high. Books lined every wall, and camped on the footstools and coffee table and kitchen counter. They were stacked in the closet where she threw their coats.

'I just had the last cup of coffee and don't intend to make anymore.'

What a bitch, thought Nichol.

'We just have a few questions,' said Gamache.

'I'm not going to invite you to sit down, so you can hurry up.'

Nichol couldn't believe the discourtesy. Really, some people.

'Did Jane Neal know you'd told her parents about Andreas Selinsky?' Gamache asked, and a stillness settled on the home.

Ruth Zardo might have had a very good reason to want Jane Neal dead. Suppose Ruth thought if her ancient betrayal of Jane came to light her friendships in Three Pines would end. These people who loved her despite herself might suddenly see her for what she really was. They'd hate her if they knew of this horrible thing she'd done, then she'd be alone. An angry, bitter, lonely old lady. She couldn't risk it, there was too much at stake.

Gamache knew from years of investigating murders there was always a motive, and the motive often made absolutely no sense to anyone other than the murderer. But it made absolute sense to that person.

'Come in,' she said, motioning to the kitchen table. It was a garden table surrounded by four metal Canadian Tire garden chairs. Once seated she saw him looking around and volunteered, 'My husband died a few years ago. Since then I've been selling bits and pieces, mostly antiques from the family. Olivier handles them for me. It keeps my head above water, just.'

'Andreas Selinsky,' he reminded her.

'I heard you the first time. That was sixty years ago. Who cares now?'

'Timmer Hadley cared.'

'What do you know about that?'

'She knew what you'd done, she overheard you talking to Jane's parents.' As he spoke he studied Ruth's fortress face. 'Timmer kept your secret, and regretted it the rest of her life. But maybe Timmer told Jane, in the end. What do you think?'

'I think you make a lousy psychic. Timmer's dead, Jane's dead. Let the past lie.'

'Can you?

Who hurt you, once,
so far beyond repair
that you would greet each overture
with curling lip?'

Ruth snorted. 'You really think throwing my own poetry at me's going to do it? What'd you do, stay up all night cramming like a student for this interview? Hoping to reduce me to tears in the face of my own pain? Crap.'

'Actually, I know that whole poem by heart:

> *When were these seeds of anger sown,*
> *and on what ground*
> *that they should flourish so,*
> *watered by tears of rage, or grief?'*

'It was not always so,' Ruth and Gamache finished the stanza together.

'Yeah, yeah. Enough. I told Jane's parents because I thought she was making a mistake. She had potential and it'd be lost on that brute of a man. I did it for her sake. I tried to convince her; when that failed, I went behind her back. In retrospect it was a mistake, but only that. Not the end of the world.'

'Did Miss Neal know?'

'Not that I know of, and it wouldn't have mattered if she did. It was long ago, gone and buried.'

What a horrible, self-involved woman, thought Nichol, looking around for something to eat. Then Nichol awoke to a realisation. She had to pee.

'May I use your toilet?' She'd be damned if she'd say please to this woman.

'You can find it.'

Nichol opened every door on the main floor and found books, and magazines but no toilet. Then she climbed the stairs and found the only washroom in the home. After flushing she ran the water, pretending to wash her hands, and looked into the mirror. A young woman with a short-bob haircut looked back. As did some lettering, probably another God-damned poem. She leaned in closer and saw there was a sticker attached to the mirror. On it was written, 'You're looking at the problem.'

Nichol immediately began searching the area behind her, the area reflected in the mirror, because the problem was there.

'Did Timmer Hadley tell you she knew what you'd done?'

Ruth had wondered whether this question would ever be asked. She hoped not. But here it was.

'Yes. That day she died. And she told me what she thought. She was pretty blunt. I had a lot of respect for Timmer. Hard to hear a person you admire and respect say those things, even harder because Timmer was dying and there was no way to make up for it.'

'What did you do?'

'It was the afternoon of the parade and Timmer said she wanted to be alone. I'd started to explain but she was tired and said she needed to rest, and could I go to the parade and come back in an hour. We could talk then. By the time I got back, exactly an hour later, she was dead.'

'Did Mrs Hadley tell Jane Neal?'

'I don't know. I think perhaps she planned to, but felt she needed to say something to me first.'

'Did you tell Miss Neal?'

'Why would I? It was long ago. Jane had probably long forgotten.'

Gamache wondered how much of this was Ruth Zardo

285

trying to convince herself. It certainly didn't convince him.

'Do you have any idea who could have wanted Miss Neal dead?'

Ruth folded both hands on her cane, and carefully placed her chin on her hands. She looked past Gamache. Finally, after about a minute of silence, she spoke.

'I told you before I think one of those three boys who threw manure might have wanted her dead. She'd embarrassed them. I still think there's nothing like a brooding, adolescent mind for creating poison. But it often takes time. They say time heals. I think that's bullshit, I think time does nothing. It only heals if the person wants it to. I've seen time, in the hands of a sick person, make situations worse. They ruminate and brood and turn a minor event into a catastrophe, given enough time.'

'Do you think that's what might have happened here?' Ruth Zardo's thoughts so mirrored his own it was as though she'd read his mind. But did she realise this made her a perfect suspect?

'Could have.'

On their walk back across the village Nichol told Gamache about the sticker on Ruth's mirror and her own search, which had revealed shampoo, soap and a bath mat. Nichol was confirmed in her certainty Gamache was beyond it. All he did was laugh.

'Let's get started,' said Solonge Frenette, a few minutes later when Gamache, Beauvoir and Ruth had arrived. Clara and Peter were already seated. 'I called the Regie du

286

Notaries in Quebec City and they looked up the official registered wills. According to them, Miss Neal's last will and testament was made in this office on 28 May this year. Her previous will was ten years ago. It's been nullified.

'Her will is very simple. After covering burial expenses and any debts, credit card, taxes, et cetera, she leaves her home and its contents to Clara Morrow.'

Clara felt the blood race from her skin. She didn't want Jane's home. She wanted Jane's voice in her ears and her arms around her. And her laughter. She wanted Jane's company.

'Miss Neal asks Clara to have a party, invite certain people, the list is in the will, and ask each of those people to choose one item from the home. She leaves her car to Ruth Zardo and her book collection to Myrna. The rest she leaves to Clara Morrow.'

'How much?' asked Ruth, to Clara's relief. She wanted to know but didn't want to look greedy.

'I made some calls and did some calculations this morning. It's roughly a quarter of a million dollars, after tax.'

The air seemed to have been sucked from the room. Clara couldn't believe it. Rich. They'd be rich. Despite herself she saw a new car, and new bedlinens and a good dinner in a restaurant in Montreal. And . . .

'There are two more things; envelopes, actually. One is for you, Mrs Zardo.' Ruth took it and shot a glance at Gamache who'd been watching this entire process intently. 'The other is for Yolande Fontaine. Who'd like it?' No one spoke.

'I'll take it,' said Clara.

Outside the notary's office Chief Inspector Gamache approached Peter and Clara.

'I'd like your help at Miss Neal's home. Your home, now, I suppose.'

'I can't imagine ever thinking of it as anything other than Jane's home.'

'I hope that's not true,' said Gamache, smiling slightly at Clara.

'Of course we'll help,' said Peter. 'What can we do?'

'I'd like both of you to come into the home and just look.' He didn't want to say more.

It was, unexpectedly, the smells that got to Clara. That unmistakable aroma of Jane, the coffee and woodsmoke. The undercurrent of fresh baking and wet dog. And Floris, her one extravagance. Jane adored Floris eau de toilette, and ordered some from London every Christmas as her gift to herself.

Sûreté officers were crawling all over the home, taking fingerprints and samples and photographs. They made it very strange, and yet Clara knew that Jane was there too, in the spaces between the strangers. Gamache led Clara and Peter through the familiar kitchen and to the swinging door. The one they'd never been through. Part of Clara now wanted to turn around and go home. To never see what Jane had so deliberately kept from them all. To go through the door felt like a betrayal of Jane's trust, a violation, an admission that Jane was no longer there to stop them.

Oh, well, too bad. Her curiosity won out, as though there was never any doubt, and she strong-armed the swinging door and walked through. Straight into an acid flashback.

Clara's first reaction was to laugh. She stood stunned for a moment then started to laugh. And laugh. And laugh until she thought she'd piddle. Peter was soon infected and began laughing. And Gamache, who up until this moment had only seen a travesty, smiled, then chuckled, then laughed and within moments was laughing so hard he had to wipe away tears.

'Holy horrible taste, Batman,' said Clara to Peter who doubled over, laughing some more.

'Solid, man, solid,' he gasped and managed to raise a peace sign before having to put both hands on his knees to support his heaving body. 'You don't suppose Jane tuned in, turned on and dropped out?'

'I'd have to say the medium is the message.' Clara pointed to the demented Happy Faces and laughed until no sound came out. She held on to Peter, hugging him to stop herself slipping to the floor.

The room was not only sublimely ridiculous, it was also a relief. After a minute or two to compose themselves they all went upstairs. In the bedroom Clara picked up the well-worn book beside Jane's bed, C. S. Lewis's, *Surprised by Joy*. It smelled of Floris.

'I don't understand,' said Peter as they walked back down the stairs and sat in front of the fireplace. Clara couldn't help herself. Reaching out she touched the brilliant yellow Happy Face wallpaper. It was velvet. An involuntary guffaw burped out and she hoped she wouldn't erupt into laughter again. It really was too ridiculous.

'Why wouldn't Jane let us see this room?' asked Peter. 'I mean, it's not that bad.' They all stared at him in disbelief. 'Well, you know what I mean.'

'I know exactly what you mean,' agreed Gamache. 'That's my question too. If she wasn't ashamed of it, then she'd let people in. If she was, then why not just get rid of it? No, I think we're being distracted by all this, perhaps even intentionally.' He paused. Maybe that was the reason for the horrid wallpaper. It was a ruse, a red herring, put there deliberately to distract them from the one thing Jane didn't want them to see. Finally, he felt, he might have the answer to why she put up this gruesome paper.

'There's something else in this room. A piece of furniture, perhaps, the pottery, a book. It's here.'

The four of them split up and started searching the room again. Clara made for the Port Neuf, which Olivier had taught her about. The old clay mugs and bowls made in Quebec were one of the first industries back in the 1700s. Primitive images of cows and horses and pigs and flowers were sponged on to the rough earthenware. They were valuable collector's items and Olivier would certainly shriek. But there was no need to keep them hidden. Gamache had a small desk upside-down and was searching for hidden drawers, while Peter examined a large pine box closely. Clara opened the drawers of the armoire, which were stuffed with lace doilies and picture placemats. She took them out. They were reproductions of old paintings of Quebec village scenes and landscapes from the mid-1800s. She'd seen them before, on Jane's kitchen table during her dinners, but also elsewhere. They were very common. But maybe they weren't reproductions after all? Is it possible these were the originals? Or that they'd been altered to include some hidden code?

She found nothing.

'Over here, I think I have something.' Peter stood back from the pine box he'd been examining. It stood on sturdy little wooden legs and came to hip height. Wrought iron handles were attached to either side, and two small, square drawers pulled out from the front. From what Peter could see, not a single nail had been used on the honey pine piece, all the joints were dovetail. It was exquisite and very maddening. The main body of the box was accessible by lifting the top, only it wouldn't lift. Somehow, and for some reason, it had been locked. Peter yanked on the top again, but it wouldn't lift. Beauvoir shoved him aside and tried it himself, much to Peter's annoyance, as though there was more than one way to open a lid.

'Maybe there's a door on the front, like a trick or a puzzle,' suggested Clara, and they all searched. Nothing. Now they stood back and stared, Clara willing it to speak to her, like so many boxes seemed to recently.

'Olivier would know,' said Peter. 'If there's a trick to it, he'll know it.'

Gamache thought for a moment and nodded. They really had no choice. Beauvoir was dispatched and within ten minutes he returned with the antiques dealer.

'Where's the patient? Holy Mary, Mother of God.' He raised his eyebrows and stared at the walls, his lean, handsome face looking attractively boyish and quizzical. 'Who did this?'

'Ralph Lauren. Who do you think?' said Peter.

'Certainly no one gay. Is that the chest?' He walked over to where the others were standing. 'Beautiful. A tea chest, modeled on one the British used back in the 1600s, but this is Quebecois. Very simple yet far from primitive. You want to get in?'

'If you don't mind,' said Gamache and Clara marveled at his patience. She was about to slap Olivier. The antiques dealer walked around the box, knocked on it in a few places, holding his ear to the polished wood, then came to rest directly in front of it. Putting out his hands he grabbed the top and yanked. Gamache rolled his eyes.

'It's locked,' said Olivier.

'Well, we know that,' said Beauvoir. 'How do we unlock it?'

'You don't have a key?'

'If we had a key we wouldn't need you.'

'Good point. Look, the only way I know is to take the hinges off the back. That could take a while since they're old and corroded. I don't want to break them.'

'Please start,' said Gamache. 'The rest of us will continue our search.'

Twenty minutes later Olivier announced he had the last hinge off. 'It's fortunate for you I'm a genius.'

'What luck,' said Beauvoir, and showed a reluctant Olivier to the door. At the chest Gamache and Peter took hold of either side of the large pine top and lifted. It came up and all four of them peered in.

Nothing. The chest was empty.

They spent a few minutes making sure there were no secret drawers then the disheartened group flopped back into their seats around the fireplace. Slowly Gamache sat up. He turned to Beauvoir, 'What did Olivier ask? Who decorated this place?'

'So?'

'Well, how do we know it was Jane Neal?'

'You think she hired someone to do this?' asked Beauvoir, amazed. Gamache just stared at him. 'No, you're thinking someone else who stayed here did it. My God, what an idiot I am,' said Beauvoir. 'Yolande. When I interviewed her yesterday she said she'd been deco-rating here –'

'That's right,' said Clara, leaning forward in her seat, 'I saw her lugging in a step ladder and bags full of stuff from the Reno Depot in Cowansville. Peter and I talked about whether she planned to move in.' Peter nodded his agreement.

'So Yolande put up the wallpaper?' Gamache got up and looked at it again. 'Her home must be a real monstrosity if this is how she decorates.'

'Not even close,' said Beauvoir. 'Just the opposite. Her home is all off-whites and beiges and tasteful colors, like a Decormag model home.'

'No Happy Faces?' asked Gamache.

'Probably never.'

Gamache stood up and paced slowly, his head down, hands clasped behind his back. He took a couple of quick strides over to the Port Neuf pottery, speaking as he went, and was standing facing a wall like a naughty schoolboy. Then he turned to face them. 'Yolande. What does she do? What drives her?'

'Money?' suggested Peter after a moment's silence.

'Approval?' said Beauvoir, coming up beside Gamache, the chief's excitement transmitting itself to everyone in the room.

'Close, but it goes deeper. In herself.'

'Anger?' Peter tried again. He didn't like being wrong but he was again, he could tell by Gamache's reaction. After a moment's silence Clara spoke, thinking out loud, 'Yolande lives in a world of her own making. The Decormag perfect world, even though her husband's a criminal and her son's a thug and she lies and cheats and steals. And she's not a real blonde, in case you hadn't figured it out. She's not a real anything from what I can tell. She lives in denial –'

'That's it.' Gamache almost jumped up and down like a game-show host. 'Denial. She lives in denial. She covers things up. That's the reason for all her make-up. It's a mask. Her face is a mask, her home is a mask, a sad attempt to paint and paper over something very ugly.' He turned to face the wall then knelt down, his hand on a seam of wallpaper. 'People tend to be consistent. That's what's wrong here. Had you said', he turned to Beauvoir, 'that Yolande had this same wallpaper at home, that'd be one thing, but she doesn't. So why would she spend days putting this up?'

'To hide something,' said Clara, kneeling down beside him. His fingers had found a small corner of the wallpaper that was already peeling back.

'Exactly.' Carefully Gamache pulled back on the corner and it rolled off, exposing about a foot of wall, and more wallpaper underneath.

'Could she have put two layers on?' Clara asked, feeling herself deflating.

'I don't think she had time,' said Gamache. Clara leaned in closer.

'Peter, look at this.' He joined them on his knees and peered at the exposed wall. 'This isn't wallpaper,' he said, looking at Clara, stunned.

'I didn't think so,' said Clara.

'Well, what is it, for God's sake?' said Gamache.

'It's Jane's drawing,' said Clara. 'Jane drew this.'

Gamache looked again and could see it. The bright colors, the childish strokes. He couldn't tell what it was, not enough had been revealed, but it had indeed been put there by Miss Neal.

'Is it possible?' he asked Clara as the two stood and looked around the room.

'Is what possible?' asked Beauvoir. '*Voyons*, what are you talking about?'

'The wallpaper,' said Gamache. 'I was wrong. It wasn't meant to distract, it was meant to cover up. Where you see wallpaper, that's where she drew.'

'But it's everywhere,' protested Beauvoir. 'She couldn't—' He stopped, seeing the look on the chief's face. Maybe she did. Was it possible, he wondered, joining the others and turning around and around. All the walls? The ceiling? The floors even? He realised he'd far under-estimated *Les Anglais* and their potential for insanity.

'And upstairs?' he asked. Gamache caught his eye and it was as though the world paused for an instant. He nodded.

'*C'est incroyable*,' whispered the two men together. Clara was beyond speech, and Peter was already over at another seam across the room, tugging.

'There's more here,' he called, standing up.

'This was her shame,' said Gamache, and Clara knew the truth of it.

Within an hour Peter and Clara had spread tarpaulins and moved the furniture. Before leaving, Gamache gave his approval for them to remove the wallpaper and as much of the covering paint as possible. Clara called Ben and he readily volunteered. She was delighted. She would have called Myrna, who would definitely have been a far harder worker than Ben, but this was a job that called for delicacy and the touch of an artist, and Ben had that.

'Any idea how long this'll take?' asked Gamache.

'Honestly? Including the ceiling and the floors? Probably a year.'

Gamache frowned.

'It's important, isn't it?' said Clara, reading his expression.

'Could be. I don't know, but I think it is.'

'We'll go as fast as we dare. Don't want to ruin the images underneath. But I think we can get a lot of the stuff off, enough to see what's underneath.'

Fortunately Yolande, proving slapdash to the end, hadn't prepped the wall, so the paper was peeling off already. Nor had she used primer under the painted bits, to Peter and Clara's great relief. They started after lunch and continued with only a break for beer and chips mid-afternoon. In the evening Peter rigged up some floodlights and they continued, except Ben who felt maybe his elbow was acting up.

At about seven a tired and bedraggled Peter and Clara decided to break for food and joined Ben by the fireplace. He'd at least managed to lay it and light it, and now they found him, his feet on the hassock, sipping red wine and reading Jane's latest copy of *The Guardian Weekly*. Gabri arrived with Szechwan take-out. He'd heard rumors of the activity and wanted desperately to see for himself. He'd even rehearsed.

The huge man, made even more enormous by his coat and scarves, swept into the room. Stopping dead in the center, and making sure he held his audience, he looked around and declared, 'Either that wallpaper goes, or I do.'

His appreciative audience roared their approval, took the food and kicked him out feeling that Jane and Oscar Wilde made one dead person too many in the room.

They worked into the night, and finally gave it up around midnight, too tired to trust themselves anymore and both slightly nauseous from inhaling paint remover. Ben had long since gone home.

The next morning, in the light of day, they saw they'd done about four square feet upstairs and a quarter of one wall downstairs. It looked as though Gamache had been right. Jane had covered every inch of her home. And Yolande had covered that. By midday a little more had been uncovered. Clara stood back to admire the few feet of wallpaper she'd stripped and Jane's work underneath. Enough was emerging now to make it quite exciting. There seemed to be a pattern and purpose to Jane's work. But what that purpose might be wasn't clear, yet.

'For God's sake, Ben, is that all you've done?' A disheartened Clara couldn't help herself. Upstairs Peter had managed to get a couple of feet done, but Ben had hardly done anything, though, granted, what he had done was brilliant. Crystal clear and beautiful. But not enough. If they were going to solve the murder they needed to uncover all the walls. Quickly. Clara could feel her anxiety rising and knew she was becoming obsessed.

'I'm sorry,' they both said at once then Ben stood up and looked down at her, hang-dog. 'I'm sorry, Clara. I'm slow, I know, but I'll get better. Practice.'

'Never mind.' She put her arm around his slim waist. 'It's Miller time. We can get back to work soon enough.' Ben perked up and put his arm around her shoulder. The two of them walked by Peter, leaving him to watch their retreating backs and walk down the stairs alone.

By that night a fair amount of the living-room walls had been exposed. They called Gamache, who brought beer and pizza and Beauvoir.

'The answer's here,' said Gamache, simply, reaching for another beer. They ate in front of the fireplace in the living room, the aroma of three extra large 'All Dressed' from Pizza Pizza just masking the mineral spirits they'd used to remove the paint. 'In this room, with this art. The answer's here, I can feel it. It's too much of a coincidence that Jane would invite you all here on the same night her art's being shown, then be murdered within hours of telling everyone this.'

'We have something to show you,' said Clara, brushing off her jeans and standing up. 'We've uncovered more of the walls. Shall we start upstairs?'

Grabbing pieces of pizza they trooped upstairs. In Peter's room the lighting was too dark to really appreciate what Jane had done, but Ben's work was different. Though tiny, the area he'd uncovered was astonishing. Brilliant, bold strokes leapt from the walls as people and animals came alive. And, in some cases, people as animals.

'Is that Nellie and Wayne?' Gamache was looking at a patch of wall. There, clear as day, was a stick-figure woman leading a cow. It was a very thick stick, and a skinny, happy cow, with a beard.

'Wonderful,' Gamache murmured.

They went back into the darkness downstairs. Peter had turned off the industrial floodlights he'd hooked up earlier in the day to allow them to work. Through dinner they'd eaten by firelight and the warm glow of a couple of table lamps. The walls had been in darkness. Now Peter went to the switch and flooded the room with light.

Gamache screwed his eyes tight shut. After a few moments he opened them.

It was like being in a cave, one of those wondrous caves explorers sometimes found filled with ancient symbols and depictions. Running caribou and swimming people.

Gamache had read all about them in *National Geographic*, now he felt as though he'd been magically transported into one, here in the heart of Quebec, in a settled and even staid old village. As with cave drawings, Gamache knew the history of Three Pines and its people was depicted here. Slowly, hands clasped behind his back, Gamache walked around the walls. They were covered floor to ceiling with village scenes and rural scenes and classrooms and children and animals and adults singing and playing and working. A few of the scenes were of accidents, and there was at least one funeral.

He no longer felt he'd walked into a cave. Now he felt surrounded by life. He took a couple of steps back and could feel tears stinging his eyes. He screwed them shut again, hoping they'd think him bothered by the strong light. And in a way he was. He was overwhelmed by emotion. Sadness and melancholia. And delight. Joy. He was lifted right out of himself. It transcended the literal. This was Jane's long house. Her home had become her long house, where every one, every event, every thing, every emotion was present. And Gamache knew then the murderer was there as well. Somewhere on those walls.

The next day Clara took the envelope to Yolande at home. Ringing the gleaming faux-brass bell and hearing the Beethoven chimes, Clara steeled herself. Just this one thing for Jane, just this one thing for Jane.

'Bitch,' a furious Yolande screamed. There followed a stream of insults and accusations, ending with a promise to sue Clara for everything she had.

Just this one thing for Jane, just this one thing for Jane.

'You're a goddamned thief, *tête carrée*. That home belongs to me. To my family. How can you sleep at night, you bitch?'

Just this one thing.

Clara held up the envelope until it caught Yolande's attention, and like a child presented with something shiny and new, Yolande stopped screaming and stared, mesmerised by the slim white paper.

'Is that for me? Is that mine? That's Aunt Jane's writing, isn't it?'

'I have a question for you.' Clara waved it back and forth.

'Give it to me.' Yolande lunged, but Clara flicked it out of her reach.

'Why did you cover up her drawings?'

'So you found them,' Yolande spat. 'Filthy, insane things. Everyone thought she was so wonderful but her family knew she was nuts. My grandparents knew she was crazy since she was a teenager and doing those hideous drawings. They were ashamed of her. All her art looked retarded. My mother said she actually wanted to study art but my grandparents put an end to that. Told her the truth. Told her it wasn't art. It was an embarrassment. They told her never to ever show anyone her scrawls. We told her the truth. It was our duty. We didn't want her to get hurt, did we? It was for her own good. And what did we get for it? Thrown out of the family home. She actually had the nerve to say I'd be allowed back the moment I apologised. The only thing I was sorry about, I told her, was that she ruined our home. Crazy old lady.'

Clara saw again Jane sitting in the Bistro, crying. Tears of joy that someone, finally, accepted her art. And Clara knew then what it had taken for Jane to expose one of her works.

'She fooled you, didn't she? You didn't know your friend was a freak. Well, now you know what we've had to put up with.'

'You have no idea, have you? No idea what you've thrown away? You're a stupid, stupid woman, Yolande.' Clara's mind went blank, as it always did in confront-ations. She was vibrating and on the verge of losing it completely. She paid for her outburst by being forced to listen to a string of accusations and threats. Oddly enough, Yolande's rage was so deeply unattractive Clara could feel her own anger ease.

'Why that particular wallpaper?' she asked into Yolande's purple face.

'Hideous, wasn't it? It seemed fitting to cover one monstrosity with another. Besides, it was cheap.'

The door slammed. Clara realised she was still holding the envelope so she slipped it under the door. Done. Just this one thing for Jane. And it wasn't so hard, after all, standing up to Yolande. All those years she'd stood silent in the face of Yolande's sly and sometimes outright attacks, and now to find it's possible to speak out. Clara wondered whether Jane knew this would happen when she addressed the envelope. Knew Clara would be the one to deliver it. Knew Yolande would react the way she always did to

Clara. And knew she'd given Clara one last chance to stand up for herself.

As she walked away from the perfect, silent house, Clara thanked Jane.

Yolande saw the envelope appear. Tearing it open she found a single playing card. The Queen of Hearts. The same one Aunt Jane had put out on the kitchen table at night when tiny Yolande had visited her and Aunt Jane had promised that in the morning that card would be different. It would have changed.

She peered into the envelope again. Surely there was something else? Some inheritance from her aunt? A cheque? A key to a safety deposit box? But the envelope was empty. Yolande examined the card, trying to remember whether it was the same one from her childhood. Were the markings on the Queen's robes the same? Did her face have one eye or two? No, Yolande concluded. This wasn't the same card. Someone had switched them. She'd been cheated again. As she made for the bucket to clean off the front stoop where Clara had stood, she threw the Queen of Hearts on the fire.

Worthless.

TWELVE

~

'Yolande Fontaine and her husband André Malenfant,' Beauvoir said as he wrote their names in tidy capitals on the sheet of paper. It was 8.15 on Tuesday morning, almost a week and a half since the murder, and the investigators were reviewing the list of suspects. The first two were obvious.

'Who else?'

'Peter and Clara Morrow,' said Nichol, looking up from her doodling.

'Motive?' he asked, writing the names.

'Money,' said Lacoste. 'They have very little. Or had. Now they're rich, of course, but before Miss Neal died they were practically paupers. Clara Morrow comes from a modest background, so she's used to being careful with money, but not him. He's a Golden Mile boy, born and bred. A Montreal Brahmin. Best schools, St Andrew's Ball. I spoke to one of his sisters in Montreal. She was circumspect, as only these people can be, but she made it quite clear the family wasn't thrilled with his choice of career. Blamed Clara for it. They wanted him to go into business. The family considers him a disappointment, at least his mother does. Too bad, really, because by Canadian art standards he's a star. Sold ten thousand dollars' worth of art last year, but that's still below the poverty level. Clara sold about a thousand dollars. They live frugally. Their car needs major repair work as does their home. She teaches art in the winter to pay the bills, and they sometimes pick up contracts to restore art. They scrape by.'

'His mother's still alive?' Gamache asked, trying to do some quick calculations.

'Ninety-two,' said Lacoste. 'Pickled, by all accounts, but breathing. An old tartar. Probably outlive them all. Family lore has it she found her husband next to her one morning, dead, and she rolled over and went back to sleep. Why be inconvenienced?'

'We only have Mrs Morrow's word for it that they didn't know what was in the will,' said Beauvoir. 'Miss Neal might have told them they'd inherit, *n'est-ce pas?*'

'If they needed money, wouldn't they have gone to Miss Neal for a loan instead of murdering her?' Gamache asked.

'Maybe they did,' said Beauvoir. 'And she said no. And, they had the best chance of luring her to the woods. If either Clara or Peter had called her at 6.30 in the morning and asked to see her without the dog, she'd have gone. No questions asked.'

Gamache had to agree.

'And', Beauvoir was on a roll, 'Peter Morrow's an accomplished archer. His specialty is the old wooden recurve. He says he only target shoots, but who knows? Besides, as you found out, it's easy enough to replace the snub-nosed tip with the killer tip. He could have gotten them from the clubhouse, killed her, cleaned the equipment and returned it. And even if we found his prints or fibers, it'd mean nothing. He used the equipment all the time anyway.'

'He was on the jury that chose her art work,' Lacoste was warming to the possibility, 'suppose he was jealous of her, saw her potential and, I don't know, flipped out or something.' She sputtered to a stop. None of them could see Peter Morrow 'flipping out'. But Gamache knew the human psyche was complex. Sometimes people reacted to things without knowing why. And often that reaction was violent, physically or emotionally. It was just possible Peter Morrow, having struggled with his art and his family's approval all his life, saw brilliance in Jane Neal's work and couldn't take it. Was consumed with jealousy. It was possible, not probable, but just possible.

'Who else?' asked Gamache.

'Ben Hadley,' said Lacoste. 'He's also a good archer, with access to the weapons. And trusted by Miss Neal.'

'But without a motive,' said Gamache.

'Well, not money, anyway,' admitted Lacoste. 'He's worth millions. All inherited from his mother. Before that he was on a generous allowance.'

Nichol snorted. She hated these 'trust fund' kids who

did nothing with their lives except wait for Mommy and Daddy to die.

Beauvoir chose to ignore the snort. 'Could he have had another motive besides money? Lacoste, anything in the papers you found in Jane Neal's home?'

'Nothing.'

'No diary?'

'Except the diary where she made a list of people who wanted to kill her.'

'Well, you might have mentioned it.' Beauvoir smiled.

Gamache looked at the list of suspects. Yolande and André, Peter and Clara and Ben Hadley.

'Anyone else?' Beauvoir was closing his notebook.

'Ruth Zardo,' said Gamache. He explained his thinking.

'So her motive,' said Lacoste, 'would be to stop Jane from telling everyone what she'd done. Wouldn't it've been easier to just kill Timmer to shut her up?'

'Actually, yes, and that's been bothering me. We don't know that Ruth Zardo didn't kill Timmer Hadley.'

'And Jane found out about it?' asked Lacoste.

'Or suspected. She was the type, I think, who would've gone directly to Ruth and asked her about her suspicions. She probably thought it was a mercy killing, one friend relieving another of pain.'

'But Ruth Zardo couldn't have actually fired the arrow,' said Beauvoir.

'True. But she might have enlisted the aid of someone who could, and would do anything. For a fee.'

'Malenfant,' said Beauvoir with a certain glum glee.

*

Clara sat in her studio with her morning coffee, staring at the box. It was still there, only now it stood on four legs, made of tree branches. Initially she'd seen it on a single leg, like the trunk of a tree. Like the blind. That's the image that had come to her in the woods during the ritual, when she'd looked over and seen the blind. It was such a perfect and appropriate image. Of being blind. Of the people who use the blind not seeing the cruelty of what they did, not seeing the beauty of what they were about to kill. It was, after all, a perfect word for that perch. A blind. And it was how Clara felt these days. Jane's killer was among them, that much was obvious. But who? What wasn't she seeing?

But the single tree trunk idea hadn't worked. The box had looked unbalanced, off-putting. So she'd added the other legs and what had been a perch, a blind, now looked like a home on great long stilts. But it still wasn't right. Closer. But there was something she needed to see. As always when faced with this problem Clara tried to clear her mind, and let the work come to her.

Beauvoir and Agent Lacoste were in the process of searching the Malenfant home. Lacoste had been prepared for filth, for a stench so thick she could see it. She hadn't been prepared for this. She stood in Bernard's bedroom and felt ill. It was perfect, not a dirty sock, not a plate of congealing food. Her kids were under five and their rooms already looked, and smelled, like the beach at low tide. This kid was, what? Fourteen? And his room smelled of Lemon Pledge. Lacoste felt like retching. As she put on her gloves and began her search she wondered if there wasn't a coffin in the basement which he slept in.

Ten minutes later she found something, though not what she'd expected. She walked out of Bernard's room and into the living room, making sure to catch the boy's eye. Rolling up the document she discreetly put it in her evidence bag. Not so discreetly, though, that Bernard didn't see. It was the first time she'd seen fear on his face.

'Well, look what I found.' Beauvoir came out of the other bedroom holding up a large manila folder. 'Oddly enough,' he said into Yolande's lemon-sucked face and André's lean leer, 'it was taped to the back of a picture, in your bedroom.'

Beauvoir opened the folder and flipped through the contents. They were rough sketches, Jane Neal's rough sketches of the county fair all the way back to 1943.

'Why did you take these?'

'Take? Who said anything about take? Aunt Jane gave them to us,' said Yolande in her most convincing, 'the roof is nearly new' real estate agent's voice.

Beauvoir wasn't buying. 'And you taped it behind that print of a lighthouse?'

'She told us to keep them out of the light,' said Yolande in her 'the plumbing isn't lead' voice.

'Why not just wallpaper over them?' André actually gave a snort of laughter before being silenced by Yolande. 'All right, take them in,' said Beauvoir. It was getting close to lunch and he longed for a beer and a sandwich.

'And the boy?' asked Lacoste, picking up the cue. 'He's a minor. Can't stay here without parents.'

'Call Children's Aid.'

'No.' Yolande grabbed Bernard and tried to put her arms around him. They wouldn't go. Bernard himself didn't seem all that upset at the thought of a foster home. André looked as though he thought this might be a good idea. Yolande was apoplectic.

'Or', said Beauvoir in his best, 'you'd better make an offer before the owners change their minds' voice, 'you can tell us the truth right now.' He held up the folder. Part of him felt badly about using Bernard but he figured he'd get over it.

The beans spilled. She'd found the folder sitting on the coffee table in Aunt Jane's home. In full view. Yolande described this as though she'd found an S and M magazine. She was about to toss it on the fire but she decided, out of respect and love for dear Aunt Jane, to keep the pictures.

'Why did you take them?' Beauvoir repeated, walking toward the door.

'OK, OK. I thought maybe they'd be worth something.'

'I thought you hated your aunt's work.'

'Not as art, you great shit,' said André. 'I thought I could sell them to her friends, maybe Ben Hadley.'

'Why would he buy them?'

'Well, he has lots of money and maybe if I threatened to burn them he'd want to save them.'

'But why take them out of the house? Why not keep the sketches there?'

'Because they disgust me.' Yolande was transformed. All the make-up in the world, and she was pretty close to wearing it all, couldn't hide the hideous person underneath. In an instant she became a bitter middle-aged woman, twisted and made grotesque like a metalwork sculpture. All rust and sharp edges. Even Bernard edged away from her. 'I needed them where I knew no one else would see them.'

On a slip of paper Beauvoir wrote a receipt for the folder and gave it to Yolande who took it in her manicured hand as though he'd passed her a sheet of toilet paper.

Clara had given up waiting for her tree house to speak and had gone to Jane's to do more work. She'd begun to see Jane's work as a masterpiece. One giant mural, like the Sistine Chapel or Da Vinci's *Last Supper*. She didn't hesitate to make the comparisons. Jane had captured the same elements as those master works. Awe. Creation. Wonderment. Longing. Even logging, in Jane's case.

Ben couldn't be moving more slowly if he tried. Still, Clara had to remind herself that it didn't really matter. It would all be revealed, eventually.

'Oh, my God, it's a disaster,' Ruth's voice rang loud and clear. Clara came up from the basement with her bucket. Ruth and Gamache were standing in the center of the living room and Clara was a little disheartened to see Ben also there, lounging by the desk.

'Did you do this?' Ruth wanted to know.

'I helped uncover it. Jane did the drawings.'

311

'I never thought I'd say it, but I'm on Yolande's side. Cover them up.'

'I want to show you something.' Clara took Ruth's elbow and guided her to the far wall. 'Look at that.' Unmistakable, there was a picture of Ruth as a child, holding her mother's hand in the schoolhouse. Little Ruth, tall and gawky, school books for feet. Encyclopedia feet. Piglets dancing in her hair. Which could mean one of two things.

'I had pigtails as a child,' said Ruth, apparently reading her thoughts. But Clara thought Jane's message was that even then Ruth was pig-headed. The other children were laughing but one child was coming over to hug her. Ruth stood, transfixed, in front of Jane's wall:

> *'Jenny kissed me when we met,*
> *jumping from the chair she sat in;*
> *time, you thief, who love to get*
> *sweets into your list, put that in:*
> *say I'm weary, say I'm sad,*
> *say that health and wealth have missed me;*
> *say I'm growing old, but add,*
> *Jenny kissed me.'*

Ruth recited the poem in a whisper, and the still room heard. 'Leigh Hunt. "Rondeau". That's the only poem I wish I'd written. I didn't think Jane remembered, I didn't think it'd meant anything to her. This is my first day here, when my father came to work in the mill. I was eight years old, the new kid, tall and ugly, as you can see, and not very nice even then. But when I walked into that schoolhouse, terrified, Jane walked all the way down the aisle and she kissed me. She didn't even know me but it didn't matter to her. Jane kissed me when we met.'

Ruth, her brittle-blue eyes glistening, took a breath and then took a long look around the room. Then slowly shook her head and whispered, 'It's extraordinary. Oh, Jane, I'm so sorry.'

'Sorry for what?' Gamache asked.

'Sorry she didn't know we loved her enough to be trusted with this. Sorry she felt she had to hide it from us.' Ruth gave a hurrumph of unamused laughter. 'I thought I was the only one with a wound. What a fool.'

'I think the key to Jane's murder is here,' said Gamache, watching the elderly woman limp around the room. 'I think she was killed because she was about to let everyone see it. I don't know why but there you have it. You knew her all her life, I want you to tell me what you see here. What strikes you, what patterns you see, what you don't see –'

'Most of the upstairs, for starters,' said Clara, and watched Ben flinch.

'Well, spend as much time as you can here.'

'I don't know,' said Ruth. 'I'm supposed to address the United Nations and Clara, aren't you accepting the Nobel prize?'

'That's right, for art.'

'I canceled both engagements,' said Gamache, thinking little Ruthie Zardo was a bad influence on Clara. They smiled and nodded. Ben and Clara went back upstairs

313

while Ruth inched along the walls, examining the images, occasionally hooting when one struck her as particularly apt. Gamache sat in the big leather chair by the fire and let the room come to him.

Suzanne picked Matthew up late in the day at his sister's in Cowansville where he'd stayed until the Provincial Guardians Office had finished its investigation. Even though Philippe had recanted his accusation of abuse, the Office was obligated to investigate. It found nothing. In his heart Matthew was disappointed. Not, of course, at being exonerated. But so much damage had been done he wished they'd made a public statement that he was, in reality, a wonderful father. A kind, compassionate, firm parent. A loving father.

He'd long since forgiven Philippe, he didn't even need to know why Philippe had done it. But standing now in the kitchen that had held so many birthday parties, and excited Christmas mornings, and had been the scene of so many batches of 's'mores' and 'yes yes' cookies, standing here, he knew life would never be the same. Too much had been said and done. He also knew, with work, it could actually be better. The question was, was Philippe willing to put the work in? A week and a half ago, in anger, he'd waited for his son to come to him. That had been a mistake. Now he was going to his son.

'Yeah?' came the sullen answer to his tentative knock.

'May I come in? I'd like to talk with you. No yelling. Just clear the air, OK?'

'Whatever.'

'Philippe.' Matthew sat on the chair by the desk and turned to face the boy, who was lying on his crumpled bed. 'I've done something that's hurt you. My problem is I don't know what it is. I've racked my brains. Is it the basement? Are you angry about having to clean up the basement?'

'No.'

'Did I yell at you, or say something to hurt your feelings? If I did please tell me. I won't be angry. I just need to know and then we can talk about it.'

'No.'

'Philippe, I'm not angry about what you did. I never have been. I was hurt and confused. But not angry at you. I love you. Can you talk to me? Whatever it is, you can tell me.'

Matthew looked at his son and for the first time in almost a year he saw his sensitive, thoughtful, kind boy. Philippe looked at his father and longed to tell him. And he almost did. Almost. He stood at the cliff, his toes over the edge, and he looked into oblivion. His father was inviting him to step over and trust that it would be all right. He would catch him, wouldn't let him fall. And to give Philippe credit, he considered it. Philippe yearned to close his eyes, take that step and fall into his father's arms.

But in the end he couldn't. Instead he turned his face to the wall, put his headphones back on, and retreated.

Matthew dropped his head and looked down at his dirty old work boots and saw in excruciating detail the mud and bits of leaves stuck there.

*

Gamache was sitting in Olivier's Bistro, by the fireplace, waiting to be served. He'd just arrived, and the people who'd been in the choice location had just left, their tip still on the table. Gamache had the momentary desire to pocket the money himself. Another bit of weirdness from the long house.

'Hi, may I join you?'

Gamache rose and bowed slightly to Myrna, then indicated the sofa facing the fireplace. 'Please.'

'Quite a lot of excitement,' said Myrna. 'I hear Jane's home is wonderful.'

'You haven't seen it?'

'No. I wanted to wait until Thursday.'

'Thursday? What's happening Thursday?'

'Clara hasn't asked you?'

'Are my feelings going to be hurt? Sûreté homicide officers are notoriously sensitive. What's happening on Thursday?'

'Thursday? Are you going too?' Gabri asked, standing over them wearing a little apron and channeling Julia Child.

'Not yet.'

'Oh well, never mind. I hear Hurricane Kyla's hit land in Florida. Saw it on Météo Media.'

'I saw that, too,' said Myrna. 'When's it supposed to get here?'

'Oh, a few days. 'Course it'll be a tropical storm by then, or whatever they call it by the time it hits Quebec. Should be quite a storm.' He looked out the window as though he expected to see it looming over the nearby mountain. He looked worried. Storms were never good.

Gamache toyed with the price tag dangling from the coffee table.

'Olivier's put price tags everywhere,' confided Gabri, 'including our private toilet, thank you very much. Fortunately I have enough elegance and good taste to overcome this one flaw of Olivier's. Greed, I think it's called. Now, can I interest you in a glass of wine, or perhaps a chandelier?'

Myrna ordered a red wine while Gamache took a Scotch.

'Clara's organising Jane's party for Thursday, just the way Jane had planned,' said Myrna, once the drinks had arrived. A couple of licorice pipes also appeared. 'After the *vernissage* at Arts Williamsburg. Now, if Clara asks, you have to say you tortured me.'

'Trying to get me suspended again? The Sûreté torturing a black woman?'

'Don't they promote you for that?'

Gamache caught and held Myrna's eye. Neither smiled. They both knew the truth in that. He wondered whether Myrna knew his particular role in the Arnot case, and the price he'd paid. He thought not. The Sûreté was good at finding other people's secrets, and keeping its own.

'Wow,' said Clara, taking the big chair on the other side of the fireplace. 'This feels good. Nice to be out of the stink of the mineral spirits. I'm on my way home to make supper.'

'Isn't this a little out of your way?' asked Myrna.

'We artistic types never take a straight line, unless you're Peter. He starts at A and paints and paints and ends up

317

at B. Without even a hesitation. Enough to drive you to drink.' She flagged down Gabri and ordered a beer and some nuts.

'How's the restoration?' asked Gamache.

'Fine, I think. I left Ben and Ruth there. Ruth has found Jane's liquor cabinet and is writing verse while staring at the walls. God knows what Ben's doing. Probably applying paint. I swear to God he seems to be going backwards. Still, it's great to have him there and actually the work he does do is fantastic, brilliant.'

'Peter isn't helping anymore?' asked Myrna.

'Oh yes, but we're taking turns now. Well, mostly he's taking turns. I spend most of the day there. It's kind of addictive. Peter loves the work, don't get me wrong, but he needs to do his own work.'

Gabri appeared with her beer. 'That'll be a hundred thousand dollars.'

'Well, you can kiss your tip goodbye.'

'If I could kiss my tip I wouldn't need Olivier.'

'We were talking about Thursday,' said Gamache. 'I hear there's a party.'

'Do you mind? I'd like to hold it just as Jane had planned.'

'Hope the Hurricane doesn't ruin it,' said Gabri, pleased to find melodrama.

Gamache wished he'd thought of it. Clara was doing it as a tribute to her friend, he knew, but it could have another very practical purpose. It could rattle the murderer.

'As long as I'm invited.'

*

Isabelle Lacoste looked up from her computer where she'd been writing her reports on the Fontaine/Malenfant search and her visit to Timmer's doctor. He'd brought up Timmer's file on his computer and finally, with extreme caution, admitted it was a remote possibility someone had helped her into the next life.

'With morphine; that would be the only way. Wouldn't really take much at that stage, she was already on it, just a little more could have put her over the top.'

'You didn't check?'

'Saw no need.' Then he'd hesitated again. Lacoste was a good enough investigator to wait. And wait. Eventually he spoke again. 'It happens a lot in cases like this. A friend, or more often a family member, gives the person a fatal dose. Mercy. Happens more often than we know or want to know. There's a kind of unwritten agreement that in terminal cases, at the end of life, we don't look too closely.'

Lacoste could certainly sympathise and privately thought this was probably a good thing, but this was business, and in this case they weren't talking about mercy.

'Is there any way to check now?'

'She was cremated. Her own wishes.' He closed his computer.

And now, two hours later, she was closing hers. It was 6.30 and pitch black outside. She needed to speak with Gamache about what she'd found in Bernard's room before heading home. It was a cold night and Lacoste buttoned her field coat before setting out across the bridge that spanned the Rivière Bella Bella and headed into the heart of Three Pines.

'Give it to me.'

'*Bonjour*, Bernard.' She'd recognised the surly voice even before she saw him.

'Gimme.' Bernard Malenfant was leaning against her.

'Do you want to tell me about it?'

'Fuck off. Give it here.' He brought his fist to her face, but didn't strike.

Isabelle Lacoste had faced down serial killers, snipers, and abusive, drunken husbands, and she was under no illusion. A furious, out-of-control fourteen-year-old was as dangerous as any of them.

'Drop that fist. I'm not going to give it to you, so it's no use threatening.'

Bernard grabbed her satchel, trying to yank it away but she'd expected this. She'd found that most boys, and even some not very bright men, underestimated women. She was strong and determined and smart. She kept her cool and twisted the satchel out of his grip.

'Bitch. It's not even mine. Do you really think I'd have shit like that?' The last word was screamed into her face so she could feel his spittle on her chin and the stench of his warm breath.

'Then whose is it?' she said evenly, trying to control her gag response.

Bernard gave her a malevolent leer. 'Are you kidding? I'm not going to tell.'

'Hey, are you all right?' A woman and her dog were walking quickly toward them from the direction of the bridge.

320

Bernard swung around and saw them. He yanked up his bike and rode away, swerving so that he headed toward the dog, but just missed it.

'Are you all right?' the woman repeated, and reached out and touched Isabelle's arm. Lacoste recognised the woman as Hanna Parra. 'Was that young Malenfant?'

'Yes. We had a few words. I'm fine, but thanks for checking.' And she meant it. This wouldn't have happened in Montreal.

'Anytime.' They walked over the Bella Bella into Three Pines, separating at the Bistro and waving goodbye.

The first thing Lacoste did upon reaching the cheerful lights and warmth of the Bistro was head to the washroom, to scrub her face with the fragrant soap and fresh water. Once clean she ordered a Martini and Rossi and caught the chief's eye. He nodded toward a small, secluded table. The Martini and Rossi, a bowl of nuts and her chief in front of her, Lacoste relaxed. She then told him about her search of Bernard's room, handing him the item she'd taken as she spoke.

'Phew,' said Gamache, examining the item. 'Get this fingerprinted. Bernard denies it's his? Did he say whose it was?'

Lacoste shook her head.

'Did you believe it's not his?'

'I don't know. I think I don't want to believe him, but some instinct tells me he's telling the truth.'

Only with Gamache could she talk about feelings, intuition and instinct without feeling defensive. He nodded and offered her dinner before she headed back to Montreal, but she declined. She wanted to see her family before they went to bed

Gamache awoke to a pounding on his door. His bedside clock said 2.47. Putting on his dressing gown he opened the door. Yvette Nichol stood there in an impossibly fluffy pink and white number.

She'd been lying awake, tossing and turning, and finally just curling on her side, staring at the wall. How had it come to this? She was in trouble. Something had gone wrong. Something always went wrong, it seemed. But how? She'd tried so hard.

Now, in the tiny new day the familiar old voice spoke to her, It's because you're Uncle Saul, after all. Stupid Uncle Saul. They were counting on you, your family, and you've fucked up again. Shame on you.

Nichol felt the lump in her chest harden and she turned over. Looking out the window she saw a light go on across the village green. She leapt out of bed, threw on a dressing gown, and ran up the stairs to Gamache's room.

'There's a light on,' she said without preamble.

'Where?'

'Across the way, at Jane Neal's home. It went on a few minutes ago.'

'Get Inspector Beauvoir. Have him meet me downstairs.'

'Yes, sir.' And she left. Five minutes later he met a disheveled Beauvoir on the stairs. As they were leaving they heard a noise and saw Nichol descending.

'Stay here,' commanded Gamache.

'No, sir. It's my light.' She might have said, 'purple

door candlestick', for all the sense that made to Gamache or Beauvoir.

'Stay here. That's an order. If you hear shots, call for help.'

As the two men walked briskly across the green toward Jane Neal's home, Gamache thought to ask, 'Did you bring your gun?'

'No. Did you?'

'No. But you've got to know Nichol had her's. Oh, well.'

They could see two lights in the home, one upstairs and another in the living room. Gamache and Beauvoir had done this hundreds of times before, they knew their routine. Gamache was always the first through, Beauvoir on his heels, ready to throw the chief out of any line of fire.

Gamache entered the dark mudroom silently and crept up the two steps into the kitchen. He tiptoed to the living-room door and listened. He could hear voices. A man's and a woman's. Unrecognisable, and unintelligible. He signaled to Beauvoir, took a breath, and shoved the door open.

Ben and Clara stood stunned in the middle of the room. Gamache felt as though he'd stumbled into a Noël Coward drawing-room comedy, all Ben needed was an ascot tied around his neck and a Martini glass. Clara, though, belonged more in a circus. She was wearing a bright red single-piece flannel outfit, complete with feet, and probably a hatch at the back.

'We surrender,' said Clara.

'So do we,' said Beauvoir, looking at her outfit, amazed. You'd never find a francophone woman in that.

'What're you doing here?' Gamache went right to the point. It was 3 a.m. and he'd just geared himself up for some unpleasantness. He wanted to go back to bed.

'That's what I was asking Ben. I haven't been sleeping so well since Jane died, so I got up to use the bathroom and saw the light. I came over to see.'

'By yourself?'

'Well, I didn't want to disturb Peter, and besides, this is Jane's home,' she said, as though that explained it. Gamache thought he understood. Clara considered it a safe place. He'd have to have a talk with her.

'Mr Hadley, what are you doing here?'

Ben was looking very embarrassed by now. 'I set my alarm to come here. I wanted to, well, sort of go upstairs, you know.'

This was so deeply uninformative and uninteresting Beauvoir thought he might actually fall asleep on his feet.

'Go on,' said Gamache.

'Well, to do more work. On the walls. You'd said yesterday how important it was to see everything, and well. Then there's Clara, of course.'

'Go on,' said Gamache. In his peripheral vision he could see Beauvoir swaying.

'You tried to hide it, but I could tell you were getting impatient with me,' Ben said to Clara. 'I'm not a very fast worker. I'm not a very fast person, I guess. Anyway, I wanted to surprise you by doing some work tonight. It was probably a dumb idea.'

'I think it's a beautiful idea,' said Clara, going over and giving Ben a hug. 'But you'll just exhaust yourself, you know, and be slow again tomorrow.'

'I hadn't thought of that,' admitted Ben. 'Do you mind, though, if I just put in a couple of hours?'

'That's fine with me,' said Gamache. 'But next time, please tell us.'

'Should I stay and help?' Clara offered. Ben hesitated and seemed on the verge of saying something, but simply shook his head. As he left Gamache looked back at Ben standing alone in the living room. He looked like a little lost boy.

THIRTEEN

—~—

I t was Thursday evening and Arts Williamsburg was
enjoying a record turnout for a *vernissage*. The tail of
Hurricane Kyla was forecast to hit later that night and
the expectation added a frisson to the event, as though
going to the opening meant taking your life in your
hands and reflected both character and courage. Which
wasn't, actually, all that far off the mark for most Arts
Williamsburg shows.

At past openings only the artists themselves and a few
scraggly friends would show up, fortifying themselves
with wine from boxes and cheese produced by a board
member's goat. This night a gnarly knot of people
surrounded Jane's work, which was sitting cloaked on an
easel in the center of the room. Around the white walls
the other artists' works were ranged, as were the artists
themselves. They'd had the misfortune to be chosen for
an exhibition in which their work was clearly upstaged
by that of a murdered woman. A few might have agreed

326

their misfortune was eclipsed by that of the person actually dead, but even then she'd bested them, even in misfortune. Life as an artist was indeed unfair.

Gamache was waiting for *Fair Day* to be unveiled. The board of Arts Williamsburg had decided to make it an 'event', so they'd invited the press, which meant the Williamsburg County News and now the chairperson of the jury was waiting for *'le moment juste'*. Gamache glanced enviously at Jean Guy, sprawled on one of the comfortable chairs, refusing to give it up to an elderly man. He was exhausted. Bad art did this to him. Actually, he had to admit, any art did this to him. Bad wine, stinky cheese and pretty smelly art took the will to live right out of him. He looked around and came to the sad but inevitable conclusion that the building wouldn't collapse when Kyla finally blew into town later that night.

'As you know, a tragic event has robbed us of a fine woman and as it turns out, a gifted artist,' Elise Jacob, the jury chair, was saying.

Clara sidled up between Ben and Peter. Elise was going on, and on, and on about the virtues of Jane. She practically had her sainted. Then, finally, just as Clara's eyes began to bulge she said, 'Here, without further ado' – Clara, who knew and loved Jane, figured there'd been plenty of doodoo already – 'is *Fair Day* by Jane Neal.'

The veil was whisked off and *Fair Day* was finally revealed, to gasps. Then a silence which was even more eloquent. The faces staring slack-jawed at *Fair Day* were variously amused, repulsed and stunned. Gamache wasn't looking at the easel, he was staring at the crowd, at their reactions. But the only reaction that was even close to odd was Peter's. His anxious smile faded as *Fair Day* was revealed, and after a moment's contemplation he cocked his head to one side and furrowed his brow. Gamache, who'd been watching these people for almost two weeks, knew that for Peter Morrow this was the equivalent of a scream.

'What is it?'

'Nothing.' Peter turned his back on Gamache and walked away. Gamache followed.

'Mr Morrow, my question wasn't about aesthetics, but about murder. Please answer it.'

Peter was brought up short, as were most people who thought Gamache was incapable of forceful speech. 'The painting disturbs me. I can't tell you why because I don't know why. It doesn't seem to be the same work we judged two weeks ago, and yet, I know it is.'

Gamache stared at *Fair Day*. He'd never liked it so he wasn't a good judge, but unlike the work on Jane Neal's walls, this piece moved him not at all.

'So what's changed?'

'Nothing. Maybe me. Is that possible? Like that card trick of Jane's with the Queen of Hearts. Does art change too? I know at the end of a day I'll look at my work and think it's great, then next morning look at it and think it's crap. The work didn't change, but I did. Maybe Jane's death changed me so much that whatever I saw in this painting isn't there anymore.'

'Do you believe that?'

Damn the man, thought Peter. 'No.'

The two men stared at *Fair Day*, then slowly, lowly, a noise was heard unlike any anyone there had heard before. It grew and magnified until it reverberated around the circle of spectators. Clara could feel the blood race from her face and hands. Was it the storm? Was this what the tail end of a disaster sounded like? Had Kyla joined them after all? But the rumbling seemed to be coming from inside the building. Inside the room. In fact, right beside Clara. She turned and found the source. Ruth.

'That's me!' Ruth jabbed a finger at the dancing goat in *Fair Day*. Then the rumbling burst into a geyser of laughter. Ruth roared. She laughed until she had to steady herself on Gabri. Her laughter infected the entire room until even the sour-faced and forgotten artists were laughing. Much of the rest of the evening was taken with people recognising themselves or others in Jane's work. Ruth also found Timmer's parents and her brother and sister, both now dead. There was the first-grade teacher and Timmer's husband, and the exercise class they all belonged to. They were the chicks. Over the course of the hour or so just about every figure had been identified. Still, Peter stared, not joining in the laughter.

Something was wrong.

'I've got it!' Clara pointed at the painting. 'This was painted at the closing parade, right? The day your mother died. In fact, isn't that your mother?' Clara showed Ben the cloud with trotters. The flying lamb.

'You're right,' laughed Myrna. 'It's Timmer.'

'Do you see? This was Jane's tribute to your mother. Everyone in this picture was meaningful to her. From her grandparents to her dogs, to everyone in between.' Now Clara turned to Peter. 'Remember that last dinner we all had together?'

'Thanksgiving?'

'Yes, that's it. We were talking about great art, and I said I thought art became art when the artist put something of themselves into it. I asked Jane what she'd put into this work, and do you remember what she said?'

'Sorry, I can't.'

'She agreed that she'd put something in it, that there was some message in this work. She wondered if we'd figure it out. In fact, I remember she looked directly at Ben when she spoke, as though you'd understand. I'd wondered why at the time, but now it makes sense. This is for your mother.'

'You think?' Ben moved closer to Clara and stared at the picture.

'Well, that doesn't make any sense,' said Agent Nichol, who'd wandered over from her post by the door, drawn to the laughter as though to a crime. Gamache started making his way toward her, hoping to cut her off before she said something totally offensive. But his legs, while long, were no match for her mouth.

'Who was Yolande to Timmer? Did they even know each other?' Nichol pointed at the face of the blonde woman in the stands next to the acrylic Peter and Clara. 'Why would Jane Neal put in a niece she herself despised? This can't be what you said, a tribute to Mrs Hadley, with that woman there.'

Nichol was clearly enjoying getting one up on Clara.

And Clara, despite herself, could feel her anger rising. She stared speechless at the smug young face on the other side of the easel. And what made it worse was that she was right. There was the big blonde woman, undeniably in *Fair Day*, and Clara knew that if anything Timmer disliked Yolande even more than Jane did.

'May I see you, please?' Gamache placed himself between Clara and Nichol, cutting off the young woman's triumphant stare. Without another word he turned and walked toward the exit, Nichol hesitating an instant then following.

'There's a bus for Montreal tomorrow morning at six from St Rémy. Take it.'

He had no more to say. Agent Yvette Nichol was left shaking with rage on the cold dark stoop of Arts Williamsburg. She wanted to pound on the closed door. It seemed all her life doors were being shut in her face and here she was again, on the outside. Throbbing with fury she took two steps over to the window and looked in, at the people milling around, at Gamache talking to that Morrow woman and her husband. But there was someone else in the picture. After a moment she realised it was her own reflection.

How was she going to explain this to her father? She'd blown it. Somehow, somewhere, she'd done something wrong. But what? But Nichol was beyond reasoning. All she could think of was walking into her miniscule home with the immaculate front yard in east end Montreal, and telling her father she'd been kicked off the case. Shame on you. A phrase from the investigation floated into her head.

You're looking at the problem.

That meant something. Something significant she was sure. And then, finally, she understood.

The problem was Gamache.

There he was talking and laughing, smug and oblivious to the pain he caused. He was no different than the police her father had told her about in Czechoslovakia. How could she have been so blind? With relief she realised she needn't tell her father anything. After all, it wasn't her fault.

Nichol turned away, the sight too painful, of people having fun and her own lonely reflection.

An hour later the party had emigrated from Arts Williamsburg to Jane's home. The wind was picking up and the rain was just beginning. Clara stationed herself in the middle of the living room, just as Jane might have, so that as everyone arrived she could see their reactions.

'Oh. My. God.' was heard a lot, as was 'Holy shit' and *'Tabarouette'*. *'Tabarnouche'* and *'Tabarnac'* bounced off the walls. Jane's living room had become a shrine to multilingual swearing. Clara felt pretty much at home. A beer in one hand and cashews in the other, she watched as the guests arrived and were swept away by amazement. Most of the downstairs walls had been exposed and there, swooping and swirling before them, was the geography and history of Three Pines. The cougars and lynx, long since disappeared, the boys marching off to the Great War, and straight on to the modest stained-glass window of St Thomas's, commemorating the dead. There were the dope plants growing outside the Williamsburg police station, a happy cat sitting on the window looking down at the healthy growth.

The first thing Clara did, of course, was find herself on the wall. Her face poked out from a bush of Old Garden Roses, while Peter was found crouching behind a noble statue of Ben in shorts, standing on his mother's lawn. Peter was in his Robin Hood outfit and sported a bow and arrow, while Ben stood bold and strong, staring at the house. Clara looked quite closely to see whether Jane had painted snakes oozing out of the old Hadley home, but she hadn't.

The home was quickly filling with laughter and shrieks and howls of recognition. And sometimes a person was moved to tears they couldn't explain. Gamache and Beauvoir worked the room, watching and listening.

'. . . but what gets me is the delight in the images,' Myrna was saying to Clara. 'Even the deaths, accidents, funerals, bad crops, even they have a kind of life. She made them natural.'

'Hey, you,' Clara called out to Ben who came over eagerly. 'Look at yourself.' She waved at his image on the wall.

'Very bold.' He smiled. 'Chiseled, even.'

Gamache looked over at Ben's image on Jane's wall, a strong man, but staring at his parent's home. Not for the first time he thought Timmer Hadley's death might have been quite timely for her son. He might finally get away from her shadow. Interestingly, though, it was Peter who was standing in shadow. Ben's shadow. Gamache wondered what that could mean. He was beginning to appreciate that Jane's home was a kind of key to the community. Jane Neal had been a very observant woman.

Elise Jacob arrived at that moment, nodding to Gamache as she walked in. 'Phew, what a night—' but her eyes quickly refocused to the wall behind him. Then she spun around to examine the wall behind her.

'Christ,' said the lovely, soignée woman, waving to Gamache and the room in general as though perhaps she was the first to notice the drawings. Gamache simply smiled and waited for her to gather herself.

'Did you bring it?' he asked, not altogether sure her ears were working yet.

'*C'est brillant*,' she whispered. '*Formidable. Magnifique.* Holy shit.'

Gamache was a patient man and he gave her a few minutes to absorb the room. Besides, he realised he had developed a kind of pride about the home, as though he had had something to do with its creation.

'It's genius, of course,' said Elise. 'I used to work as a curator at the Musée des Beaux Arts in Ottawa before retiring down here.' Gamache again marveled at the people who chose to live in this area. Was Margaret Atwood a garbage collector perhaps? Or maybe Prime Minister Mulroney had picked up a second career delivering the mail. No one was who they seemed. Everyone was more. And one person in this room was very much more.

'Who'd have thought the same woman who painted that dreadful *Fair Day* did all this?' Elise continued. 'I guess we all have bad days. Still, you'd have thought she'd have chosen a better one to submit.'

'It was the only one she had,' said Gamache, 'or at least the only one not on construction material.'

'That's strange.'

'To say the least,' agreed Gamache. 'Did you bring it?' he repeated.

'Sorry, yes, it's in the mudroom.'

A minute later Gamache was setting *Fair Day* on to its easel in the center of the room. Now all of Jane's art was together.

He stood very still and watched. The din increased as the guests drank more wine and recognised more people and events on the walls. The only one behaving at all oddly was Clara. Gamache watched as she wandered over to *Fair Day* then back to the wall. Then over to *Fair Day* and back to the same spot on the wall. Then back to the easel. But this time with more purpose. Then she practically ran to the wall. And stood there for a very long time. Then she very slowly came back to *Fair Day* as though lost in thought.

'What is it?' Gamache asked, coming to stand beside her.

'This isn't Yolande,' Clara pointed to the blonde woman next to Peter.

'How do you know?'

'Over there,' Clara pointed to the wall she'd been examining. 'That's Yolande as painted by Jane. There are similarities, but not many.'

Gamache had to see for himself, though he knew Clara

would be right. Sure enough the only thing she'd been wrong about was saying there were similarities. There were none, as far as he could tell. The Yolande on the wall, even the child, was clearly Yolande. Physically, but also emotionally. She radiated contempt and greed and something else. Cunning. The woman on the wall was all those things. And just a little needy. In the painting on the easel the woman in the stands was simply blonde.

'Then who is she?' he asked when he got back.

'I don't know. But I do know one thing. Have you noticed that Jane never made up a face? Everyone on these walls was someone she knew, someone from the village.'

'Or a visitor,' said Gamache.

'Actually,' said Ruth, joining their conversation, 'there are no visitors. People who moved away and would come home to visit, yes, but they're considered villagers. Everyone on the walls she knew.'

'And everyone in *Fair Day* she knew, except her.' Clara pointed a cashew at the blonde woman. 'She's a stranger. But there's more. I've been wondering what's wrong with *Fair Day*. It's clearly Jane's, but it's not. If this was the first thing she'd done I'd say she just hadn't found her style. But this was the last.' Clara leaned into the work. 'Everything in it is strong, confident, purposeful. But taken as a whole it doesn't work.'

'She's right,' said Elise. 'It doesn't.'

The circle around *Fair Day* was growing, the guests attracted by the mystery.

'But it worked when we were judging it, right?' Clara

turned to Peter. 'It's her. Jane didn't paint her.' Clara pointed a ramrod straight '*J'accuse*' finger at the blonde in the stands next to Peter. As though sucked down a drain, all heads leaned into the center of the circle, to peer at the face.

'That's why this picture doesn't work,' continued Clara. 'It did before this face was changed. Whoever changed it changed the whole picture without realising it.'

'How do you know Jane didn't paint this face?' Gamache asked, his voice becoming official. Across the room Beauvoir heard it and went over, taking out his notepad and pen as he arrived.

'First of all, it's the only face in here that doesn't look alive.' Gamache had to agree with that. 'But that's subjective. There's actual proof if you want.'

'It would make a nice change.'

'Look.' Clara pointed again at the woman. 'Jesus, now that I look more closely I must have been blind not to see it before. It's like this huge carbuncle.' Try as they might none of them could see what she meant.

'For God's sake, just tell us, before I spank you,' said Ruth.

'There.' Clara zigzagged her finger around the woman's face, and sure enough, looking more closely, they could see a tiny smudging. 'It's like a wart, a huge blemish on this work.' She pointed to nearly invisible fuzzy marks. 'That's done by a rag and mineral spirits, right, Ben?'

But Ben was still peering almost cross-eyed at *Fair Day*.

'And look at that, those brush strokes. All wrong. Look at Peter's face beside her. Totally different strokes.' Clara

337

waved her whole arm back and forth then up and down. 'Up and down. Jane doesn't do up and down strokes. Lots of sideways, but no straight up and down. Look at this woman's hair. Up and down strokes. A dead give-away. Do you notice the paint?' She turned to Peter, who seemed uncomfortable.

'No. Nothing strange about the paints.'

'Oh, come on. Look. The whites are different. Jane used Titanium white here, here and here. But over here,' she pointed to the woman's eyes, 'this is Zinc white. That's Ochre Yellow.' Clara was pointing to the woman's vest. 'Jane never used Ochre, only Cadmium. So obvious. You know, we've done so much art, teaching it, and even sometimes picking up extra money restoring things for the McCord, that I can tell you who painted what, just by their brush strokes, never mind their choice of brushes and paints.'

'Why would someone paint in a face?' Myrna asked.

'That's the question,' agreed Gamache.

'And not the only one. Why add a face, yes, great question, but whoever did it also took out a face. You can tell by the smudges. They didn't just paint on top of the existing face, the one Jane did, they actually erased that whole face. I don't get it. If Jane, or anyone, wanted to erase a face it would be easiest to just paint over the existing one. You can do that with acrylic, in fact, everyone does that with acrylic. You almost never bother erasing. Just paint over your mistakes.'

'But if they did that could you remove that face and find the original underneath?' Gamache asked.

'It's tricky,' said Peter, 'but a good art restorer could. It's like we're doing upstairs here, taking off one layer of paint to find the image underneath. With a canvas, though, you can also do it with x-ray. It's a little blurry, but you might get an idea of who's there. Now, well, it's destroyed.'

'Whoever did this didn't want the face found,' said Clara. 'So she removed hers and painted in another woman's.'

'But', Ben jumped in, 'they gave themselves away when they erased the original face and drew a new one on top. They didn't know Jane's work. Her code. They made up a face not realising Jane never did that –'

'And they used the wrong strokes,' said Clara.

'Well, that lets me out,' said Gabri.

'But why do it at all? I mean, whose face was erased?' Myrna asked.

There was silence for a moment while they all considered.

'Can you take this face off and get an idea of the original?' Gamache asked.

'Maybe. Depends how thoroughly the original face was removed. Do you think the murderer did this?' Clara asked.

'I do. I just don't know why.'

'You said, "she",' said Beauvoir to Clara. 'Why?'

'I guess because the new face is female. I assumed the person who did this would paint the easiest thing and that's what we see in the mirror every day.'

'You think this is the murderer's face?' Beauvoir asked.

'No, that wouldn't be very smart. I think it's the murderer's gender, that's all. Under pressure a white man is most likely to paint a white man, not a black man, not a white woman – but the thing he's most familiar with. The same here.'

It's a good point, thought Gamache. But he also thought that if a man was painting to deceive he might very well paint a woman.

'Would it take skill to do this?' he asked.

'Remove one face and replace it with another? Yes, quite a lot. Not necessarily to take the first face off, but then again most people wouldn't know how. Would you?' she asked Beauvoir.

'No, not a clue. You mentioned mineral spirits and a rag, but the first time I ever heard of mineral spirits was a few days ago when you needed them for your work here.'

'Exactly. Artists know these things, but most people don't. Once the face is off she'd have to paint on another, using Jane's style. That takes skill. Whoever did this is an artist, and I'd say a good one. It took us quite a while to find the mistake. We probably never would have if your Agent Nichol hadn't been so obnoxious. She said this was Yolande. I was so pissed off I went in search of Jane's Yolande to see if it was true. And it wasn't. But it forced me to look more closely at the face to see who it might be. That's when I noticed the differences. So you can tell Nichol she helped solve the case.'

'Anything else you'd like us to tell her?' Beauvoir smiled at Clara.

340

Gamache knew he wouldn't lead Nichol to believe her rudeness had paid off, and yet he knew if he'd sent her away earlier they'd never be this far now. In a sense Clara was right but she'd failed to give herself enough credit. Her own need to prove Nichol wrong had played quite a role as well.

'You thought *Fair Day* was good enough for the exhibition when you judged it on the Friday before Thanksgiving?' he asked Peter.

'I thought it was brilliant.'

'It had changed by Thanksgiving Monday,' said Clara, turning to Gamache and Beauvoir. 'Remember when you two came in and I showed you *Fair Day*? The magic was gone then.'

'Saturday and Sunday,' said Beauvoir. 'Two days. Somewhere in there the murderer changed this painting. Jane Neal was killed Sunday morning.'

They all stared at it, willing it to tell them who did this. Gamache knew that *Fair Day* was screaming at them. The reason for Jane Neal's murder was in that picture. Clara could hear a tap tap tapping on the living-room window and went over to see who was out there. Staring into the darkness a branch suddenly appeared and hit the glass. Hurricane Kyla had arrived, and wanted in.

The party broke up quickly after that, everyone racing for their homes or cars before the worst of the storm hit.

'Don't let a house fall on you,' Gabri shouted after Ruth, who may or may not have given him the finger as she disappeared into the dark. *Fair Day* was taken to the B&B where a group now sat in the large living room sipping liqueurs and espresso. A fire had been laid and lit and outside Kyla moaned and called the leaves from the trees. Rain now whipped against the windows causing them to tremble. Inside the group instinctively huddled closer, warmed by the fire, the drinks and the company.

'Who knew about *Fair Day* before Miss Neal was killed?' Gamache asked. Peter and Clara were there, as were Ben, Olivier, Gabri and Myrna.

'The jury,' said Peter.

'Didn't you talk about it at your Thanksgiving dinner that Friday night?'

'We talked about it a lot. Jane even described it,' confirmed Clara.

'It's not the same thing,' said Gamache. 'Who saw *Fair Day* before tonight?'

They looked at each other, shaking their heads.

'Who was on the jury again?' Beauvoir asked.

'Henri Lariviere, Irenée Calfat, Elise Jacob, Clara and me,' said Peter.

'And who else might have seen it?' Gamache asked again. It was a crucial question. The murderer killed Jane because of *Fair Day*. He or she had to have seen it and seen the threat, enough to alter the picture, enough to murder.

'Isaac Coy,' said Clara. 'He's the caretaker. And I guess it's possible anyone who came in to see the other exhibition, the abstract art, could have wandered into the storeroom and seen it.'

'But not likely,' said Gamache.

'Not by mistake,' Clara agreed. She got up. 'I'm sorry,

but I think I've left my purse at Jane's. I'm just going to nip over and get it.'

'In the storm?' Myrna asked, incredulous.

'I'm going home as well,' said Ben. 'Unless there's something else I can do?'

Gamache shook his head and the gathering broke up. One by one they made their way into the black night; arms instinctively up to protect their faces. The night air was filled with driving rain and dead leaves and running people.

Clara needed to think, and for that she needed her safe place, which happened to be Jane's kitchen. She turned on all the lights and sank into one of the big old chairs beside the wood stove.

Was it possible? Surely she'd gotten something wrong. Forgotten something, or read too much into something. It'd struck her first staring at *Fair Day* during the cocktail, though the beginnings of the idea had started at Arts Williamsburg earlier in the evening. But she'd rejected the thought. Too painful. Too close. Much too close.

But the damning idea had come back with force in the B&B just now. As they'd stared at *Fair Day* all the pieces had come together. All the clues, all the hints. Everything made sense. She couldn't go home. Not now. She was afraid to go home.

'What do you think?' Beauvoir asked, sitting in the chair opposite Gamache. Nichol was lounging on the sofa reading a magazine, punishing Gamache with her silence. Gabri and Olivier had gone to bed.

'Yolande,' said Gamache. 'I keep coming back to that family. So many lines of enquiry lead us back there. The manure throwing, papering the walls. André has a hunting bow.'

'But he doesn't have a recurve,' said Beauvoir, sadly.

'He'll have destroyed it,' said Gamache, 'but why use it at all, that's the problem. Why would anyone use an old bow instead of a new compound-hunting bow?'

'Unless it was a woman,' said Beauvoir. This was his favorite part of the job, sitting with the chief late at night with a drink and a fireplace, hashing out the crime. 'A recurve is easier to use and an old recurve easier still. We saw that with Suzanne Croft. She wasn't able to use the modern bow, but she'd obviously used the older one. We're back to Yolande. She'd know her aunt's art, probably better than anyone, and art runs in the family. If we dug we'd probably find she's done some painting in her life. Everyone around here does, I think it's a law.'

'OK, so let's follow this through. Why would Yolande want to kill Jane?'

'For money, or the home, which comes to the same thing. She probably thought she inherited, she probably bribes that crooked notary in Williamsburg for information and God knows she'd be highly motivated to find out about her aunt's will.'

'Agreed. But what's the connection with *Fair Day*? What was in the painting that would make Yolande change it? It's of the closing parade of this year's fair, but it seems to be a tribute to Timmer Hadley. How could Yolande have seen it, and even if she did see it, why would she need to change it?'

This met with silence. After a few minutes Gamache moved on.

'OK, let's look at others. What about Ben Hadley?'

'Why him?' Beauvoir asked.

'He had access to the bows, has the skill and local knowledge, Miss Neal would have trusted him, and he knows how to paint. Apparently he's very good. And he's on the board of Arts Williamsburg, so he had a key to the gallery. He could have let himself in any time to see *Fair Day*.'

'Motive?' asked Beauvoir.

'That's the problem. There's no clear motive, is there? Why would he need to kill Jane Neal? Not for money. Why?'

Gamache stared into the dying flames, racking his brain. He wondered whether he was trying too hard, trying not to come to the other conclusion.

'Come on. Peter Morrow did it. Who else?'

Gamache didn't have to look up to know who spoke. The pumpkin on the cover of *Harrowsmith Country Life* had found its voice.

Clara stared at her reflection in the window of Jane's kitchen. A ghostly, frightened woman looked back. Her theory made sense.

Ignore it, the voice inside said. It's not your business. Let the police do their work. For God's sake, don't say anything. It was a seductive voice, one that promised peace and calm and the continuation of her beautiful life in Three Pines. To act on what she knew would destroy that life.

What if you're wrong? cooed the voice. You'll hurt a lot of people.

But Clara knew she wasn't wrong. She was afraid of losing this life she loved, this man she loved.

He'll be furious. He'll deny it, shrieked the now panicked voice in her head. He'll confuse you. Make you feel horrible for suggesting such a thing. Best not to say anything. You have everything to lose and nothing to gain. And, no one need know. No one will ever know that you said nothing.

But Clara knew the voice lied. Had always lied to her. Clara would know and that knowing would eventually destroy her life anyway.

Gamache lay in bed staring at *Fair Day*. Conversations and snippets of conversations swirled in his head as he stared at the stylised people and animals and remembered what each person had said at one time or another over the past two weeks.

Yvette Nichol had been right. Peter Morrow was the likeliest suspect, but there was no evidence. Gamache knew that their best chance of catching him lay with this picture and the analysis tomorrow. *Fair Day* was their smoking gun. But as he stared at each face in the picture something suggested itself, something so unlikely he couldn't believe it. He sat up in bed. It wasn't what was in *Fair Day* that would prove who murdered Jane Neal. It was what wasn't in *Fair Day*. Gamache leapt out of bed and threw on his clothes.

Clara could barely see for the rain, but the wind was the worst. Kyla had turned the autumn leaves, so beautiful on the trees, into small missiles. They whipped around her, plastering against her face. She put an arm up to protect her eyes and leaned into the wind, stumbling over the uneven terrain. The leaves and twigs smacked her raincoat, trying to find her skin. Where the leaves failed the frigid water succeeded. It poured up her sleeves and down her back, into her nose and pelted her eyeballs when she squinted them open. But she was almost there.

'I was getting worried. I expected you earlier,' he said, coming over to hug her. Clara stepped back, out of his embrace. He looked at her surprised and hurt. Then he looked down at her boots, puddling water and mud on the floor. She followed his gaze and automatically removed her boots, almost smiling at the normalcy of the action. Maybe she'd been wrong. Maybe she could just take off her boots, sit down, and not say anything. Too late. Her mouth was already working.

'I've been thinking.' She paused, not sure what to say, or how to say it.

'I know. I could see it in your face. When did you figure it out?'

So, she thought, he's not going to deny it. She didn't know whether to be relieved or horrified.

'At the party, but I couldn't get it all. I needed time to think, to work it out.'

'Was that why you said "she", when describing the forger?'

'Yes. I wanted to buy some time, maybe even throw the police off.'

'It threw me off. I was hoping you meant it. But then at the B&B. I could see your mind working. I know you too well. What're we going to do?'

'I needed to see if you'd really done it. I felt I owed you this, because I love you.' Clara felt numb, as though she was having an out of body experience.

'And I love you,' he said in a voice that struck her as suddenly mincing. Was it always like this? 'And I need you. You don't have to tell the police, there's no evidence. Even the tests tomorrow won't show anything. I was careful. Once I put my mind to something I'm very good, but you know that.'

She did. And she suspected he was right. The police would have a hard time convicting him.

'Why?' she asked, 'why did you kill Jane? And why did you kill your mother?'

'Wouldn't you?' Ben smiled, and advanced.

Gamache had woken Beauvoir and now the two were banging on the Morrows' door.

'Did you forget your key?' Peter was saying as he unlocked it. He stared, uncomprehending, at Gamache and Beauvoir. 'Where's Clara?'

'That's what we wanted to ask you. We need to speak with her, now.'

348

'I left her at Jane's, but that was', Peter consulted his watch, 'an hour ago.'

'That's a long time to search for a purse,' said Beauvoir.

'She didn't have a purse, it was just a ruse to leave the B&B and go into Jane's home,' explained Peter. 'I knew it, but I figured she wanted time alone, to think.'

'But she's not back yet?' Gamache asked. 'Weren't you worried?'

'I'm always worried about Clara. The instant she leaves the house I'm worried.'

Gamache turned and hurried through the woods to Jane's home.

Clara awoke with a throbbing head. At least, she assumed she was awake. Everything was black. Blinding black. Her face was on a floor and she was breathing in dirt. It was sticking to her skin, wet from the rain. Her clothes under her raincoat clung to her body where the rain had driven in. She felt cold and sick. She couldn't stop shivering. Where was she? And where was Ben? She realised her arms were tied behind her. She'd been at Ben's home, so this must be Ben's basement. She had a memory of being carried, drifting in and out of consciousness. And of Peter. Of hearing Peter. No. Of smelling Peter. Peter had been close by. Peter had been carrying her.

'I see you're awake.' Ben stood above her holding a flashlight.

'Peter?' Clara called in a reedy voice. Ben seemed to find this funny.

'Good. That's what I was hoping, but bad news, Clara.

Peter isn't here. In fact, this is pretty much a night of bad news for you. Guess where we are.'

When Clara didn't speak Ben slowly moved the flashlight around so it played on the walls, the ceiling, the floors. It didn't have to go far before Clara knew. She probably knew earlier but her brain wouldn't accept it.

'Can you hear them, Clara?' Ben was silent again, and sure enough Clara heard it. A slithering. A sliding. And she could smell them. A musky, swampy smell.

Snakes.

They were in Timmer's home. Timmer's basement.

'But, the good news is, you won't have to worry about them for long.' Ben brought the flashlight up so she could see his face. She could also see he was wearing one of Peter's coats. 'You came here, and fell down the stairs,' he said, in a reasonable voice, as though expecting her to agree with him. 'Gamache may suspect, but no one else will. Peter would never suspect me, I'll be the one comforting him in his loss. And everyone else knows I'm a kind man. And I really am. This doesn't count.'

He turned away from her and walked toward the wooden stairs, the flashlight throwing fantastic shadows across the dirt floor. 'The electricity's been turned off and you stumbled and fell. I'm just fixing the steps now. Rickety old things. Asked Mother for years to repair them, but she was too mean to part with the money. Now you're paying the tragic price. Happily, if Gamache doesn't buy that I've sprinkled enough clues so that Peter'll be charged. I expect a whole lot of fibers from his jacket are on you now. You probably breathed some in too. They'll find those in the autopsy. You'll help to convict your own husband.'

Clara rocked herself to a sitting position. She could see Ben working on the stairs. She knew she had a matter of minutes, maybe moments. She strained against the cords binding her wrists. Fortunately, Ben hadn't tied them tightly. He probably didn't want to cause bruising, but it meant she was able to work her wrists loose though not free.

'What you doing over there?' Ben turned the light on Clara, who leaned back to mask her movements. Her back touched the wall and something brushed into her hair and neck. Then was gone. Oh God. Dear Mother of God. The instant the light turned back to the steps Clara worked frantically, more desperate to get away from the snakes than from Ben. She could hear them slithering, moving along the beams and ventilation shafts. Finally her hands burst free and she scrambled off into the dark.

'Clara? Clara!' The light flashed back and forth wildly searching. 'I don't have time for this.'

Ben left the stairs and started frantically searching. Clara backed further and further into the basement, toward the rank smell. Something brushed her cheek then fell on to her foot. She bit through her lip, trying not to scream, the metallic taste of blood helping her focus. She kicked hard and heard a soft thump as it hit a nearby wall.

Gamache, Beauvoir and Peter ran through Jane's home, but Gamache knew she wouldn't be there. If something bad was going to happen to Clara, it wouldn't be in this home.

'She's at Hadley's place,' said Gamache, making for the door. Once out Beauvoir quickly sped by him, as did Peter. Their footsteps sounded like wild horses as they raced through the storm toward the home with its welcoming lights.

Clara wasn't sure whether the roaring she heard was Kyla, furious Kyla, or her own terrified breath. Or blood pounding in her ears. The whole home above her seemed to shudder and moan. She held her breath but her body screamed for oxygen and after a moment she was forced to breathe, hungrily and noisily.

'I heard that.' Ben swung around, but he moved so fast he lost his grip on the flashlight and the thing flew out of his hand, landing with two thumps. The first sent the light bouncing, hitting Clara full in the face. The second thump plunged the basement into total darkness.

'Shit,' hissed Ben.

Oh God, Oh God, thought Clara. Complete and utter darkness descended. She was frozen, petrified. She heard a movement to her right. This was just enough to get her going. She crawled quietly, slowly left, feeling along the base of the rough stone wall, looking for a rock, a pipe, a brick, anything. Except . . .

Her hand closed around it and it in turn curled up and closed around her. With a spasm she hurled it into the darkness and heard it bounce across the room.

'Here I come,' Ben whispered. As he spoke Clara realised

she'd crawled right up to him in the darkness. He was a step away, but blind as well. She squatted frozen in place, waiting for his hands to grip her. Instead she heard him moving off across the room. Toward the tossed snake.

'Where is she?' Peter pleaded. They'd searched Ben's home and found only a puddle. Now Peter was striding in concentric circles around Ben's living room, coming ever closer to Gamache, who was standing stock still in the center.

'Be quiet, please, Mr Morrow.' Peter stopped pacing. The words were spoken softly, with authority. Gamache was staring ahead. He could barely hear himself think for the force of the storm outside, and the force of Peter's terror inside.

Clara knew she had two chances, which was better than she'd had a few minutes ago. She needed to find the stairs, or she needed to find a weapon and get Ben before he got her. She knew Ben. He was strong, but he was slow. This wasn't a big help since a race probably wasn't on the cards, but it was something.

She had no idea where to find a weapon, except maybe on the floor. But while a brick or pipe might be lying on the floor, she knew what else certainly was. She could hear Ben stumble a few feet ahead of her. She turned and dropped to her knees, scuttling across the dirt floor, waving her hands ahead of her hoping, dear God, please, to grip something that didn't grip back. Again Clara heard a pounding, and wished her heart quieter, though not completely still. Her hand brushed against something and in a flash she knew what it was. But too late. With a snap the mousetrap whacked against her fingers, breaking the middle two and forcing a shout of pain and shock out of her. Adrenaline shot through her and she instantly pulled the trap off her wounded hand and flung it away. She rolled sideways, knowing mousetraps are laid against walls. A wall must lie directly ahead. If Ben was rushing through the darkness to grab her . . .

Peter heard Clara's cry of pain and its abrupt end. He and the policemen had arrived a few moments earlier to find Timmer's front door banging open in the wind. Gamache and Beauvoir pulled flashlights from their coats and played them on the hardwood floor. Watery steps trailed into the heart of the dark home. They followed at a run. Just as they rounded into the kitchen they heard the scream.

'Over here.' Peter opened a door into darkness. The three big men plunged down the basement stairs together.

Clara rolled then stopped just as Ben ploughed head-long into the stone wall. He hit it at full run and Clara had been wrong. He was fast. But not so much now. The impact had sent a shudder through the basement. Then Clara heard another noise.

Stairs breaking.

FOURTEEN

―◡

E verything seemed to happen very slowly. Gamache's flashlight hit the floor first and winked out, but not before he had a glimpse of Beauvoir sprawled across the now collapsed stairs. Gamache tried to twist out of the way and almost managed it. One foot fell between the risers of the broken stairs, and he both heard and felt his leg snap as his weight bore down. The other foot fell on something much more comfy, though just as noisy. Gamache heard Beauvoir bark in pain, and then Peter crashed down. He was swan-diving, head first, and Gamache felt their heads bang together and saw a whole lot more light than the basement, or the universe, contained. Then he passed out.

He woke up a short time later with Clara staring down at him, her face filled with fear. She radiated terror. He tried to get up, to protect her, but couldn't move.

'Chief? You all right?' He shifted his blurry eyes and saw Beauvoir also looking down at him. 'I've called for help on the cell phone.' Beauvoir then reached out and held the Chief's hand. For an instant.

'I'm good, Jean Guy. You?' He looked into the worried face.

'I think an elephant landed on me.' Beauvoir smiled slightly. A bit of bright red blood bubbled from his lip and Gamache lifted one shaky hand to gently wipe it away.

'You must be more careful, boy,' Gamache whispered. 'Peter?'

'I'm stuck, but I'm OK. You hit me with your head.'

This wasn't the time to argue over who hit whom.

'There it is again. A slithering.' Clara had found a flashlight, not all that difficult since the basement was now littered with flashlights, and men. She played it madly around the ceiling and the floor and wished it had power to do more than illuminate. A nice flamethrower would come in handy. She held Peter's hand with her own broken hand, exchanging physical pain for emotional solace.

'Ben?' Gamache asked, and hoped soon he'd be able to form full sentences. His leg was shooting pain and his head throbbed, but he recognised that some threat was still out there, in the dark, in the basement with them.

'He's out cold,' said Clara. She could have left them. The stairs had collapsed, true, but there was a step ladder not far away and she could have used that to climb out.

But she didn't.

Clara had never known such fear. And anger. Not against Ben, yet, but against these morons who were supposed to have saved her. And now she had to protect them.

'I hear something,' said Beauvoir. Gamache tried to raise himself to his elbows, but his leg sent so much pain into his body it took his breath and strength away. He fell back and reached out his hands, hoping to find something to grab on to to use as a weapon.

'Upstairs,' said Beauvoir. 'They're here.'

Gamache and Clara had never heard such beautiful words.

A week later they were gathered in Jane's living room, which was beginning to feel like home to all of them, including Gamache. They looked like a Fife and Drum Corps, Gamache's leg in a cast, Beauvoir bent over with broken ribs, Peter's head bandaged and Clara's hand in plaster.

Upstairs, Gabri and Olivier could be heard quietly singing 'It's Raining Men'. From the kitchen came the sounds of Myrna humming while preparing fresh bread and homemade soup. Outside snow was falling, huge wet flakes that melted almost as soon as they landed and felt like horse kisses when they touched a cheek. The last of the autumn leaves had blown off the trees and the apples had fallen from the orchards.

'I think it's beginning to stick on the ground,' said Myrna, bringing in cutlery and setting up TV tables around the crackling fire. From upstairs they could hear Gabri exclaiming over things in Jane's bedroom.

'Greed. Disgusting,' said Ruth and made her way quickly to the stairs and up.

Clara watched as Peter got up and stirred the perfectly

fine fire. She'd held him that night as he sprawled on the dirt floor. That had been the last time she'd gotten that close. Since the events of that horrible night he'd retreated completely on to his island. The bridge had been destroyed. The walls had been constructed. And now Peter was unapproachable, even by her. Physically, yes, she could hold his hand, hold his head, hold his body, and she did. But she knew she could no longer hold his heart.

She watched his handsome face, lined with care now, and bruised by the fall. She knew he'd been hurt the worst, perhaps beyond repair.

'I want this,' said Ruth, coming down the stairs. She waved a small book then tucked it into a huge pocket in her worn cardigan. Jane in her will had invited each of her friends to choose an item from her home. Ruth had made her choice.

'How'd you know it was Ben?' Myrna asked, taking a seat and calling the boys down to lunch. Bowls of soup had been put out and baskets of fresh rolls steamed on the blanket box.

'At the party here it came to me,' said Clara.

'What did you see we didn't?' Olivier asked, joining them.

'It's what I didn't see. I didn't see Ben. I knew *Fair Day* was a tribute to Timmer. All the people who were important to Timmer were in it –'

'Except Ben!' said Myrna, buttering her warm roll and watching the butter melt as soon as it touched the bread. 'What a fool to have missed it.'

'Took me a long time too,' admitted Gamache. 'I only saw it after staring at *Fair Day* in my room. No Ben.'

'No Ben,' repeated Clara. 'I knew there was no way Jane would've left him out. But he wasn't there. Unless he had been there and it was his face that'd been removed.'

'But why did Ben panic when he saw *Fair Day*? I mean, what was so horrible about seeing his face in a painting?' Olivier asked.

'Think about it,' said Gamache. 'Ben injected his mother with a fatal dose of morphine on the final day of the fair, actually while the parade was on. He'd made sure he had an alibi, he was off in Ottawa at an antiques show.'

'And was he?' Clara asked.

'Oh yes, even bought a few things. Then he raced back here, it's only about three hours by car, and waited for the parade to start –'

'Knowing I'd leave his mother? How could he have known?' asked Ruth.

'He knew his mother, knew she'd insist.'

'And she did. I should have stayed.'

'You weren't to know, Ruth,' said Gabri.

'Go on,' said Olivier, dipping his roll in the soup. 'He looked at the painting and –'

'He saw himself, apparently at the parade,' said Gamache. 'There in the stands. He believed then that Jane knew what he'd done, that he'd been in Three Pines after all.'

'So he stole the painting, erased his face, and painted in a new one,' said Clara.

'The strange woman was sitting next to Peter,' Ruth pointed out. 'A natural place for Jane to put Ben.'

Peter made a conscious effort not to lower his eyes.

'That night at the B&B after the *vernissage* it all came together,' said Clara. 'He didn't lock his door after the murder. Everyone else did, but not Ben. Then there was the speed, or lack of it, with which he was uncovering the walls. Then that night we saw the light here, Ben said he was catching up on stripping the walls, and I accepted it but later I thought it sounded a little lame even for Ben.'

'Turns out,' supplied Gamache, 'he was searching Jane's home for this.' He held up the folder Beauvoir had found in Yolande's home. 'Sketches Jane did of every county fair for sixty years. Ben thought there might be some rough sketches for *Fair Day* around, and he was looking for them.'

'Do the sketches show anything?' Olivier asked.

'No, too rough.'

'And then there were the onions,' said Clara.

'Onions?'

'When I'd gone to Ben's home the day after Jane was killed he was frying up onions, to make chili con carne. But Ben never cooked. Egoist that I am I believed him when he said it was to cheer me up. I wandered into his living room at one stage and smelt what I took to be cleaning fluid. It was that comforting smell that means everything's clean and cared for. I figured Nellie had cleaned. Later I was talking to her and she said Wayne had been so sick she hadn't cleaned anywhere in a week or more. Ben must have been using a solvent and he fried the onions to cover up the smell.'

'Exactly,' confirmed Gamache, sipping on a beer. 'He'd taken *Fair Day* from Arts Williamsburg that Saturday after your Thanksgiving dinner, stripped away his own face and painted in another. But he made the mistake of making up a face. He also used his own paints, which were different to Jane's. Then he returned the work to Arts Williamsburg, but he had to kill Jane before she could see the change.'

'You', Clara turned to Gamache, 'put it beyond doubt for me. You kept asking who else had seen Jane's work. I remembered then that Ben had specifically asked Jane at the Thanksgiving dinner if she'd mind him going to Arts Williamsburg to see it.'

'Do you think he was suspicious that night?' Myrna asked.

'Perhaps a little uneasy. His guilty mind might have been playing tricks on him. The look on his face when Jane said the picture was of the parade and it held a special message. She'd looked directly at him.'

'He also looked odd when she quoted that poem,' said Myrna.

'What poem was that?' Gamache asked.

'Auden. There, in the pile by her seat where you're sitting, Clara. I can see it,' said Myrna. '*The Collected Works of W. H. Auden.*'

Clara handed the hefty volume to Myrna.

'Here it is,' said Myrna. 'She'd read from Auden's tribute to Herman Melville:

Evil is unspectacular and always human,
and shares our bed and eats at our own table.'

Peter reached out for the book and scanned the beginning of the poem, the part Jane hadn't read:

'Towards the end he sailed into an extraordinary
   mildness,
and anchored in his home and reached his wife
and rode within the harbour of her hand,
and went across each morning to an office
as though his occupation were another island.
Goodness existed: that was the new knowledge.
His terror had to blow itself quite out.'

Peter looked into the fire, listening to the murmur of the familiar voices. Gently he slipped a piece of paper into the book and closed it.

'Like a paranoid person he read hidden messages into everything,' said Gamache. 'Ben had the opportunity and skill to kill Jane. He lived practically beside the schoolhouse, he could go there without being seen, let himself in, take a recurve bow and a couple of arrows, change the tips from target to hunting, then lure Jane and kill her.'

The movie played in Peter's head. Now he dropped his eyes. He couldn't look at his friends. How had he not known this about his best friend?

'How'd he get Jane there?' Gabri asked.

'A phone call,' said Gamache. 'Jane trusted him

completely. She didn't question when he asked her to meet him by the deer trail. Told her there were poachers so she'd better leave Lucy at home. She went without another thought.'

This is what comes of trust and friendship, loyalty and love, thought Peter. You get screwed. Betrayed. You get wounded so deeply you can barely breathe and sometimes it kills you. Or worse. It kills the people you love most. Ben had almost killed Clara. He'd trusted Ben. Loved Ben. And this is what happened. Never again. Gamache had been right about Matthew 10:36.

'Why did he kill his own mother?' Ruth asked.

'The oldest story in the book,' said Gamache.

'Ben was a male prostitute?' Gabri exclaimed.

'That's the oldest profession. Where do you keep your head?' asked Ruth. 'Never mind, don't answer that.'

'Greed,' explained Gamache. 'I should have twigged earlier, after our conversation in the bookstore,' he said to Myrna. 'You described a personality type. The ones who lead what you called "still" lives. Do you remember?'

'Yes, I do. The ones who aren't growing and evolving, who are standing still. They're the ones who rarely got better.'

'Yes, that was it,' said Gamache. 'They waited for life to happen to them. They waited for someone to save them. Or heal them. They did nothing for themselves.'

'Ben,' said Peter. It was almost the first time he'd spoken all day.

'Ben.' Gamache gave a single nod. 'Jane saw it, I think.' He got up and hobbled to the wall. 'Here. Her drawing of Ben. Did you notice he's wearing shorts? Like a little boy. And he's in stone. Stuck. Facing his parent's home, facing the past. It makes sense now, of course, but I didn't see it earlier.'

'But why didn't we see it? We lived with him every day,' Clara asked.

'Why should you? You were leading your own busy lives. Besides, there's something else about Jane's drawing of Ben.' He let them consider for a moment.

'The shadow,' said Peter.

'Yes. He cast a long and dark shadow. And his darkness influenced others.'

'Influenced me, you mean,' said Peter.

'Yes. And Clara. And almost everyone. He was very clever, he gave the impression of being tolerant and kind, while actually being very dark, very cunning.'

'But why did he kill Timmer?' Ruth asked again.

'She was going to change her will. Not cut him out entirely, but give him just enough to live on, so that he'd have to start doing something for himself. She knew what sort of a man he'd become, the lies, the laziness, the excuses. But she'd always felt responsible. Until she met you, Myrna. You and Timmer used to talk about these things. I think your descriptions got her to thinking about Ben. She'd long known he was a problem, but she'd seen it as a kind of passive problem. The only person he was hurting was himself. And her, with his lies about her—'

'She knew what Ben was saying?' Clara asked.

'Yes. Ben told us that during his interrogation. He admitted to telling lies about his mother since he was a child, to get sympathy, but didn't seem to think there was anything wrong with that. "It could have been true," was how he put it. For instance,' Gamache turned to Peter, 'he told you his mother had insisted on sending him to Abbott's, but the truth was he'd begged to go. He wanted to punish his mother by making her feel she wasn't needed. I think those discussions with you, Myrna, were a real turning point in Timmer's life. Up until then she'd blamed herself for how Ben had turned out. She half believed his accusations that she'd been a horrible mother. And she felt she owed him. That's why she let him live in her home all his life.'

'Didn't that strike you as weird?' Myrna asked Clara.

'No. It's incredible to look back now and see it. It was just where Ben lived. Besides, he said his mother refused to let him leave. Emotional blackmail, I thought. I bought everything he said.' Clara shook her head in amazement. 'When he moved to the caretaker's cottage Ben told us she'd kicked him out because he'd finally stood up to her.'

'And you believed that?' Ruth asked quietly. 'Who bought enough of your art so you could buy your home? Who gave you furniture? Who had you over for dinners those first years to introduce you around and to give you good meals when she knew you were barely eating? Who sent you home with parcels of leftovers? Who listened politely every time you spoke, and asked interested questions? I could go on all night. Did none of this make an impression? Are you that blind?'

There it was again, thought Clara. The blind.

This was far worse than any injuries Ben had given her. Ruth was staring at them, her face hard. How could they have been so gullible? How could Ben's words have been stronger than Timmer's actions? Ruth was right. Timmer had been nothing but tolerant, kind and generous.

Clara realised with a chill that Ben had begun to assassinate his mother long ago.

'You're right. I'm so sorry. Even the snakes. I'd believed the snakes.'

'Snakes?' said Peter. 'What snakes?'

Clara shook her head. Ben had lied to her, and used Peter's name to add legitimacy to it. Why had he told her there were snakes in his mother's basement? Why had he made up that story about himself and Peter as boys? Because it made him even more of a victim, a hero, she realised. And she'd been more than willing to believe it. Poor Ben, they'd called him. And poor Ben he'd wanted to be, though not literally as it turned out.

Timmer's basement had proven, once the electricity had been restored, to be clean, absolutely fine. No snakes. No snake nests. No indication anything had ever slithered in or out of there, except Ben. The 'snakes' dangling from the ceiling had been wires, and she'd kicked and tossed pieces of garden hose. The power of the imagination never ceased to amaze Clara.

'Another reason I was slow to catch on,' admitted Gamache, 'was that I made a mistake. Quite a big one. I thought he loved you, Clara. Romantically. I even asked him about it. That was the biggest mistake. Instead of asking him how he felt about you, I asked him how long he'd loved you. I gave him the excuse he needed for all his guarded looks. He wasn't sneaking peeks at you out of passion, but fear. He knew how intuitive you are, and that of anyone, you'd figure it out. But I let him off the hook and fooled myself.'

'But you came to it in the end,' said Clara. 'Does Ben realise what he's done?'

'No. He's convinced he was totally justified in what he did. The Hadley money was his. The Hadley property was his. His mother was simply holding them until they were passed on to him. The idea of not getting his inheritance was so unimaginable he felt he had no choice but to kill her. And because she put him in that position, well it wasn't his fault. She brought it on herself.'

Olivier shivered. 'He seemed so gentle.'

'And he was,' said Gamache, 'until you disagreed with him, or he didn't get what he wanted. He was a child. He killed his mother for the money. And he killed Jane because he thought she was announcing it to the world with *Fair Day*.'

'It's ironic,' said Peter, 'he thought his face in *Fair Day* gave him away. But what gave him away was erasing his face. Had he left the picture as it was he'd never have been caught. He'd been passive all his life. The one time he actually acts he condemns himself.'

Ruth Zardo walked slowly and painfully up the hill, Daisy on a lead beside her. She'd volunteered to take Ben's dog, surprising herself more than anyone else when she'd made the offer. But it felt right. Two stinky, lame old ladies.

They picked their way along the uneven path, being careful not to slip on the gathering snow and twist an ankle or aggravate a hip.

She heard it before she saw it. The prayer stick, its brightly colored ribbons catching the wind, sending their gifts into the air, knocking against each other. Like true friends. Bumping, and sometimes hurting, though never meaning to. Ruth took hold of the old photograph, the image almost worn off by the rain and snow. She hadn't looked at this picture in sixty years, since the day she'd taken it at the fair. Jane and Andreas, so joyous. And Timmer behind, looking straight at the camera, at Ruth holding the camera, and scowling. Ruth had known then, years ago, that Timmer knew. Young Ruth had just betrayed Jane. And now Timmer was dead. And Andreas was dead, and Jane was dead. And Ruth felt, maybe, it was time to let go. She released the old photograph and it quickly joined the other objects, dancing and playing together.

Ruth reached into her pocket and took out the book she'd chosen as her gift from Jane. With it she withdrew the envelope Jane had left her. Inside was a card, hand-drawn by Jane, a near duplicate of the image on the wall of Jane's living room. Except, instead of two young girls embracing, they were now old and frail. Two elderly women. Holding each other. Ruth slipped it into the book. The worn little book that smelled of Floris.

In a tremulous voice Ruth started to read out loud, the words taken by the wind to play among the snowflakes and bright ribbons. Daisy looked at her with adoration.

*

Gamache sat in the Bistro, having come in to say goodbye, and maybe buy a licorice pipe, or two, before heading back to Montreal. Olivier and Gabri were having a heated discussion about where to put the magnificent Welsh dresser Olivier had chosen. Olivier had tried not to choose it. Had spoken with himself quite sternly about not being greedy and taking the best thing in Jane's home.

Just this once, he begged himself, take something symbolic. Something small to remember her by. A nice bit of *famille rose*, or a little silver tray. Not the Welsh dresser. Not the Welsh dresser.

'Why can't we ever put the nice things in the B&B?' Gabri was complaining, as he and Olivier walked around the Bistro, looking for a place for the Welsh dresser. Spotting Gamache, they went over to him. Gabri had a question.

'Did you ever suspect us?'

Gamache looked at the two men, one huge and buoyant, the other slim and self-contained. 'No. I think you've both been hurt too much in your lives by the cruelty of others to ever be cruel yourselves. In my experience people who have been hurt either pass it on and become abusive themselves or they develop a great kindness. You're not the types to do murder. I wish I could say the same for everyone here.'

'What do you mean?' asked Olivier.

'Who do you mean?' asked Gabri.

'Now, you don't expect me to tell you, do you? Besides, this person may never act.' To Gabri's observant eye Gamache looked unconvinced, even slightly fearful.

Just then Myrna arrived for a hot chocolate.

'I have a question for you.' Myrna turned to Gamache, after she'd ordered. 'What's with Philippe? Why'd he turn on his father like that?'

Gamache wondered how much to say. Isabelle Lacoste had sent the item she'd found taped behind a framed poster in Bernard's room to the lab and the results had come back. Philippe's fingerprints were all over it. Gamache hadn't been surprised. Bernard Malenfant had been blackmailing the young man.

But Gamache knew Philippe's behavior had changed before that. He'd gone from being a happy, kind boy to a cruel, sullen, deeply unhappy adolescent. Gamache had guessed the reason but the magazine had confirmed it. Philippe didn't hate his father. No. Philippe hated himself, and took it out on his father.

'I'm sorry,' said Gamache. 'I can't tell you.'

As Gamache put on his coat Olivier and Gabri came over.

'We think we know why Philippe's been acting this way,' said Gabri. 'We wrote it on this piece of paper. If we're right, could you just nod?'

Gamache opened the note and read. Then he folded it back up and put it in his pocket. As he went out the door he looked back at the two men, standing shoulder to shoulder, just touching. Against his better judgment, he nodded. He never regretted it.

They watched Armand Gamache limp to his car and drive away. Gabri felt a deep sadness. He'd known about Philippe for a while. The manure incident, perversely, had confirmed it. That's why they'd decided to invite Philippe to work off his debt at the Bistro. Where they could watch him, but more importantly, where he could watch them. And see it was all right.

'Well,' Olivier's hand brushed against Gabri's, 'at least you'll have another munchkin if you ever decide to stage *The Wizard of Oz*.'

'Just what this village needs, another friend of Dorothy.'

'This is for you.' From behind her back Clara brought a large photograph, stylised, layered by video and taken as a still off her Mac. She beamed as Peter stared at it. But slowly the smile flattened. He didn't get it. This wasn't unusual, he rarely understood her work. But she'd hoped this would be different. Her gift to him was both the photograph and trusting him enough to show it to him. Her art was so painfully personal it was the most exposed she could ever be. After not telling Peter about the deer blind and the trail and holding back other things she now wanted to show him that she'd been wrong. She loved and trusted him.

He stared at the weird photo. It showed a box on stilts, like a treehouse. Inside was a rock or an egg, Peter didn't know which. So like Clara to be unclear. And the whole thing was spinning. It made him feel a little nauseous.

'It's the blind house,' she said, as though that explained it. Peter didn't know what to say. Recently, for the last week, there hadn't been a lot to say to anyone.

Clara wondered whether she should explain about the stone and its symbolism with death. But the object might be an egg. Symbolic of life. Which was it? That was the glorious tension in the luminous work. Up until that morning the treehouse had been static, but all that talk of people being stuck had given Clara the idea of spinning the house, like a little planet, with its own gravity, its own reality. Like most homes, it contained life and death, inseparable. And the final allusion. Home as an allegory for self. A self-portrait of our choices. And our blind spots.

Peter didn't get it. Didn't try. He left Clara standing there with a work of art that, unbeknownst to either of them, would one day make her famous.

She watched him wander almost aimlessly into his studio and shut the door. One day she knew he'd leave his safe and sterile island and come back to this messy mainland. When he did she'd be waiting, her arms open, as always.

Now Clara sat in the living room and took a piece of paper from her pocket. It was addressed to the minister of St Thomas's church. She crossed out the first bit of writing. Below it she carefully printed something, then she put on her coat and walked up the hill to the white clapboard church, handed the paper to the minister and returned to the fresh air.

The Revd James Morris unfolded the slip of paper and read. It was instructions for the engraving on Jane Neal's headstone. On the top of the page was written, 'Matthew 10:36.' But that had been crossed out and something else had been printed underneath. He took out his Bible and looked up Matthew 10:36.

'And a man's foes shall be they of his own household.'
Below it was the new instruction.
'Surprised by Joy.'

At the top of the hill Armand Gamache stopped the car and got out. He looked down at the village and his heart soared. He looked over the rooftops and imagined the good, kind, flawed people inside struggling with their lives. People were walking their dogs, raking the relentless autumn leaves, racing the gently falling snow. They were shopping at M. Beliveau's general store and buying baguettes from Sarah's boulangerie. Olivier stood at the Bistro doorway and shook out a tablecloth. Life was far from harried here. But neither was it still.

ACKNOWLEDGEMENTS

—

This is for my husband Michael, who has created a life for us full of love and kindness. He allowed me to quit my job, pretend to write, then gave me unstinting praise even when what I produced was drivel. I've realised that anyone can be a critic but it takes a remarkable person to offer praise. Michael is that person. As is Liz Davidson, my wonderful friend and inspiration. She allowed me to steal her life, her time, her poetry and her brilliant art. And in return she got to hear about every burp from my book-baby. What luck. I'm grateful to her husband, John Ballantyne, who also allowed me to steal his life; Margaret Ballantyne-Power – more a sister than a friend – for her encouragement spanning years; and Sharon and Jim, who never failed to celebrate. Thank you to the lively and caffeinated members of Les Girls: Liz, France, Michele, Johanne, Christina, Daphne, Brigitte, and a special thank you to Cheryl for her love and her prayer stick ritual for *Still Life*. Thank you to the No Rules Book Club, to Christina Davidson Richards, Kirk Lawrence, Sheila Fischman, Neil McKenty, Cotton Aimers and Sue and Mike Riddell. Thank you to Chris Matthews for giving me archery lessons and not mocking, I think.

My brothers, Rob and Doug, and their families have offered love and support without qualification.

Still Life would never have been noticed beyond the other wonderful unpublished novels out there had it not been for the generosity of the Crime Writers' Association in Great Britain. The CWA has created the Debut Dagger award for an unpublished first novel. I'm almost certain mine would never have been noticed had *Still Life* not been short-listed and then 'Very Highly Commended', coming in second for the CWA Debut Dagger in 2004. It was one of the most remarkable things to have happened to me. Here is a group of successful authors who take time to read, support and encourage new crime writers. They gave me an opportunity most of them never had, and I'll be forever grateful. I also know it's a gift designed to be given away.

Kay Mitchell of the CWA has been wonderful and her own novels have given me such pleasure. Thank you as well to Sarah Turner, a heroine in our household, and to Maxim Jakubowski.

My editor at Hodder Headline is Sherise Hobbs and at St Martin's Minotaur it is Ben Sevier. They have made *Still Life* so much better through their critiques, firm suggestions and enthusiasm. It's both an education and a pleasure to work with them.

Thank you to Kim McArthur, for taking me under her literary wing.

And, finally, my agent is Teresa Chris. It is solely because of her that *Still Life* is in your hands now. She is brilliant and fun, a great editor, pithy in the extreme and a superb agent. I am particularly fortunate to be working with her, considering I almost ran her over the first time we met – not a strategy I would recommend to new writers, but it seemed to work.

Thank you, Teresa.

I went through a period in my life when I had no friends, when the phone never rang, when I thought I would die from loneliness. I know that the real blessing here isn't that I have a book published, but that I have so many people to thank.

If you enjoyed *Still Life*,
read on for the beginning
of the next Gamache case,
A Fatal Grace!

ONE

—

Had CC de Poitiers known she was going to be murdered she might have bought her husband, Richard, a Christmas gift. She might even have gone to her daughter's end of term pageant at Miss Edward's School for Girls, or 'girths' as CC liked to tease her expansive daughter. Had CC de Poitiers known the end was near she might have been at work instead of in the cheapest room the Ritz in Montreal had to offer. But the only end she knew was near belonged to a man named Saul.

'So, what do you think? Do you like it?' She balanced her book on her pallid stomach.

Saul looked at it, not for the first time. She'd dragged it out of her huge purse every five minutes for the past few days. In business meetings, dinners, taxi rides through the snowy streets of Montreal, CC'd suddenly bend down and emerge triumphant, holding her creation as though another virgin birth.

'I like the picture,' he said, knowing the insult. He'd taken the picture. He knew she was asking, pleading, for more and he knew he no longer cared to give it. And he wondered how much longer he could be around CC de Poitiers before he became her. Not physically, of course. At forty-eight she was a few years younger than him. She was slim and ropy and toned, her teeth impossibly white and her hair impossibly blonde. Touching her was like caressing a veneer of ice. There was a beauty to it, and a frailty he found attractive. But there was also danger. If she ever broke, if she shattered, she'd tear him to pieces.

But her exterior wasn't the issue. Watching her caress her book with more tenderness than she'd ever shown when caressing him, he wondered whether her ice water insides had somehow seeped into him, perhaps during sex, and were slowly freezing him. Already he couldn't feel his core.

At fifty-two Saul Petrov was just beginning to notice his friends weren't quite as brilliant, not quite as clever, not quite as slim as they once were. In fact, most had begun to bore him. And he'd noticed a telltale yawn or two from them as well. They were growing thick and bald and dull, and he suspected he was too. It wasn't so bad that women rarely looked at him any more or that he'd begun to consider trading his downhill skis for cross country, or that his GP had scheduled his first prostate test. He could accept all that. What woke Saul Petrov at two in the morning, and whispered in his ears in the voice that had warned him as a child that lions lived under his bed, was the certainty that people now found him boring. He'd take deep dark breaths of the night air, trying to reassure himself that the stifled yawn of his dinner companion was because of the wine or the *magret de canard* or the warmth in the Montreal restaurant, wrapped as they were in their sensible winter sweaters.

But still the night voice growled and warned of dangers ahead. Of impending disaster. Of telling tales too long, of an attention span too short, of seeing the whites of too many eyes. Of glances, fast and discreet, at watches. When can they reasonably leave him? Of eyes scanning the room, desperate for more stimulating company.

And so he'd allowed himself to be seduced by CC. Seduced and devoured so that the lion under the bed had become the lion in the bed. He'd begun to suspect this self-absorbed woman had finally finished absorbing herself, her husband and even that disaster of a daughter and was now busy absorbing him.

He'd already become cruel in her company. And he'd begun despising himself. But not quite as much as he despised her.

'It's a brilliant book,' she said, ignoring him. 'I mean, really. Who wouldn't want this?' She waved it in his face. 'People'll eat it up. There're so many troubled people out there.' She turned now and actually looked out their hotel room window at the building opposite, as though surveying her 'people'. 'I did this for them.' Now she turned back to him, her eyes wide and sincere.

Does she believe it? he wondered.

He'd read the book, of course. *Be Calm* she'd called it, after the company she'd founded a few years ago, which was a laugh given the bundle of nerves she actually was. The anxious, nervous hands, constantly smoothing and straightening. The snippy responses, the impatience that spilled over into anger.

Calm was not a word anyone would apply to CC de Poitiers, despite her placid, frozen exterior.

She'd shopped the book around to all the publishers, beginning with the top publishing houses in New York and ending with Publications Réjean et Maison des cartes in St Polycarpe, a one-*vache* village along the highway between Montreal and Toronto.

They'd all said no, immediately recognizing the manuscript as a flaccid mishmash of ridiculous self-help philosophies, wrapped in half-baked Buddhist and Hindu teachings, spewed forth by a woman whose cover photo looked as though she'd eat her young.

'No goddamned enlightenment,' she'd said to Saul in her Montreal office the day a batch of rejection letters arrived, ripping them into pieces and dropping them on the floor for the hired help to clean up. 'This world is messed up, I tell you. People are cruel and insensitive, they're out to screw each other. There's no love or compassion. This', she sliced her book violently in the air like an ancient mythical hammer, heading for an unforgiving anvil, 'will teach people how to find happiness.'

Her voice was low, the words staggering under the weight of venom. She'd gone on to self-publish her book, making sure it was out in time for Christmas. And while the book talked a lot about light Saul found it interesting and ironic that it had actually been released on the winter solstice. The darkest day of the year.

'Who published it again?' He couldn't seem to help himself. She was silent. 'Oh, I remember now,' he said. 'No one wanted it. That must have been horrible.' He paused for a moment, wondering whether to twist the knife. Oh, what the hell. Might as well. 'How'd that make you feel?' Did he imagine the wince?

But her silence remained, eloquent, her face impassive. Anything CC didn't like didn't exist. That included her husband and her daughter. It included any unpleasantness, any criticism, any harsh words not her own, any emotions. CC lived, Saul knew, in her own world, where she was perfect, where she could hide her feelings and hide her failings.

He wondered how long before that world would explode. He hoped he'd be around to see it. But not too close.

People are cruel and insensitive, she'd said. Cruel and insensitive. It wasn't all that long ago, before he'd taken the contract to freelance as CC's photographer and lover, that he'd actually thought the world a beautiful place. Each morning he'd wake early and go into the young day, when the world was new and anything was possible, and he'd see how lovely Montreal was. He'd see people smiling at each other as they got their cappuccinos at the café, or their fresh flowers or their baguettes. He'd see the children in autumn gathering the fallen chestnuts to play conkers. He'd see the elderly women walking arm in arm down the Main.

He wasn't foolish or blind enough not to also see the homeless men and women, or the bruised and battered faces that spoke of a long and empty night and a longer day ahead.

But at his core he believed the world a lovely place. And his photographs reflected that, catching the light, the brilliance, the hope. And the shadows that naturally challenged the light.

Ironically it was this very quality that had caught CC's eye and led her to offer him the contract. An article in a Montreal style magazine had described him as a 'hot' photographer, and CC always went for the best. Which was why they always took a room at the Ritz. A cramped, dreary room on a low floor without view or charm, but the Ritz. CC would collect the shampoos and stationery to prove her worth, just as she'd collected him. And she'd use them to make some obscure point to people who didn't care, just as she'd use him. And then, eventually, everything would be discarded. As her husband had been tossed aside, as her daughter was ignored and ridiculed.

The world was a cruel and insensitive place.

And he now believed it.

He hated CC de Poitiers.

He got out of bed, leaving CC to stare at her book, her real lover. He looked at her and she seemed to go in and out of focus. He cocked his head to one side and wondered whether he'd had too much to drink again. But still she seemed to grow fuzzy, then sharp, as though he was looking through a prism at two different women, one beautiful, glamorous, vivacious, and the other a pathetic, dyed-blonde rope, all corded and wound and knotted and rough. And dangerous.

'What's this?' He reached into the garbage and withdrew a portfolio. He recognized it immediately as an artist's dossier of work. It was beautifully and painstakingly bound and printed on archival Arche paper. He flipped it open and caught his breath.

A series of works, luminous and light, seemed to glow off the fine paper. He felt a stirring in his chest. They showed a world both lovely and hurt. But mostly, it was a world where hope and comfort still existed. It was clearly the world the artist saw each day, the world the artist lived in. As he himself once lived in a world of light and hope.

The works appeared simple but were in reality very complex. Images and colors were layered one on top of the other. Hours and hours, days and days must have been spent on each one to get the desired effect.

He stared down at the one before him now. A majestic tree soared into the sky, as though keening for the sun. The artist had photographed it and had somehow captured a sense of movement without making it disorienting. Instead it was graceful and calming and, above all, powerful. The tips of the branches seemed to melt or become fuzzy as though even in its confidence and yearning there was a tiny doubt. It was brilliant.

All thoughts of CC were forgotten. He'd climbed into the tree, almost feeling tickled by its rough bark, as if he had been sitting on his grandfather's lap and snuggling into his unshaven face. How had the artist managed that?

He couldn't make out the signature. He flipped through the other pages and slowly felt a smile come to his frozen face and move to his hardened heart.

Maybe, one day, if he ever got clear of CC he could go back to his work and do pieces like this.

He exhaled all the darkness he'd stored up.

'So, do you like it?' CC held her book up and waved it at him.